CORSAIRE

RICHARD L. MONTGOMERY

June 2014

America Star Books

Hardcover 9781611028447
Softcover 9781611026450
PUBLISHED BY AMERICA STAR BOOKS, LLLP
www.americastarbooks.com

Printed in the United States of America

Dedicated to my friends in Fort Edward, New York,
and in particular, to the Class of 1960.

I want to thank my daughter, Casey Bushey, for her continued support, untiring effort, dogged determination and unparalleled ability to keep me on track with the plot, twists and myriad of characters portrayed in this book. Her amazing ability to catch the inconsistencies and identify subtle changes to avoid the difficulties associated with a major rewrite, is only surpassed by her willingness to read and re-read the manuscript.

I also want to thank my friend, Colonel Marty C. Higgins (USMC Retired), for his dedicated service to this country and for being the inspiration for my character, Roy Higgins.

And finally, I want to again thank my friend, Oliver Dimalanta, for his imagination and artistic talent in designing the cover for *Corsaire*.

FOREWORD

"Like all of Richard Montgomery's novels, *Corsaire* starts fast and picks up speed with every page, but with this stiletto-sharp book about Somali pirates off the Horn of Africa, Montgomery, an ex-US Navy pilot, expands his range and style in a perfectly-brilliant foray into espionage territory that used to belong to Clancy and Cussler, but Montgomery brings a sleek unadorned prose free of Clancy's jargon and Cussler's bombast. *Corsaire* is full of fascinating insider details about everything from the international shipping trade to the boulevards of Paris and the beaches of Florida as he constructs a complex and sophisticated book that exceeds all the thriller pulse-points except one—a wild ending that I never saw coming. *Corsaire*, the latest outstanding novel from a sure-handed pro in full command of his art."

—*Carsten Stroud, New York Times Best-Selling Author of THE NICEVILLE TRILOGY*

Better Homes and Gardens®

2014

January

S	M	T	W	T	F	S
			1	2	3	4
5	6	7	8	9	10	11
12	13	14	15	16	17	18
19	20	21	22	23	24	25
26	27	28	29	30	31	

February

S	M	T	W	T	F	S
						1
2	3	4	5	6	7	8
9	10	11	12	13	14	15
16	17	18	19	20	21	22
23	24	25	26	27	28	

March

S	M	T	W	T	F	S
						1
2	3	4	5	6	7	8
9	10	11	12	13	14	15
16	17	18	19	20	21	22
23	24	25	26	27	28	29
30	31					

April

S	M	T	W	T	F	S
		1	2	3	4	5
6	7	8	9	10	11	12
13	14	15	16	17	18	19
20	21	22	23	24	25	26
27	28	29	30			

May

S	M	T	W	T	F	S
				1	2	3
4	5	6	7	8	9	10
11	12	13	14	15	16	17
18	19	20	21	22	23	24
25	26	27	28	29	30	31

June

S	M	T	W	T	F	S
1	2	3	4	5	6	7
8	9	10	11	12	13	14
15	16	17	18	19	20	21
22	23	24	25	26	27	28
29	30					

#130014

Better Homes and Gardens

2014

July

S	M	T	W	T	F	S
		1	2	3	4	5
6	7	8	9	10	11	12
13	14	15	16	17	18	19
20	21	22	23	24	25	26
27	28	29	30	31		

August

S	M	T	W	T	F	S
					1	2
3	4	5	6	7	8	9
10	11	12	13	14	15	16
17	18	19	20	21	22	23
24	25	26	27	28	29	30
31						

September

S	M	T	W	T	F	S
	1	2	3	4	5	6
7	8	9	10	11	12	13
14	15	16	17	18	19	20
21	22	23	24	25	26	27
28	29	30				

October

S	M	T	W	T	F	S
			1	2	3	4
5	6	7	8	9	10	11
12	13	14	15	16	17	18
19	20	21	22	23	24	25
26	27	28	29	30	31	

November

S	M	T	W	T	F	S
						1
2	3	4	5	6	7	8
9	10	11	12	13	14	15
16	17	18	19	20	21	22
23	24	25	26	27	28	29
30						

December

S	M	T	W	T	F	S
	1	2	3	4	5	6
7	8	9	10	11	12	13
14	15	16	17	18	19	20
21	22	23	24	25	26	27
28	29	30	31			

CHAPTER ONE
Wilmington, North Carolina
Day 1
0900 Hours

James Theodore Blackwell, or "JT" as he was known by his friends, sat behind the large teak desk that had been a fixture in the Blackwell family since the early eighteen hundreds. He had been sitting motionless for several long minutes. The color in his face was beginning to return, although he still had a clammy feeling that had lingered way too long. His large, strong hands gripped the armrests of the chair as if he were bracing for heavy seas. The age spots on the back of his hands were numerous. Several were pronounced and needing the attention of a dermatologist. They matched the color of the desk and gave the eerie appearance of a jungle warrior blending in with his environment. He continued to stare at the center of the desk. His grip strengthened. His knuckles tightened and turned white. He didn't blink as the intensity of his stare increased. He was focused as the anger overwhelmed his thought.

JT's father, Theodore Blackwell, had run the family shipping business from that very desk, as did his father before him. As a young boy, JT would jump onto the desk and beg his dad, "Tell me the story—tell me the story. Pleeease! Right from the beginning."

JT would always make sure that his dad told him the entire story without leaving out one salient word. Although Theodore had told the story many times, he would always make time for the young lad. He was good about that, no matter how busy he was. Theodore would stop whatever he was doing, smile broadly, and lean back into his chair as JT ceremoniously took up his customary position in the middle of the desk.

JT would sit cross-legged with his elbows propped on his knees and his face cupped in his hands. His eyes were wide with delight as if he were hearing the story for the very first time. No matter how many times he had heard the story, it always seemed to be a brand new adventure. It was a story that he would never forget—one that he would someday ceremoniously tell his son, being sure not to leave out one single word or phrase.

Before his dad would start the story, he always took a large swallow of coffee and cleared his throat. He would look at JT as he leaned forward and placed his crusty elbows on the desk, his large forearms crossed in front of him. He would look straight into JT's eyes. Their gaze would be locked in anticipation of the first word. Theodore would shift his gaze back and forth from eye-to-eye challenging young JT to blink—to break the concentration. The boy would never blink as he looked back intently, knowing every word his dad was about to recite. He wouldn't let his dad leave out one word—not even one syllable.

JT's dad would always begin the tale with Edward Teach, the notorious pirate better known as Blackbeard. The tale would begin with how Blackbeard captured the French merchant vessel, *La Concorde*. Blackbeard renamed the ship, *Queen Anne's Revenge*, and had purposely run it aground near Beaufort, North Carolina. His purpose was to separate himself from his crew in order to receive a royal pardon. Following Blackbeard's departure, many of the local fishermen tried, in vain, to free the ship.

When they finally realized that they could not move it, they began removing the contents, including most of the wood from Blackbeard's cabin. As they continued to strip *Queen Anne's Revenge*, a nor'easter interrupted their endeavor. Unfortunately, Mother Nature accomplished what the men could not do. The ship was swept from the sandbar out to sea where it was torn apart by the storm, sunk, and was hidden in a watery grave.

"Tell me more," begged the young JT, knowing that his dad would always tell him the whole story. Theodore would take another swallow of coffee and continue as young JT's eyes widened again, waiting for the words he knew were to follow.

A local carpenter by the name of Barnum Hitchcock bought the best pieces of wood and built a desk for his own personal use. The desk was the centerpiece of his small business, until he went off to fight the British. Unfortunately, he was killed during the Siege of Charleston in

March of 1780. Consequently, the desk was purchased by JT's great, great, great uncle, Joseph Hewes, who was one of the signers of the Declaration of Independence. Joseph Hewes had purchased the desk from Barnum Hitchcock's widow, Maude. The desk still contained all of the letters written to Maude detailing stories of the valiant men under Hitchcock's command—men who lost their lives in the battle for independence. Joseph Hewes had carefully placed the letters in a leather pouch, which he stored in the bottom left-hand drawer of the desk, and where they remain to this very day.

The desk became the focal point of Joseph Hewes' new adventure as a shipbuilder. In fact, the desk was the very first piece of office furniture that he had purchased. It was used for everything from a drafting table, to a storage bin, to a footrest that Joseph Hewes would use when he would take his afternoon nap. And now, it was the proud possession of JT Blackwell as he continued in the family business that was established so many years ago.

As he continued to stare at the center of the desk, he subconsciously rubbed his hand over several deep notches that had served Joseph Hewes as a reminder of the fate of those men of conviction who willingly gave their lives in the fight against the British. There were initials scratched into the desk next to each of the dark furrows that had become smooth with the passage of so many years. Each time Theodore told JT the story of Blackbeard, he would let JT pick out one set of initials. Theodore would then proceed to tell him the story of the man behind those initials. The fate of each man was chronicled in the letters that were safely tied together and stored in the leather pouch.

JT had thought about turning the letters over to the museum in Charleston; however, the pouch had become a permanent part of the great teak desk. In fact, they were the only contents allowed in the lower left-hand drawer. That drawer was sacred. As JT looked at the notches, he repeated their names over and over in his mind—Avery Mister, Trace Meekins, Louis Atwell, Tommy Daniels…the list went on. Their legacy would live on forever, or at least as long as there was someone in the Blackwell family to carry on their memory. As far as JT was concerned, those valiant men would never be forgotten.

JT pushed back from the desk and stood up. He was a man of stature. At six feet three inches, he tried to stand straight but leaned a bit forward. His weight had varied only a few pounds over the years. He was proud of the fact that he could still fit into the trousers he wore when he graduated from The Citadel. He didn't suffer from the debilitating arthritis that seemed to conquer many of his peers, or at least the ones who were still alive at eighty-five years of age. Fishing was a tough business. It wasn't a vocation for the weak or timid. They all started as fishermen. He contributed his good health to hard work, a diet of fresh fish, only a few eggs, and an occasional porterhouse steak. His night was always capped with a healthy tumbler of Jack Daniel's Black Label. He had never been a beer or wine drinker. "Real men drink the hard stuff," he would boast as he would throw his head back, emptying the contents of a double shot glass. No one ever challenged his exclamation. They knew better.

As he looked out of his third-story window, his eyes moved from vessel to vessel. He subconsciously counted each one, as he always did. All of the shrimp boats were out to sea. A few had returned with their holds filled with jumbo shrimp. It appeared that it was going to be a good fishing season. A slight smile crossed his face as he noted that Blackwell Shipbuilding had built nearly all the vessels in port. There were a few renegades, but the greater majority were Blackwell ships.

JT went back and sat behind the large teak desk. He took a sip of coffee that had been sitting on the desk for nearly an hour or so. The tepid black coffee brought a scowl to his face. He would only drink his coffee piping hot. He normally drank a few sips and then poured out the rest just before refilling with more fresh hot coffee. It had been his daily routine for his entire life. He got up and went to the Bunn coffee maker where two pots of coffee were sitting in anticipation of attention. He emptied his cup into the small sink and refilled it to the brim. He immediately took a healthy swallow, which brought a temporary smile to his face. He went back to the desk, sat down and began re-living the events of the morning. It was not the start he had expected.

He cradled the cup in both hands as the steam rose in front of his eyes. The wrinkles in his forehead deepened as he looked over at the phone in anticipation of it ringing again. An hour earlier it had rung. He had been expecting a call to confirm an order for no less than six fishing trawlers. However, this wasn't the call he was looking forward to—no, not at all. The call caught him totally by surprise, totally off guard. The voice on the other end of the line was deep. The man spoke with an accent that JT was all too familiar with. He had had dealings in that part of the world where your word meant nothing—a part of the world where men only dealt in cash, guns, knives and false promises. A part of the world where you never started anything until the cash was in hand, and then you continued to look over your shoulder.

CHAPTER TWO

Pensacola, Florida
Day 2
0900 Hours

Carl stepped out onto the balcony just as four F-18s from Sherman Field flew overhead at about five hundred feet. The blue and gold aircraft were in a tight diamond formation. Rick and Carlos were already on their feet, hands cupped over both ears, as they watched the aircraft commence a high performance climb punctuated by a coordinated roll to the right. The sound of the F-18s was overwhelming. The oval patio table vibrated in harmony as it danced several inches across the rough patio surface. Circular ripples formed in sympathy on the surface of tepid coffee, which was about to be replaced. Carl didn't have the luxury of covering his ears, since he was carrying the tray with fresh coffee and assorted scones.

Carl placed the tray on the large, glass-topped patio table just in time to cover his ears as two solo planes screamed by at full power on their way to loosely join the formation. Their wingtip vortices carved a curious white pattern in the sky as both planes weaved back and forth, shooting straight up, as each performed several aileron rolls side by side, seemingly defying all the rules of aviation. The Blue Angels were an elite group of aviators chosen for their proven performance, demeanor, good looks and physical strength.

"Did you ever want to be a Blue Angel?" asked Carl as he sat down across from Rick. Carlos remained standing as he watched the other two aircraft join the formation. Carl had already chosen a blueberry scone and taken a large bite, which affected his diction. He caught a few of the crumbs in his left hand as he continued to munch on the day-old scone.

"There was no way that the Blues were going to accept, or even consider, anyone from the Anti-Submarine Warfare community. Besides, in many cases, it was not the best career choice," responded Rick as he continued to watch the aircraft maneuver off in the distance.

"So, there was discrimination among the airdales," said Carlos mockingly as he turned toward Rick. He knew that there was indeed discrimination among the airdales.

Rick smiled as he chose a cinnamon scone and sat down across from Carl.

"It always boils down to individual performance, and more importantly, the needs of the Navy. All the pilots are good, but there are always the best ones in every community. The Blues certainly take the best ones," responded Rick. "There's no denying that. So Carl, have you made any decisions concerning a trip to London?" he asked, changing the subject.

"I haven't ruled it out. I did contact our new friend Alastair Sims at MI6 to see if he would keep tabs on the illusive twin. He said he would...for a slight consideration."

"It's always for a *slight consideration*," retorted Carlos somewhat sarcastically as he took his seat at the table.

"By the way, I understand she has taken a leave of absence from the airlines," added Carl as he pointed to the diamond formation that was flying just above the water close to the horizon.

"She must have moved part of the lottery money without Tarek Haddad's knowledge," offered Carlos as he moved the chair closer to the table. "Seems they all wanted a piece of that pie," he added with a smirk.

"It was a good-sized pie. Greed is always a very strong motive," said Rick.

The three of them sat there enjoying the weather. It was a perfect Florida morning. There were no clouds in the sky, and the coffee was fresh and hot. Rick and Lynn had invited Carlos and Ann to enjoy a little getaway with them at their Destin condo. Ann and Lynn had developed a very good friendship, and the four of them really enjoyed spending time together. Carl had flown in for a little getaway himself and to meet with Rick and Carlos about some upcoming business.

"I may have a new project for you by the end of the week," said Carl, directing his comment to Rick. "It appears that Savage wants to expand Homeland Security's coverage of the Mexican drug trade.

That whole fiasco with Fast and Furious has been a tremendous embarrassment and has placed added emphasis on the border," said Carl as he finished his second cup of coffee.

"I'm surprised that whole thing didn't end it for Holder," stated Rick.

"If he were a Republican, it would have," said Carl. "The press would've been unmerciful," he added.

"What's Savage looking for?" asked Rick.

"I believe he wants us to put together a delivery order under our current contract's statement of work that requests the identification and implementation of a surveillance system to effectively monitor the entire border between the U.S. and Mexico. Additionally, I believe he'll want the delivery order to include a determination of the best vehicle to provide a rapid response capability to complement the surveillance system," answered Carl.

Rick shook his head slightly as he poured a fresh cup of coffee.

"One of my last projects at the Operational Test and Evaluation Command was working with Customs on a very similar project," responded Rick. "It involved the use of tethered blimps to monitor the border," he added as a slight smile crossed his face.

"Seems I remember that project," said Carl, "but I believe it was never completed," he added as he poured a cup of fresh coffee from the large chrome carafe.

Carlos got up and leaned against the railing as he searched the sky for the Blues. He didn't seem to be interested in their conversation.

"The project was moving along well until they were just south of Tampa. Seems the construction crew hit water while digging a hole for the anchoring system," continued Rick.

"What a surprise," laughed Carlos as he turned his attention toward Rick and Carl. "Hitting water when digging a hole in Florida," he added, shaking his head. "Who'd have thunk it?"

Carlos *was* listening.

"Certainly no surprise for the diggers," said Rick. "But the real surprise was how fast the environmentalists showed up and claimed the site to be wetlands."

"And that's what stopped the project," said Carl. It was more of a statement than a question.

"That stopped the *whole* project," said Rick as he finished his scone.

"You've got to be kidding me. The whole freaking state is a wetlands area," said Carlos as he spotted the diamond formation off in the distance.

Carl poured the remainder of the carafe's contents into Rick and Carlos's cup and headed back into the kitchen.

"She must have moved that money to an offshore account while Tarek Haddad was still alive," said Carlos, changing the subject back to the twins. He was still wondering how and when the money was moved. "She must have moved it before they converted it all to gold," he added.

"There are still many unanswered questions with that project," said Rick. "I have a feeling we'll catch up to her one of these days. Carl isn't going to let several million dollars just disappear. You can bet on that."

"So when will the girls be back?" asked Carl as he reappeared with the carafe in hand.

"No telling. You know Lynn. She doesn't like time constraints. She wears a watch for decoration purposes only," said Rick.

"I think she's rubbing off on Ann with all the shopping," added Carlos, clearly less amused.

Rick thought to himself that these two must have been having an interesting time together. Lynn was looking for the boutiques; however, Ann would be very happy in a Bass Pro Shop checking out the guns and knives. Secretly, Ann really was enjoying the boutique shopping with Lynn. The good news was that they truly liked one another. Their new friendship was genuine as evidenced by their time together.

"Yeah, I'm sorry about that buddy," laughed Rick. "They'll probably call later and want us to meet them for dinner."

"I could handle McGuire's," offered Carlos, quickly forgetting about the shopping. "Ann loves to carve up a steak," he said with a smile.

"She even uses her own knife," laughed Carl.

"That always gets a rise from the servers," laughed Carlos.

"Patrons too," said Rick as they all had a good laugh.

"So Carlos, when is the big date?" asked Carl.

"What big date?" questioned Carlos, pretending not to understand the question.

"Yeah right," said Rick.

Carlos took a drink of fresh coffee.

"We don't want to rush into anything," he said, trying to feign a serious expression.

"Rush into anything?" questioned Rick. "You've only known the girl for the past twenty years or so."

"Let the poor boy alone Rick. He'll get married when Ann says it's time," consoled Carl, patting Carlos on the back. He was about to say something else when his phone rang. He looked at the caller ID. It was his executive secretary, Elaine Drew.

"Morning Elaine," answered Carl.

"Morning to you," she said in a cheerful voice. "How's Florida?"

"Relaxing," responded Carl. "Not a whole lot of phone calls. So what's up?"

"You just got a call from a fellow by the name of JT Blackwell. Said that he met you last year during a conference hosted by George Steinbrenner."

Carl remembered the conference. He had known George Steinbrenner when Steinbrenner was active in the shipbuilding business. Carl had been to several of his gatherings up until George began losing the battle with Alzheimer's.

"Off the top of my head, I don't remember him. What was his reason for calling?" asked Carl as he took a drink of coffee and searched his mind, trying to conjure up an image of Blackwell.

"He said that he had a problem and that he actually preferred to talk with you in person. I told him that you were not in the office and that I didn't expect you back for a few days. He asked if you would please give him a call in order to set up a meeting. He sounded quite desperate. I have his toll free number."

"They all sound desperate. Hold on, let me get something to write on," said Carl as he went into the den. Elaine could hear him shuffling through a drawer. "Okay," he said, "shoot."

"Number is 877-555-6454," said Elaine deliberately.

"I've got it," said Carl. "Anything else?"

"Savage called again. Said there was no rush."

"I think I know what he wants. I'll give him a call," responded Carl.

"That's it on this end. Everything here is going smoothly. When are you planning on coming back?" asked Elaine.

"In a couple of days. We'll probably take the boat over to Destin, do a little fishing, and have a nice meal at Marina Café. I'll let you know. Talk with you later."

Carl looked at the number he wrote down and tried to visualize JT Blackwell. He had been to several conferences in New York City, only one at George Steinbrenner's in the past couple of years. As he walked back out onto the patio, the Blues flew by in right echelon. It appeared that the practice session was over, and they were going in for landing. The sound of freedom followed well behind the aircraft as they headed for Sherman Field at fifteen hundred feet and two hundred fifty knots.

Rick and Carlos were standing at the railing watching the aircraft as Carl took his seat at the table. As the quiet returned, Carl dialed the number given to him by Elaine. The phone rang several times. Carl was about to hang up and try later when he heard a strong voice on the other end of the line.

"Good morning Mr. Peterson. I appreciate your quick response."

"Mr. Blackwell. And how may I be of assistance?" asked Carl, avoiding the usual pleasantries. Besides, he still couldn't place Blackwell.

"I'm not sure you remember me, but I was one of the presenters at the Steinbrenner conference last year. After the conference, we had a conversation and discussed the capabilities offered by container ships—in particular, the ability to provide a rapid response capability in nearly any scenario," offered Blackwell.

Carl did remember the presentation and conversation following. There were several ship builders that took part in the conversation, including one three-star admiral that said the Navy was already staging containers with "unique" capabilities to meet certain unspecified contingencies. For some reason, Carl still couldn't visualize Blackwell.

"I do remember the conversation," said Carl, not wanting to admit that he couldn't specifically remember Blackwell.

"You handed me your business card. I did a little bit of research on your company. I believe you and your people have the capability, and where with all, to provide the results I am looking for," said Blackwell.

"And what is it that you are looking for?" asked Carl.

There was a long pause on the line. Carl wasn't sure if he had lost the connection. He looked at his phone. It appeared that he was still connected. He still couldn't visualize Blackwell, although he could remember a couple of the other participants who had joined in the conversation.

"Mr. Blackwell?" said Carl, confirming that Blackwell was still on the line.

"My granddaughter, her cousin and another couple have been kidnapped by pirates off the African coast," responded Blackwell. There was a slight hint of remorse in his voice that rapidly faded.

The old man had tried to talk his granddaughter out of taking the trip. He had pleaded, but to no avail. He knew the dangers.

"You are absolutely sure of this?" asked Carl after a slight pause. "Has someone contacted you?" continued Carl before Blackwell had a chance to answer his first question.

"I'm sure. They used her satellite phone," replied Blackwell.

"Have you talked with your granddaughter?" asked Carl.

"I have. At this point it seems they're all okay but quite afraid, as you can imagine," responded Blackwell.

"And what are their demands?" asked Carl.

"They want five million dollars," responded Blackwell.

"Five million dollars," repeated Carl. "Have you talked with the State Department?"

"I have, but since my granddaughter is already a captive, they're powerless, short of a full-blown invasion," offered Blackwell. "Which, will not happen," he added.

"I assume they're in Somalia. Is that correct?" asked Carl.

"I believe so," responded Blackwell.

"Is money an issue?" asked Carl.

"No, I have the resources."

"Why not meet their demands to ensure your granddaughter's safe return?" asked Carl after a long pause.

"Mr. Peterson, I've been around a long time. I'm sitting at a desk fashioned from the wood taken from Blackbeard's flagship. My family has been in the shipping business for over one hundred and fifty years. I do have the resources and could do as you say, but I strongly believe my granddaughter was specifically targeted. And for that reason, I am assuming she will be safe. I want to know how she was singled out and who is responsible. And I want them…dealt with accordingly."

As a C-130 went overhead, Carl got up and motioned for Rick and Carlos to follow him into the den. Both Rick and Carlos had been listening, as well as they could without being too obvious, to Carl's side of the conversation. Carlos was mumbling something about Mogadishu as Rick closed the sliding glass door.

"Somalia," said Carlos. "I really hate Somalia. I hate the skinnies," he said loud enough for Rick and Carl to hear. Carl covered the mouthpiece of the phone. In principle, Rick agreed with Carlos's assessment. The news media had filmed our troops going ashore in Somalia. War wasn't serious anymore. The landing had looked like a Hollywood set. Carl removed his hand and placed his forefinger against his lips as he continued the conversation with Blackwell.

"I wasn't planning on leaving Pensacola for a couple of days," Carl confessed. His response seemed to be an apology rather than an answer to a question.

There was a slight pause before Blackwell continued the conversation.

"I'm a very wealthy man Mr. Peterson. I'm quite sure that we can come to some sort of an arrangement that will be acceptable to each of us," said Blackwell. He had caught the conciliatory tone in Carl's response.

Carl hesitated momentarily as he looked over at Rick and Carlos. Rick could tell by Carl's expression that Blackwell had just dangled a carrot in front of him. From the look on Carl's face, it was probably a very convincing carrot. Carl was an easy read when it came to money. Carl could never resist the prospect of a lucrative contract, no matter what the mission required. Rick's expression was confirmation that if Carl needed to cut the vacation short, it was all right with him. Besides, Rick, Carlos and the girls were staying at Rick's condo in Destin.

"I can be back in Washington tomorrow morning," offered Carl. Having made that offer, it dawned on him that he had no idea where Blackwell was located. "Forgive me Mr. Blackwell, but quite honestly, I can't remember if you have an office in the D.C. area," continued Carl, trying to give the impression that he actually knew Blackwell. It was really a statement rather than a question…a statement to which he hoped Blackwell would provide a revealing answer.

"I'm in Wilmington, North Carolina," responded Blackwell. "And Mr. Peterson, please understand that I do not want to disrupt your vacation in any way," he tendered in defense of his position.

"I'm on a very informal vacation with two of my closest friends— friends who will understand and who, by the way, I would like you to meet," responded Carl.

"If it wouldn't be an inconvenience, I could fly to Pensacola this afternoon. I could easily be there in say…four hours," offered Blackwell. "Since time is of the essence, I need to meet with you as soon as possible," he pleaded. "I can fill you in concerning my thoughts on this matter and answer any preliminary questions you may have."

There was a slight hint of desperation in his voice. The desperation was genuine. Carl had purposely held the phone away from his ear so that Rick and Carlos could hear Blackwell's side of the conversation. Rick nodded his concurrence with Blackwell's offer to fly into Pensacola.

"That will work for me," said Carl after a slight pause.

"Is Pensacola the closest airport?" asked Blackwell.

"Pensacola will be fine," responded Carl. "I'm less than thirty minutes from the airport."

"Then I will see you at two," confirmed Blackwell.

"Mr. Blackwell, one other thing," said Carl, catching Blackwell before he hung up the phone. "What *is* the status of your negotiation?"

"I haven't responded to them at this point. They have given me a couple of days. The ball appears to be in my court," responded Blackwell.

"I strongly believe you should attempt to diffuse the situation. I encourage you to maintain contact, and start the ransom process. At least make them believe you are serious about meeting their demands. These people have been known to deal harshly with their captives... and sometimes for no apparent reason other than sending a message," offered Carl.

Carl could hear Blackwell in the background shuffling through some papers. It was the first time Carl could hear Blackwell take a deep breath.

"I do appreciate your recommendation. The only reason I have not responded yet is because I have had dealings in that part of the world...and with not so favorable results. However, I understand the intent and will get my people working on it. I should have some answers when I see you. I assume that Pensacola has facilities to receive a corporate aircraft?" asked Blackwell, changing the subject.

"They do," responded Carl.

"I will be at Pensacola by two this afternoon," confirmed Blackwell, sounding somewhat relieved as well as encouraged.

"Two it is," said Carl as he hung up the phone.

Rick and Carlos didn't say anything as Carl poured another cup of coffee. He offered the carafe to Rick. Rick filled Carlos's cup then his own. All three tipped their cups in unison as if to consecrate their invisible agreement. They didn't say anything for several seconds. Rick broke the silence.

"So his granddaughter has been kidnapped by Somali pirates," it was purely a rhetorical statement.

"From what I could hear, he sounds to me like a guy with strong convictions," said Carlos.

"He is probably a very determined and stubborn old man. For the life of me, I still can't seem to place him," said Carl, his face showing the strain of thought.

"He probably is a stubborn guy. But I totally agree that he needs to communicate his willingness to negotiate with these people. Short of a full-blown military operation, there's no way to provide a successful extraction at this stage of the game without significant risks," offered Rick.

"I hate the skinnies," said Carlos again, thinking back to his involvement in rescue operations in Mogadishu. "They're a bunch of cowards who hide behind women and children," he added.

"There are weapon systems that can be employed effectively in that situation," offered Rick.

"Listen to us…we are already planning an invasion, and we have no idea what Blackwell really wants us to do," said Carl.

"I hate the skinnies," said Carlos yet again and with more conviction. It was obvious to Rick and Carl that Carlos would be more than happy to drop a nuclear bomb on the whole bunch and be done with it.

CHAPTER THREE
Pensacola International Airport
1400 Hours

The Gulfstream came to a full stop in front of the operations building and almost immediately, the hatch opened. A well-dressed older man was already standing in the doorway ready to disembark. As soon as the ramp hit the tarmac, JT Blackwell was on his way to meet Carl. As he got closer, Rick and Carlos could hear Carl say, "I remember this guy." Carl increased his pace as he walked out on the tarmac. Rick and Carlos lagged a few steps behind.

Blackwell was much taller than Carl had remembered him to be. Blackwell wore gray trousers and a dark-blue long-sleeve shirt that was open at the collar. His sleeves were turned up twice at the cuff, exposing a light gray colored lining that nearly matched his trousers. Blackwell appeared to be well tanned. He had thick wrists, and he walked briskly as he approached. It was clear he was fatigued from obvious lack of sleep. As he extended his right hand to greet Carl, there was a hint of relief that briefly crossed Blackwell's face. Carl grasped Blackwell's hand, making sure of firm contact. Carl couldn't help but notice the gold Rolex Presidential watch on Blackwell's right wrist. The old man's grip was sincere and strong.

"Mr. Peterson, it has been a while," he said in a deep, clear and confident voice.

"Good afternoon Mr. Blackwell. I trust that you had a good flight," responded Carl as he looked over at the Gulfstream.

"I did," said Blackwell. "I really don't like flying commercial anymore. The TSA personnel are rude at best and treat the passengers like cattle. Most of them murder the English language. Fortunately, I have the resources to forego that pleasure," he added as he looked in the direction of his aircraft.

"Let me introduce my friends," said Carl as he turned and motioned with his right hand. "This is Rick Morgan and Carlos Garcia. I have known them for…well, let's just say for too many years," he added with a fond smile.

The men exchanged the usual pleasantries as Carl began to steer them toward the operations building.

"We can go to one of the local restaurants or head back to my place. In fact, there is a nice restaurant in the terminal," offered Carl.

"Actually, if you don't mind, I have everything we need on board the aircraft," responded Blackwell as he stood his position. "I travel with a very attentive crew," he said as he started toward the aircraft.

It was obvious that JT Blackwell was a man of decision as he led the way toward the aircraft. "Besides, we can save some time," he added as he looked over his shoulder.

The interior of the plane was plush. It was laid out similar to Carl's, but the modifications were more suitable for a businessman's purpose. The seats were covered in cream-colored soft Italian leather. They were spotless and probably recently replaced. There was a medium-sized table centered between semi-circular bench-style seats near the cabin door. The table was already set with coffee, tea, bottled water and assorted petits fours. There were also several pads of paper and pens stacked neatly on one side of the table.

Blackwell motioned for the men to take a seat. Rick slid in first followed by Carlos. Carl took a position on the left side near the aisle. Blackwell took up a position on the right side next to Rick. A flight attendant seemed to appear out of nowhere. She was in uniform and appeared to be Korean, although she was quite tall. Her perfume left a sweet aroma as she walked past the table.

"Will there be anything else Mr. Blackwell?" she asked in a British accent.

"No TiLee. That will be all. We do need a bit of privacy…you understand?" he said.

Her smile was genuine as she, the pilot and co-pilot disembarked. The pilot and co-pilot nodded without saying anything as they quietly slipped past the table.

"They have been with me for over ten years," Blackwell announced proudly as he poured a cup of coffee and passed the carafe to Rick.

"We are alone. This conversation will be strictly private," continued Blackwell as he reached for one of the petits fours. "By the way, I took your advice. One of my people has already made contact with the Somalis. I understand they are making progress as we speak."

"I believe that was a smart move. That should give us a little time, and more importantly, your granddaughter will be safe," responded Carl.

"At least for the time being," added Blackwell.

"And what is it exactly that you want us to do?" asked Carl directly.

"First of all, I want you to ensure the safe return of my granddaughter and her friends. Then I want you to find out who orchestrated this kidnapping," responded Blackwell.

"So you believe your granddaughter may have been specifically targeted. Is that correct?" asked Carl.

"Everyone sailing around the world basically takes one of two routes. Depending upon the time of year, many end up traveling east to west. They had made contact with the authorities at the Suez Canal. With that in mind, I find it difficult to believe that the Somalis just came upon them—that they were some random target of opportunity," offered Blackwell.

No one said anything for several seconds. Carl made a few notes as did Rick.

"I agree with you," said Rick as he put his pencil down.

He looked directly at Blackwell and then to Carl.

"I have never accepted the randomness of their targets. I also believe that somewhere along your granddaughter's route, and probably at one of their port visits, someone took notice and marked them as a potential target."

"I agree with that scenario, and *that* is exactly what I want you to find out," responded Blackwell.

"Assuming all goes well with your granddaughter's return, and let me assure you that the only thing the Somalis are interested in at this point is the money, how far do you want to go with this?" asked Carl.

"First of all, let me make it very clear. For me personally, the money is not the issue. I have been a man of the sea my whole life, as was my father and his father before him," said Blackwell as he poured another cup of coffee. He topped off Rick's cup and handed the carafe to Carlos. "The Somalis are a bunch of kids—fifteen to twenty years old with a twenty-five year old in charge at best. Somewhere there are adults behind this. It is the adults I really want to find. And I want to deal with them accordingly," said Blackwell as he looked around the table.

"Walk the plank so to speak," offered Carlos.

"That's one way to put it," responded Blackwell. "Is that in the realm of your capabilities?" he asked after a slight pause.

Blackwell's eyes indicated that he was quite serious.

"It can be," responded Carl without hesitation. "However, it's imperative that your granddaughter is in friendly hands before we commence any operation of that nature. Rick, what do you think?" asked Carl.

"It would help if we were part of the ransom negotiations," said Rick.

"That will be no problem," responded Blackwell.

"In the meantime, we'll need you to provide us with everything you know or have concerning your granddaughter's trip," said Rick.

"That will also be no problem," responded Blackwell as he got up and retrieved a briefcase from the galley area. "I'm sure you'll find everything you need in here," he added as he placed the briefcase in the aisle next to Carl's right leg. "So what do you see as the next step?"

"You need to put us in contact with your negotiator," said Carl.

"Then?" asked Blackwell.

"Then we follow the money," said Rick.

CHAPTER FOUR

Pensacola, Florida

1630 Hours

The meeting with Blackwell had gone very well. Carl was finally able to put a face with the name. He did remember Blackwell. During the conference, Blackwell was second to speak. His presentation had focused on the expansion of the Panama Canal to accommodate vessels capable of carrying up to twelve thousand five hundred containers as well as the impact that particular expansion would have on U.S. ports. Blackwell went on to explain out how difficult it would be to provide adequate security to ensure the containers didn't carry contraband, or worse yet, a nuclear bomb. He was quick to point out that many U.S. ports would be ready to accept the larger vessels by the year 2015 and that some were ready now, including Norfolk, Los Angeles, Long Beach, Oakland and Seattle. The security aspect got everyone's attention. Additionally, Blackwell had presented some very interesting ideas on the use of containers to meet specific military needs and objectives.

Carl and Rick had had an interesting conversation on the very subject of container ships a couple of months before the conference in New York. Since Rick's primary residence was in Virginia Beach, he certainly had a vested interest in the security of the numerous military commands home-ported in the Tidewater area. In particular, Rick had expressed concern that the Norfolk Naval Base was extremely vulnerable to a terrorist action that, if executed properly, could isolate the fleet. A well-placed explosion at Thimble Shoals would take all the ships at Norfolk out of action. And if a container ship just happened to blow up at Thimble Shoals, the Navy would be blocked in for several months. Certainly an option would be to remove a portion of the Chesapeake Bay Bridge Tunnel, but that could take a fatal amount of time in a real war scenario.

The short trip back to Carl's condo provided just enough time to determine what needed to be done in the short term. It was decided that Carl would head back to Old Town, and Rick and Carlos would remain in Destin. They would go over the material provided by Blackwell. Anything that required immediate attention could be handled via video conferencing, or informally via Skype. Carl would make contact with Blackwell and Blackwell's negotiator to ensure that he would play an integral part during the ransom negotiations. Rick and Carlos would develop the initial project scenario and determine the preliminary composition of team requirements. They would identify potential assets and make the initial contact with them. It seemed to be a clear course of action. However, it was always clear on paper.

As they entered Carl's condo, Rick went into the kitchen to make a fresh pot of coffee. Carlos turned the TV on and was checking the weather when Rick's phone rang. It was Lynn.

"Hey honey, are you on the way back?" he asked as he poured out the contents of the carafe.

"Not yet. Have you guys thought about dinner?" she asked, knowing that they probably had discussed their options.

"We are leaning toward McGuire's if that's all right with you and Ann?" questioned Rick.

Rick could hear Lynn as she said to Ann, "They're so predictable. I told you the boys would want to go to McGuire's."

Rick always got a kick out of Lynn referring to him, Carl and Carlos as "the boys."

"That's okay with us. Why don't we meet you there at six-thirty," responded Lynn.

"Predictable, huh? Well, *the boys* will be there. How's the shopping?"

"It's Pensacola," responded Lynn. "I guess I could use another pair of overalls," she teased. "There are a couple of other shops we want to look into. We'll see you at six-thirty. Love you."

Rick poured a cup of fresh coffee as Carl entered the room.

"Have we decided on dinner?" Carl asked.

"Seems we are a predictable bunch," said Rick. "It's McGuires," he added as he watched Carlos flipping through the channels. They all loved a good steak, and McGuire's was by far the best in town.

Carlos mumbled the word *predictable* a couple of times.

"That sounds good to me," responded Carl as he made a call to Elaine Drew.

Elaine was in the process of tidying up the office. She picked up on the second ring, "Good afternoon Carl," she answered in a perky voice, signaling that she truly enjoyed hearing from Carl even though the end of the day was at hand. Carl was never demanding...at least not with Elaine.

"Afternoon Elaine. By chance, is Roland still there?" he asked, sounding somewhat apologetic, although he was certain that Roland Carpenter was indeed still in the office.

"Yes he is. Hold on, and I will get him for you."

Roland Carpenter was usually the last to leave the office.

"Good afternoon Mr. Peterson," answered Roland.

"Roland, I need you to do some research on the Somali pirates. Basically, I would like to know how many ships have been seized by them, the frequency, and in particular, the outcome."

"Any particular timeframe?" asked Roland.

"You're the analyst. We just need enough information in order to provide a meaningful analysis—one that will help us determine if there is a common thread connecting the victims other than the pirates themselves."

"I'll get started on it. How soon do you need the information?" asked Roland.

"Unfortunately, I need it as soon as possible. We have a client whose granddaughter was recently taken captive by pirates and, we believe, taken to Somalia. He has hired us to ensure her safe return, and as part of the deal, he wants us to find out who may have orchestrated the piracy."

"I will get started on it right away. Do you need to talk with Ms. Drew?" asked Roland.

"Yes. And thanks Roland," said Carl as Roland transferred the call.

"Yes Carl?"

"Elaine, I will need to get back to the office early tomorrow morning. Rick and Carlos will be staying in Destin working on a new project."

"I'll schedule the aircraft and let you know when they'll be there. Is there anything else?" she asked.

"Yes, one other thing. Give Blackwell a call and ask him to set up a meeting with his negotiator," responded Carl.

"Negotiator?" questioned Elaine.

"He'll know. I'll fill you in when I see you. Let Blackwell know that I'll be more than happy to meet with him in Wilmington. In fact, I could make a stop at Wilmington tomorrow morning on my way back to D.C. His call."

"Will do. Is that it?" asked Elaine.

"That's it," said Carl as he hung up the phone and joined Rick and Carlos. They had been listening as well as they could. Rick had already opened the briefcase that Blackwell had given them and was thumbing through the material.

"We should get Roland to check the satellite imagery of the ports and harbors around Somalia. According to this information, Blackwell's granddaughter had a Beneteau Idylle series fifty-one-foot sailboat. There can't be too many of them in Somalia. I can't imagine the boat would be tied up to a pier, but you never know," said Rick.

"Probably anchored in some obscure harbor," offered Carl.

"That would certainly make it much easier to find," responded Rick.

"What do they do with the ships?" asked Carlos.

"Who knows. They probably sell them. Just another source of revenue," said Carl. "I'm sure Roland will find some information on that particular subject."

Rick continued to peruse the information provided by Blackwell. There were a few articles concerning recent events in Somalia that Blackwell had obviously printed from the Internet.

"If we are going to follow the money, you really need to control the negotiation. I have no idea how sophisticated these people are, but chasing around an electronic fund transfer can be challenging at best if we want to get eyes on who's getting the money," offered Rick.

"I agree. Blackwell certainly doesn't seem to be the kind of guy who'll go off half-cocked. Being a lifelong seafaring man, I'm sure he's well aware of how these modern-day pirates operate," said Carl.

"I hope you guys don't consider going into Somalia," said Carlos. "You know, we don't blend in very well," he added with raised eyebrows as he stuck out his arm. "I'm dark, but I'm not *that* dark."

"Let's see how the negotiation process goes before we make any rash decisions. We need to find out who and what we are dealing with. Then we'll have a better idea how to handle things," said Carl.

"Seems I read an article where an English couple was attacked by a gang within hours of arriving at a beach resort in Kenya. The resort was just a few miles from the border with Somalia. The husband was killed and the wife taken captive," said Rick.

"Hold on," said Carl as he made a few keystrokes on his laptop.

"Here it is. They had just arrived at the Kiwayu Safari Village. Seems they were taken by an Islamist group called Harakat al-Shabaab al-Mujahideen."

"That's a mouthful," responded Carlos.

Carl read the whole article out loud to Rick and Carlos. The article included reference to another couple who had been held captive for over a year. They were finally released when the ransom was paid.

"I suspect that time is not an issue with the pirates," observed Rick.

"They certainly aren't a refined bunch," added Carl.

"They have no regard for life," said Carlos, making his distaste for this group well known.

"I'm sure Roland will come across the information we need in order to determine a timeline and decide upon a course of action," responded Carl as he went over to the patio door.

A light afternoon rain began to fall as Carl looked out at the Gulf. The only clouds were in the vicinity of Carl's condo. Hopefully it wasn't an omen of things to come. The rest of the sky was blue. The sun was getting close to the horizon. Carl knew that there was probably a rainbow to the east. He thought about going out on the patio to look.

A rainbow wouldn't be there for long. Maybe the end of the rainbow was over his condo. Carl looked up but didn't see anything but rain. He went back inside and continued the conversation with Rick and Carlos.

"We'll follow the money, but our priority has to be the granddaughter," said Carl. "I don't want them ending up like the English couple."

Rick put one of the folders down and thought for a few seconds before responding to Carl.

"There's a very good chance that we'll be executing this project on two fronts. We'll probably need one team to follow the money and the other team to ensure the safe return of the granddaughter," said Rick as he looked over at Carlos. He knew what Carlos was thinking and what he was about to say.

"I volunteer to follow the money," announced Carlos without looking up.

Carlos also knew that Rick was expecting that declaration.

"Yeah, right," said both Carl and Rick nearly in unison.

"I wonder what Higgins is doing," said Carl.

"I was just thinking the same thing. He and his team would certainly be my first choice," responded Rick. "I would bet he has connections in that part of the world. In fact, he probably has connections right in Somalia."

"He seems to have connections all over the world," agreed Carl.

Rick continued to look through the material that Blackwell had provided. The material was quite thorough. Blackwell had also provided a brief overview of his granddaughter and the companions that had accompanied her on her voyage. The information also included a tentative schedule of their transit. Rick was impressed with the detail.

"Seems there were four of them on the boat," he said without looking up. "The granddaughter's name is Courtney Evans."

"I assume she's married," said Carl. It was actually a question.

"I'm not sure," responded Rick as he thumbed through the material.

"Well, it really doesn't matter," said Carl.

"Hold on a second," said Rick as he read a hand-written note from Blackwell. "Seems her husband was a cancer victim. She promised to spread his ashes around the world."

No one said anything as Rick continued to read the note.

"Looks like they bought the boat in Saint Lucia, spent a few days there, and then started their journey."

"I assume they went through the Panama Canal. What was their next stop?" asked Carl.

"The Galápagos Islands. Looks like they planned to spend a few days there," responded Rick.

"How long does it take to sail around the world?" asked Carlos.

"It depends," said Rick.

"Says here that the average is two hundred to five hundred days," responded Carl.

Carl had already brought up an around-the-world sailing site that provided the overall route and sailing particulars.

"So if they headed west, they probably went to Tahiti and Fiji," offered Rick.

"That appears to be the route," responded Carl.

"Let's also look into the seller of the boat," said Rick as he made a note.

CHAPTER FIVE
Destin, Florida
Day 3
0900 Hours

As Carl was on his way to Wilmington for a ten hundred meeting with JT Blackwell, Lynn, Ann, and *the boys* were sitting out on Rick's balcony enjoying the morning view of the Gulf. The weather in Destin was ideal…as usual. The visibility was only limited by the horizon. Lynn was about to say something when Carlos blurted out, "Porpoise off the starboard bow!" He looked back at Ann as he pointed in the direction where several porpoise could be seen breaking the surface of the water. They were about fifty yards off shore. Rick looked through his binoculars and then handed them to Carlos. No matter how many times they had seen porpoise, new sightings in the wild were always welcomed with enthusiasm.

"There are at least five of them," reported Carlos.

"Can I see, can I see?" asked Ann as she slid her chair back, stood up, and moved next to Carlos. She began tapping him on his right shoulder. Carlos continued to watch as several pelicans began diving in the vicinity of the porpoise.

"They must be into a school of baitfish," said Rick as he leaned against the railing. Several more pelicans joined the feast.

Ann continued to tap Carlos on the shoulder until he finally relented and handed her the binoculars. *Sometimes she's like a little kid,* he thought to himself. He smiled as he continued to watch the porpoise roll in among the baitfish. The fish were being overwhelmed as they tried desperately to avoid the sea and air predators. Many in the school, if not all, would be unsuccessful in their attempt at escape and evasion. The sea was beautiful but certainly treacherous depending upon one's position in the food chain, and that included man.

"They're heading toward the Destin Bridge," said Rick. "They'll head back east later this afternoon. Seems to be a daily ritual," he added.

"Looks like four adults and at least one calf in the pod," said Ann.

"A pod," declared Carlos, glancing at Ann.

Having worked with porpoise as a Navy SEAL, he was very familiar with the proper nomenclature. He was somewhat surprised that Ann knew.

"That's right Garcia, a *pod*," retorted Ann defiantly as she lowered the binoculars, resting them against her ample bosom. There was an unmistakable hint of a gotcha moment. "If you would leave the *pride* once in a while, you would realize that there's more to me than just a pretty face," she added as she repositioned the binoculars. She wondered if Carlos would pick up on the pun.

"You forgot to add a nice body to boot," he said as he continued to look at her well-defined figure. He then let out a jungle-sized roar.

He had indeed picked up on the pun.

Lynn smiled as she and Rick began removing the morning dishes.

"Anyone for another cup of coffee?" asked Lynn.

Rick and Carlos nodded their desire for a fresh cup.

Rick accompanied Lynn into the kitchen and selected two Vermont Country Blend K-Cups. Lynn rinsed the coffee cups, dried them, and placed them side by side on the counter. She took one and placed it on the Keurig.

"They really are great together, aren't they," remarked Lynn.

"That they are," responded Rick as he looked back out on the balcony. Carlos was now tapping Ann on the shoulder. She wasn't acquiescing to the moment.

"So what's the new project?" asked Lynn.

Rick had been waiting all too patiently for her to ask.

"Looks like we may be looking into a piracy off the coast of Somalia. Carl is meeting with the client, a man by the name of Blackwell, again this morning."

"A piracy? I thought that piracy has really slowed down?"

"It has slowed down quite a bit—but not stopped."

"So who was captured?" asked an inquisitive Lynn.

"Blackwell's granddaughter and the people who were with her," responded Rick not wanting to get into a long discussion on what little details he actually knew at this point.

Lynn didn't say anything as she continued to make the fresh cups of coffee. Rick could tell that she was pondering the piracy situation and developing several scenarios in her mind, each of which would generate a million questions. She would think of the many *what ifs* that Rick would be forced to address.

"You're not going to Somalia are you?" she asked without looking at him.

One of the scenarios had just surfaced.

"No, not to worry honey. Hopefully, no one will have to set foot in Somalia."

"And how can you avoid going?" she asked.

"We'll push for an at sea transfer."

"And if your pirate friends don't agree?"

"My pirate friends?" questioned Rick.

Lynn didn't say anything.

"Then we'll put together the right team," he responded.

"I hope so. You're too old for this sort of thing," she said raising her eyebrows.

Rick smiled. He knew that was coming. He had just won a million dollars from an imaginary wager.

"*The boys* are too old?" he questioned.

"You know what I mean," she said as she brushed by him with the fresh coffee.

Rick understood her concern. He never told her everything, and she knew that he never told her everything. There were things that she didn't want to know, and there were certainly things she would never know.

"Ann, did you still want to go for a walk?" asked Lynn looking over at Ann.

"Rick, do you need me here for anything?" asked Ann before committing to Lynn.

"No, you go enjoy your walk. If we need you, Carlos will bring you up to speed," replied Rick.

"Well, what about you guys? Would you like to go with us?" Lynn asked.

"We'd love too, but we have some work to do," responded Rick.

"Yeah we'd love too," added Carlos. His smile and enthusiasm were far from convincing.

"Then you don't mind if Ann and I go?

"Of course not," responded Rick.

Carlos nodded in agreement. He was relieved. A walk with Lynn and Ann was never just a walk. Keeping up with the two of them was a chore at best. Usually Rick and Carlos would let the girls go on ahead. Within fifteen minutes, they would be at least a hundred yards ahead of them. Rick never viewed a walk on the beach as exercise. He believed it was a time to enjoy nature—at least he was determined to stick with that story no matter what.

As Lynn and Ann prepared for their walk, Rick and Carlos went into Rick's office where they had the contents of Blackwell's briefcase spread out on the desk. Everything was neatly stacked into several piles.

"Did Courtney have a crew member on board or just friends?" asked Carlos.

"From what I can gather, she was an accomplished sailor. The couple with her were friends, and the guy with her was her first cousin," said Rick.

"So, she lost her husband," said Carlos as he looked at a picture of Courtney Evans. She was striking.

"She was on a mission," responded Rick as he continued to look through the material.

"One that was interrupted by the skinnies," retorted Carlos.

"The cousin's name is Scotty Blackwell. He is also an experienced sailor. Says here that he has circumnavigated the globe nine times— five times on the Race Route and four times on the Canal Route," offered Rick.

"With that much experience, you'd think he would have known better than to sail them into the vicinity of pirates," said Carlos.

Rick continued to look at the material as he thought about what Carlos had just said. Several years back he had been involved in a three-day conference that focused on piracy in the Gulf of Aden. He certainly was no expert, but there were certain aspects that strongly suggested that the attacks were far from random. Rick never believed that they were merely targets of opportunity. Someone was feeding the pirates specific information, and that someone could very well be in a position of authority.

The conference included information on methods being employed to provide protection. Many shipping companies were currently employing ex-military personnel to provide onboard security. Although the pirates were well armed, they were no match for experienced military personnel who were better armed and well prepared to repel an attack. The effort was paying off. Piracy was indeed down from previous years. As a result, the pirates had become much more selective. The fact that the pirates were able to board certain oil tankers without confrontation was further evidence that the pirates were being fed intelligence from an outside source.

Targeting Courtney Evans' sailboat was not a mere coincidence. It was certainly not public knowledge that Courtney Evans was JT Blackwell's granddaughter and that she came from a family with considerable wealth. So why did they target her? She did have a very nice sailboat. However, the pirates' main objective was to collect a substantial ransom, one that JT Blackwell could afford. The one thing the pirates did not fully appreciate was the fact that the same wealth could, and in the case of JT Blackwell, would be used to hire a team capable of going after them.

Wilmington, North Carolina
0915 Hours

The Peterson Group aircraft landed at 0915 hours and was directed to the corporate facility. A lineman in a clean blue jumpsuit with bright orange wands parked The Peterson Group aircraft two spaces from Blackwell's aircraft. As Carl got off the plane, he noticed that a couple of mechanics were removing a cowling from the number one engine on Blackwell's plane. *There's always something to fix on an aircraft,* he thought to himself.

As he was about to enter the operations building, a young man in a dark suit and chauffeur's hat approached. He introduced himself and directed Carl to a white limousine that JT Blackwell had provided. Blackwell was obviously sparing no expense to entice Carl into taking on the project. Carl had already resolved to take on the assignment. He and Blackwell just needed to formalize the contract and agree to the terms.

The twenty-minute drive through Wilmington brought back a few memories for Carl. He hadn't been there for many years. Some things change, but Wilmington was the same city he had visited just before he had met the young Rick Morgan in Miami. He had never told Rick about his weekend in Wilmington. That weekend changed the direction of his life—for good.

The sound of breaking shells under the weight of the tires brought Carl back to the present, as the limo pulled into the parking area next to a building where JT Blackwell's office occupied a good portion of the third floor. Blackwell was already outside and leaning against a Range Rover that had just been detailed. He smiled as the driver opened the door for Carl.

"I trust you had a good flight," said Blackwell as he shook hands with Carl.

"A very good flight," responded Carl. "Like the limo," he added as he looked back at the vehicle.

"I rented it to impress you," said Blackwell as he handed the driver a folded bill.

Blackwell's honesty was refreshing.

"Thank you Mr. Blackwell," responded the driver as he put the bill into his pocket. "What time would you like me to return?" the driver asked.

"Actually, I will drive Mr. Peterson to the airport. Tell your boss thank you for the quick response."

"Will do Mr. Blackwell," responded the driver as he got into the limo and drove off. The sound of the shells crushing under the wheels continued to remind Carl of his visit many years ago.

Blackwell's office was not what Carl had expected. It was quite modern in all respects except for Blackwell's large teak desk that bore the scars of many years of service. Carl couldn't help but return his gaze to the desk. He felt the texture of the wood.

"It was made from the wood salvaged from Blackbeard's ship, *Queen Anne's Revenge*," offered Blackwell, noticing that the desk had captured Carl's attention.

"I thought it might be special," responded Carl. "And these notches?" he asked.

"A reminder of some of the men who were killed during the Revolutionary War," responded Blackwell as he opened the lower drawer and placed the packet of letters on top of the desk.

"Maybe when this is over you would like to read these," Blackwell enticed. "There is one letter for each notch. There are few men of their character these days. The letters are priceless," he continued after a short pause.

"I'll take you up on that when your granddaughter is safe," responded Carl with sincerity.

"So I take it you're going to take on this project," said Blackwell as he motioned for Carl to take a seat.

"Of course we will Mr. Blackwell."

"Please, call me JT. And as I mentioned before, I'm a very wealthy man. Cost is not an issue. You do whatever is necessary to ensure the safe return of my granddaughter and her friends."

"And the ransom?" asked Carl.

"If you can recoup the ransom, that would be an unexpected benefit. I would be very generous with a commission. My interest in the ransom is only to find out who else is involved, which reminds me," he said as he reached for his phone. "Carter, please come up," summoned Blackwell.

Carl didn't say anything as Blackwell got up and opened the door and then went over and retrieved a coffee pot from a Bunn coffee maker. "Would you like a cup?" he asked.

"I would indeed," responded Carl as he got up and joined Blackwell.

As he was fixing his own coffee, a young man came into the office. JT Blackwell introduced him as Carter Stanton. Stanton was short in stature and overweight, but well dressed. He shook hands with Carl. Carter's grip was weak and unassuming.

"So where are we?" asked Blackwell as the three men sat down.

"Quite frankly Mr. Blackwell, this type of transaction is out of my area of expertise. To act responsibly, we need a professional negotiator familiar with this sort of thing," responded Stanton.

Blackwell looked over at Carl who appreciated Stanton's candidness.

"And what do you suggest Mr. Peterson?" asked Blackwell.

"I agree with Stanton," responded Carl without hesitation.

Blackwell rubbed his hand over the notches on the desk as he pondered the situation.

"Can, and will you provide the negotiation?" asked Blackwell, directing his question to Carl.

"I can put together an experienced negotiation team. Might take a few days."

"Then, let's do it. Thank you Stanton," said Blackwell as he dismissed Carter Stanton from any further negotiation.

Stanton got up and nodded to Carl Peterson. He looked relieved.

Carl didn't say anything as he waited for JT Blackwell to continue.

"Stanton is a good man. He's young. I knew this was way over his head, but as you suggested, we needed to start the process."

"By the way, what is the name of Courtney's sailboat?' asked Carl.

"*A Pirate's Dream,*" responded Blackwell. A slight smile crossed the old man's face.

CHAPTER SIX
Destin, Florida
1100 Hours

Carlos handed the last of the documents to Rick and sat back in his chair, appearing to be in deep thought. *For sure he is thinking about Somalia*, Rick thought to himself as he looked over at Carlos. Carlos made brief eye contact, then stood up, stretched, yawned, and didn't say anything as he walked over to the patio door and looked out in the direction of the Destin-Fort Walton Beach Airport. A small twin-engine corporate jet could be seen taking the active runway. It did a rolling takeoff. Carlos watched the aircraft as it climbed out straight ahead. The sound followed close behind. It was out of sight within seconds. Rick placed everything back into the briefcase and was about to close it when his laptop sounded a message alert. The message was from Roland. It was brief:

Have attached several files for your review, please call at your earliest convenience. By the way, what was the make of the sailboat? VR—Roland.

Rick remembered seeing pictures of the sailboat. He shuffled through the material and soon found what he was looking for. He then dialed Roland.

"Good morning Mr. Morgan. I trust you received the material."

"That I did. It would appear that you have put a lot of effort into this," said Rick. "I plan on going through it right away."

"There is a lot more to piracy than one would expect," responded Roland. "It has been an education to say the least," he added.

Rick was aware of the many issues facing Somalia, including the reasons to justify their actions. The fact that there was no real government in place stifled any meaningful cooperation that one would normally expect from a country run by a legitimate government.

"She has a fifty-one foot Beneteau."

"A fifty-one foot Beneteau," repeated Roland just loud enough that Rick heard him repeat the name. "Actually, I have some footage on a target of interest that size," he added as he pulled the keyboard toward his chest.

Rick could hear Roland making a few key strokes followed by an audible tone—one that he recognized from the past.

"Mr. Morgan, would you hold on for a couple of minutes. I'm looking at a live satellite feed, and I just want to determine if there are any other sailboats fitting that description in Somali waters. It shouldn't take long at all."

"No problem," said Rick as he put the phone on speaker and went to look for Carlos.

Carlos had gone into the den and was looking through the binoculars. He appeared to be scanning the beach for the girls. Roland was back on the line before Rick could get Carlos's full attention.

"There's only one fifty-one foot sailboat that the feed identified. It's anchored at Eyl. In fact, I had taken notice of that particular boat a few hours ago. Looks like it's in very good condition," said Roland.

"Is it a Beneteau?" asked Rick. "Can you make out the name on the stern?" he continued before Roland could respond.

"I'm checking that as we speak."

Rick walked back into the office and sat behind his desk. He slowly swung his chair around as an aircraft could be heard doing a run up just prior to taking the active runway. It brought back fond memories of his early days as a Navy pilot. Rick was imagining himself in the cockpit of an A-4 Skyhawk when Roland interrupted his daydream.

"The stern is covered by a canvass, but I would be willing to bet that the sailboat I'm looking at is your boat," said Roland as he continued to scan the Beneteau.

"Probably why the stern is covered. Are there any other boats in the area?" asked Rick.

"There are a few, but nothing even close to a fifty-one footer," responded Roland.

"You said that you took notice of it a few hours ago."

"I did. Probably wouldn't have paid it much attention, but I noticed some action around that particular boat. I recorded an event that may be more than just a mere coincidence," said Roland.

"And?" asked Rick.

"There is a rusty old Liberty ship run aground a few hundred yards to the south. About two hours ago, a small johnboat left the beach area by the ship and went directly over to the sailboat. A guy went onto the sailboat and retrieved something that appeared to be a small sea bag. He then went back to the ship, pulled the johnboat onto the beach, and went on board. The johnboat is still there."

Rick didn't respond immediately. In his mind, the conclusion was obvious.

"Could be that Blackwell's granddaughter is being held on the ship," offered Rick.

"Maybe so, but I would feel much more comfortable if I had a visual to make that determination," said Roland.

"Can you play that again?" asked Rick.

Rick continued to scrutinize the recording. Roland was right. This was just too much of a coincidence to ignore. However, the pirates were known for moving the captives to new locations—and moving them quite frequently. Besides, it wouldn't be wise to even attempt an extraction based upon an observation with no confirmation.

"Are you tied into a geo-stationary satellite?" asked Rick.

"Yes sir," responded Roland somewhat tentatively after a short pause.

"It's okay Roland. Several years ago I wrote the Test and Evaluation Master Plan for those very satellites. At that time, there were eighteen of them. The plan was to put up twenty-four in all. I'm a little surprised they're still in service."

"They're not...or at least they aren't supposed to be," responded Roland.

"Will you keep an eye on the ship and let me know if there is any more suspicious activity? Maybe you can get some close-ups of anyone going on or off the ship."

"I can do that. And if you have a current picture of the sailboat, including any of the people on the boat, I can make a positive identification through autocorrelation," responded Roland.

Rick was very familiar with the use of autocorrelation techniques to find a particular target among many targets of similar size and shape. There were always subtle differences that could be used to distinguish among targets and make a positive identification.

"I'll scan the pictures I have," responded Rick.

"Even a partial photograph will work," offered Roland.

"I believe Somalia is eight hours ahead of Eastern Standard Time," said Rick, changing the subject.

"That's correct," responded Roland.

"Do you have night vision capability?"

"It's limited, but there are periods when I can piggyback on an orbiting satellite with that capability," responded Roland.

"If they have any sophistication at all, they're probably aware of the window," said Rick.

"From the material I've read so far, it appears that the pirates have moved into the twenty-first century. They seem to employ the right people for the right job," responded Roland.

"No more eye patches, peg legs and parrots...eh, Roland," laughed Rick.

"Probably a few parrots," responded Roland.

"I can't imagine they would make any moves during daylight hours, but you never know," said Rick.

"If they do, there's a good chance that I can make a positive identification. I can certainly track where they move the captives."

"Let me know how your surveillance goes. I'll send the pictures to you in a couple of minutes. Thanks Roland."

There were several pictures of the sailboat. One was obviously a commercial picture of a Beneteau. All the other pictures were current and of Courtney and her friends. One picture showed her holding a gold urn. A couple of the pictures were taken as they boarded the sailboat in St. Lucia. Rick scanned all of them and forwarded them to Roland. As he was scanning the pictures, Carlos came into the room.

"So what did Roland have to say?"

"He sent quite a bit of information. There's a strong possibility that he has located our sailboat."

"Where did he find it?" asked Carlos.

"Eyl," responded Rick.

Carlos didn't say anything. Rick started to look through the material that Roland had provided.

"Would you like a cup of coffee?" asked Carlos as he headed for the kitchen.

"That would be nice, and I think there is a Danish roll in the refrigerator," responded Rick.

Five minutes later, Carlos returned with two Starbucks city mugs and a plate with two Danishes. Rick had been collecting the city mugs for several years and had a fairly large selection in the condo. Carlos placed a Florida cup on the desk in front of Rick. Rick smiled as he took a drink and noticed Carlos's selection. Carlos was cradling a cup from Phuket, Thailand.

"Are you trying to tell me something?" asked Rick as he motioned to the cup from Thailand.

"Depends upon how you want to pronounce it. I prefer the phonetic pronunciation myself," smiled Carlos.

"I love that cup. Most people don't get it," responded Rick. "So what's bothering you my friend?" asked Rick as he put his pencil down and sat back in the chair.

Carlos took a long drink from the cup as he looked out at the airport. Rick didn't want to press him, but he knew that Carlos had something on his mind that involved Somalia. Carlos took a seat across from Rick.

"I spent some time in Djibouti, at Camp Lemonnier, a short time after it was abandoned by the French Foreign Legion. We had flown in for a joint mission with the French—a quid pro quo thing. The place was a mess. The buildings had been plundered, the swimming pool was filled with garbage, and there was goat and bird shit everywhere. I got to stay a few nights in one of the containerized living units that were set up in rows. It was known as CLUville. I would have preferred to set up my own accommodations, but you couldn't trust the locals. They'd slit your throat for a candy bar. Our mission was to rescue a couple of French nationals that had been taken captive by the al-Shabaab Islamist group. We had what we thought was reliable HUMINT that pinpointed the two in Berbera. There were six of us Navy SEALS and a French Foreign Legion lieutenant by the name of Maurice Bovier. Bovier actually led the mission. He was the epitome of the Hollywood stereotypical legionnaire. He was tough, resourceful, smelled badly, but he was the guy you wanted standing next to you in a dark alley."

Carlos took a bite of Danish and followed it with a drink from the Phuket cup. He looked at the name on the cup, took another swallow of coffee, and then continued.

"Everything went as planned until we went to the extraction point. Then all hell broke loose. It was obvious that we had been set up. We held our own. Bovier made it possible for us to complete the mission. He was captured. We dropped off the two Frenchmen and went back for him. We found his head on a pole. We never did find his body. We took his head back with us. Later that day, I accompanied his remains to France. With a little help from the Foreign Legion, I purchased a cadaver. Lieutenant Bovier was buried with full honors. His family never knew that he wasn't all there."

Rick didn't say anything as Carlos got up and went back into the kitchen. Carlos was one of the toughest guys that Rick had ever known. A few years ago he had placed third in the Double Ironman competition at the young age of fifty-three. But Carlos had strong reservations about Somalia, and it was evident to Rick. Carlos returned with another cup of coffee.

"Would you like a refill?"

"I'm fine," responded Rick.

"I just don't like these people. I'd rather deal with the Serbs or the Russians for that matter. You know what to expect from them. But with these guys…I'd have a hard time negotiating with a guy that I wanted to shoot."

"So the only good skinny is a dead skinny?" observed Rick. It was purely a rhetorical question.

"I believe so," said Carlos as he pointed to the name on his cup.

Rick didn't say anything. He continued to look through the material and made a few notes. He wouldn't push Carlos. He understood where Carlos was coming from. They had all been there—lost people they respected. Some things never changed.

"From what I have gleaned so far, the pirates operate on a very different time schedule. There seems to be no urgency...until they decide that there is urgency."

"Meaning?" questioned Carlos.

"Meaning they want to give the impression that they are willing to negotiate. And *that* will give us enough time to come up with a plan."

CHAPTER SEVEN
Cartagena, Colombia
Day 4
0900 Hours

Roy Higgins was sitting at a glass-top table for two outside the Hilton Cartagena when his cell phone rang. He looked at the caller ID. A slight smile briefly crossed his face.

"Carl," he answered, just as a couple of young women wearing black thongs and white-lace cover-ups, with nothing underneath, brushed by him and headed across the street to the beach area that served the hotel. The air around him was suddenly filled with a faint aroma of lilacs. Their leather sandals made slapping sounds as they bounced across the highway. The sun fostered little beads of perspiration that added a shred of mystery to their glistening bodies. One of the girls looked back and gave a sheepish smile. They had knowingly captured the full attention of the older gentleman.

"Mr. Higgins," said Carl, sounding somewhat relieved that Roy had answered the call, and even more relieved that he didn't have to leave a message. He probably wouldn't have left a message anyway. "Are you able to talk?"

"That I am," answered Roy somewhat rhythmically. He was still in step with the young women.

"Am I catching you had a bad time?" asked Carl, perceiving the musical tone in Higgins' voice.

"No, not at all. I'm taking a few days off and enjoying the local scenery…if you know what I mean," he responded as he stood up to watch the girls wrestle with their bamboo beach blankets. The girls were young, firm, and obviously quite uninhibited as they bent over without bending their knees. Roy shook his head slightly and then sat down. At his age, he could continue to look with a sense of satisfaction. Gratification would not be on the menu.

"Are you in the states?" asked Carl.

"I'm in Cartagena. Just finished a tractor deal in Bogotá and will be heading back to Miami early tomorrow."

Carl was very familiar with Cartagena. Cartagena was Miami's sister city. He and Rick had been there on several occasions. All were in connection with business...and mostly at night. Carl smiled to himself as he conjured up an image of the local scenery—scenery that he suspected had fully captured Roy's attention.

"You be careful with the local scenery," cautioned Carl.

"Right," laughed Roy. "Actually, I was just looking through some invoices. It has been a very profitable trip," he added as he shook the local newspaper to give the impression that he was indeed looking through some papers. It didn't fool Carl.

Carl was aware that Roy Higgins' listed occupation was that of a heavy equipment sales representative. In fact, Roy Higgins was quite good at it. He had sold millions of dollars worth of tractors and associated earth moving equipment throughout Central and South America. He was well known, and for many, he was a welcomed visitor. For others, he was the angel of death.

"Will you be available for some contract work?" asked Carl, getting right to the point.

"Depends," said Higgins as he finished what was left of his café con leche. "What's the gig?" he asked as he signaled a barista and pointed to his empty cup. He punctuated his desire with a repetitive motion of his left forefinger.

The barista smiled and did a smart about face, although he pivoted on the wrong foot.

"My client's granddaughter has been kidnapped by Somali pirates and has hired my firm to negotiate the ransom along with her safe return."

Roy didn't respond for several seconds. He subconsciously picked up the cup, and then remembered that it was empty. His mind wondered to the Horn of Africa. He had been there on many occasions...too many. He was always very happy and relieved when he left. The seconds of silence lingered on long enough, prompting Carl to look at the LED display.

"You still there?" asked Carl, thinking that he may have lost the connection.

"I'm here," responded Roy. "I've had a few dealings with Somali pirates. I'm all too familiar with them and their tactics. They're not a refined bunch. For the most part, they're a young, pissed off bunch who carry guns, and they all happen to look alike. My immediate recommendation for your client would be to pay the ransom and hope that his granddaughter is returned in one piece."

Carl was not at all surprised by Roy's directness or recommendation.

"Well, I have to agree with you, but my client is hell-bent on finding out who is behind it."

"Behind it?" questioned Roy.

"My client believes that his granddaughter was specifically targeted by someone who took the time to look into her background and potential resources."

"Well, that's certainly a possibility in this day and age. In the past couple of years, piracy has waned considerably. The pirates have become more cautious and much more selective with their targets. Targets of opportunity are a thing of the past. I assume you're bringing Morgan and his team into this."

"Rick is going over the particulars as we speak."

There was another long pause as Roy took a drink from his fresh cup of café con leche that the barista had somehow placed on the table without him noticing. The revelation caused him to look around. He was usually very much aware of his surroundings. Carl could hear a discernable click as Roy put the cup down on the saucer. Roy was still somewhat surprised that he hadn't noticed the barista. He regrouped.

"Rick's a good man. Tell you what, I have to be in Miami tomorrow morning for a meeting with my supplier, then I'm free for at least a couple of weeks, maybe more. I can head up to D.C. later in the day."

"Great," responded Carl, sounding confident.

"Carl, I'm not committing to be a part of this, so don't get too excited," responded Roy, catching the tone in Carl's voice. "I just want to be in on the initial planning before I make a final decision."

"Fair enough my friend. By the way, I'm heading down to Florida tomorrow and can easily swing by Miami and pick you up."

"You don't have to pick me up. I'm traveling on the Senator's nickel."

"Senator Windell?"

"One in the same," responded Roy.

"I thought he had decided to retire."

"I think the episode with the *Search for Snake* convinced him that there were still a lot of good guys on his side."

"That's good to know. I assume he's keeping you busy?"

"Busy enough. The work is interesting, and the money…well, the money is nothing to sniff at."

"Listen Roy, I have a two-hour meeting at SOUTHCOM. It's an easy jaunt over to Miami. We can do a little catching up on the way," offered Carl.

"Sounds like we're both flying on someone else's nickel."

"It's the only way to fly."

Roy didn't have to think very long. Besides, he could save the Senator a few bucks.

"Okay, I should be through with my meeting by noon. I'll let you know a time. By the way, I'll be in South Miami. Is Homestead good for you?"

"Homestead will do just fine. I'll see you tomorrow," responded Carl. "And Roy, watch out for that jailbait."

Roy finished his café con leche, stood up, and took one last look over at the girls. They were lying on their back enjoying the late morning sun. They were tan all over. He smiled to himself thinking that days with girls that age were long gone…or not.

Destin, Florida
1015 Hours

Rick continued to go over the material that Roland had provided. He had been busy with the yellow highlighter. Carlos had gone back into the den, turned on the TV, and had dozed off on the couch. The girls hadn't returned from their morning walk on the beach. Rick was reading an article about the British couple who had been kidnapped within hours of arriving at a beach resort in Kenya. The resort was just a few miles from the Somali border. The pirates had made a beach landing, killed the husband, and kidnapped the wife. As he continued to read the article, his cell phone rang. Rick picked it up and glanced at the LED. The name *Blue Sky* filled the display.

"Morning Carl," answered Rick as he leaned back in his chair.

"Hey buddy. What's going on?" asked Carl.

"I was just going over the material that Roland provided. I assume he sent you the same information."

"I believe he did. I really haven't had an opportunity to get into it yet. So what do you think?" asked Carl. He knew the short answer.

"I think this thing could get very messy. We know what Blackwell basically wants, but you and I both know that *basically* leaves a lot to interpretation. We need to pin down what Blackwell really expects from us so that he won't have any unrealistic expectations." said Rick.

"I plan on doing just that," responded Carl.

"Getting his granddaughter back may be the easy part, as long as he's willing to forfeit the ransom."

"You don't think we can negotiate the amount?" asked Carl.

"We may be able to negotiate the amount to some small degree, but I wouldn't count on it. I wouldn't want it to be a showstopper."

"Sounds like you have done quite a bit of research already. Do you have a plan in mind?"

"Not really. Right now the pirates have all the chips. But it will be a lot easier to come up with an executable plan once Blackwell's granddaughter and her friends are safe. And the only way we can ensure their safe return is to meet the agreed upon monetary demands, and meet that demand in a timely manner."

"So as far as the money is concerned, what is our role?" asked Carl.

"Quite frankly, I think our role will be to determine how and where to deliver the money."

"What about the granddaughter and her friends?" asked Carl.

"Once the pirates have the money, they will let them go. There would be no sense in harming them at that point. If that were their modus operandi, no one would ever negotiate with them, much less pay any amount of ransom."

"I agree. What about finding out who may be behind it?" asked Carl.

"I believe that issue will be the real challenge. There are so many potential areas along the route where she could have been marked. I would love to get a good look at her sailboat. Hopefully, Roland's analysis will identify a common thread—any connection that could be used to provide a valid starting point."

"Speaking of a starting point, guess who I talked to this morning?"

"Higgins," responded Rick without one second of thought.

"Am I that transparent?"

"Sometimes you are, but Higgins was the logical choice."

"He indicated that he has had dealings with some Somali pirates in the past."

"And how did that turn out?"

"I'm not sure, but he was quick to recommend that we pay the ransom."

Rick didn't say anything for a few seconds as he heard the girls come in from their walk on the beach. He could hear Ann picking on Carlos for taking an early nap. He turned his attention back to the conversation.

"I agree with him. There is only one thing the pirates are interested in, and that is money."

"And how much," added Carl.

"Right, and how much," repeated Rick. "Higgins will know how to negotiate the release of Blackwell's granddaughter and her friends. However, being released is one thing, getting out of the country safely could be another issue we'll need to consider," added Rick.

"Do you really think that another group might try to take advantage of the situation?"

"We're on their turf. You never know, but Higgins and his team would be my choice to successfully negotiate the terms of the release and safe passage."

"He hasn't committed yet. I'm going to pick him up at Homestead tomorrow and then fly to D.C."

"Carl, why don't you guys fly into Destin? Carlos and Ann are still here. We can dial in Roland..."

"And then we can adjourn to Marina Café for a few drinks," interrupted Carl. "I love that place, especially during happy hour," he added.

"You like the half-price menu," teased Rick.

"Well that too, and the view is great," he added with a laugh. "Is Wally still there?"

"He is. Did you know that he's from Beirut?"

"I suspected that he was Lebanese. Wally is probably short for Walid. He's really a good guy," stated Carl.

"That he is," responded Rick.

"Will Lynn be okay with us flying in?"

"She'll be okay with it. Besides, she and Ann are having a good time together. They would probably like to do some more shopping anyway. More of that girl bonding thing."

"Check with her first just to make sure," said Carl.

"Will do, but just plan on coming here. By tomorrow I should be well up to speed on the project. You just need to pin Blackwell down," Rick reminded Carl.

"I'll call him today," responded Carl. "See you tomorrow."

Rick put the phone down and brought up the last article in the attachments from Roland. It was an article about a British couple who spent quite a long time in Somali captivity while the British government was trying to negotiate their release. One item caught his attention. He looked at his watch and made a note to call Alastair Sims at MI6 first thing in the morning.

CHAPTER EIGHT
Destin, Florida
Day 5
0900 Hours

A ray of sunlight made its way into the bedroom through a slight separation where one of the large room darkeners didn't quite make it to the wall. Although it was short-lived, the ray's life was long enough to wake Rick. He couldn't fall asleep the night before. He was unable to slow down the parade of thoughts marching through his mind. He had put himself in Blackwell's shoes. It was always like that with a new client—with a new project. A myriad of scenarios had joined the parade. He went over each one several times as they passed by. No matter how he played it, how the scenario developed, one thing was very clear; the best initial course of action would be to pay the ransom and then focus the team's effort on ensuring the safe passage of Blackwell's granddaughter and her friends.

The fact that there was no real governing authority in Somalia left the local groups in a constant struggle. Somalia was like the American old west. Cooperation, if at all, was minimal at best. It was always survival of the fittest. The most ruthless gangs would have their way. Nothing ever changed. As Rick lay there, he slowly began to doze off. His thoughts went to man's constant inward struggle. The Christians believed that the return of Jesus was immanent. The non-Christians didn't know or care for that matter. Rick cared. He would always care. He started counting backwards from one hundred. Each time he would get to eighty-three, eighty-two, he would start thinking about the project again. On the third try, he finally fell asleep.

As Rick slowly woke to the small ray of light peeking into the curtains, he reached over to touch Lynn, but he felt nothing but empty sheets. She was already up. Rick looked at the clock. He couldn't believe that it was nearly nine. He rose up on his elbows and looked over at the other clock just to make sure. As he got up, he could hear the girls talking in the den. It sounded like they were planning a shopping trip down 30A. There were several shops that Lynn liked to visit on a regular basis. She wouldn't buy anything unless it was on sale. Sooner or later, everything was on sale. At the end of the day she loved to stop by *Vue on 30a* for a glass of wine and to enjoy the sunset. That would be the part that Ann would like.

As he went into the bathroom, it dawned on him that he hadn't said anything to Lynn about Carl or Roy Higgins. Lynn didn't know Roy Higgins; however, she was always a good first-time hostess no matter what. She would most likely ask him a million questions. Lynn actually really liked Carl, but Rick loved pulling Carl's chain. When it came to being liked, Carl's chain was short.

Carlos was inserting a K-Cup into the Keurig when Rick joined them in the kitchen.

"Hey Rick," said Carlos. His greeting alerted Lynn that Rick was finally up.

"Looks who's up," she exclaimed as she looked over her left shoulder. She didn't make eye contact.

It's that southern thing, he thought to himself. He smiled.

"Had a hard time falling asleep last night," Rick said in a failed attempt to defend his "sleeping-in."

"Thinking about the project?" asked Carlos. It was more of a rhetorical question. He knew that Rick would wrestle with it until he had all those little rectangles, squares and decision blocks on paper. Every contingency would be covered...one-way or another.

"Sometimes I find it difficult to just clear my mind and fall asleep."

"You have to have a clear conscience," said Lynn.

She was listening. Women hear everything. Rick pretended to ignore her. Carlos removed the Phuket cup from the Keurig. Rick smiled.

"You like that cup," said Rick as he selected one of the K-Cups.

"It speaks volumes," responded Carlos. "Thought I heard you talking with Carl last night," he added as he raised the cup and smelled the freshly brewed coffee. He took a small sip. His expression confirmed that it was just right.

"That's right!" exclaimed Rick as if he just remembered it. "Hey honey, do you have a problem if Carl stops by here later this afternoon?"

"Of course not," she responded. "Is he planning on staying here or in Pensacola?"

"I assume he will be staying in Pensacola. Roy Higgins will be with him."

"Do I know Roy Higgins?" asked Lynn as she got up from the couch and walked over to the counter that separated the kitchen and den. She had a questioning look on her face. She was in full listening mode.

"I have mentioned him, but you have never met him," answered Rick.

"He's a good guy," said Carlos. "He's one of us."

"A house full of spies," laughed Ann without looking up.

"Do you know Roy Higgins?" asked Lynn as she looked over at Ann.

"Yes, but I haven't seen him for many years," she responded.

"You'll like him," offered Carlos convincingly.

Lynn thought for a few seconds. Her day was probably going to change, but living with Rick Morgan was never routine. She had given up a long time ago on making long-term plans. Even short-term plans could be in jeopardy.

"Well then, I'm looking forward to meeting this Mr. Higgins," she said as she went back to the couch and sat next to Ann. They continued to look through a local magazine featuring the restaurants on 30A.

Rick wasn't sure if she had just surrendered or acquiesced to the moment. However, he was glad that Ann and Carlos were there. Otherwise, he would be the one answering a million questions.

"Well I guess that's settled," Rick said as he retrieved his fresh cup of coffee from the Keurig.

"How is Higgins these days?" asked Carlos.

"I suspect he's doing well. He seems to stay off the radar."

"Doesn't he have a pretty good cover job?" asked Carlos.

"From what I remember, he sells earth moving equipment."

"Probably handy in his line of business," responded Carlos with raised eyebrows.

Lynn turned and looked over at Rick. Rick smiled as he put his cup down and looked at his watch.

"I think it's fifteen thirty hours in London. I need to give our friend, Alastair Sims, a call."

"The MI6 Mr. Sims? Do you think he can help us with this project?" asked Carlos not knowing where Rick was heading."

"I was reading one of the articles that Roland provided. It was about a British couple who was captured by Somali pirates in the vicinity of the Seychelles. The article mentioned that the couple had initially flown to Tortola. After touring the islands they bought a large sailboat and commenced their around-the-world trip."

"And you think there may be a connection somehow to the Blackwell project?"

"The article said they flew in to Tortola then bought the sailboat. You just don't decide all of a sudden to sail around the world. It must've been their plan all along. I'd like to know where they bought the boat, the make of the boat, and who sold it to them."

"Didn't Blackwell's granddaughter pick up her boat in Saint Lucia?"

"That she did."

"That's a long way from Tortola. Seems like a stretch."

"Maybe. I'm hoping Sims can fill in the blanks," said Rick as he headed for his office.

"I'll be right in," said Carlos as he put his coffee cup in the microwave. Carlos loved his coffee piping hot. It cooled quite rapidly in the large Starbucks cup.

Rick took his little green wheel book from his briefcase and found Alastair Sims' number under the *M* tab. There was a note under Sims' name that simply stated, *count your fingers*. The meaning was clear. Nothing ever came without a price. Rick dialed the number. He didn't need to go through an overseas operator or any special channels. The number went directly to Sims' satellite phone.

"Morgan," answered Sims just after the first ring. "I take it you're still alive?"

"That I am Sims."

"How is it there in The Colonies?" he asked, never losing an opportunity for a dig.

"Much the same as you well know. We are free."

"Maybe not for long," quipped Sims. "I think your president wants to be king," he laughed. Unfortunately, he was serious.

Rick agreed with him.

"When that happens, I'll move to England."

"England is not so bad," responded Sims. "Have you thought about Canada?"

"Actually, I have. Is it all right if I put you on speaker? Carlos is here with me."

"That will be fine. So what can I do for you?"

"We have a client whose granddaughter has been captured by Somali pirates. I was..."

"Pay the ransom," interrupted Sims.

"That seems to be the conventional wisdom," responded Rick.

"It's a no-win situation. These people are uneducated and ruthless—makes for a very bad combination and very little room for negotiation. They are only interested in the money. And Morgan, when it comes to piracy, the whole country is your enemy. Pay the ransom and extract your pound of flesh some other way."

Rick didn't say anything for several seconds. His gut told him that Sims was probably right.

"Were you at all involved with negotiating the release of the Coughlins?" asked Rick.

"I was on the periphery. That was a mess. They were in captivity well over a year as the family refused the pirates' first demands. After not hearing a word for several months, the family finally agreed on a sum. The Coughlins were released a month after the ransom was paid."

"A month later," repeated Rick.

"The pirates don't do anything until the money is in place and distributed."

"Distributed?" questioned Rick.

"As I said, the whole country is dirty. Everyone gets a piece of the pie," responded Sims. "That's why they are so hard to deal with."

"The article mentioned the Coughlins flew to Tortola and bought a sailboat on one of the islands. Do you know what make of sailboat, and where they actually bought it?"

"Off the top of my head, I don't remember the answer to either of those questions. It seems to me after their tour of the British Virgin Islands, they flew to Saint Thomas. I can get you that information in a few days."

"A few days."

"The wife and I are on holiday in the Galápagos Islands. Scheduled to leave in a couple of days. Let me see what I can find out from this end," responded Sims, hearing the urgency in Rick's voice.

"Thanks Sims. I'll owe you one."

Rick laid the phone down and looked over at Carlos. Carlos had a pensive look on his face.

Homestead, Florida
1230 Hours

Roy Higgins was sitting outside the operations terminal when The Peterson Group Gulfstream came to a full stop. He stood up and retrieved a small brown satchel from behind the bench as he waited for the aircraft engines to shut down. He held a light khaki colored Panama hat in his right hand. He looked very South American in his off-white cotton trousers and brown silk shirt with large yellow leaves. The top two buttons were open, exposing a large gold Figaro chain, which complemented a gold Rolex on his right wrist. He wore brown sandals that appeared to match the color of his shirt. He was well tanned. Roy Higgins fit right in with the Miami crowd. As the line crew was chocking the wheels, the hatch opened. Carl started down the ladder as soon as it was secured in place.

Carl and Roy hadn't seen each other in quite a long time, although they were both involved indirectly with the same project a couple of years back. Roy's team had been contracted by a secret coalition led by Senator Paul Windell. The mission involved a covert operation to assassinate a rogue world leader in South America. The successful accomplishment of that mission was dependent upon The Peterson Group's retrieval of a smart sniper system known as *Snake*. Snake had been hijacked in an attempt to foil the coalition's present and future operations.

Carl had a broad smile on his face as he shook hands with Higgins. Higgins' grip was strong. His hands were rough. His days as an active sniper were probably past.

"How long has it been?" asked Carl.

"At least ten years," responded Higgins.

"Time is going by too fast my friend," said Carl. "You're looking quite fit," he added as they boarded the plane.

Higgins was indeed fit. At five feet eleven inches, he was a little shorter than Carl. His weight had never varied more than a couple of pounds from his usual weight of one hundred seventy-five pounds. He weighed exactly one hundred seventy-five when he graduated from the University of Florida.

"In our business you have to stay in shape."

"And especially at our age," added Carl.

They both smiled. Age was always the real discriminator.

"So, did you ever get married?" asked Carl.

"Wanted to once or twice, but business always interrupted my plans. How about you?"

"No, not yet," responded Carl.

"Not yet," laughed Higgins.

CHAPTER NINE
Destin, Florida
1430 Hours

Rick and Carlos were standing outside the corporate terminal when The Peterson Group Gulfstream came to a full stop. There were several other aircraft being prepared for their clients. The Destin-Fort Walton Beach Airport had become quite busy in the past few years. Several well-known celebrities, along with a few prominent political figures, had homes in the area.

Following the usual greetings, they headed south on Airport Road. At Carl's insistence, Roy sat up front with Rick. He held his Panama hat in his left hand as he adjusted the band. Rick noticed the small single-shot derringer that he had given to Roy some years ago. The twenty-two caliber couldn't have been more than two inches in length.

"I notice you still have that hatband gun," said Rick.

"I do. You gave it to me many years ago in Miami. It has saved my life on two occasions—one, just a year ago."

"May I see it?" asked Carl.

Roy took it from the band and handed it back to Carl.

"Be careful—it's ready to go," said Roy.

"I've never seen one quite like this," said Carl as he handed it to Carlos.

Carlos twisted the barrel revealing a twenty-two short round. He then closed the barrel as he moved his hand, judging the weight of the little weapon.

"Rick told me that it belonged to Al Capone. Claims that Capone always had it with him in his hatband," offered Roy.

"Is that right?" asked Carl, motioning to Carlos that he wanted to see it again.

Carlos handed it back.

"Well, that's the story my father-in-law told me," said Rick. "Seems there is some truth that Capone did carry such a weapon. My father-in-law had always believed that it was indeed the weapon that Capone carried," he added.

"Might really be worth something. Did you ever try to trace it?" asked Carl.

"I did, but got sidetracked," answered Rick.

"If you don't mind, let me take a few pictures. I can get Roland to do some research," said Carl as he handed it back to Roy.

"Fine with me," nodded Roy as they approached the traffic light on Highway 98. They just missed the green light. As they stopped, Roy leaned forward to look up at the two towers known as Silver Beach.

"That looks fairly new," he said.

"It's about ten years old," responded Rick.

"Man, this place has really changed. I remember when you wouldn't see a car for at least 10 minutes," added Roy as he looked in both directions.

"Do you remember the little cottages that use to be there?" asked Rick.

"Vaguely," responded Roy, the lines in his forehead deepening as he strained to remember.

"There used to be a very nice restaurant there that looked out over the beach. They only served breakfast," said Rick.

"Yes, I do remember. In fact they served the best french toast in town—anywhere for that matter."

"That was a long time ago," responded Rick as the light changed.

Rick headed east on the Emerald Coast Parkway as Roy continued to take in the sights.

"Now I do remember Grand Mariner. Spent two weeks there in the eighties," he said as he continued to look fondly at the building. "Should have married that girl," he said under his breath. There was regret in the tone.

"They did an extensive facelift on the building a couple of years ago. Although it's one of the older buildings, it's really quite nice," said Rick. "Lynn and I almost bought one of the units a few years back," he added.

"Why didn't you?" asked Carl.

"Never got the other half of the money from the sale of my company," responded Rick.

"And why was that?" asked Carl.

"Seems we had an earnout that had to be met in order to trigger the other half of the payout."

"That's a routine business practice. Was the earnout realistic?" asked Carl.

"Basically, just had to do the same revenue we did the year before," answered Rick.

"And you didn't make it?" asked a surprised Carl.

"We didn't," Rick responded simply.

"Sounds to me that you got taken," said Carlos.

"Maybe we need to look into it," offered Carl. By the tone of his voice he wasn't kidding.

"I let it go a long time ago. It just wasn't meant to be," said Rick.

Rick made the right turn into the Silver Shells complex. Roy was impressed with the fact that there was a Ruth's Chris Steak House sitting at the entrance to the property.

"This complex wasn't here either," said Roy.

Rick parked the car on the upper level at St. Barth. They entered through the lobby area and took the elevator up to Rick's floor.

The entrance to Rick's unit provided a spectacular view of the Gulf. Roy was enjoying the panoramic view and was about to say something when Lynn and Ann greeted him. Lynn was all smiles as Roy and Ann hugged. They hadn't seen one another for several years. The girls had prepared a large platter of fruit, cheese, honey-baked ham and assorted crackers. Following the usual pleasantries and several questions from Lynn, Rick showed Roy around the condo. The guys then adjourned to Rick's office as Lynn and Ann prepared to head out to finish the day shopping on 30A.

"We'll meet you at Marina Café," Lynn said as she kissed Rick goodbye. "Nice to meet you Roy," she added with a broad smile. Her smile was genuine.

Ann went over to Carlos and gave him a big hug and whispered something into his right ear that made him smile.

"I'll take you up on that later," he said as he kissed her softly.

"That you will," she smiled.

They all assumed that Carlos would be getting something special later. Their assumption would be correct.

"I'll give you a call say around five," said Rick as the girls headed out the door. The guys could hear them talking all the way to the elevator.

"You did well Rick," Roy said as he looked around Rick's office. "Really nice digs, and what a view," he added as he looked out at the airport and Indian Bayou Country Club. "You've got it all here," Roy added.

"I've been fortunate. Could have made some bad mistakes."

"When did you and Ann hook up?" asked Roy as he sat down next to Carlos.

"A couple of years ago."

"A couple of years ago? I thought you guys had been an item for many years."

"We sorta got sidetracked," responded Carlos as he glanced toward Carl. Carl didn't take notice.

"She hasn't changed much—still one good-looking woman. She as tough as she used to be?"

"She's tougher," laughed Carlos.

Rick pulled out a small note pad and took a drink from his cup.

"Well let's get down to business. Carl, did you happen to get a chance to talk with Blackwell and determine his priorities?" asked Rick.

"That I did. Nothing has changed. He wants his granddaughter released and then he wants us to find out who, if anyone, set her up."

"And he is aware that we may never recover any of the ransom?"

"He is. He made it very clear that money, or the amount for that matter, was not an issue," responded Carl.

"What about the sailboat?" asked Carlos.

"If they haven't sold it already, they will. It's just another source of revenue for them," responded Roy.

Rick looked over at Carl.

"Actually, Blackwell never mentioned the sailboat," said Carl, anticipating Rick's unspoken question.

"Maybe he just assumes the pirates will let them sail it out of there," said Carlos.

"We can include it in the ransom negotiation," said Rick.

"I wouldn't make it a priority," said Roy.

"According to Roland, it was still anchored in the harbor as of yesterday," offered Rick.

"We could put a team on it and take it," offered Carlos.

"That's an option, but you would need quite a bit of backup," said Roy.

Rick made a couple of notes and sat back in the chair.

"Roy, how many dealings have you had with Somali pirates?" asked Rick.

"Four in all. Two involved oil tankers. One involved a merchant vessel, and the other involved a sailboat."

"And how did they turn out?" asked Carl.

"The tankers and merchant vessels were fairly easy. The companies paid the ransom, and the ships and their crews were released. The sailboat was another issue. The family didn't have enough liquid assets to come up with the ransom. They needed time to raise the funds. We tried to negotiate the amount, but the Somalis said they had all the time in the world. However, they made it quite clear that there would be a time limit."

"Meaning?" asked Carl.

"Meaning that they would kill the captives," responded Roy. "The family made a down payment to buy some time. And a little over two months later, the family was able to put together the rest of the ransom."

"Did you guys ever consider just taking the sailboat?" asked Carl, reflecting on Carlos's comment.

"We did. But you have to understand...there are no friendlies in Somalia. Everyone is your enemy. Money is the only friend. Money buys friends, and then only temporarily," said Roy.

No one said anything for a few minutes as Rick made a few more notes.

"Is there any possibility of recovering the ransom?" asked Carl.

"As I said, money buys friends. As soon as they receive the ransom, they start paying off their support system. Everybody gets a cut of the action, right down to the guy who is cutting bait and watching the sailboat."

"Were you able to negotiate the amount of the ransom?" asked Carl.

"Not at all. They hold all the cards."

A look of disappointment took over Carl's face.

"How was the ransom delivered?" asked Rick.

"The ransom for the tankers was hand delivered at the pier. It was all in cash and old currency. No new bills or bills with sequential numbers. No bills larger than a fifty. The ransom for the family was airdropped in a canvass bag to a location that was provided when our helicopter was in the air."

"Did they release the people right away?" asked Rick.

"About ten days later," responded Roy.

"Is there always a delay?" asked Carlos.

"They move the captives around frequently. We concluded that once the captives were taken into custody, the pirates themselves went back out to the mother ship. Another group held the captives from that point on. The ransom had to be distributed among all the players before anyone was willing to release them."

"Probably the reason for the assorted bills," offered Carl.

No one said anything for several more minutes as Rick made a few more notes. He tapped the pad several times with the eraser head of the pencil.

"So there are many players," recapped Rick.

"Too many to try a successful extraction," commented Roy. "They may be an unrefined bunch, but they run a sophisticated operation."

"How so?" asked Carl.

"They have the latest high tech equipment, including GPS, satellite phones, rocket-propelled grenades, AK-47s, and they use speedboats with high power outboards to attack," responded Roy.

Rick drew a few rectangles on a fresh piece of paper. Carl got up, walked over to the sliding glass door, and watched as an aircraft similar to his took the active runway.

"So this whole negotiation process is basically an exercise in futility," responded Carl as he turned around. The look of disappointment was still in residence. Hopefully it wasn't a long-term lease. He wanted more than to just pay the ransom. He agreed with Blackwell, and he wanted to extract a pound of flesh for each day that Blackwell's granddaughter had to endure captivity.

"Maybe not," responded Rick. "The pirates themselves may be unsophisticated, but someone with sophistication is calling the shots. That is the person we want to find."

"It's a starting point, or more accurately, it's a data point for Roland," said Carl, his face showing a sign that the lease was about to end.

"Roy, is it possible that Blackwell's granddaughter was merely a target of opportunity?" asked Rick. He was sure that he knew the answer.

"Well it's possible, but I doubt it. I agree with Blackwell's premise that someone marked her. It's a well-known fact that the pirates receive tip-offs from contacts at ports in the Gulf of Aden. They're all in cahoots."

"Another data point," said Carl as he licked his forefinger and made a striking motion.

Rick made a few more notes.

"Okay. As far as the ransom is concerned, we'll play the game and pay it. Then we'll focus on ensuring safe passage," concluded Rick.

"Once it's paid, is there really a concern for their safe passage?" asked Carl, looking at Roy.

"These people are like hyenas. The lion makes the kill, and the lesser group sit around waiting for the scraps," responded Roy.

"So you're saying there's an outside chance that once our people are released, they could be taken captive by another group?" asked Carl.

"There's no such thing as a non-compete clause in Somalia, if you know what I mean," said Roy.

"Can we control or have any input regarding the release point?" asked Rick.

"No. They will give you no time to set up a counter action. We'll need a couple of helicopters to make the pickup, and then we'll have to provide the necessary safe passage," said Roy.

"*We?*" asked Carl, placing heaving emphasis on the word.

"Yes, we," responded Roy after a slight hesitation.

"So you're on board with us?" asked Carl.

"I am," responded Roy.

Rick sat there for a few minutes as Carlos patted Roy on the back. Rick didn't like not being in control of a situation. It was always much easier to be on the giving end rather than the receiving end.

"Roy, do they ever split the captives up?" asked Rick.

"Not that I'm aware of."

"And what if they haven't moved them?" asked Rick. It was purely a rhetorical question.

"Then we have another option," responded Carl before Roy could respond. The lease was finally up.

CHAPTER TEN
Destin, Florida
1800 Hours

Lynn and Ann met the guys at Marina Café. The guys had already secured two high-top tables and had positioned them for a nice view of the harbor and sunset. Several boats were returning from a day of fishing. Relatives and friends lined the pier in anticipation of a successful day at sea.

There was a group of elderly people over by the piano. A rather large woman with bouffant hair was reading something to them from a notepad. Her voice was husky from too many years of smoking. She tried to maintain control, but only a few of the older folks seemed to be listening. It appeared that they were getting ready to move into the main dining room.

The server, Angela, had already brought the guys two glasses of wine and two beers. Rick was seated on Roy's right side, so Lynn took the seat to Roy's left. Before sitting down, she had already started in on the questions. Roy was accommodating. Carl leaned over to Rick and whispered something in his ear that made Rick smile and glance over at Lynn. Lynn caught the gesture by Carl. Later, she would question Rick. He would have to tell her what Carl had said. *Carl has a way of always getting himself into trouble with Lynn,* Rick thought to himself. Some things would never change.

As Lynn continued to ask Roy questions, Rick took the liberty of ordering two margherita pizzas and four sushi rolls for the group. As the older folks made their way into the dinning area, Rick decided that it was time to rescue Roy and ask him a few questions about Somalia. When Lynn took a drink of wine, Rick seized the moment.

"Do you still have contacts in Somalia that might be able to provide some information?" asked Rick.

"I have a couple of people there."

"Can you trust them?"

"As long as I pay them more than the competition."

"We have reason to believe that Blackwell's granddaughter and her friends are being held on an old Liberty ship. Could your contacts find out if that assumption is correct?"

"I'm sure they could," responded Roy.

Rick thought for a few minutes as he swirled his wine around in the glass. He held it up in the light looking for the fingers. Carl remarked that it was going to be a nice sunset. His timely observation was all that Lynn needed. She glanced over at Ann who could easily see the invite on Lynn's face. They excused themselves and went outside to enjoy the momentary event.

"From your earlier comments, I assume you have resources that could be employed during a rescue attempt. Is that also correct?" asked Rick.

Roy smiled.

"I provide security for tankers owned by the Saudis. As part of the deal, they provide two Black Hawk helicopters, a large modified *cigarette* boat, a couple of Zodiacs and an interesting assortment of weapons."

"And you have access to the helicopters?" asked Carl.

"I guess you might say that, for all practical purposes, they are mine. I have full control of them."

"Where do you keep them?" asked Rick.

"At the Djibouti-Ambouli International Airport. In fact, they are maintained by the U.S. Africa Command under a dual contract with the Saudi royal family."

"Camp Lemonnier," lamented Carlos as unpleasant memories of a time long ago resurfaced. Carlos shook his head in an attempt to repress the images.

"Sweet deal," responded Carl as he looked over at Rick. "But I thought we had decided to pay the ransom," he added. It was more of a question than a statement.

"I hate giving in to these people," said Rick after a slight pause.

Carl smiled. There were always alternatives, none of which included giving up.

"What do you have in mind?" asked Roy.

"I was just thinking that we might be able to use a tanker escort as cover for an extraction operation," said Rick.

"That's certainly a possibility," responded Roy.

"We would need to confirm that Blackwell's granddaughter is indeed on the ship," said Carl.

"And we would need to confirm that *all* of them are on the ship," reiterated Rick.

"Yes, if they are all on the ship, and with the water to our back, our chances of a successful extraction are very good," concluded Carl.

"Our chance of success would be improved greatly if we could put a couple of guys on the ship before we make the full assault," offered Carlos.

"That's a good point," responded Rick. "Do you have assets?" asked Rick, directing his question to Roy.

Roy checked the date on his watch.

"I can have a couple of guys in Djibouti within forty-eight hours," he responded.

"For what I have in mind, we'll need a couple more guys," said Rick.

"I know a couple of ex-Navy SEALS who were working for Blackwater. Heard from them a couple of weeks ago. They were looking for work. There's a possibility they might still be available," said Carlos.

Rick took a drink of wine and noticed that the girls were on their way in from the deck.

"We clearly have some options. Obviously, this is not the time or place to plan the extraction. Let's work on it tomorrow," said Rick as Lynn and Ann returned from watching the sunset.

"You guys missed it," said Lynn.

"Darn," responded Rick. He had an aw-shucks look on his face that was far from convincing.

Lynn punched him in the arm just as Angela arrived with the two pizzas. She said that the sushi was on the way as she smiled at Lynn and made a little fist in support.

"Are you planning on spending the night with us?" asked Lynn. Her question was directed at Carl. "We have plenty of room," she added sincerely.

Carl looked over at Rick for confirmation.

"Why not? Then we could finish the preliminary planning in the morning," said Rick.

"Fine with me. Is that okay with you Roy?"

"You're the boss. I'm riding with you," responded Roy.

"It's settled then," said Rick.

"Let me give my flight crew a call. They can get a room for the night," said Carl as he got up from the table and walked outside with phone in hand.

"So, have you guys solved the world's problems?" asked Lynn as she finished what was left of her Pinot Noir.

"Some of the problems," responded Carlos.

Lynn knew she only got part of the story when it came to The Peterson Group projects. Rick would always keep sensitive project information close to the chest. He never wanted to worry Lynn, but he knew she would always be concerned for his safety. He had told her not to worry on the last project and then ended up in the South Miami Hospital.

Rick's Condo
Day 6
0800 Hours

Ann helped Lynn as she prepared biscuits with tomato gravy, scrambled eggs, bacon and assorted fruits for breakfast. They had the large patio table set up. It was another beautiful day in Destin. The Gulf was calm. Several fishing boats were slowly cruising eastward. There were fishermen on each of the observation towers looking for fish. Roy had the binoculars up to his eyes. He checked out each boat as he swept the area. A large container ship was clearly visible on the horizon. It was heading in the direction of Tampa.

"By the looks of their rigs, it must be cobia season," said Roy as he continued to look through the binoculars.

"It will be as soon as somebody hooks the first one," responded Rick.

"Don't they usually have a cobia tournament about this time of year?" asked Carl.

"They do. The Cobia World Championship is being sponsored by Harbor Docks," responded Rick.

"Maybe we should enter the tournament," remarked Carl.

"Can you shoot the fish?" asked Carlos jokingly as he looked fondly at Ann.

"Funny Garcia," she said before he could make fun of her fishing skills.

"It ends May fifth," responded Rick.

"That settles that," Carl responded sadly.

"Cobia is a great tasting fish," offered Roy. "Caught many of them in my fishing days."

"If we get a chance, we should do some fishing," said Carl. "We caught one last year that weighed sixty-four pounds. Still have some fillets in the freezer."

Following breakfast, everyone carried a plate to the kitchen. Lynn said that she would take care of the dishes.

"Anyone want a refill?" asked Rick as he made himself a fresh cup of coffee.

Following the refills, the guys headed for Rick's office. Lynn and Ann prepared for their morning walk. Carlos was keeping Ann updated on the side, just in case she was needed down the road. Roy took one last look with the binoculars and announced that one of the boats had something on the line. They all took a turn looking out at the Gulf. Cobia season had begun.

"Carl, have you made contact with the Somalis?" asked Rick.

"I talked with a guy named Mohamed yesterday. I gave him a number that Roland set up on my satellite phone. He said he would call back with instructions."

"They all use the name Mohamed," offered Roy.

"Is Roland confident that he can trace the calls?" asked Rick.

"He is," answered Carl.

"They are very much aware of the technology. They will keep on the move when communicating with you," responded Roy.

"We need to get them to put Blackwell's granddaughter on the line to verify that she's okay," said Rick.

"They will do that, but if they use a local phone, you'll never have enough time to pinpoint her location," responded Roy.

"No, but if she is on the Liberty ship, and they take her off to make a call, then we may be able to get a visual confirmation from the satellite," said Rick.

"Good point," said Carl.

"They'll jack you around a bit just to get your attention and to let you know they are in full control," said Roy.

"Then we'll use that to our advantage. It'll give us time to put our plan in motion," said Rick.

"And what if we can't locate the girl?" asked Carl.

"Then we will go, as they say, to plan B," replied Rick.

"And what is plan B?" asked Carl.

"We'll position assets to ensure safe passage, and we'll deliver the ransom."

"How much do they want?" asked Roy.

"Five million," responded Carl.

"That's quite a chunk of change," responded Roy. "They must have done their homework on the granddaughter to demand that much."

"Somebody did the homework," offered Rick.

"Maybe we could take a couple of prisoners and do a little water boarding," said Carlos.

"They won't know enough. They can only give you the guy above them. There are too many layers to deal with. You'd be water boarding half the town," said Roy.

"The whole country is dirty," mumbled Carlos, loud enough for all to hear.

"You have to understand where they're coming from. They feel justified in their piracy," offered Roy.

"How so?" asked Carl.

"The Somalis will tell you that the illegal fishing by international trawlers off their coast, including the illegal dumping of toxic waste, is the reason they have resorted to piracy."

"That's an excuse," said Carlos.

"Maybe, but the illegal fishing costs the Somalis hundreds of millions of dollars every year. When you're a fisherman, and you can't feed your family, you resort to desperate measures," responded Roy.

"They wouldn't have a problem if the country would get its act together," said Carl.

No one said anything for a few moments as they thought about what Roy and Carl had said. Roy had certainly made a good point. It was basically a matter of record and which side of the coast you lived on. Somalia hadn't had a functional government in place since 1991. Civil war was destroying the very fabric and foundation of the country. With no governing authority, there was no one to enforce or protect the territorial waters. The fishermen had to take matters into their own hands to bring attention to the situation. Piracy was their means to do just that and recoup some of their losses. Carlos had listened, but a few mitigating comments were not enough to change his mind. He was first to speak.

"I really hate the skinnies," mumbled Carlos as he got up. "Anyone else like a refill?" he offered.

"Let's all take a break," said Rick as he put down his pencil.

They all headed back into the den. Carlos was already looking through the binoculars. The boats had turned and were now heading west. Several pelicans were diving into a school of baitfish. One of the boats was heading in that direction. The beach was filling up with spring breakers. Destin was in full swing mode. As Rick was making a cup of coffee, his satellite phone rang. The name *Sims* filled the LED display. He was looking forward to the call.

"Morning Mr. Sims," answered Rick. "Are you back in England?"

"No, I'm still on holiday but was able to get you some information concerning the Coughlins."

"Great, let me grab a pencil and paper. So how's the trip going?" asked Rick as he went into his office.

"Quite well. Seen more giant tortoises and strange animals than I care to remember. But, the wife is happy and that's all that counts."

"I can understand that," responded Rick.

"Have you ever been to the Galápagos Islands?" asked Sims.

"Never been there," responded Rick.

"Ah, you should make the trip. Lots of skinny women with long stringy hair, wire rim glasses, flowery shirts and sandals."

"Sounds like I would really enjoy that," responded Rick. His lack of enthusiasm was all too obvious.

"I take it you're not a fan of the Mother Earth crowd."

"Hardly," responded Rick. "Okay, I'm ready to write."

"The Coughlins had a fifty-one foot Beneteau."

Rick didn't have to write it down. He just stared at the paper and didn't say anything for a few seconds.

"You there Morgan?" asked Sims.

"Yes, I'm here. And where did they pick up the boat?" he asked as he put the pencil down.

"Saint Lucia. They bought the boat in Saint Lucia."

CHAPTER ELEVEN
Destin, Florida
Day 6
0930 Hours

The revelation by Alastair Sims caught Rick totally by surprise. It was the break he was looking for—the one that The Peterson Group needed in order to have a valid starting point—one that would eventually lead to the person or persons ultimately responsible for targeting Blackwell's granddaughter and orchestrating the piracy.

Rick sat at his desk making a few notes while the guys remained out on the patio taking turns with the binoculars. Carl was the first to return to the office. He sat down across from Rick and took a drink of fresh coffee. Rick was so focused on his thoughts and notepad that he didn't even notice that Carl was sitting there, watching him intently. Rick continued to make a few notes and drew a couple of rectangles on the paper. He was in the process of connecting two of the rectangles with a line when Carl broke the silence.

"So, what did our friend, Sims, have to say?" asked Carl, cradling the coffee mug in both hands.

The question seemed to startle Rick. He looked up and looked around. He was genuinely surprised that he hadn't noticed that Carl had entered the office, or sat down across from him for that matter. A slight smile crossed Rick's face as he regained his composure and slid back in his chair. The smile remained. It was the kind of smile that Carl had seen many times before when Rick knew something that Carl didn't know—something that would start the game. From Rick's expression, Carl had the feeling that Rick was about to blow things wide open.

"Guess what make of sailboat the Coughlins owned?" asked Rick, just as Carlos and Roy came into the room. They had heard the question and sat down without saying anything.

"By the look on your face, I suspect that you are going to tell me they had the same make of sailboat as Blackwell's granddaughter," responded Carl as he took another swallow of coffee.

"Not only was it the same make, it was exactly the same size," said Rick.

"A fifty-one foot Beneteau," responded Carl as he moved forward in the chair.

"One in the same."

Rick held the pencil between the thumb and forefingers of both hands. He rolled the pencil around as he watched the reaction of his three friends. Carl leaned further forward and rested his forearms on the desk.

"Could be a coincidence," he offered cautiously.

"Could be," responded Rick, his tone signaling that *could be* was not the correct answer.

"That is a popular choice of sailboat for circumnavigating the globe," Carl added in support of his supposition.

"I agree," said Rick hesitantly.

"And?" asked Carl anxiously waiting for the next tidbit.

"Guess where the Coughlins bought the boat?" asked Rick.

Rick was indeed on a roll. The little smile on his face had broadened. It was almost a victory smile. It was a question that needed no answer.

"No. No way," responded Carl.

"St Lucia!" exclaimed Carlos before Carl had a chance to answer.

Roy gave Carlos a high five.

"Yes, Saint Lucia. The Coughlins and Ms. Courtney Evans both purchased fifty-one foot Beneteaus in Saint Lucia. Do you still think that's a coincidence?" asked Rick.

"If it is…it's certainly a remarkable one," surrendered Carl.

"You know what would be even more remarkable?" asked Rick.

It was purely a rhetorical question—one that he intended to answer before anyone responded. Actually, he answered it with another question.

"What if they both had purchased the *same* sailboat?" asked Rick.

"The same sailboat," repeated Carlos. He hadn't meant to say it out loud.

Rick had emphasized the word *same*. Carl leaned back in his chair, placed both elbows on the armrest, and rested his chin on folded hands. The lines in his forehead deepened. No one said anything for several minutes as they mulled over Rick's question. Was it really possible that the Coughlins and Ms. Evans had purchased the same sailboat? Was it just a coincidence that they both bought the sailboat in St. Lucia? Was it also a coincidence that they were both taken into captivity by Somali pirates basically in the area of the Seychelles?

"You know...it very well could be the same sailboat, especially if your premise that she was specifically targeted is correct," said Roy.

"How can we be absolutely sure?" asked Carlos.

"Roland will be able to make that determination. All he would need is an actual picture of the Coughlins' boat. Then he could make a positive identification through autocorrelation techniques," responded Rick.

"Don't they all look alike?" asked Carlos.

"No two boats are exactly alike," responded Rick. "There are subtle differences, especially in sailboats—differences that Roland would easily be able to identify through autocorrelation," added Rick.

"I wonder how many marinas are in Saint Lucia," mused Carl.

"Can't be too many," responded Roy.

"It really doesn't matter. We just need to find out who brokered the boat," said Rick.

"That shouldn't be too hard," responded Carl.

"It won't be. We already have that information on Courtney's boat," said Rick.

"And the Coughlins?" asked Carl.

"Sims can probably provide that information."

"And if they are the same, we have narrowed our starting point," said Carl.

"Not only that, if they are indeed the same boat, and were sold by the same brokerage firm, we have pinpointed the actual starting point," added Rick.

"Touché," responded Carl.

"Do we even need to connect the brokerage firm to the pirates?" asked Carlos.

"It would complete the circle," said Rick.

"Knowing these guys, I would assume that they use the same agent, so to speak, to take the sailboats off their hands," offered Roy.

"Another player in the game," said Carl.

"We can deal with him later," said Rick.

"He probably works for the brokerage firm anyway," said Carl.

"If we can determine that the Coughlins and Ms. Evans purchased the sailboat through the same brokerage firm, we're in business," said Rick confidently.

"Yes, as far as finding out who may have marked her as a target," said Carl.

"You know Rick, if the brokerage firm is dirty, they're probably just a front," said Roy.

"We'll let Roland figure that one out," said Rick.

"Could be a lot of players," said Carlos.

"Mostly suits at that level," offered Carl.

"If there are suits, then there are guys like us in the wings providing protection," said Roy.

"You're right, but they won't know that we're on to them and that we'll be coming after them. We just have to be patient. We'll have the element of surprise on our side," offered Rick.

"And we can extract more than a pound of flesh," said Carl. "So what's our next step? Where do you see this thing going?"

"Why don't you guys take a break while I put a few things down on a whiteboard. I think a visual will make things much clearer," said Rick.

Carl agreed, and he, Carlos and Roy headed into the den. As Carlos was making a fresh cup of coffee, Lynn and Ann returned from their morning walk on the beach. Lynn went into the office and asked Rick if they had thought about lunch. Rick indicated that they would probably just snack for lunch. Lynn said that she and Ann would take their showers and get cleaned up. They were going to head back to a few shops on 30A. She knew not to press Rick when he was deep into a project.

"Why don't you and Ann pick out a nice place on Thirty-A for dinner," said Rick. "Then maybe we'll hit Vue for after-dinner drinks and possibly catch the sunset if it's not too late," he added.

"Sounds good to me," responded Lynn with a soft kiss to his forehead.

Rick smiled as she left the room. Lynn was quite easy to please. Twenty minutes later, Rick got up and went into the kitchen. He made a cup of coffee and told the guys he was ready. When they came into the room, Rick had the whiteboard set up on a small easel. The usual rectangles, squares and decision blocks were clearly marked. Lines with arrows clearly depicted the various course of action. Rick had a small pen-sized pointer in his right hand. Carl, Roy, and Carlos sat down and were digesting the information on the board. Rick gave them a few minutes and then proceeded.

"In review," said Rick as he moved to the side of the easel. "This whole thing started with the taking of *A Pirate's Dream* and her crew. As you know, Mr. Blackwell has hired us to accomplish two main goals. The first and foremost goal is to ensure the safe return of his granddaughter and her friends—Scott Blackwell and Lisa and Dan Bradley. The second goal is to determine who was responsible for orchestrating the piracy. Mr. Blackwell has the resources to fully meet the pirates' demands and has given us the authority to proceed, as we see fit, to achieve both goals. I would like to focus our attention to the first goal. Any questions so far?" asked Rick.

No one had any questions. Rick continued.

"As I see it, the first goal can be accomplished in one of three ways. The easiest for us would be to pay the ransom and provide a safe escort for Ms. Evans and her friends. Take our fee and be done with it. The second way would be to determine where they are being held and then put together an extraction team to rescue them. Obviously, the second way would require thorough planning and additional resources, including experienced personnel."

"And the third way?" questioned Carlos. He had a puzzled look on his face.

"Actually, the third way would be to pay the ransom, ensure safe passage, and then go back in and try to recover as much of the ransom as possible. However, as Roy pointed out, there are many fingers in the ransom pie, which would probably prove to be a massive undertaking with questionable return on our investment."

"So why even consider it?" asked Carl.

"Because, one way or the other, it becomes part of the second goal. Once we find out who is behind the operation, I believe we'll find the bulk of the money, and we can recover it from them."

"I like it," said Carlos.

"As far as the first goal is concerned, my gut tells me we should focus on the extraction," offered Rick.

"I agree," said Carl.

"Okay, if we're all in agreement, then the first thing we need to do is confirm they are holding Ms. Evans and her friends on the old Liberty ship. Roy, are your contacts in Eyl?" asked Rick as he went over to his desk and made a few keystrokes on his laptop.

"Actually, they are in Mogadishu. They go back and forth on a fairly regular basis."

"Isn't that quite a distance from Eyl?" asked Carl.

"It is, but they fly on a weekly basis to Garoowe, which is less than a hundred miles from Eyl," responded Roy.

"And I take it that their unexpected presence in Eyl would not raise suspicion?" asked Rick.

"Let's just say they are…respected," responded Roy, searching for the right word.

"We need a map," said Carl.

"Check the printer," said Rick.

Carl retrieved a color printout of the Horn of Africa as Rick made a few more notes. Carl handed the map to Carlos.

"Carl, you need to make contact with the negotiator and demand that you speak with Ms. Evans. Tell him that there will be no more negotiation until you can verify that she and her friends are okay," said Rick

"And what if he won't comply?" asked Carl.

"He probably won't. So hang up. He'll call you back," said Rick confidently.

"How can you be so sure?" asked Carlos.

"Statistically, all they want is the money. There have been only a couple of captives who have been killed over the years. We have assumed, and I believe correctly, that they know Ms. Evans has considerable resources at her disposal. They want money. They'll call back," responded Rick.

"I agree," said Roy.

Carl concurred.

"As soon as we're done here, I will give Roland a call and ensure that he continues to keep eyes on the old ship. They'll either move her off the ship or let her call from the ship. Either way, we'll be in business," offered Rick.

"And my people?" asked Roy.

"How soon can they be in Eyl and in viewing distance of the ship?" asked Rick.

"About four hours from my call."

"Good. And you do have a couple of assets that can be in Djibouti within forty-eight hours?" asked Rick.

"From my call," responded Roy confidently.

"When is the next tanker coming out of Saudi Arabia?" asked Rick.

Roy pulled out a small notebook and looked through his notes.

"I have the *Seychelles Princess* scheduled to depart Ras Tanura in two days," responded Roy.

"And how long before it'll be in our area?" asked Rick.

"About three days."

"Good, we have five days," said Rick.

"Carlos, the two SEALS you mentioned—find out if and when they'll be available. If they are, we need to get them to Djibouti in the next two days."

"I'll give them a call right now," said Carlos as he got up and went into the other room.

"Are we getting a little ahead of ourselves?" asked Carl.

Rick thought for a few minutes before answering.

"We need to be ready. Once they allow you to talk with Ms. Evans, they're going to expect results. We need to have everyone in position when the tanker is in proximity to Eyl. The pirates won't be surprised to see a helicopter escort. What they won't expect is for one of the helicopters to break off and head into Eyl to make the extraction."

"And Carlos's people?" asked Carl.

"Roy, we need to get them on the ship prior to the assault. As SEALS, they'll know how to get on without being seen, especially at night. We need the right logistics to get them there before the assault."

"I have two Zodiacs. We routinely use them during the tanker escort. They can easily drop off a couple of guys outside the harbor."

"Good. You'll need to coordinate that effort with Carlos," responded Rick. "We need to have them on board the freighter when we bring in the helicopter."

"What if they do move Ms. Evans?" asked Carl.

"I'm betting they won't, but if they do, Roy's people can follow them. Once we're sure where they are, we can re-evaluate our options."

No one said anything for a couple of minutes.

"Any other questions?" asked Rick as Carlos returned and gave a thumbs-up.

"Okay, we have a basic plan to meet the first objective. Now we have to refine it."

CHAPTER TWELVE
Santa Rosa Beach, Florida
1800 Hours

Rick and the guys met Lynn and Ann at Stinky's Fish Camp on 30A. The guys went through several dozen raw oysters in less than thirty minutes. Lynn had her usual one oyster, a cracker and hot sauce. She pretended to like it. Ann, on the other hand, nearly kept up with Carlos. All of them had started with a Bloody Mary. Following dinner, they headed east on 30A and stopped at *Vue on 30a* for an after-dinner drink in anticipation of a beautiful sunset.

The weather was perfect. There were a few cirrus clouds in the western sky that would become golden brown just after the sun sank into the Gulf. The porch area was nearly full. There was one table for four that needed to be cleared. Rick signaled one of the servers and indicated that they were going to sit there. The server recognized Rick and Lynn and immediately began clearing the table.

Lynn and Ann sat next to each other. Rick and Carlos sat down as Carl and Roy went over to the bar. All the stools were taken. Several guys stood close to the bar eyeing the scenery. There were several women sitting there enjoying their drinks, seemingly oblivious to anyone outside their immediate space. Carl ordered a Napoleon brandy for himself. He ordered a Modelo Especial for Roy at Roy's request. The Napoleon brandy caught the interest of the lady sitting next to where Carl had slipped in to place his order.

"Napoleon brandy," she said as she looked up at Carl. She had noticed him in the mirror behind the bar. "I haven't had one of those in years. My dad was a great fan of Napoleon," she continued.

Carl was surprised that she had addressed him. She was a very attractive woman, probably in her mid-to-late forties. She had blonde hair, blue eyes, a smooth tan and a wonderful smile that framed a perfect set of very expensive teeth. Carl looked down at her ring finger. She caught the casual glance.

"Lost my husband several years ago," she smiled. "You married?" she asked, not looking at his ring finger.

Carl liked her directness. No sense in wasting time or meaningless conversation.

"No...never have been," he responded after a short pause. There was a slight hint of regret in the tone of his voice that she picked up.

"Never? Really? I find that hard to believe," she continued as she looked Carl over. She didn't try to hide her inspection.

She was indeed deliberate. He held in his stomach, enjoying the eye scan. Roy stood there pretending to look out at the approaching sunset. He was also enjoying the friendly banter.

"Came close once, but it wasn't meant to be," responded Carl as the bartender delivered his Napoleon brandy.

Carl picked up the snifter, held it at an angle in his left hand, and placed the flame from his lighter under the glass. He moved the flame back and forth for several seconds. The whole process had fully captured his new lady friend's attention. She couldn't help but notice the four stars on the lighter.

"Would you like to try this?" he asked as he swirled the contents of the snifter.

"I would," she responded as she reached for the snifter. "That is really nice," she added as she handed the glass back to Carl.

He was surprised that there was no lipstick stain on the edge of the glass. She was not the typical cougar found sitting in many of the bars along the *Redneck Riviera*.

"I'm Veronica," she said extending her right hand.

Her hand was dainty, smooth and well manicured. Her perfume was subtle and quite expensive.

"Carl Peterson," he responded with a competitive smile. "And this is my friend Roy Higgins," he added as he turned to Roy.

"Nice to meet you Roy Higgins," she said with a pleasant smile.

Roy shook hands and took the opportunity to excuse himself. There was certainly the gentleman side to Roy Higgins.

"The pleasure is all mine," he said as he tipped his hat. "I'll be at the table," he added as he slipped away. He looked back at Veronica and smiled.

"*Blue Sky*," sang out Carlos from the table. He said it just loud enough for Carl to hear.

Carl purposely ignored him.

"So how did you manage to stay single all these years, *Carl Peterson?*" she asked as she thoughtfully repeated his name.

"Unfortunately, my job kept me on the go. Just never had the time to cultivate a serious relationship."

"Do you live in the area?" she asked, knowing that most locals end up at Vue sooner or later.

"Actually, I live in McLean, Virginia. But I have a condo in Pensacola."

"Pensacola? That's a pretty long drive for a night out on Thirty-A."

"I'm staying the night with friends," he responded as he motioned toward the table.

She looked in the direction of the table and took a sip of her martini. She placed the near empty glass on the bar next to a clutch purse.

"And what is that you do Mr. Peterson?" she asked as she turned her body in his direction and moved a bit closer into his personal space.

She was wearing a black silk dress that ended just below her knees. Her high heels complemented the dress. She wore one small gold necklace with a gold cross, a ruby ring and matching tennis bracelet. She appeared to have little or no makeup on. Carl was impressed. He took another swallow of the brandy and checked her ankles. They were small.

"Do I pass?" she asked.

Carl tried to suppress a smile.

"Am I that obvious? Guess I have lost the ability to sneak a peek. And please, call me Carl."

"So Carl, what is it that you do in McLean?" she asked again as she looked over at the table.

"I do contract work...for a number of clients," he responded after giving his answer some obvious thought.

Normally he would just make up some story about being a traveling salesman for an information technology firm or some other innocuous occupation that everyone seemed to do at one time or another. But, for some reason, he felt Veronica deserved a more honest answer.

"Contract work. That narrows it down," she said as she turned and finished her martini.

Carl signaled the bartender for refills.

"Would you like another brandy?" asked the bartender as he removed the glasses and wiped the bar top with a dry cloth. Wiping the bar top was a habit.

"I'll have one more, and the lady will have..."

"A dirty martini...very dry please," she interrupted, placing her hand on Carl's right forearm.

"And your friends over there? Are they just friends?" she asked.

Carl smiled.

"Actually, they are close friends. We work together."

"Contractors," she said with a telling smile as she looked back at the table. "The guy with the mustache looks like an ex-Ranger, Delta Force...maybe a SEAL. The guy with the Panama hat could be a covert operative in Central America. The one girl looks...European. The other two I'm not sure about," she said as she continued to evaluate Carl's friends.

"You are observant. You should have been a lawyer."

"I was," she responded as she put the olive in her mouth. She twirled it around, pulled out the little sword, and made a thrusting gesture toward Carl's heart.

Carl didn't say anything for a few seconds as he thought about this woman. She was good. She was fascinating. He liked her.

"So, tell me something about you, since you seem to have me figured out. How long have you been in the area?" he asked as he warmed the brandy.

"I've been here nearly my whole life. My dad was stationed at Eglin and then came back to Hurlburt Field for his twilight tour. I finished law school, worked for a few years in D.C., and came back down here when my dad had a mild stroke. Been here ever since."

That explains why she hasn't asked where McLean was located, he thought to himself. She didn't say anything about her marriage. Carl wasn't about to ask.

"Would you like to meet my friends?"

"That would be nice," she responded as she stood up.

She said something to the woman next to her as she retrieved her small purse from the bar top. She was about five foot ten with the heels. She was slender and striking to say the least. Carl placed his hand in the middle of her back as he guided her in the direction of his friends. Her back was firm, no bulges around her bra strap. He suspected that she worked out on a regular basis. She looked back at him. She knew exactly what he was doing. He was caught again. As they walked to the table, Rick, Carlos and Roy stood up. Carl made the introductions. She made solid eye contact as she shook each one's hand. Carl retrieved a couple of chairs that were not being used and positioned them near the table.

"Veronica's dad finished his career at Hurlburt Field," offered Carl, hoping to stimulate conversation.

Since all of them, with the exception of Lynn, had a connection to Hurlburt at one time or another, the revelation got their attention.

"What did he do there?" asked Rick.

"I'm really not sure what he did in his early years, but he was the base commander until he retired," she responded as she sipped the martini.

"No kidding," said Carl. "What's your dad's name?"

"Charles Lake," she responded.

Rick glanced over at Carl. They didn't respond immediately. Not only did they know the notorious Charlie Lake, but they had also been on several missions to Central and South America with him.

"Your Colonel Lake's daughter...Ronnie Lake?" asked Carl.

She was genuinely surprised that he knew her nickname. Most of her friends knew her as Verney. Only her high school friends knew her as Ronnie, and most of them had left the area a long time ago. Even her friends at the bar didn't know her childhood name.

"You know my father?" she questioned Carl.

"We all know your father. We know him well," answered Carl as Rick, Carlos and Roy held up their glasses in salute.

"Contractors," she smiled. "Yeah, right."

"So how is your dad?" asked Rick.

"He had some health issues, but he's doing better now. Does a lot of yelling at the TV. He actually shot the brand new TV that mom had mounted above the fireplace. Shot it dead center during the Presidential debates. Put a big hole in the fireplace. Mom wasn't too happy to say the least."

"That sounds like Charlie. Not a fan of the President, I take it," said Carl.

"Actually, he was mad that Romney hadn't brought up Benghazi," she responded.

"I think we were all disappointed that he didn't bring up Benghazi," said Rick.

"You know what we used to call your dad?" asked Carl.

"I have no idea," she responded. Her expression indicated that she wanted to know more about her father, especially the early years when he would disappear for short periods of time.

"Crazy Charlie," responded Carl.

"Crazy," she repeated, somewhat in defense of her father.

"Well, not in the sense of actually being crazy. He was..."

"Fearless," interrupted Rick, rescuing Carl out. "Your dad was fearless."

"That he was. He was indeed fearless," confirmed Carl.

"But, *Fearless* Charlie just didn't have the same ring as *Crazy* Charlie," offered Rick.

"We were all a bit crazy in those days," said Carl.

"And you're not now?" teased Ann.

"Hopefully not now," added Lynn.

"With age comes caution," said Rick.

"Russian," said Veronica with a big smile as she toasted Ann.

Ann smiled.

"You are good," said Carl. "How did you know?"

"I'm paid to know those things. When you work analyzing potential jurors, you have to know everything about them. A lot of it comes from researching public records, but the real clincher comes from observation. It's my gift."

"Could be a curse," offered Ann with raised eyebrows.

Veronica knew exactly what Ann had implied. It was a curse especially when meeting a potential suitor. Most of them never got past her initial glance in the mirror. The rest would fail at about the second question. For a beautiful woman, she was living a very lonely life.

"So you're still working?" asked Rick.

She smiled. She was sure that Rick meant that she was evaluating each one of them. Actually, she was. It was difficult for her to separate work from pleasure.

"I do contract work," she smiled.

They all had a good laugh as they toasted Carl's newfound friend.

CHAPTER THIRTEEN
Destin, Florida
2145 Hours

The sunset proved to be all that was expected…and more. It provided a romantic backdrop for Carl's new interest. He had passed the test…and so did she. Rick hadn't seen Carl this excited in several years. Carl was good at pretending to have fun, but this chance encounter had all the earmarks of the real thing. It was genuine. They shared many of the same interests. He and Ronnie exchanged phone numbers and agreed to meet in Washington in a couple of weeks. She was going to be up there on business and expected to be there for several weeks. Carl was delighted at the prospect of spending some quality time with her. Carl noticed that she left when they left. That was a good sign.

They all sang "Lazy River" on the way back to Rick and Lynn's condo. Carl joined in when they got to the "blue skies up above; everyone's in love" part. It was the only part he actually knew. Roy didn't quite understand the significance, or why they all seemed to emphasize *blue skies*, but he thoroughly enjoyed their enthusiasm. He joined in even though he really didn't know any of the words. He could at least hum along and tap his foot. The rest of them didn't know all the words either for that matter, but it didn't stop them from making up new lyrics…most of them directed at Carl's expense. They all sang off-key except for Lynn, and surprisingly Carlos.

By 2145, Lynn was getting ready for bed. Rick and the team were deep into the Blackwell project again. After several iterations, Rick had developed an initial scenario that looked really good on paper. It always looked *really good* on paper…until the shooting started.

Carlos and Roy would continue to refine the scenario when the extraction team joined up in Djibouti. Rick, Carl and Ann would man the command center that was located inside the Sensitive Compartmented Information Facility in The Peterson Group in Old Town, which was commonly referred to as the SCIF. Carlos would coordinate the final scenario with Rick. Roland would enter the scenario's parameters into a wargaming software program that The Peterson Group had developed in support of the Pentagon's strategic programs. The Peterson Group had developed an Iranian scenario that would provide a good foundation for their mission in Somalia. The Iranian scenario was being used as a training exercise. Someone in the Pentagon had unceremoniously renamed the Iranian scenario, *Operation Arabian Nights*. Since the Iranians were not Arabs, Carl's team determined that the exercise was doomed from the start.

Roland had added a feature that he had been working on that provided a real-time interface with satellite imagery. Although untested, Roland was convinced the modification would provide valuable tactical information and allow the team to have unfettered superiority over the pirates.

Carlos had confirmed that his contacts, Shaun Spencer and Cody Taylor would be on their way to Djibouti first thing in the morning. Carlos had provided a short overview of the project. Shaun and Cody were excited about the opportunity to work with The Peterson Group.

Two of Roy's covert operatives, Guillermo Bonafonte and Rafael Gonzaléz, had just completed a mission in Libya and were scheduled to depart on a C-130 that was assigned to the Horn of Africa Command. Roy had also confirmed that his contacts in Mogadishu would make an unscheduled trip to Eyl. Their names were Osman Mohamed Ali and Mohammed Hammat Yusef. Since their names were a mouthful, the team would fondly refer to them as Ozzie and Harriet. Roy believed that they would have no trouble finding out if Courtney Evans and her friends were currently being held on the old ship. However, Rick and Carlos didn't like working with operatives they didn't know. Roy tried to assure them that they could trust Ozzie and Harriet.

"Ozzie and Harriet I trust," said Carlos. His reference to the old TV show was obvious.

"I assure you that they can be trusted," said Roy.

Carlos's expression indicated that he had serious reservations.

"I trust *you* Roy," responded Carlos. His emphasis was clear.

Roy didn't respond verbally. He just made a facial gesture that confirmed his understanding of the situation.

Osman Ali had ensured Roy that he and Mohammed Yusef would be in visual contact with the ship when Carl spoke with the negotiator. Carl would then demand to speak with Courtney Evans. Carl was very good at negotiating. One way or the other, he would convince the Somali negotiator that Mr. Blackwell had full intentions of meeting their demands but if, and only if, he was allowed to speak with his only granddaughter. Once he confirmed that she and her friends were okay, he would pay the ransom.

Rick and Carl were convinced that the pirates would acquiesce to Carl's demands. There was no reason not to comply. The pirates held all the cards—they owned the deck. They were only interested in the money, and Blackwell had plenty of money. One way or the other, The Peterson Group would have enough time and information to decide whether or not to proceed with the extraction mission as planned.

Since the pirates were aware that many of the oil tankers were being escorted, the presence of helicopters and various surface vessels would be expected. Therefore, Rick had determined that the best time to commence the mission would be when an oil tanker, by the name of *Seychelles Princess,* was in the vicinity of the Gulf of Aden and known pirate activity. Since night was their friend, the team would use the cover of darkness to make a beach landing. They would stay well out of range of the entrance to the small harbor. There was no way to enter through the narrow passage without being seen and causing an unnecessary confrontation.

The scheduled transit time of the *Seychelles Princess* would provide at least a four-hour window of opportunity. If everything went according to schedule, the team would commence the with the extraction operation at exactly zero two hundred hours. In support of the operation, Shaun, Cody, Guillermo and Rafael would make a beach landing the night before, approximately one mile south of the harbor. They would secure the Zodiac. Shaun and Cody would then proceed to the Liberty ship, while Guillermo and Rafael would make their way to a predetermined location that would provide a clear view of the ship as well as the makeshift brow that provided access on and off the ship.

Once Shaun and Cody were safely aboard the ship, they would determine how many pirates were on board along with their location. They would also determine where Courtney Evans and her friends were being held. Then they would go back into hiding until zero two hundred hours the next morning. Shaun and Cody would provide the initial assault, eliminate the onboard threat, and free the hostages. Guillermo and Rafael would provide sniper coverage if needed from their hidden location. Every Somalian with a weapon would be considered a target. There would be no questions...and there would be no prisoners. Roland would provide real-time information on the location and movement of potential targets picked up by the satellite. Once Shaun and Cody had freed Courtney Evans and her friends, the six of them would precede to the extraction point, where they would be picked up by the helicopter. Guillermo and Rafael would continue to provide coverage.

When the helicopter was well clear of the harbor, Guillermo and Rafael would make their way back to the Zodiac, and leave the shoreline under the cover of darkness. A second helicopter would provide additional coverage. It was known that the pirates had RPGs, but by the time they had figured out what had happened, the team would be long gone.

As usual, the plan was fairly basic. Rick always maintained that the simpler the plan, the less that could go wrong. However, they were all familiar with Murphy's Law—if anything can go wrong, it will. The successful accomplishment of the mission hinged upon three very crucial elements: the confirmed whereabouts of Courtney Evans and her friends; the successful insurgency by the team the night prior; and the most important element, surprise. The rest, although dangerous, was mostly routine—bang-bang in and out. The whole operation should take less than twenty minutes once the *Seychelles Princess* was in the area. *Should* and *would* were sometimes miles apart. Rick sat down in his chair looking at the whiteboard.

"Are we missing anything?" he asked.

"Don't forget that these guys sleep with their weapons," said Roy.

"Do they all have RPGs?" asked Carlos.

"They seem to have a pecking order when it comes to weapon lethality," responded Roy. "Unfortunately, many of the inhabitants of Eyl are very sympathetic with the pirates' cause. They are part of the pecking order," added Roy with a wry smile.

"Is it possible that some of the 'civilians' have RPGs? What about the people that live close to the harbor?" asked Rick.

"It's not only possible...you can bet on it," responded Roy. "We could end up engaging half the town if we're not careful."

"What about Ozzie and Harriet? I assume they have their contacts—ones they can trust. Could they provide that kind of intelligence information?" asked Carl, directing his question to Roy.

"They probably could, but questions along those lines would certainly raise suspicion. As I said, many of the inhabitants are sympathetic with the pirates' cause. We could end up losing the element of surprise."

"And our people," added Carlos.

"What about the Horn of Africa Command?" asked Rick. "They must have some intelligence along those lines," he added.

"I'm sure they do, but as you know, they hold that information close to the chest," responded Roy.

"Even from you?" questioned Carl.

"Unfortunately...even from me," Roy confessed.

"From what I understand, the command employs drones. Do you have any drones or access to a drone?" asked Rick.

"I do. We use them as decoys during our escort operation. The pirates have no idea which ones are carrying live ordnance. Keeps them at bay."

"And could you make one with live ordnance available...just in case?" asked Rick.

"I believe that can be arranged."

"Good. Why don't you and Carlos throw a drone into the mix. We can coordinate a flyover once we have everyone's feet wet," offered Rick.

"Will do," responded Roy.

Carlos nodded in agreement.

"And you are absolutely sure that you can trust Ozzie and Harriet? An awful lot hinges on their integrity and full cooperation," asked Rick. "Carlos and I have been sold out before," he added as he looked over at Carlos.

"As much as you can trust anyone that you are paying. They have always come through in the past," responded Roy. "They have been part of my team since I took the contract with the Saudis. I pay them very well," he added.

"Hopefully the pirates aren't paying them more," said Carlos.

"I understand your concern, but I fully trust them. Osman Mohamed Ali is related to Abdiweli Mohamed Ali, the current President of Puntland. Before the presidential election, Ali was the Prime Minister of Somalia. He is trying very hard to unite Somalia and is an outspoken critic of the pirates," said Roy in defense of his people.

No one said anything for a minute or so as Rick made a few notes.

"I hope you understand *our* concern," said Rick. "Five million in ransom can buy a lot of trust," he added.

"Rick, believe me, I understand," responded Roy.

"And they have all the necessary communication equipment?" asked Rick.

"They do, and they also have night vision capability," answered Roy.

"Can they pre-position another vehicle for us to use just in case we have a problem with the helicopter—one that will be large enough to accommodate at least six people, and one that Guillermo and Rafael can cover from their position?" asked Rick.

"I'm sure they can and will...for a price," said Roy with a smile.

"Let's make that happen," said Rick. "And I don't care how you do it, but let's make sure the damn thing is in good working order," directed Rick.

Rick thought for a few minutes before continuing. He took a deep breath and slid forward in the chair.

"As you all know, extractions can go really well, or they can go very badly. There never seems to be very much in-between," he offered as he stood up.

"Just ask Jimmy Carter," offered Carl.

"A sand storm might be just what we need," said Roy.

The team sat there in silence for a few minutes as they continued to look at the list on the whiteboard.

"Anything else?" asked Rick after a few minutes.

"We need to go over the things that can go wrong," said Carl.

"Let's take a break, and I'll start making a list," said Rick. "Hopefully we won't need a larger board," he added with a smile.

Carl and Roy went into the kitchen. Carlos remained behind as Rick started making a list on the white board. Carlos had been involved with Mogadishu. He knew that nothing ever went as planned...as did Rick. Planning was just that. Within five minutes, Carl and Roy were back. Rick had started a list, which included everything from failure of the *Seychelles Princess* to arrive on time, to the weather deteriorating.

"Kind of makes you wonder if we should attempt this without military support," said Carl as he studied the list.

"It is a bit overwhelming. We have to trust our instincts and the equipment," said Rick.

"I can assure you that my equipment is well maintained. Besides, we have very good backup systems," offered Roy.

"They all appear to be the normal concerns," said Carl.

"I don't want us to focus on all that can go wrong. Let's focus on what we want to do. What do you see as the show stoppers?" asked Rick.

"Failure to positively locate where Ms. Evans and her friends are being held," said Carlos.

"Roy, assuming that they're on the Liberty ship, what's the probability that they'll keep them there?" asked Rick.

"I think it's highly probable that they're still on the ship. However, the pirates are known to move the captives around on a fairly frequent basis."

"Then we need to make sure that Blackwell talks with all of them," said Rick as he looked over at Carl. "My only fear is that they might decide to move them once the call is complete," he added.

"I'll work on it," responded Carl.

"The one thing we have going for us is that they were taken into custody quite recently. They're probably on the ship and will be there for another week or two," offered Roy.

"What about the Zodiac?" asked Carlos. "I don't like leaving it unguarded."

"I agree," said Roy. "I have an operative who can man the Zodiac as well as provide any additional support. We can drop off our people, move offshore, and then pick them up when the helicopter is safely out of range."

"Let's do that," agreed Rick.

Everyone seemed to be satisfied with the initial planning session. Following a short break, they determined that they would all fly out to D.C. in the morning. When the planning session was over, Rick grabbed Carlos by the arm. He was about to say something when his cell phone rang. He looked at the LED display. It was Roland.

"Roland," answered Rick. "You can't still be at work," he added.

"I'm at home, but I have been monitoring the harbor at Eyl. Think you would want to know that two guys just boarded the sailboat and are underway."

CHAPTER FOURTEEN
Old Town
Day 7
0930 Hours

By 0930 hours, Carl, Rick and Ann were in the SCIF at The Peterson Group office in Old Town. Carlos and Roy were at Andrews Air Force Base and in the process of boarding a flight to Rota, Spain, where they would make a connecting military flight to Djibouti. Roland was sitting at the conference table making a few keystrokes on his laptop while looking up at the screen. Elaine Drew entered the room with a tray of assorted rolls, butter and jellies that would suffice as a continental breakfast. She placed the tray in the center of the conference table just as a satellite image popped up on the large screen. Roland used the joystick to zero in on a sailboat that was fully underway. From the wake and angle of list to the starboard side, there appeared to be a fairly strong westerly wind.

"There's our sailboat," announced Roland as he zoomed in on the boat.

Westward Ho could be clearly seen on the stern. From the swirl marks around the name, it was quite obvious that it had been recently prepared and painted. The cleanup of the stern could have been much better. It was probably done in haste, just prior to the boat being moved from the harbor at Eyl.

"You're certain that this is indeed *A Pirate's Dream*?" asked Carl.

"I'm absolutely certain we are looking at Ms. Evans' sailboat," responded Roland emphatically.

They all watched the sailboat as Elaine poured three cups of coffee from a silver carafe. Carlos already had his hand on the cup.

"I assume you'll be able to maintain contact with the sailboat," said Rick.

"No problem. I have created an algorithm that will locate the boat via satellite any time we need to confirm its whereabouts," responded Roland matter-of-factly as he panned the deck.

Two crew members could be seen working the sails. They were shirtless, trim and appeared to be quite fit. Both had dark hair and were well tanned from many years in the sun. Their coordinated effort confirmed that they knew what they were doing.

"Were you able to get any good facial shots of these guys?" asked Carl.

"Not yet, but I will sooner or later," responded Roland.

"Do you think there are anymore than just two crew members aboard the sailboat?" asked Ann.

"I believe there are only these two," responded Roland. "They boarded the boat early this morning—Somalia time. I have pictures of them as they prepared to get underway. They left the harbor during high tide."

"They certainly don't look like Somali pirates," said Carl.

"Not in the usual sense," responded Rick.

"Just another data point," said Carl under his breath as he sipped the hot coffee.

"I need to call Sims and get the info on the Coughlin's sailboat. If Roland can determine that this boat and the Coughlin's boat are one in the same, we're in business," said Rick as he hit the send button on his satellite phone.

Everyone continued to watch the sailboat and enjoy the impromptu breakfast as Rick got up. Sims answered the call on the second ring.

"Morgan," he answered deliberately. "I can't seem to get away from you," he said. His laugh was forced. "You are worse than my wife."

"You know us Colonists. We are a persistent bunch," responded Rick, fending off any attempt by Sims to gain the upper hand with one of his usual Colonial digs.

The comment was successful. It caught Sims a bit off-guard. He hesitated for several seconds before regrouping.

"You shot at us from behind the trees."

"Yeah, and we didn't even wear red coats," responded Rick.

After several long seconds of silence, Sims responded in surrender.

"Persistence is good. And before you ask, I let my assistant know that you needed information concerning the Coughlin's sailboat. I thought that you would've heard from her by now. She did say that there were some very good pictures of the boat along with information on the seller."

"Great. Is it okay if I give her a call?"

"Certainly. Her name is Melissa Kent. You may reach her at the MI6 headquarters number. I assume you still have it," said Sims somewhat sarcastically.

"I do, and thanks for your help Sims," said Rick, wanting to end the conversation. He really didn't like Sims and, in fact, had discarded the number some time ago. Elaine would have it.

"Any time Morgan. And keep me in the loop. I would love to know what you discover and where you're going with this."

Rick ended the call and asked Elaine to call MI6 and get Alistair Sims' assistant, Melissa Kent, on the line. She nodded and left the room. Roland was still panning the sailboat trying to get a good facial shot of the crew members. By now, they were sitting back. One was smoking a rather large cigar. The wheel was lashed. The sailboat was on a steady course.

Could be a doobie, Rick thought to himself as he noticed the mannerisms of the sailor who was smoking. He was enjoying it way too much for it to be just an oversized cigar.

"Are they heading for the Suez Canal?" asked Ann.

"I'm sure they are," responded Roland.

"Do they have to register the sailboat?" she asked.

"From what I understand, there seems to be a lot of latitude when it comes to sailboats. It depends upon the country of origin. Some require licensing and some don't. Some only require registration when the sailboat has a motor," offered Rick.

"What about Saint Lucia?" asked Carl.

"From what I've read, Saint Lucia is fairly lax," responded Rick.

"Don't they require permission to enter the Suez Canal?" asked Ann, still thinking about the licensing and registration process.

"Roland, what do you have on the canal procedures?" asked Rick.

Roland made a few keystrokes, which divided the presentation on the large screen. The sailboat occupied the left side. A list appeared on the right side. It was titled, *Suez Canal Transit Procedures*.

Roland was prepared. Rick and Carl smiled as Roland started his short presentation. Carl glanced at Roland's penny loafers—still no socks.

"Ms. Peters is quite correct. There are very specific procedures that start with the Canal Authority. For those traveling north through the canal, they start the process at Suez. For those traveling south through the canal, they would start at Port Said."

Roland gave the team a few minutes to look over the list. Rick made a few notes as Roland went over and stood by the screen. He was fully prepared to answer their questions.

"Arrival forms, insurance certificate, immigration, departure forms, customs, port clearance certificate, passports...on and on," said Carl. "That would take some time, preparation and experience," he added.

"It does...usually about three days. The Canal Authority strongly recommends that you hire an agent to help with the process," said Roland. "They even provide a couple of names on their website," he added as he brought up a screen with two names clearly displayed.

"So if they just sail straight into the canal, then someone is being paid off," concluded Ann.

"It's not that simple. They have to be accompanied by a pilot. All the ships heading north start out at zero six hundred hours on the day of transit. They all travel together," answered Roland.

"Sort of like an armada. So how long does it take to transit the canal?" asked Ann.

"Approximately fifteen hours," responded Roland as he looked back at the screen.

"Can you *retrieve* some of their documents from the Small Craft Department," asked Rick. He hesitated before tentatively saying the word retrieve.

Roland smiled without saying anything.

"I know nothing," said Carl, covering his ears. He knew that Roland would have no problem accessing the Small Craft Department computers.

Ann was about to say something when Elaine Drew opened the door and announced that she had Ms. Melissa Kent on line two. Rick got up from the conference table and took the call. The others took the opportunity to take a break and stretch their legs.

"Ms. Kent, Rick Morgan here."

"Yes, Mr. Morgan. I was about to ring you. I have the information you requested. I can email or fax it to you."

"Email will be fine. Do you have my email address?" asked Rick.

"If it hasn't changed within the last year, then I do."

"It's the same."

"Info is on the way," she responded as she hit the send button.

"Thank you for the information," said Rick.

"My pleasure."

The email arrived before Rick had placed the phone on the cradle.

Tripoli, Libya
1400 Hours Local Time

Guillermo Bonafonte and Rafael Gonzaléz were the last to board the C-130. The plane had waited for them to arrive. They were both exhausted from their mission to Benghazi. Although it was a quick in and out, the timing didn't give them much chance to recoup following their previous mission to Colombia. They both took sling seats on the port side of the aircraft.

There were several young Army soldiers already strapped in sitting across from them. They were young and had the look of innocence on their faces. One looked to be a female, but Guillermo wasn't quite sure. He tried not to stare, but his curiosity got the best of him. The soldier's smile wasn't conclusive. In today's Army, Guillermo wasn't sure. As he looked at each of the young soldiers, he suddenly felt quite old. Rafael was snoring before Guillermo was fully situated.

The young soldiers hugged their sea bags for security as they stared at Guillermo and Rafael, trying hard to figure out what was so special about these two guys that they had enough pull to delay the flight on the tarmac—these two guys in desert fatigues with long hair and scruffy beards. They appeared to be traveling light, but the rifle cases were a dead give away to the one lone sergeant who was obviously in charge. He nodded at Guillermo who returned his unspoken greeting. They shared a common heritage.

As the C-130 taxied out to the active duty runway, Guillermo thought about the mission to Benghazi. The State Department had been jumping through hoops trying to cover their ass in what appeared to be a complete failure on their part to provide adequate security for the late Ambassador to Libya. Somewhere along the line, his requests for additional security fell through the proverbial crack...or were purposely ignored. Why the Ambassador was in Benghazi in the first place was not totally clear. Someone knew.

However, looking back at the events, it appeared that the Ambassador had become somewhat complacent to the dangers inherent in the Islamic world. Although he did express trepidation, the fact that he proceeded on an unspecified mission without proper security was further evidence that he didn't fully grasp the severity of the situation, or he didn't want to...or he was sold out. Guillermo wondered if the truth would ever come out.

The administration tried to blame the events in Benghazi on a video that did not paint Muhammad in a favorable light. Although the Administration continued to promote the video connection, everyone knew that the fifteen-minute video had absolutely nothing to do with the assault. From the very beginning, anyone in a position of authority knew that it was an affiliate of al-Qaeda known as Ansar al-Sharia, which was responsible for the assault—an assault that resulted in the death of the Ambassador along with three others that included two former Navy SEALS.

Officially, and for purely political reasons, the Administration was not backing down from blaming the uprising in Benghazi on the video. Unofficially, Senator Windell's coalition provided information on two of Ansar al-Sharia's top lieutenants who the CIA believed were responsible for orchestrating the assault. The CIA had kept up with their whereabouts. Although the coalition was not one hundred percent sure that the intelligence information was correct, they had decided to send the Libyans a clear message that would require no interpretation or video for clarification.

Roy Higgins was tasked with the mission to eliminate the two lieutenants. Accordingly, Guillermo and Rafael were sent to Benghazi. On their way into Benghazi, they were provided with the coordinates of a house known to be a frequent meeting place of the group's leadership. Guillermo and Rafael had staked out the house for two full days when they received intelligence information that a meeting was to be held later in the afternoon on the third day.

By 1600 hours, one of the targets arrived. Several minutes later another man who fit the description of one of the lieutenants arrived along with two bodyguards. Rafael confirmed that he was their second target. As the two men embraced on the porch, Guillermo and Rafael took their shots. Both men were dead before they hit the ground.

In the confusion, Rafael shot the other two men that were on the porch. A fifth man exited the rear of the house and was shot by Guillermo as he tried to scale a small fence that led to a culvert. There was no more activity around the house. It was suddenly very quiet. Guillermo and Rafael watched for another couple of minutes, then packed up and departed.

Guillermo looked over at the young recruit again. He still couldn't figure out the gender. Not being able to tell the men from the women had never been one of his problems. How things had changed. He fell asleep as the aircraft leveled off and reduced power. The vibration was soothing. Guillermo and Rafael both woke up, as if on cue, as the aircraft began its approach into Djibouti.

CHAPTER FIFTEEN
Camp Lemonnier
Day 8
2100 Hours

Carlos and Roy had arrived early in the evening. Guillermo Bonafonte, Rafael Gonzaléz, Shaun Spencer and Cody Taylor met them as scheduled at the club that served both the officers and enlisted troops. Cody Taylor knew both Guillermo and Rafael. Their paths had crossed many times over the years. The last time Cody and Guillermo met was in 1989 during Operation Just Cause in Panama. Cody was a member of SEAL Team Four. Guillermo was there in support of the Rangers during follow-up operations.

SEAL Team Four's mission was to secure the Punta Paitilla Airport and destroy Noriega's private jet. The mission, known as *Nifty Package*, appeared to be straightforward. However, the Team encountered exceptionally strong resistance from a large contingent of the Panamanian Defense Forces that had been dispatched to guard the airport. During the heavy firefight, four Navy SEALS were killed and eight were wounded.

In retrospect, a much larger Ranger force should have handled the operation. The Rangers would have had the manpower to completely overwhelm Noreiga's troops. However, rice bowls prevailed—every flag officer wanted a piece of the action regardless of the tactical situation or *unintended* consequences.

Cody had been wounded several times, the worst of which nearly tore off his left calf muscle. The rehab process was painful and lengthy. Although he had a near full recovery, he was qualified for fifty percent disability. He figured that he had cheated death long enough, so he decided to retire from the military and work for someone where his input would, at the very least, be considered more seriously.

At thirty-two, Shaun Spencer was the youngest of the group. He had met Carlos one time before when Carlos was a consultant to SEAL Team Six at Little Creek. At five feet nine inches, Shaun was of average height. He weighed one hundred and sixty-five pounds, had a full head of red hair that was comb free, and had an abundance of freckles that would always give him the appearance of innocence...at first glance. His newfound friends stopped referring to him as *Howdy Doody* after the first week of BUD/S in Coronado.

His ability to drink beer was a living testimony to his Irish heritage—a heritage that he was quick to embrace and defend on a moment's notice. He could have been the poster child for the phrase, "in a New York second." Although he was born in Saratoga Springs, New York, his family moved to San Diego, California, right after his dad finished Nuclear Power School in Ballston Spa.

It was in Coronado where, as a young boy, he would watch the Navy SEALS training along the beach. He was fascinated by their physical prowess, dogged determination, and unbridled enthusiasm. He knew that one day he would be a Navy SEAL, and it would be him on the beach carrying his swim buddy on the quarter-mile run.

Shaun had never been wounded in combat. He was the only Navy SEAL on the team without a Purple Heart. Sometimes it would bother him; although, his dad had reminded him that it was always better if your enemy got the Purple Heart equivalent. That actually made a lot more sense. However, he did have a bullet wound that he never talked about. His buddies would have never let him live down the fact that his best friend, Maury Thompson, had accidentally shot him in the forearm with a twenty-two when they were shooting rats in a landfill in Chula Vista.

After a couple of successful kills, Maury ceremoniously blew on the end of the barrel, smiled broadly, and in an attempt to imitate the television undercover cops, he tucked the twenty-two into his belt behind his back. Unfortunately, Maury was a skinny kid. His ass just wasn't big enough to provide the necessary support for the heavy revolver. It fell through to the ground and discharged. The bullet hit Shaun in the meaty part of his forearm, traveled upward, and fortunately came to rest just below his right elbow. Both he and Maury threw up at the sight of the wound and blood...so much for machismo.

The hard part was explaining to his mom what had happened. His dad, being a pragmatic guy, was more understanding. He saw the humor in the situation, took a picture of the wound, and then called the rescue squad. Shaun would subconsciously cover the nearly faded wound when the guys started the "you show me yours and I'll show you mine" thing after a few rounds of beers. Many of the wounds were impressive.

Although Shaun loved being a Navy SEAL, he had decided that too many SEALS were being killed on missions that were understaffed, underfunded, and planned by bureaucrats who had absolutely no idea about field operations. Even though the funding didn't directly affect the SEAL Teams, it did have a negative impact on the forces providing the necessary support.

As far as Shaun was concerned, the handwriting was on the wall. Additionally, he was not at all happy with several of his former colleagues who decided to go public with information that he believed should not have been shared in the public domain. It seemed to him that everyone had a price. Many were working on books that would solicit a lot of initial attention, and then rapidly fade into obscurity. For him, Benghazi was the last straw. His commitment was over, and he decided it was time to leave.

Both he and Cody had worked for Blackwater. However, Blackwater had taken a few hits politically, and with the so-called sequester, Blackwater was forced to scale down their operation. It was only a matter of time and he would be on the street again. He remembered the old adage that it was easier to find a job while you still had a job. He decided to look, and was actually working for Blackwater, when he accepted Carlos's offer.

Guillermo and Rafael were experienced snipers and had worked with Higgins in and around the Horn of Africa for many years. They were certainly familiar with Somalia, the tribal culture, and how difficult it was to negotiate with the young pirates. Since their role would be limited to providing the necessary cover for the main operation, their role in the planning phase was more observational in nature.

As the six men sat there solving the world's problems, Roy's phone vibrated. He looked at the message and announced to the group that the *Seychelles Princess* was underway.

"How much time do we have?" asked Cody as he finished his second beer and signaled for another round.

"Roughly seventy-two hours. However, we'll need to be in the op-area in forty-eight hours," responded Carlos. "We'll finalize everything first thing in the morning after a good night's sleep," he added.

Roy nodded in approval.

"That'll give us plenty of time to be on station," Carlos added.

No one said anything as the guy behind the bar delivered six assorted bottles of ice-cold beer. The empties identified each man's preference. Shaun finished a third of his new bottle before the rest of the group finished what was left of their second round.

"So what's the overall plan? Can you give us a little overview?" asked Cody as he finished his second bottle.

"We believe that Ms. Evans and her three friends are being held captive on an old Liberty ship that is anchored in the harbor at Eyl," responded Carlos.

"An old Liberty ship. Is it seaworthy?" asked Cody as he took a long drink. Little beads of water dripped down on his shirt.

"Not at all. It's basically a rust bucket. It's grounded and appears to have a slight port list," responded Carlos.

"It's been there for years," interrupted Roy. "The pirates use it for everything from a storage locker to a holding cell for the occasional captives."

"And you're sure that our people are being held on board?" asked Cody.

"Quite sure. We are also monitoring the ship via satellite imagery and have people on station that will provide additional surveillance operations. Carl will be making contact with the negotiator just prior to the mission. He'll demand that Mr. Blackwell talks directly with his granddaughter. If the negotiation goes as we expect, we'll be able to confirm her location."

"And if not?" asked Cody.

"We won't proceed with the mission as planned unless we are absolutely positive that Ms. Evans and her friends are indeed on the ship," responded Carlos.

"From what I understand, the pirates move the captives around quite often," stated Cody. "And never on a regular basis," he added as he tipped the bottle in Carlos's direction.

"That's true, but we are fairly certain that Ms. Evans and her party are currently on the ship," stated Carlos.

Cody didn't say anything. It was obvious that he wasn't convinced that Ms. Evans and her friends were still on the ship.

"How many guards?" asked Shaun.

"No more than three at any one time," responded Carlos.

"How soon could the pirates respond?" asked Cody.

"There are several small huts on the north side of the harbor— many of them are occupied by pirates. The one advantage we have is that there is only one brow attached to the ship, so we know who comes and goes," responded Carlos.

"A single access point," said Cody somewhat hesitantly.

No one said anything for several minutes as they visualized the old Liberty ship. They continued to enjoy the beer and some of the local color who were allowed to frequent the club. Surprisingly, it wasn't very noisy. Most of the conversations appeared to be of a personal nature...they just had to agree upon the price.

"Using that same logic, getting off the ship could be a real problem," offered Cody.

"That's true, but we'll have the element of surprise on our side. We should be well on our way to the extraction point by the time the pirates realize that something is going on," responded Carlos.

Cody smiled as he thought back to several of his covert operations that were designed to rescue hostages. Quite frankly, most went as planned. The ones that didn't go well were the plans that were modified to satisfy some politician's personal last minute desires. However, no politicians were directly involved in this operation. The chain of command ended with Carl Peterson.

The Peterson Group Office
Old Town
Day 8

The material provided by Melissa Kent was brief but quite informative. She had obviously taken time to put the material together in a chronological format. The pictures of the Coughlin's boat were of excellent quality. Using autocorrelation techniques, it took Roland less than ten minutes to determine that the Coughlin's sailboat was, in fact, the same sailboat purchased by Courtney Evans in St. Lucia.

Within the hour, Roland had also determined that there were three separate shell organizations involved in the transaction process. A further analysis of the accounting information led to a company named Lafitte Holdings. His announcement got an immediate reaction from Rick and the team.

"Lafitte Holdings," said Rick with a broad smile. "You are kidding?" he stated. It was more of a declaration than a question.

"No kidding," responded Roland quite seriously. He didn't quite connect the same dots.

"Is it irony, or just plain brazenness on the part of someone who is involved in piracy to name their company after a famous French pirate?" said Rick as he looked around the room.

"Jean Lafitte," said Carl as he remembered the name from history. "The Battle of New Orleans," he added.

Roland Smiled.

"Where are they headquartered?" asked Rick.

"Cannes, France," responded Roland as he continued to dig deeper into the information on Lafitte Holdings. "The CEO appears to be a man by the name of Patrice Boucher."

"See what you can find on this guy," said Rick. "It could be an alias," he added.

"Patrice Boucher," repeated Carl. "Why does that name sound familiar to me?" he asked.

Rick looked over at Carl. Carl had an inquisitive look on his face that seemed to deepen by the second.

"You think you may know, or have known, this guy?" asked Rick.

"Just sounds familiar to me," responded Carl as he took a drink of tepid coffee.

"How old is he?" asked Rick as he looked over at Roland.

Roland made a few keystrokes on his laptop. His eyes rapidly scanned the material looking for information. Carl got up and emptied the contents of his coffee cup into the stainless steel sink and poured a fresh cup. Ann and Rick joined him. Rick was about to say something when Roland announced that he had more information. He also had a picture pulled up on the screen.

"Does his picture ring any bells?" asked Rick, looking at Carl.

"There's something so familiar...I just can't place him," replied Carl.

"Says here that he was born in Paris, France, on June nineteenth, nineteen sixty-two. Father was a career diplomat, and his mother a French maid by the name of Michelle Giroux," offered Roland.

"A French maid," repeated Carl.

Everyone except Roland knew what Carl was thinking. Rick shook his head.

"Mostly benign information," responded Roland as he continued to peruse the material.

"The kind of information that could fit anyone's background," offered Rick. It wasn't meant to be a question.

"Probably," responded Roland. "I'll check for continuity and aliases."

"Let's take a break," said Carl. "I need to give Blackwell a call and prepare him for the negotiation process with our pirate friends."

Rick looked at his watch.

"Good idea. I need to give Carlos a call," he said as he pulled his chair out of the way as Ann stood up.

"I suspect they are getting ready to proceed on station," she said.

Camp Lemonnier
Day 8
2200 Hours Local Time

Carlos was just about to call Rick when his satellite phone rang. He smiled as he looked at the LED display.

"Just about to call you," he answered.

"How's it going?" asked Rick.

"Everything is on track. The *Seychelles Princess* is underway."

"And the plan?" asked Rick.

"We went over it several times this afternoon...pretty straightforward. I'll email the particulars for your review," said Carlos.

"What about the new guys?" asked Rick.

"Well, I've known Cody for many years. Shaun is new to me, but Cody vouches for him. That's good enough for me," responded Carlos.

"And your confidence level?" asked Rick.

"I have full confidence in their ability to complete their part of the mission. Besides, Cody has been involved with several boarding operations and is thoroughly familiar with the Liberty ship layout," added Carlos.

"How's Roy's setup?"

"Impressive, to say the least. He has all kinds of neat weapons, including drones, helicopters, Zodiacs, state-of-the-art communications equipment, and full access to real-time satellite coverage. We're set," responded Carlos.

"Good. We'll provide you with backup from this end. Roland will be monitoring the satellite coverage as well. Anything else?" asked Rick.

"No, I believe we have it covered," responded Carlos.

"By the way, does the name Patrice Boucher ring any bells with you?"

Carlos thought for several seconds before answering.

"Doesn't ring any bells with me. Who is he?"

"He's the CEO of the holding company that brokered the sailboat purchased by Ms. Evans."

"So we have a connection," said Carlos. It was more of a statement.

"Not only that, Roland verified that it was the *same* sailboat that the Coughlin's had purchased a few years ago."

"Interesting," responded Carlos as he subconsciously began connecting the dots.

"When are you guys heading out?" asked Rick.

"Within the hour," responded Carlos.

"I'll be in touch," said Rick as he handed the phone to Ann.

CHAPTER SIXTEEN
Eyl, Somalia
Day 9
1400 Hours Local

Courtney Evans opened her eyes. The room was nearly pitch-black except for a sliver of light that stole its way through a small hole in the steel door. Dust sparkled in the ray of light. It was miserably hot. The small fan seemed to work only occasionally. She reached over and fumbled for the keychain flashlight that she was allowed to keep. She turned it on and panned the small room that now served as her cell. In the light, she caught a glimpse of two small red eyes. They stared intently as she held the light steady. By now, her hand didn't shake. She took a deep breath and slowly moved the light over to the tinfoil plate. The few morsels were gone. She slowly panned back only to catch a shadow in the corner. It disappeared almost as quickly as she had caught sight of it in the faint light.

Until now she hadn't seen the rat, but she knew it was there. She could hear it gnawing on something that was close to her bunk. Having grown up near the shipyards in Wilmington, North Carolina, she had grown accustomed to rats, or as accustomed as one could be with a rat. She knew that rats weren't dangerous as long as they were not hungry, or accidentally backed into a corner. The wharf rats were the biggest and most dangerous.

When she was little, her tomcat, Brutus, had cornered one in the tool shed behind her grandpa's marina. Surprisingly, the rat made short work of Brutus. She had a guarded respect for them from that day forward. Hopefully, she was dealing with a small rat that was satisfied with the little bits of food she would share from her daily meal. She took a deep breath and turned off the small flashlight to conserve what was left of the single triple A battery.

She hadn't been allowed to go outside. She had seen her cousin, Scotty, and her best friends, Lisa and Dan, on only one occasion since they were taken captive. They weren't allowed to talk. There were times she thought she could hear one of them tapping on the bulkhead. She had learned Morse code as a kid but could only remember a few of the letters. Everyone knew the code for SOS. She could only assume that they were okay. There was certainly no profit in hurting any of them. Her only fear was that Scotty could be hardheaded. He was a big tough guy who could easily handle the pirates in a fair fight, but the fight wouldn't be fair. Scotty wasn't stupid. She had convinced herself that he wouldn't try anything foolish. Besides, where would he go? Where would any of them go?

The one small light that hung from a frayed cord would come on sporadically. There seemed to be no rhyme or reason to its schedule other than it must have been tied into another light that was used infrequently. It had a mind of its own and made a strange humming sound when it did decide to come on. The fan and the light provided an eerie chorus to a ballad that was yet to be written.

She wasn't exactly sure how long she had been in the room, or even what day it was, but she had a pretty good idea. By the number of meals, she calculated that she had been in there for six days, counting today. She turned the flashlight on again and panned the room looking for the rat. She had unceremoniously named it Mickey. The name wasn't very original, but it was benign, it was safe, it was friendly, and it reminded her of a better time. She would carry on a one-way conversation. Mickey didn't care. As long as she kept Mickey fed, they were both safe—at least for the time being.

Courtney was certain that she and her friends were being held on the old rusted Liberty ship that was grounded near the beach at the southern end of the harbor. It was leaning subtly to the port side, which was typical of a boat that had run aground. She had noticed the Liberty ship along with several small boats that haphazardly lined the shore.

She took in as much of the surroundings as possible as they were brought in, just before they were handed over to another small group of well-armed pirates. They were all young, tall and painfully thin. Only one spoke. He used few words, but they were clearly understandable.

She was sure that he was fully capable of communicating, but he didn't.

When they first arrived, the pirates had blindfolded them, and drove them around for an hour or so. However, the sound of small boats entering and leaving the harbor was unmistakable. Since her stateroom had the same port list she had observed of the Liberty ship, she was certain they were all being held aboard that old rusty ship.

As she sat on the edge of the bunk bed, she thought back to the day they sailed away from St. Lucia and the excitement as they emerged from the Panama Canal. The open ocean was inviting—it was theirs to conquer. She had an urn with her husband's ashes. She had promised him that she would spread his ashes around the world. It was going to be a voyage to remember and a tribute to a wonderful husband who loved the sea.

Everything had gone nearly according to plan until they entered the Seychelles. They heard the speedboat before they saw it. It seemed to come out of nowhere. There were five men on board. All had weapons—one held an RPG. It was pointed in their direction. They had read the warnings. They all knew what to expect, but they never thought that it would happen to them. It always happened to someone else.

Instinctively, Scotty had gone below to retrieve his weapon. However, they were severely outgunned, and they knew it. Dan pushed the barrel of the rifle toward the deck and convinced Scotty that it would be more prudent to do nothing.

"The pirates only want money," Dan emphasized in support of surrendering.

Reluctantly, Scotty acquiesced.

It seemed so long ago. She shook her head in disbelief as she panned the room again. She knew her situation. The old ship was used as a home for some, a prison for others, and a playground for Mickey and his many friends. She would never get used to the musty smell and deplorable condition of the room. She could only imagine what it would look like in full light.

The only time she was let out of the room was to use the small head at the end of the dimly lit passageway. It was on the starboard side. It was obviously shared by the other inhabitants of the ship. Their hygiene was questionable at best. The stench of urine was overwhelming. Toilet paper, and that description was being charitable, was at a premium. It appeared to be cut from old newspapers—very old newspapers. She could only image what her butt must have looked like. She gave up a long time ago trying to cover the seat. She was good at hovering. She did her best to conserve.

On one occasion when she reached for a strip of paper, she noticed a long strand of brown hair that had been carefully tied to the edge of the rickety holder. It had obviously been fastened there for her to find. Since she hadn't seen it the last time she was in there, she assumed it was a sign from her friend Lisa. It was a sign that she was all right. Why the pirates had split them up was a mystery. There was certainly nowhere for any of them to go and nowhere to hide.

She was about to lie back down when she heard someone at the door. Her stomach told her that it was probably time for the daily meal, or maybe it was just a Pavlovian response. The door swung open. The sudden burst of light made her squint. She could just make out two shapes in the passageway. Two pirates with AK-47s motioned for her to come out of the room. She hesitated.

"Come out," yelled the older of the two. She hadn't seen him before. He was tall and well muscled. He wasn't thin like the others.

Courtney got up slowly and put on her sandals. As she went to the door, the younger of the two pirates grabbed her by the hair and pulled her into the hallway. He was rough. The older pirate said something to him that she didn't understand as he put a dirty black blindfold over her eyes and tied it tightly. It had the texture of wool and an odor that she couldn't identify. He grabbed her by the arm and began to lead her down the passageway. She pulled back.

"Where are you taking me?" she demanded.

Neither of the pirates said anything. Courtney did her best to hold her position and again demanded to know where she was being taken. She fully expected to feel the butt end of a gun.

"You'll find out," said the older pirate as he yanked her down the passageway.

The heat was nearly unbearable. It had to be well over one hundred degrees in the passageway. Beads of sweat ran down her sides. The pirates led her into a larger room and removed her blindfold. Scotty, Dan and Lisa were already in the room. Their hands were tied behind their backs. Lisa broke down in tears when she saw Courtney. Courtney wanted to say something, but the pirates wouldn't let them talk. One of them pointed to a chair and motioned for Courtney to sit down. As she sat down, she looked over at Lisa and mouthed the words, "I love you."

The pirates huddled together and were talking when another pirate entered the room. The other three pirates made a lame attempt to come to attention. Courtney had never seen the new pirate. He was very tall, and much older than the other three. His skin was very dark, wrinkled and bore the scars of numerous battles. His hair was beginning to gray. He wore linen khaki trousers, a tropical white shirt, brown sandals and a large gold watch. The trousers and shirt were badly wrinkled. Several sweat rings were clearly visible under his arms. There was a small gold chain around his neck. He had obviously sprayed on too much cologne. It didn't work.

"Which one of you is Evans?" he asked in a gruff voice.

He looked at both women and walked toward Courtney before she had a chance to answer.

"You are Evans," he declared. "Get up," he yelled as he grabbed her by the arm.

His eyes were cold. His hands were rough. *There is nothing even remotely refined about this man*, she thought to herself. He led her to the corner of the room. He reached into his pocket and pulled out a small cell phone. He dialed a number and waited for a few seconds.

"I have her here," he said into the phone.

He looked down at her as he seemed to be waiting for a response on the line.

"Yes," he said as he covered the phone with his right hand.

"Just answer the questions," he said as he handed her the phone. "Do not offer any information or say where you are being held."

She reached for the phone. He pulled it back.

"Do you understand me? Say nothing about where you are being held," he repeated loudly. His eyes indicated that he was quite serious. She nodded that she fully understood his demand.

"Hello?" she answered, not knowing who was on the other end.

"Courtney," gasped JT Blackwell, overwhelmed with relief and joy at the sound of her voice. "Are you okay?" he asked, regaining his composure.

Her heart raced. She held back tears of joy just hearing her granddad's voice. She hesitated slightly before answering. She nearly choked up but fought her tears hard. She cleared her throat.

"Yes, we are okay," she answered, letting him know that they were all okay.

"I'm making arrangements to pay the ransom. You should be released very soon," he said. "Hang in there honey," he added as his voice began to crack.

She was about to say something when the older pirate grabbed the phone from her hand.

"Pay the ransom, and you will have your family back."

"I want to talk with the others," demanded Blackwell.

The older pirate hesitated and looked in their direction. He walked to the other side of the room.

"Just state your name," he said as he held the phone in front of Scotty.

CHAPTER SEVENTEEN
Wilmington, North Carolina
Day 9
0630 Hours Local, 1430 Hours Somalia Time

JT Blackwell slowly put down the phone that had been given to him by Carl Peterson. He carefully placed it on the right side of the desk. He looked at it, wondering if it were more than a mere phone. He had never seen a satellite phone before. Out of habit, he ran his fingers across the notches that had been a part of the desk for nearly two centuries.

The call had been brief—way too brief. The old man wanted to ask more questions, but as instructed, he followed Carl's directions to the letter. It was difficult to stay on script. However, JT knew that it was imperative. Carl and Rick had listened to the conversation from The Peterson Group office in Old Town. Roland had recorded the entire exchange of information and had clearly marked the time when each person was allowed to speak. It didn't take Roland long to determine that the call had originated from the old Liberty ship. The trace was the vital confirmation that the team needed to proceed with the mission as planned.

JT slowly walked over to the Bunn coffee machine and poured a fresh cup. He was about to take a sip when the satellite phone rang again for the second time. He spilled some of the coffee as he put down the cup and briskly walked to the desk. He knew it would be Carl Peterson.

"Well, what do you think?" he asked. The tone of his voice indicated that he wasn't totally satisfied with the call. He was hoping for some positive assurance at Carl's end.

"It went as well as I would have expected," responded Carl. "At least we know that Courtney and her friends are okay, and we have confirmed they are being held on the old Liberty ship," he added.

"So you believe they are all right?" asked JT, knowing that Courtney was obviously having a difficult time maintaining her composure.

"I believe they are okay considering their surroundings," responded Carl.

"Do you think they'll keep them together on the ship?"

"I think they will for the time being. We have a surveillance team in sight of the ship. Rick is calling them as we speak," said Carl as he looked over at Rick.

Rick's body language indicated that he had not yet made contact with Ozzie and Harriet. Carl was about to say something when Rick snapped his thumb and forefinger together several times to gain Carl's attention. Carl subconsciously snapped the thumb and forefinger of his left hand in response.

"Let me call you back JT. It appears that Rick has our people on the line. I'll have some more information in a few minutes," said Carl as he ended the call before JT had an opportunity to respond.

Carl didn't like cutting the old man off, but he needed to talk with his surveillance team. He didn't want to take a chance of losing the connection.

"I have no idea who is on the line," said Rick as he handed the phone to Carl.

"Peterson here," he answered. "With whom am I speaking?" he asked as he put the phone on speaker.

Carl shrugged his shoulders and smiled at Rick.

Rick mouthed the words "with whom am I speaking." It brought a slight smile to Rick's face.

"Mr. Peterson, this is Mohammed Yusef."

Without prompting, Roland made a few keystrokes on his computer and the names Yusef and Ali, a.k.a. Ozzie and Harriet, were clearly displayed along with photographs of each man. Carl looked at the screen. Knowing what the men looked like helped to put the conversation on a more personal level. He really didn't know the men very well, but Roy vouched for them and their integrity.

"The negotiator just spoke with our people," said Carl. "Can you verify the time of his arrival?"

"He arrived at fourteen twenty hours. He left at exactly fourteen thirty-eight hours."

"Hold on a second Mohammed, I have you on speaker. My people are checking the timeline," said Carl. "I want to be absolutely sure," he added.

Within ten seconds, Roland gave a thumbs-up to Carl.

"The time corresponds with the call to Blackwell," said Carl. "We have also confirmed that the call did come from inside the Liberty ship. Was the negotiator alone?" asked Carl.

"Yes, but you should know that the man your people talked with is not the negotiator," responded Yusef.

"Not the negotiator?" questioned Carl.

"No. The man your people talked with is Yusuf Naji. He is, what you would call, a lieutenant. He does the dirty work for the negotiator," answered Mohammed Yusef.

"Do you know who the negotiator is?" asked Carl.

"Of course. There are several; however, Yusuf Naji works for a guy by the name of Mohamed Ibrahim. I can assure you that Ibrahim is the one handling your people, and he is the one you will be dealing with."

Carl didn't say anything for several seconds. Roland commenced a search on his computer. Rick scribbled on the pad and showed it to Carl. Carl nodded in agreement that it didn't really matter who the negotiator was. Carl would be communicating with him soon enough.

"How about the captives? Did you happen to see them?" asked Carl.

"No," responded Yusef.

"Okay. We need you to continue the surveillance. Let me or Higgins know if Naji shows up again, and more importantly, if anyone moves the captives," directed Carl.

"Will do," responded Yusef. "Mr. Peterson, Ibrahim is a tough character. He is not someone you can push around. He will bend only slightly. When the negotiation is over, he will expect near immediate results. That is when your captives could be in jeopardy," warned Mohammed Yusef.

"I understand. We'll be in touch," responded Carl.

Carl put the phone down and looked over at Rick and Ann. They had heard the conversation. Rick was still taking notes.

"What do you guys think?" asked Carl, directing his question to Ann.

"I believe we're on track. However, based upon previous intelligence, there's a strong possibility that the pirates will move Ms. Evans within the next couple of days," she responded.

"And you Rick?"

Rick leaned back in the chair. He put his pencil on top of the note pad.

"I'm not so sure they'll move them anytime soon. They certainly don't seem to follow any rigid time schedule. They have no reason to believe that anyone would be foolish enough to try and make an extraction right under their nose. However, I do agree with Yusef. Once the drop point has been established…time will be of the essence. I agree that once that determination has been made, they'll waste no time moving the captives to a new location—probably one that is in the vicinity of the exchange point."

"So how do we control the timing? How do we keep them from moving them prior to the commencement of our operation?" asked Carl.

Rick looked at his notepad. He had written and underlined the names Yusuf Naji and Mohamed Ibrahim.

"Considering the communication this morning with Naji, it's apparent that the next move is ours. I suggest you make contact with the negotiator just prior to our people moving ashore. Say that Blackwell has suffered a medical setback and will be hospitalized for a few days—that he is going to be all right, but he will need some time to finish gathering the ransom. That should give us the time we need to complete our mission."

Carl thought for a few seconds and then nodded in agreement. He looked at his watch.

"I need to get back to Blackwell," he said as he picked up the satellite phone.

Rick and Ann got up from the conference table and walked over to the small refrigerator and retrieved two bottles of water as Carl dialed Blackwell. The old man must have been sitting on the phone. He answered it before Carl heard the first ring. Blackwell didn't offer any greeting. He was understandably anxious.

"So where are we?" he asked impatiently.

JT Blackwell was a man who had always been in control. He didn't like being on the periphery. He was known to be a proactive guy. He hadn't mellowed with age.

"We're on track. We know where your granddaughter and her friends are being held. We know that they're okay, and we have a plan in place to rescue them," said Carl.

"I don't want to take any risks. As you know, I have the resources. I'll gladly pay the ransom," reminded Blackwell.

"I assure you, we don't intend to take any unnecessary chances," responded Carl. "If it looks like we cannot effect a safe extraction, we will immediately back off," he added.

The old man was silent for several seconds. Carl could only imagine what was going through Blackwell's mind.

"So what's the next step?" asked Blackwell softly.

"I'll be talking with the negotiator to set up the particulars of the exchange," responded Carl.

Carl purposely didn't mention that Naji was not the negotiator, nor did he offer any other information concerning the plan to delay payment of the ransom. Again, Blackwell was silent. He didn't say anything for nearly a minute or so. Carl could hear him taking a few deep breaths. Actually, the old man had a million questions. However, Blackwell was fully aware that The Peterson Group was extremely competent. Reluctantly, he would defer to Carl Peterson's discretion.

"Okay," he finally said. "Please keep me in the loop. This is my only granddaughter," he pleaded. "She's my life. She means the world to me," he added.

Carl could hear the desperation in Blackwell's voice.

"I will. And don't worry Mr. Blackwell. My people are the best at what they do. You'll be talking with Courtney before you know it," affirmed Carl. "I'll talk with you later," he added.

The old man acknowledged Carl's words of encouragement and hung up with a guarded "thank you."

For a moment, Carl thought about scrubbing the rescue attempt and just paying the ransom. That was certainly the most benign way to treat the situation. Everyone would be safe, but the old man would be out five million. Blackwell could certainly afford it. The thought had a brief life. Rick and Ann sat back down at the conference table as Carl again looked at his watch. Rick got up and went over to Roland. It was time to contact Roy and Carlos.

"Is the *Seychelles Princess* on schedule?" Rick asked.

Roland made a few keystrokes and brought up a visual of the operational area. There was a course superimposed that depicted the planned route of the *Seychelles Princess*. Roland expanded the scale and pointed to a blip, which was the actual position of the ship. The timeline along the proposed course indicated that the ship was on course and schedule.

"The *Seychelles Princess* will enter the op-area in thirty-three and a half hours," said Roland.

"What about our people?" asked Rick.

"Our people are already in the vicinity of the rendezvous point," responded Roland.

"Let's bring Roy and Carlos online," said Carl, motioning to Roland.

Roland made a few more keystrokes, and a visual of Roy's Combat Information Center, more commonly referred to as the CIC, popped up on the video display. The room was a little larger than normal. Roy and Carlos were standing by a large whiteboard that was not clearly visible from the current setup. Upon hearing the connecting tone, Roy and Carlos took up a position in front of the camera.

"Good afternoon from Djibouti," Roy answered as he checked his watch.

"How's it going," asked Carl.

"Going well. We're on schedule. Our guys are already in the op-area. *Seychelles Princess* is a day and a half out. We'll be putting the team ashore in about eight hours. Perfect night, partial moon and miserably hot."

"How is your communications package?" asked Rick.

"Everything is working five by five. We have full satellite coverage and a primary and backup communication system. Also, have an open line to Ozzie and Harriett. How about at your end?" asked Roy.

"Same here. Starting tomorrow, we'll be manned around the clock and provide backup communications if you need it," said Rick.

"I assume there has been no change in the location of Ms. Evans or her friends?" asked Roy. It was a rhetorical question.

"Still on the Liberty ship," responded Rick.

"Would you happen to know Mohamed Ibrahim?" asked Carl, changing the subject.

"I don't know him personally, but I do know him by reputation. He's a pretty rough character. Is he the one you'll be dealing with?" asked Roy somewhat incredulously.

"According to Ozzie and Harriett, it appears that he'll be handling the negotiation," responded Carl.

"He may be negotiating the ransom, but I can't imagine that the buck stops with him. He's just one step up from carrying an RPG in a speedboat. I'd bet a year's pay that he takes direction from higher up the food chain," said Roy.

"How extensive is this food chain?" asked Carl.

"As I said before, everyone gets a piece of the pie. It could go all the way up into the existing political structure," responded Roy.

Carl was about to ask another question when Roland put up a picture of Mohamed Ibrahim on the screen. The picture looked like a mug shot. Ibrahim bore many facial scars. The most distinguishing feature was that he had only one ear.

CHAPTER EIGHTEEN
Somali Coast
Day 9
2300 Hours

The Zodiac skimmed across the water at nearly full throttle. The airflow provided a welcomed relief from the one hundred and seven degree temperature that hung over the area like a heavy wool blanket. Climate change had nothing to do with the temperature and humidity that were normal during this time of year. The heat didn't seem to bother the five men aboard the dull black Zodiac. All of them had been involved in desert operations over the years. And all were seasoned veterans of covert operations. They had made numerous landings in all parts of the world under various conditions…and usually during the middle of the night when not expected. Four of the men had landed ashore in Mogadishu in 1993 during the operation known as *Gothic Serpent.* They were all too familiar with the political situation in Somalia, the illegal poaching, the plight of the people, and the fighters they unceremoniously referred to as the "skinnies."

The pilot at the helm was Raul Sanchez. He was a former Army staff sergeant who had been with the 75th Ranger Regiment during *Gothic Serpent.* He had the distinction of being directly involved in the capture of warlord Mohamed Farrah Aidid. Unfortunately the capture, showing Raul firmly holding a confused and ruffled warlord firmly by the upper arm, was immortalized on film. Still shots had appeared on the cover of several foreign publications along with numerous simulcasts of the film over and over by Aljazeera. Within a very short period of time, a sizeable bounty had been placed on Raul Sanchez's head. And in that part of the world, *on his head*, was meant quite literally.

Following the second attempt on his life, which resulted in the death of two French legionnaires, the Army decided that it was not only in Raul's best interest, but also in the best interest of the Army to transfer Raul to the Pentagon. The French strongly endorsed the U.S.

Army's decision—a decision they had been trying to influence for some time. They had considered Sanchez a magnet for every young wannabe terrorist.

Within three months, and after several run-ins with Washington bureaucrats who Raul referred to as pencil-neck assholes, Raul's head was again on a platter. This time, he knew his days in the Army were numbered. It was just a matter of time before he would piss off the wrong politician and find himself in an untenable situation. Although he loved the Army, and in particular field operations, he couldn't stand the thought of continuing to shine a chair with the seat of his pants. He was an operator. Besides, as a staff sergeant in the Pentagon, he had about as much authority as one of the janitors on Saturday night.

Duty in the Pentagon was not for him. Moreover, he did not want to be discharged for less than honorable reasons. Thus, he decided that it would be prudent to put in his papers and save what was left of his waning career. The Army gladly accepted his resignation, and he was on the street in less than two weeks.

Several months later, Raul ran into Roy Higgins at a recruiting seminar sponsored by Blackwater. Roy knew and had worked with Raul on several occasions. The last time was in Colombia when the CIA, and an unnamed Ranger unit, took out a drug lord in Cali. Raul had led the unit. Roy offered Raul a job on the spot. Without knowing what the job would be, Raul jumped at the opportunity to be back in cammies and carry a weapon again…legally.

Raul was very familiar with the Somali coastline. He knew where all the small harbors were, and a couple in particular that would provide a serendipitous landing. The harbor he selected was far enough away from the area of operation that it would be off the radar coverage of any unfriendly. Although the landing point was well to the south of the harbor where the Liberty ship was grounded, the team could easily cover the two-mile trek in plenty of time to board the ship and provide the necessary intelligence to effect a successful extraction. Besides, there was certainly no rush.

The current plan was for Shaun and Cody to be in place aboard the Liberty ship twenty-four hours in advance of the arrival of the

Seychelles Princess. That would give them plenty of time to search the ship, locate Courtney Evans and her friends, and find a secure place to become invisible until they were given the go-ahead.

Guillermo and Rafael would go ashore 2200 hours the next night. They would make their way to a position approximately six hundred yards from the Liberty ship. They had already selected the site based upon a thorough examination of current terrain guidance mapping along with real-time satellite imagery. The location they selected would give them a clear view of the Liberty ship and the makeshift brow. It was also well within the range of the XM-3 sniper weapon system. By waiting twenty-four hours, they would minimize both their exposure to the elements and the possibility of being seen.

As the Zodiac continued on its journey, Shaun, Cody, Guillermo and Rafael checked their gear. All four men wore modified Desert Combat Uniforms. Much to Roy's dismay, Shaun and Cody had cut off the sleeves, as did many Navy SEALS involved in desert operations. Guillermo and Rafael left their uniforms intact. All four men wore Salomon Quest boots. However, in order to eliminate weight, all four men opted to leave the ballistic armor plates behind.

Both Shaun and Cody selected SIG Sauer P229s from Roy's impressive collection of weaponry. Cody also grabbed his favorite weapon, an HK416 with a ten-inch barrel and suppressor. Although both men subscribed to the motto, "light is right," they both had enough magazines to fight a small war. Shaun nearly filled all ten pockets with various goodies from Roy's locker, including explosive breaching charges, a Gerber multitool, two fixed blade knives, and a small medical kit.

Roy also had a modest supply of night vision goggles that had been recently surveyed by Seal Team Six just after they were issued the new four-tube version. How he had come by them was a bit of a mystery. Although Shaun and Cody would have preferred the four-tube night vision goggles, both men were comfortable with the two-tube version.

Guillermo and Rafael carried camouflaged XM-3 sniper rifles, a healthy supply of water, and enough 7.62mm ammunition to fight the same small war alongside Shaun and Cody. Additionally, Rafael was in charge of the satellite communications equipment. He would maintain satellite communications with Roy and Carlos. All four men checked their headsets during the transit. Rafael made contact with Roy, and also did a five by five check with Rick Morgan's team in The Peterson Group office. The communications gear worked as advertised. As usual, the team would communicate only when necessary.

Shaun and Cody had memorized the layout of this particular Liberty ship. Roland had certainly done his homework. He had no problem tracing the remaining markings that were still visible on the stern of the ship. He discovered that the ship had been sold to the Greeks during World War II.

From the information that Roland was able to glean on this particular ship, he discovered that it had been modified to carry troops on the deck just below the main deck. He suspected that this deck, known as the tween deck, was probably now being used to hold Ms. Evans and her friends. There was also a slight possibility that other captives were being held.

Although there was no evidence that anyone else was being held on the ship, it was one of the contingencies that Rick and the team had considered and addressed. If there were other captives, Cody would make a recommendation considering their situation and physical condition. However, the primary mission was to rescue Courtney Evans and her three friends...and no others.

Roland had developed an algorithm to identify and record activity aboard the ship. Satellite imagery of the ship indicated that the pirates normally hung out in the vicinity of the bridge deck, located on the upper deck at the center of the ship. There were usually only three pirates on the ship at any one time. There was also a gun mount on the stern of the ship. A large bird nest occupied the place where a 5-inch gun had been mounted. By the amount of bird droppings and small bones that graced the deck, the nest appeared to be an active home for an osprey. It was probably two to three months old.

Guillermo and Rafael didn't say much on the trip. They were both still tired from their mission into Libya. There were numerous large ships scattered about the horizon. Most were tankers and cargo ships on their way to transit the Suez Canal. The ship captains had learned to travel in convoys and take advantage of the contractors who had been hired by many of the ship owners to protect their cargo. As a result, piracy was down. The pirates were no match for the skill and weaponry carried by the hired mercenaries.

As Shaun looked back, Roy's patrol boat was easily identifiable. Roy wanted it to be highly visible as a stark reminder and stern warning to the pirates to stay away from the tankers. The patrol boat had been provided by the Saudis. It was heavily armed and had the weaponry to fend off any attempt by pirates to challenge them. Several months earlier, a speedboat with five pirates had made the fatal mistake of trying to attack the patrol boat. News of their fate spread quickly throughout Somalia. There was a new dog in town…and no one was going to mess with the big dog.

At 2330 hours, the Zodiac cruised ashore in a small harbor that offered a smooth landing for the team. The sky was clear, the stars were numerous, and the half moon provided more than enough illumination…maybe too much. It was still miserably hot, but the desert uniform worn by the team wicked away the sweat as advertised.

Guillermo and Rafael shook hands with Shaun and Cody. Nothing much was said among the team members as the two men headed inland toward a ridge that ran north and south for several miles. The ridge would provide good cover as Shaun and Cody made their way toward Eyl and the Liberty ship. Guillermo and Rafael scanned the area with their night scopes. They could see Shaun and Cody as they moved north at a steady pace. Raul waited for about fifteen minutes until they heard from Cody that everything was a go.

As Guillermo helped push the Zodiac into the surf, he thought to himself that this beach could have been anywhere in the world. It was serene. It was pleasant. The sound of the small waves coming ashore was soothing and reminded him of a time not so long ago.

Guillermo thought back to his chance encounter with Patricia Delgado. Their paths had crossed briefly when he and Rafael were on their way to Venezuela. Ms. Delgado was a CIA operative whose cover had been compromised. She was about five foot six and in her mid-thirties. She had long black hair, big brown eyes, full lips and a body that was the envy of most girls.

Although just a brief passing in the night, there was instant chemistry between them. They held each other's gaze long enough to confirm the mutual feeling. He wondered to himself if he would ever be able to enjoy her company on a beach where there wasn't turmoil just beyond the dunes.

He fell asleep with a vision of her running down the beach. Tomorrow was already here.

CHAPTER NINETEEN
The Peterson Group Office
Day 9
1600 Hours

The brief communications test with Cody and Shaun came in loud and clear. There was very little static on the line and no perceptible delay in the transmission at either end. Rick was fully satisfied with the test and gave Roland a thumbs-up. Roland continued to monitor the secure circuit as Cody and Shaun skillfully made their way along the ridge leading toward the harbor at Eyl.

Carl had already taken a seat at the conference table next to Ann. Rick continued to watch the satellite imagery for a few more minutes as Roland made some minor adjustments and added some amplifying information. A time stamp appeared in the upper right-hand corner of the display. The time was 0030 Somalia time. Out of habit, Rick looked at his watch. No synchronization was required, as he had already set up the time difference. He then patted Roland on the shoulder. It was a fatherly gesture that didn't require a response.

Rick poured a cup of coffee and then joined Carl and Ann at the conference table. The three of them continued to review the plan— *one more time*. One more time never really meant one more time. Minor changes were normal and fully expected; however, Rick would never make any major changes at this point in the mission unless all hell broke loose. So far, everything was going according to the plan and schedule.

As the three of them were reviewing the plan, Roland set up a split screen view on the large monitor. He put Shaun and Cody on the left side and Roy's command center on the right side of the large display. Shaun and Cody could be seen making their way next to the ridge. They were taking advantage of what little moon shadows were available. Roy and Carlos were sitting in front of a large monitor with nearly the same satellite view that Roland had up on the screen.

The only difference was that Roy had selected a lower scale, which provided a close-up view of Cody and Shaun.

When Roland hit the audio feed, the conversation between Roy and Carlos could be heard quite clearly. It was loud enough to get Rick, Ann and Carl's attention.

"Let them know that we have a live feed and can hear them," Carl said, glancing over at Roland.

"Will do," responded Roland as he turned down the volume.

He let Roy know that the video feed was live and that the communication was two-way. Roy turned to the camera and smiled. There were certainly no secrets among the primary team members. They had all known each other for many years. The only real unknowns were Ozzie and Harriet. Roy looked back at the screen and continued to monitor Shaun and Cody's progress. Cody and Shaun would maintain radio silence. Neither Roy nor Rick would hear from them for at least another hour and a half…unless.

The Zodiac was already one hundred yards offshore and paralleling the coastline. It moved slowly across the water as Guillermo and Rafael panned the shoreline and ridge with their night scopes. It didn't take them long to acquire visual contact with Shaun and Cody. Guillermo smiled as he checked the range. Both men were well within the range of his XM-3 sniper rifle, as would be anyone else. Cody had no idea that he was in the crosshairs. Guillermo smiled to himself and moved the crosshairs to Shaun. He targeted both men and said, "bang-bang," under his breath. It was loud enough to get Rafael's attention. Rafael looked over at Guillermo and smiled. He had done the same thing a few minutes ago.

Guillermo then scanned the terrain well out in front of the men. *No problem*, he thought to himself as he brought the weapon down and laid it across his thighs. He looked up at the night sky and wondered how many times he had been in the crosshairs. How many of his friends had targeted him as they checked their equipment and the wind.

Raul was fully prepared to head into shore at the slightest hint of trouble. Not wanting to get too far ahead of Shaun and Cody, he slowly throttled back. The nose of the Zodiac immediately lowered as the boat slowed down to a couple of knots. There was a slight breeze and an eerie silence that engulfed the Zodiac. The sea state was somewhat less than forecast. However, there were swells that easily raised and lowered the Zodiac in rhythmic fashion. Although the motion was soothing, it was the kind of movement that could make a landlubber revisit dinner.

As Guillermo looked in the direction of the shoreline, he thought about the countless number of times he had been sitting in a Zodiac, providing sniper coverage for just part of a team going ashore on a one-hour mission. Many of the missions blended into one big war that never seemed to end. It would never end. He was convinced that if there were only two people in the world, one would want to control the other—one would want what the other has. It was an endless battle. He counted to himself, timing the swells, making a mental note. On several occasions, he had made shots from a thousand yards offshore and in seas much rougher than it was on this hot and humid night.

As Raul added a little power, Guillermo and Rafael continued to pan the ridge. At the low power setting, the Zodiac hardly made a sound as it continued on a northerly course paralleling the coast. Initially, Guillermo and Rafael were concerned that the presence of a Zodiac might alert the pirates that something was brewing. Although he and Rafael could easily take out the pirates in an approaching speedboat, dealing with a couple of RPGs was another issue.

Strategically, they would take out the guy holding the most lethal weapon. The guy with the RPG would be first to go, followed by whoever was foolish enough to pick up the weapon. They would all be dead meat. Guillermo and Rafael would win the battle as long as they had ammunition.

However, Roy had assured them that the presence of a Zodiac running up and down the shoreline was common practice whenever Saudi tankers were approaching the area known as the Seychelles. The pirates had their own intelligence network—one that was quite effective. They also knew the schedules, and they would expect to see Roy's well-lit patrol boat, the ever-present helicopters, a couple of Zodiacs and an occasional drone. Besides, there were more targets of opportunity with much less protection just over the horizon. The pirates had learned one hard lesson with Roy Higgins. They weren't about to challenge his people again, unless they had a death wish.

Moreover, many of the pirates operated from a mother ship that usually remained a couple hundred miles offshore. The probability of pirates coming from the harbor at Eyl was fairly remote. In the past few years, the pirates used the mother ship as their base of operations. Roy's people always kept track of the mother ship's location and the number of speedboats tied alongside. Tonight was no different. The mother ship was where they expected it to be. Roland also had the mother ship marked clearly on his screen.

Roy would send a drone in their direction just to let them know that the big dog was in the area—a warning to stay away from the Saudi tankers. However, Roy knew not to be complacent. Although he would send assets to patrol near the entrance to the harbor at Eyl, he always varied the routine just to keep the pirates guessing. Thus the presence of the Zodiacs and the occasional helicopter would not raise any undue suspicion on the part of the pirates. This night should be no different.

Roland continued to monitor the live satellite coverage of the area. He zoomed in on Shaun and Cody. They had already covered a little over a mile and appeared to be moving at a very fast pace. Roland moved ahead and zoomed in on the Liberty ship. There was no movement around the ship. However, there were lights on around the bridge deck. There were no lights on the stern. He watched the ship for several minutes then panned the small village that was to the north of the harbor. He counted eleven small fishing boats that had been pulled up onto the beach area. Fishing nets were draped over several of the boats. A couple of the boats were obviously pirate vessels.

Of the several houses close to the beach, only one appeared to be lit. Three pickup trucks were parked haphazardly around the house. The heat signature indicated that they had been there for at least a couple of hours. They were probably in for the night. Roland continued to pan the area.

When he was satisfied that there was no activity in the small village, he zoomed in on the position where Ozzie and Harriet had been parked to observe the ship. Their vehicle was gone. He wasn't sure what their orders were. He made a note and then focused in on Shaun and Cody. He then changed the scale so that the Liberty ship was also visible. He placed a cursor between the men and the ship and determined that they would be at the harbor in about thirty minutes at their current pace. Roy and Carlos appeared to be making some calculations of their own. Everyone appeared to be on the same page.

"Are you guys getting hungry?" Carl asked as he looked at his watch. "I could have Elaine order some pizza from Bertucci's if you like," he added.

"Sounds good to me," responded Ann as she looked up for confirmation from Rick and Roland.

"How about you Roland?" asked Carl.

"I can always eat Italian," he responded, without taking his eyes off the screen. "The works for me," he added.

"Pizza it is," said Carl as he let Elaine know their desires.

Rick went over and sat down next to Roland. Both men watched the screen as Cody and Shaun continued at a fast pace. Roland panned the area again looking for bogies.

"How far out is the Zodiac?" asked Rick.

With one keystroke, Roland changed the scale and pointed to the Zodiac on the screen.

"He's about two hundred meters offshore," responded Roland.

Rick didn't say anything as Roland placed a cursor on the men and the Zodiac. The calculation gave the exact distance. Rick noted that Guillermo and Rafael were well within the range of their sniper rifles.

"What's the sea state?" asked Rick.

Roland looked at his notes.

"Supposed to be a sea state of three," responded Roland. "I would be surprised if it were more than two," he added.

Rick didn't say anything as he thought about taking a shot from a moving platform. A sea state of three would provide slight difficulty for a shot due to the small rolling waves, but anything less than a three would be relatively easy. He was certain that Raul had picked the offshore course to minimize the movement of the Zodiac. Guillermo and Rafael were both more than capable of making a shot from a moving platform, especially at a stationary target. The hardest shot is from a moving helicopter to a moving target. Guillermo had made many shots from a moving platform, and one year, he had won the sniper competition at Fort Benning. The winning shot was his shot from a moving helicopter.

"Is it quiet around the ship?" asked Rick.

"I just panned the area. Nothing out of the ordinary," responded Roland.

Rick didn't say anything as he continued to watch the screen. He was about to get up when Roland asked him about Ozzie and Harriet.

"I'll check with Roy. There's probably no reason for them to be in the area until tomorrow night," said Rick as he got up and went back to the conference table.

"How are we looking?" asked Carl.

"Good. Shaun and Cody will be at the harbor in about thirty minutes," responded Rick as he looked at his watch.

"And Guillermo and Rafael?" asked Carl.

"They're close enough to provide cover if necessary," responded Rick.

Carl didn't say anything for a few minutes. Ann got up and poured a fresh cup of coffee and then sat down next to Roland. Roland smiled as Ann placed her hand on his shoulder. Her perfume was subtle. Her closeness was momentarily distracting. Maybe Rick was right. He needed a woman in his life.

"Rick, this isn't going *too* smoothly...is it?" asked Carl, feeling some concern.

"You mean no bright lights or media illuminating the way—no cameras like it was a Hollywood set?" asked Rick.

"Mogadishu was something wasn't it," recalled Carl.

Rick's expression confirmed his disappointment with the whole Mogadishu mission.

"If this goes as we have planned, our guys will be in and out before the pirates know what's happened," offered Rick.

"You know Rick, it's a lot harder watching an operation than being there on the ground...being a part of it," said Carl.

His eyes were sincere. He missed the action, as did Rick.

"It's a young man's game," responded Rick.

"It is," lamented Carl. "It just isn't fair," he added as he looked over at the screen.

CHAPTER TWENTY
Eyl, Somalia
Day 10
0100 Hours

Shaun and Cody made it to the south end of the harbor at exactly 0110 hours. The smell of fuel and dead fish had become more pronounced with every step as they got closer to the harbor and the area where the Liberty ship was entombed. Although the area close to the harbor was fairly flat, neither man had caught sight of the old ship.

Suddenly, it seemed to appear out of nowhere. There it was, looming about fifty yards starboard of their position. At first glance in the dim moonlight, it looked like a pile of debris—debris that was now a permanent part of the landscape. As they got closer, there was an eerie silence—a silence only seafaring men understood when in the presence of a dead ship and silenced memories.

Cody reached out and stopped Shaun. He made a hand gesture to put on their night vision goggles. Both men scanned the area for several minutes until they were convinced that they were alone. Cody removed his goggles and let his eyes adjust to the darkness. He looked up at the star-studded night sky. The moon seemed to hang over the harbor like a light in an old Humphrey Bogart movie. Cody had an urge to try and reach up and touch it. The half lit moon provided just enough illumination to create shadows the men would use to their advantage. They listened for a few more minutes and then moved very slowly toward the stern.

As they approached the old ship, the port list was more noticeable, but it was subtle—just subtle enough to keep an intruder off-balance. The ship was never going anywhere but deeper into the sandy grave. The skeg was visible just above the water level. There were little mounds of sand all around the ship that were starting to disappear as the tide began to come in.

Shaun and Cody crouched down behind the remains of an old tugboat that had probably been there well before the Liberty ship. The rotting wood gave off a pungent odor. Cody knew just enough Italian to interpret the name that was trying to hang on to the weathered board that had come loose from the bow. The name brought a slight smile to his face. *Reliable One* didn't make a whole lot of sense, not even in Italian. However, the old tug did provide good cover and a suitable location to observe the area around the Liberty ship.

Their only concern now was the possibility of running into a pack of stray dogs. Roland had warned the men that dogs could be a problem. *So far so good*, Cody thought to himself. He was not fond of dogs, any dogs for that matter. Cody and Shaun were prepared to stay their position until they were sure that the area was clear. Besides, they were in no rush.

From the barnacles on what was left of the tug, it appeared that the tide wouldn't be much of a problem. Both men scanned the area again with their night vision goggles. Surprisingly, there was no activity. No activity was good, as long as it wasn't planned. Cody tapped Shaun on the shoulder.

"It's almost too quiet," he whispered.

Shaun nodded in agreement.

"Do you think they're expecting us?" asked Shaun.

"Not unless our new friends, Ozzie and Harriet, are playing both ends against the middle," responded Cody.

"I really don't like relying on a couple of guys I don't know," said Shaun. "Especially Somalis," he added in a sarcastic tone.

"I don't either. But Higgins vouches for them," said Cody.

"I really don't know Higgins either," whispered Shaun after a slight pause.

Cody smiled to himself. He agreed. In their business, trust was a precious commodity. Unfortunately, it was a commodity that could be traded...and was traded all too often.

"Let's just sit here for a little while. See if anyone shows up," Cody added.

The two men held their position and put on their night vision goggles. They hardly moved as Shaun panned the area in the direction of the small fishing village. Cody directed his attention toward the old ship. He slowly looked up and down the port side. Roland had described the ship to a tee and had provided them with a very accurate schematic.

Liberty ships were cargo ships that were built during World War II. The typical Liberty ship was just over four hundred forty feet in length and about fifty-seven feet wide. A variety of weapons could be carried aboard the ship, including a stern-mounted deck gun and several anti-aircraft guns.

The ship basically had three levels: the upper deck, the tween deck, which was located just under the upper deck, and then five separate cargo holds beneath the tween deck. The tween deck was mainly for storage, but some were modified to carry troops.

The crew accommodations were housed in a large three-deck structure located at the center of the ship on the upper deck. The highest level, or bridge deck, housed the ship's captain and radio operator. The next level was called the boat deck; this area housed the officers. The lowest level, located directly on the upper deck, housed the crew and mess facilities.

The aft gun mount was located on the stern. Beneath this was the munitions storage area. Cody and Shaun had memorized the drawings. The stern would indeed provide the best access point for boarding the ship. *But wouldn't the pirates know that,* Cody thought to himself. He scanned the stern for several minutes. He thought about the large bird's nest that was now occupying the place where a deck gun had been mounted during the Second World War. A startled Osprey could make a lot of noise…too much noise, especially at 0130 hours. *It could be an old nest,* he thought as he moved his gaze back to the stern.

The pilot ladder that hung over the side was well worn. It ended just above the skeg. From his vantage point, it looked to be sturdy enough to support a man's weight, but looks could be deceiving. Shaun, being the lighter of the two, would be first to test its integrity. Once he got to the upper deck, he would attach a rope to provide additional support and security.

Although the stern was bathed in darkness, there were several small bright lights that illuminated the bridge and the area around the makeshift brow. A generator could be heard pumping away somewhere close to the brow. Bright lights were good. Anyone in the light would make an easy target, and they would have a difficult time seeing anyone in the shadows. Cody noticed that there was a small skiff pulled up on shore next to the brow. There were no oars, but there was a small motor on the back and several wooden boxes near the front of the boat. Cody wasn't sure how long the skiff had been there. He could contact Roy and find out for sure, but he didn't want to break radio silence. Besides, they knew that there would be someone on the ship. How many were on the ship was the issue. Cody tapped Shaun on the shoulder and pointed to the skiff.

"From the size of the skiff, there are probably no more than four aboard," he whispered.

"Yeah...unless they made a couple of trips," responded Shaun as he looked back at the skiff.

Good point, Cody thought to himself.

Cody took off his goggles and looked up at the area that would have housed the crew. There was a bright light coming from one of the portholes. He continued to focus on the area. There were changes in the light that indicated movement from within. There was certainly someone moving around inside.

Cody looked at his watch. The tide was steadily moving in. It was time to board the ship if they wanted to stay as dry as possible. Although they didn't expect there would be a roving patrol, just in case, they didn't need to leave wet footprints on the deck.

He tapped Shaun on the shoulder and pointed to the stern. Shaun put most of his things into his small waterproof bag and handed it to Cody. The only weapon he chose was one of the fixed blade knives. He threw the black woven rope over his shoulder, and without a word spoken, headed for the stern.

The ground between the old tug and the ship was firm and covered with thousands of broken shells that had been there for years. Shaun hardly made a sound as he deftly made his way over the shells. The water was only ankle deep next to the ship. The top of the skeg was just above the water level. In ten minutes, it would be underwater.

Shaun stood on the skeg and tested the first rung of the pilot ladder. It was solid enough to support his weight, as were the rest of the rungs. He easily made it to the upper deck. There was no railing. The deck was still quite warm from the day's sun. The footprints would not be an issue. He looked in the direction of the nest. There didn't appear to be any birds, although an osprey could be very still.

Cody covered Shaun with the HK416. He would take out anyone approaching the stern. He continued to watch the area around the gun mount until he was convinced that Shaun was in the clear. He then moved his attention to the crew area. For the first time, he thought he could hear some music, but he wasn't sure. It was difficult to tell with the whining noise made by the generator. The light emanating from the porthole continued to flicker. The flicker was haphazard. For sure there was someone moving about inside the crew deck.

Cody looked back to the stern. Shaun was signaling for him to come aboard. He picked up both waterproof bags and headed for the skeg that was now almost underwater. He attached the bags to the rope and gave the rope two tugs. Shaun hoisted the bags to the deck. He tied the rope to an old cleat, tested it, and then let the rope down next to the pilot ladder. Cody easily made his way onto the Liberty ship. Both men moved slowly away from the stern and into the shadows.

The area around the gun mount was covered in feathers, fish bones and dried bird droppings. It appeared that the nest had been abandoned some time ago. The men were careful not to disturb the droppings. Knowing the Somalis, they probably had killed and eaten the osprey. Anyway, it didn't matter. They didn't have to deal with a pissed-off bird at 0130 in the morning.

Obviously the gun mount hadn't been used for anything…and it hadn't been used for anything for many years. The information that Roland provided included a detailed drawing of the gun mount and the modification incorporated by the Greeks. Upon examination of the drawings, the team had concluded that the gun mount would provide access to a good hiding place. Cody found the small hatch that allowed access to the munitions storage area that was located beneath the gun mount.

According to Roland, there were two other hatches located in the munitions storage area. One of the hatches was a part of the original design and provided access to one of the fuel tanks. The other hatch was part of the modification that provided a passageway into the tween deck. Normally, the tween deck would be used to carry cargo, but the Greeks had modified this particular ship to carry troops.

Cody shined a light down into the munitions storage area. He signaled Shaun.

"Keep an eye on the crew deck while I check it out," he said as he handed the HK416 to Shaun.

Shaun gave Cody a thumbs-up and directed his attention to the bridge and crew deck area.

The ladder provided adequate support as Cody carefully went down into the munitions space. The space was quite small but suitable for hiding out. It was actually a little cooler than he had expected. Cody looked around and found the access to the fuel tank. The hatch was rusted shut and would probably never be opened. On the forward bulkhead, there was a hatch that was open just enough for a man to get through. Cody tried to move the hatch, but it was stuck in position. He didn't want to force it for fear of making a noise that could resonate throughout the ship. He looked inside. It was very dark. It was the access to the tween deck that was located just above cargo hold number five. Cody panned the space with his light. The space was completely empty.

The information that Roland had obtained indicated that two spaces on the tween deck had been modified to carry troops. Roland suspected that Ms. Evans and her friends were probably being held in the tween deck just below and aft of the crew deck. That would make sense and provide easy control and access by the pirates.

Cody went into the space, keeping his light focused on the deck. The last thing he needed to do was to fall through an opening into the cargo hold of this old rusty ship. He continued to move slowly toward the forward bulkhead where another hatch was located. He ran his hand around the hatch and over the hinges. There was no seal. The hinges had been recently greased. He assumed that the hatch could be opened. He attached a listening device to the bulkhead and listened. He could hear some faint music but no other sounds.

Cody listened for a few more minutes and then headed back to the munitions storage area. He made a mental note of the number of paces across the tween deck. He visualized the drawing in his mind. *Roland was probably right*, he thought to himself. He looked around the munitions area and decided that it would provide the best location to hide out. He moved the waterproof bags to one of the corners and then went up the ladder to the gun mount.

"So what do think?" whispered Shaun.

CHAPTER TWENTY-ONE
Eyl, Somalia
Day 10
0200 Hours

Shaun got down on his knees and looked down into the munitions space. He was careful not to turn on his small charge light until he had extended his arm down into the space where it couldn't be seen from the bridge area. He slowly moved the light around from corner to corner. After about a minute, he turned the light off and stood up.

"Well, it's not the Ritz," he whispered jokingly. "But, it will have to do," he added as he put the small light back into his pocket.

Cody smiled. In the dark, Shaun couldn't quite see the smile. Cody cupped his hand over his watch, pressed the little button on the side, and took note of the time. Roy Higgins would be expecting to hear from them fairly soon. Cody was certain that Roy and Carlos had been watching via satellite. They certainly would have followed Cody and Shaun's progress as they made their way into the harbor area and onto the Liberty ship. Nevertheless, they needed to do a communications check to eliminate any surprises.

Cody looked at his watch again and decided to wait just a little longer until he had gathered some more information. If he was going to break radio silence, he wanted to provide current on-site intelligence. Cody looked in the direction of the crew deck. He could still hear the whining noise made by the generator. It was steady. He could also hear what sounded like an old phonograph. The music reminded him of a sound track from an old movie. He started to look at his watch again and then whispered to Shaun.

"I would like to get a good look inside the crew deck before we touch base with Higgins."

Before Shaun had a chance to respond, Cody handed the HK416 to him and took out his SIG. He checked the magazine and suppressor. He then chambered a round and slowly lowered the hammer.

"I can go if you'd rather cover me," responded Shaun.

Shaun was itching to look through the porthole.

"No, I got it. Watch my back. Don't shoot anyone unless it's absolutely necessary," said Cody. "We don't need to start the rest of this mission a day early," he added.

Shaun nodded somewhat disappointedly and tapped Cody on the shoulder. Cody immediately headed in the direction of the crew deck. Shaun took up a position just forward of the old gun mount. There were several good spots to observe the crew deck. Shaun stood next to an old rusted locker that was leaning to port and missing the door. It was positioned about three feet in front of a large gaping hole in the bulkhead that had once been a porthole. It looked like an errant round had taken it out. Shaun leaned back and became part of the bulkhead. He was virtually invisible to the outside world, especially in the dark.

Cody had slipped away, disappearing into the shadows. Both men were like ghosts in the night. As Cody got closer to the crew deck, he could hear voices from inside the structure. The music had stopped. The people inside were speaking in a language that he didn't understand, but he was sure that it was Somali. Whatever they were saying, they seemed to be speaking quite rapidly and interrupting one another.

There was obviously a man and a woman talking, or possibly two women. The man had no problem speaking over the women. Every once in a while there was a short period of silence, interrupted by laughter, punctuated by moaning sounds that were all too familiar. The contrast in sounds convinced Cody that there were at least three people in the space.

Cody was about to move in next to the bulkhead under one of the portholes when a door on the port side of the crew deck abruptly swung open. It banged off the bulkhead hard enough to swing back and nearly close. Cody slowly retreated into the shadows. He had a clear view of the opening.

A young Somali man walked out into the bright light. He was totally naked and still somewhat aroused. He walked briskly across the narrow deck and stood next to the brow. He widened his stance and began to pee over the side. The arousal didn't seem to hinder his ability to urinate. As he stood there swaying back and forth and humming aloud, two young Somali girls joined him. They were also naked.

The girls couldn't have been much over fourteen or fifteen years old. They were very thin and small breasted. All their weight was concentrated in their upper thighs and butt, which gave them a comical appearance. They were quite mature from the waist down. They giggled as they watch the man urinate over the side.

One of the girls squatted close to him and began peeing on the deck. The young man yelled something and pointed to the generator. She ignored him and continued to pee. He kicked her over onto her left side. The young girl continued to pee while trying to get up. She yelled something that made him raise a hand as if he were going to backhand her. He didn't hit her, but he said something to her that made her look in the direction of the generator.

Although the generator appeared to be fairly new, it was tied to the brow with an old white sheet. For whatever unexplainable reason, the generator seemed to pull at the sheet. She stared at it for a few seconds and then got up. The other girl reached around from behind the man, grabbed his penis with both hands and pretended to ring it out like it was an old wet rag. She then shook it hard and let go as he turned around and put his arms around both girls. He said something else that made all three of them laugh as they staggered back into the structure. One of the girls reached back and slammed the door shut as they entered the space.

Cody looked over at the generator and realized what the man must have said. The girl was lucky her pee avoided the shredded extension cords that were haphazardly spread about the deck. *This is not a refined bunch*, Cody thought to himself as he waited in the shadows.

However, it did remind him of the times his girlfriend would help him write his name in the snow. They weren't a refined bunch either in their younger days. After downing a six-pack of beer, Cody could write his first, middle and last name easily. "Don't eat yellow snow," they would say as they laughed aloud. He looked back in the direction of Shaun. Shaun was still invisible.

Cody waited for a few minutes before moving in under the porthole. The laughter and moaning had begun again. He put up a small mirror and looked into the space. The porthole was yellowed with age. It hadn't been cleaned in years. It was nearly opaque, but there were areas that allowed visibility. He slowly stood up and peered into the space with just his left eye. He fought the urge to wipe it off.

The young man was standing there in all his glory as both girls took their turns bending over a small wooden table. The young man was casually drinking a beer as he serviced the girls. One of the girls appeared to be stuffing qaat into her mouth. Her cheeks swelled as she started to chew the leaves. *That explains the rapid talking and excitement,* Cody thought to himself.

He moved back and used the mirror again to peer around the room. He was careful not to cause an unwanted reflection or shadow. He continued to look but didn't see anyone else. If there were anyone else, surely they would have joined the party by now. He moved away from the bulkhead and carefully made his way back to the gun mount.

"It looks like there is only one pirate and two young girls."

"Shit, they look like kids," said Shaun.

"They are kids," responded Cody. "They're in there screwing their brains out and chewing qaat," he added.

"Kids having kids," said Shaun shaking his head. "No one else?" he questioned, changing the subject.

"Doesn't appear to be anyone else," responded Cody.

Neither man said anything for a several minutes. Cody leaned back against the bulkhead. He was trying to erase the picture of the young girl urinating all over herself. She didn't even seem to care. It was fortunate that she didn't make contact with one of the frayed wires.

As the father of a teenage daughter, the sight of her nakedness was a bit disturbing. Cody had seen enough naked women in his life but never naked kids. Some things were sacred. He wanted to put one in the back of the pirate's head just for the sake of it, but he successfully fought the desire. It would have been a foolish emotional gesture from a professional. The mission to rescue Courtney Evans was much more important than a momentary lapse in judgment. Besides, when the extraction commenced, the girls were expendable.

"I'm going down below to touch base with Roy and Carlos. Keep an eye on this bunch. In their condition, I wouldn't be a bit surprised if they started wandering around the ship playing hide and seek. Last thing we need is one of these young girls dropping in on us," said Cody.

Shaun nodded as he continued to watch the bridge area. Cody went below, put on his headset, and made contact with Roy Higgins. Cody had assumed correctly. Roy and Carlos had been watching via satellite...so had Rick, Ann and Carl for that matter. They all had seen Shaun and Cody make their way onto the ship. They had also witnessed the events around the bridge area. Roland had zoomed in on the Somalis. Rick, Carl and Ann probably had a better view than Cody. As Cody made initial contact, Roland patched Cody through to the overhead speaker.

"Anything on Ms. Evans?" asked Roy.

"Not yet. Given the time, I would assume they're all asleep. We'll work on locating her and friends tomorrow. By the way, the information from Roland Carpenter was excellent."

"So there is access to the tween deck from the munitions storage area," said Roy. It was purely a rhetorical statement.

"There is, and there is also a hatch leading into the tween deck where Roland believes they're holding Ms. Evans and her friends," said Cody.

"What is the material condition of the hatch?" asked Carlos.

"It's been greased recently. Looks to be in good shape. However, it's secured, and I believe it's locked on the other side," responded Cody.

"So you tried it?" asked Roy.

"Not really. Didn't want to make any unnecessary noise," responded Cody.

"Can you gain access?" asked Carlos.

"When the time comes, we'll gain access one way or the other," responded Cody.

"You may have to blow it," said Carlos.

"We can do that, but I would prefer to take Ms. Evans and her friends off the ship via the brow."

No one said anything for several seconds.

"What about the women?" asked Rick. "They look like kids. Were you able to determine if they were staying aboard the ship?"

Cody recognized Rick's voice. He didn't acknowledge him by name but was happy to know that The Peterson Group office in Old Town would also be providing backup satellite coverage and communications if necessary.

"From what I've seen, I think they're just overnight visitors," he responded.

"If they're there tomorrow morning, you may have to deal with them. Are you comfortable with that?" asked Rick.

"They're just young kids," said Cody, seemingly in defense.

"Young kids blew up a lot of good soldiers in Vietnam. Even young girls blew up guys in Iraq and Afghanistan. Just be careful," emphasized Rick.

"Will do," responded Cody. He knew that Rick was right.

No American soldier wanted to kill young kids, but kids in backward nations were, unfortunately, a plentiful bunch...and, nobody would miss them. Both of these young girls would most likely end up pregnant. If their children survived their first few years, they would end up on the street looking into garbage cans for whatever little clothing and morsels they could salvage. Ten years later, they'd be bending over for another young pirate—probably bending over the same wooden table. *The pro-life zealots should spend some time in this part of the world*, Cody thought to himself.

Rick made a couple of notes. He knew that there was a strong possibility that prostitutes would frequent the ship. Prostitutes were always dangerous. They were known to carry razor blades in their hair and would use them at the slightest hint of a problem. The motive of these young girls was questionable. Rick would leave the final decision on how to handle them up to Shaun and Cody.

"When the action starts, knock them out. You'll be long gone by the time they come to," offered Rick. "Use your judgment," he added.

"Hopefully, they'll be gone," said Cody. "But I assure you that I won't let them get in the way," he said convincingly.

CHAPTER TWENTY-TWO
The Peterson Group Office
Day 10
0600 Hours

Roland was already sitting at the conference table when Elaine Drew entered the room and began to make the coffee. She smiled and said good morning. Rick, Carl and Ann arrived about five minutes later. They didn't seem at all surprised to see Roland sitting there first thing in the morning. Many times he would spend the night, especially when the covert teams were active.

He had already brought up the satellite imagery of the Liberty ship along with a live feed from Roy's Combat Information Center at Camp Lemonnier. Roy and Carlos could be seen looking over a large display board similar to that employed during wargaming exercises. Roy had a small toy-sized helicopter in his hand. However, this was not a game. There were new players added to the mix.

Roland sat back in the chair and clasped his hands together behind his head. He was rocking gently. Carl wondered to himself if Roland had spent the night. It wouldn't be the first time Roland had spent the night in The Peterson Group guest room. Carl couldn't remember what the kid was wearing the day before. He looked down at Roland's penny loafers…still no socks.

Rick caught Carl looking and put out his right hand. Carl reached into his pocket and peeled off a new twenty and slapped it into Rick's outstretched palm. Rick snapped the bill between both hands and held it up to the light. Carl shook his head. Roland looked back at Rick and smiled. Carl caught the exchange between Rick and Roland.

"Are you two in cahoots?" asked Carl, looking first at Roland and then over at Rick. Rick had a big smile on his face.

"Sir?" asked Roland innocently, pretending that he didn't notice the exchange of looks.

"Never mind," said Carl. "Do you even own a pair of socks?" he asked as he looked down at Roland's feet.

"Several pairs," responded Roland as he said good morning to the rest of the crew. He then leaned in toward the table and pulled his keyboard a little closer. He made a few keystrokes and brought up the sound so they could hear the conversation in Roy's command center.

"Anything new?" asked Carl as he picked up one of the coffee cups that Elaine had just filled. She handed a cup to Rick and poured one for Ann. Before Roland could respond, she asked if anyone needed anything else. Carl thanked her, and she left the room quietly. She knew the team was nearing the execution phase of the mission. Their attention would be focused on the task at hand.

"Mr. Higgins said that the *Seychelles Princess* was on schedule. It's about ten hours out from the op-area," Roland answered.

Carl looked up at the two clocks that Roland had mounted on the wall next to the large screen. One was set to Eastern Standard Time. The other was set to, and clearly marked for, Somalia time. It was just past 1600 hours in Somalia. Out of habit, Carl checked his watch. So did Ann.

"I need to call the negotiator," said Carl as he went over to his desk and thumbed through one of the many steno pads that were stacked neatly on the right side of his desk. Blackwell was written in large letters across the top of the second one down from the top. He opened it to a page with the name Mohamed Ibrahim in capital letters. The name was centered on the page and circled several times in black ink. Rick went over to where Roland was sitting.

"Is everything set up?" he asked, leaning close to Roland's right ear.

"We're set Mr. Morgan," responded Roland as he looked over at Carl. Carl didn't hear him.

Carl dialed the number given to him by JT Blackwell. There was a slight delay and then a clicking sound as the connection was established. The ringtone had a hollow sound to it. Carl felt like he was in a barrel. Hopefully, it wasn't a premonition of things to come. He could hear himself breathing, although he wasn't at all nervous. He paused and took a couple of deep breaths. He certainly didn't want to sound nervous. *It must be the feedback in the line*, he thought to himself. Mohamed Ibrahim answered after several short rings.

"Waad salaamantahay" he answered with a pronounced Arabic accent.

"Hello, this is Carl Peterson. I would like to speak with Mohamed Ibrahim," Carl announced in a loud clear voice.

In anticipation, Roland had put Mohamed Ibrahim's picture, along with a short biography, on the small monitor that was mounted in the center of the conference table. The monitor was fastened to a swivel. Roland reached over and turned it toward Carl. Carl moved closer to the conference table and focused on the picture.

Mohamed Ibrahim had a very distinguished look. He was graying at the temples, slightly balding on top, and wore a neatly trimmed beard. His two front teeth were partially visible and appeared to be outlined in gold. His shirt was unbuttoned, exposing a large gold chain—the top of what appeared to be a crescent moon was clearly visible. His skin was very dark and surprisingly smooth. The information alongside the picture indicated that he was over six feet tall and weighed one hundred eighty five pounds. His age was listed at fifty-eight years old. However, he looked like he could easily be in his late forties...or it could have been an older picture. In any case, Mohamed Ibrahim did not appear to be your typical pirate.

"Ah, Mr. Peterson. I see you have done your homework. I won't ask you how you learned my name. However, since you have, I assume you have also discovered that I am a man of experience... well educated...and with many resources at my disposal," boasted Ibrahim, setting the stage for limited negotiation.

"I'm fully aware of your resume Mr. Ibrahim," responded Carl.

"Please, call me Mohamed."

Please seems out of place, Carl thought to himself. It was meant to be disarming. Carl knew how to play the game.

"Let's dispense with the list of...shall we say...personal attributes. I'm sure they are legion," said Carl, slipping into a British-style persona.

"By all means," responded Ibrahim.

The information that Roland had provided also indicated that Mohamed Ibrahim was an Oxford graduate. He had earned an engineering degree, although he never was employed in the field. Upon returning to Somalia, he had become more disturbed by the plight of the Somali people. He became politically active and was an outspoken advocate who aggressively supported fighting against the fishermen who routinely poached in Somali waters. Frustrated with the lack of cooperation on the part of the pseudo-Somali government, he resorted to piracy to help alleviate the financial burden facing so many of the local populace. As a result, he had become somewhat of a local hero to many…and a big pain in the ass to others.

Mohamed Ibrahim was certainly no fool. Carl hesitated for a few seconds as he continued to study the man on the screen. He took a drink from the coffee cup.

"Let me be very clear. Mr. Blackwell has every intention of meeting your demands…and meeting them fully, I assure you. Unfortunately, yesterday Mr. Blackwell suffered a minor heart attack and is presently in intensive care."

"And his prognosis is good I trust?" interrupted Ibrahim.

"He'll be fine. Just needs a couple of days under the doctor's care," responded Carl. "There's an outside chance that he'll be released late tomorrow morning. In any case, we'll complete the arrangements at that time," he added.

"What hospital is he in?" asked Ibrahim after a short pause.

Carl looked over at Rick. Although Rick could not hear Ibrahim's side of the conversation, he could tell by Carl's expression that Ibrahim wanted to know where JT Blackwell was hospitalized. Rick tried to suppress a smile, but failed. Carl had bet that Ibrahim wouldn't ask that question. Rick extended his right hand. He rubbed his thumb and first two fingers together several times. Carl didn't dignify the gesture as he turned to Roland.

"Roland, do you have the room information on Mr. Blackwell?" he asked without covering the phone. He wanted Ibrahim to hear the request.

"I'll enter it on the screen," replied Roland.

The information that Roland put on the screen had been prepared earlier at Rick's request. Although it was a facade, the hospital would confirm the information.

"Mr. Blackwell is in the New Hanover Regional Medical Center in Wilmington, North Carolina. I have his room and phone number if you want to give him, or the hospital, a call," Carl confirmed.

"No, that will be fine. You said the New Hanover Regional Medical Center. I can find the number myself," responded Ibrahim confidently.

"Your choice. By the way, we have most of the money in our possession, but there are a few securities that Mr. Blackwell must sign in person in order to authorize the distribution of funds. I trust you understand."

"I understand perfectly well. I own a few securities myself. I will give you two more days, but I strongly suggest that you don't test my patience. This will be my only consideration," said Ibrahim as he ended the call.

Carl didn't say anything as he put the satellite phone down on his desk. He wasn't at all surprised that Ibrahim had ended the call so abruptly. It was purely a textbook power play on the part of Mohamed Ibrahim. No matter what, Carl knew perfectly well the only thing that Ibrahim was really interested in was the money. Ibrahim could bluff all he wanted to, but he would be back on the phone when the time was right. Besides, there were captives in Somalia who had been there for a couple of years—a few more days wouldn't matter.

"I take it he didn't say goodbye," said Rick.

"No he didn't," smiled Carl.

"Do you think he bought it?" asked Ann.

"We'll see," responded Carl.

"You owe me twenty bucks," said Rick.

Eyl, Somalia
Day 10
1400 Hours

Cody slowly made his way across the tween deck that was above cargo hold number five. A musty odor permeated the air. He hadn't noticed it earlier. *Must have been the rain*, he thought to himself. There were numerous holes in the bulkhead that allowed little rays of light to pierce the space. They looked to be frozen as they emanated in all directions. The rays of light were full of dust particles that seemed to have a mind of their own.

Cody moved next to the bulkhead and peered through one of the larger holes that was a couple of inches to the left of the hatch that led into the space where Roland believed Courtney Evans and her friends were being held. Cody could see into a long passageway that was illuminated by several small overhead lights. However, most of the light came from the open overhead hatch at the far end of the passageway. The sun was the source.

Cody continued to look through the hole. He counted ten doors, five on each side of the passageway. There was also another door at the far end of the passageway. He flashed his light back toward the munitions storage area. He then looked back through the hole. The space was quite a bit smaller in length.

Cody made a mental note and looked through several of the other holes that populated the bulkhead. The light emanating from them wasn't as bright. As he looked through one of the holes that was fairly close to the corner, he could barely make out someone lying in a bunk bed. There was a small overhead light that was burning but putting out very little light.

The person in the bed appeared to be a young woman. Cody purposely didn't make a sound. As he tried to get a better look, he heard someone talking in the passageway. He looked back through the hole near the hatch and saw two young Somali men. They were carrying trays and a bucket. The men systematically unlocked each door, opened it, handed in a tin plate of food, and then dipped water from the bucket. Cody counted four servings.

The men were about to leave when a woman yelled that she needed to use the toilet. One of the men motioned to the other to get her. He pointed in the direction of the door at the far end of the passageway. Cody watched as a woman with long dark hair was led down the passageway. She appeared to be in good physical condition. She kept her head down and didn't say anything. Cody assumed the woman to be Lisa Bradley. He waited until she was led back to her room. After seeing her face, he was certain that it was Lisa Bradley.

After the men left, Cody grabbed the upper dog of the hatch and moved it slightly. He wanted to open the hatch, but it wasn't time. Cody looked at his watch. It was already 1500 hours. He listened at the hatch for several minutes but did not hear any more sounds. He was a little surprised that Ms. Evans and her friends didn't try to communicate with one another. *The Pirates must have warned them to remain silent*, he thought to himself.

After a few more minutes, Cody walked back to the munitions storage area. Shaun was near the top of the ladder keeping watch. The brief afternoon shower was long gone. The sun was bright. The temperature was nearly one hundred and ten degrees in the shade. Steam was rising off the deck. Shaun put his hand on the deck. It was extremely hot to the touch. *Hot enough to fry an egg*, he mused.

Cody signaled him. Shaun looked down and whispered, "Are they here?"

"I only saw Lisa Bradley. But the pirates delivered four meals, so I assume all four are on board and are being held in that area," said Cody in a low voice as he sat on the edge of a small bench.

"I need to make radio contact with Higgins," he said as he put on his headset and went back into the tween deck above cargo hold number five.

CHAPTER TWENTY-THREE
Eyl, Somalia
Day 10
2200 Hours

Raul Sanchez throttled back and began to ease the Zodiac closer to shore. His only passengers were Guillermo Bonafonte and Rafael Gonzaléz. They were sitting across from one another and finishing their third bottle of water. Both men were well hydrated, although the Somali heat could bring on dehydration with very little warning—even to those most accustomed to and experienced with desert operations. The men knew all too well that when you were thirsty, it was too late.

Both men wore modified 4-piece desert ghillie suits that weighed slightly less than the standard four pounds. Their XM-3 sniper rifles were resting across their knees. They had replaced their day optic sight with the universal night sight. They weren't planning on being in Somalia at sun up.

Both men carried enough ammunition to fight a small war, although they would prefer that the mission went as planned. The camouflage on their face was subtle. Even their eyes were not discernable in the beige strands that fell haphazardly around their faces. Neither man had bathed in several days. By western standards, they were ripe—really ripe. Even Raul took notice of their hygiene...or the planned lack thereof. They would easily blend in with the local environment.

As the Zodiac skimmed across the water, both men checked their gear one more time. Raul had loaded the Zodiac with additional tools of the trade. Higgins did have an impressive assortment of goodies. Where he got most of them would remain his secret. Guillermo and Rafael had packed a few of the items just in case, including one short-range weapon. Carrying a short-range weapon was standard operating procedure. Hopefully, they wouldn't need to use the close-up weapon.

Guillermo made one last communications check with the entire team. The communications check was brief, as everyone checked in and synchronized their watches. Guillermo and Rafael had nearly three hours to make it to the location determined to provide the best vantage point. They would make it there in much less time.

If their intelligence information was correct, they wouldn't have to dig in. There were enough rocks and crevasses where they would easily become an unrecognizable part of the topography. Fortunately, the area around the ridge was replete with good hiding places. Since they were not going up against a well-trained enemy, they would pick the best location to cover the extraction. Even in the open, they wouldn't be seen.

As Guillermo looked up into the night sky, his thoughts wandered to Patricia Delgado. She had been temporarily reassigned to the States and had planned to meet him in Miami. He had been looking forward to a real date. He couldn't remember the last time he was out with a woman who really wanted to be with him—one who didn't have her hand out when the "party" was over.

However, the events in Benghazi would keep them apart. There was always something looming over the horizon. Their chosen occupations were not favorable to pursuing a serious relationship. Guillermo was tired of one-night stands. He was ready to settle down. Their phone conversations had been long and pleasant. She seemed to share his enthusiasm. He leaned back and wondered if she was the one...and more importantly, would he ever see her again.

Raul made a gentle turn to starboard and slowly cruised into the small harbor. He added a little power and maneuvered the boat ashore. He landed in nearly the same spot where they had dropped off Cody and Shaun the night before. It seemed like just moments ago.

Without saying a word, Guillermo and Rafael jumped off the bow onto dry ground. The beach was firm and covered in small shells. Guillermo easily pushed the Zodiac away from the shoreline as Rafael moved quickly into the shadows. Guillermo gave a thumbs-up to Raul. Raul slowly added power and headed for open water. As planned, he would stay close to the shore just in case.

Guillermo joined Rafael in the shadows, tapped him on the shoulder, and both men moved quickly in the direction of the ridge.

They didn't make a sound. Raul looked back at the beach. The men had vanished into the night. He smiled as he added power.

The moon was a little lower in the sky but seemed brighter than it was the previous night. As they knelt next to the ridge, Guillermo checked his GPS. They were less than two miles from their perch. Guillermo took the lead and set a comfortable pace. There was certainly no rush, no reason to work up a sweat. They would easily make it to their set-up point well before the *Seychelles Princess* arrived in the op-area. It would give them time to observe the harbor and the immediate area around the Liberty ship.

Raul Sanchez had moved the Zodiac roughly one hundred meters offshore. He paralleled the beach and maintained contact with Roy Higgins. Roy would provide satellite coverage and was prepared to dispatch one of the two on station helicopters if necessary. The real mission had started. However, Raul and Roy's conversation focused on the *Seychelles Princess*. There would be no reference to Guillermo, Rafael, Cody or Shaun.

When Saudi tankers were in the area, communications among Roy Higgins' assets were common, frequent and expected. Roy was certain that the pirates monitored their conversations. In fact, he wanted them to hear every word…so they would know that the big dog was on station. Besides, the pirates wouldn't be able to hear the secure satellite communications between Rick Morgan's team.

By 0100 on day eleven, Somalia time, the *Seychelles Princess* was six nautical miles southeast of the area where the active escort would begin. Roy changed the scale on the satellite imagery and pointed out the salient contacts that they would be following. Carlos used a long wooden pointer shaped like a giant T to move the little wooden models in accordance with Roy's coordinates. Roy had used the wargaming board quite effectively for the past two years. He found the board leaning against the wall in an old storage area. When he realized what it was, he had it set up in his CIC.

Surprisingly, the depiction of the Horn of Africa and the adjacent waters leading to the Suez Canal were constructed to scale. Roy added latitude and longitude lines, including minute marks that would allow a precise positioning of assets. The board proved to be quite valuable during the escort operations. Being old school and all too familiar with power outages, Roy would never take a chance of losing the tactical picture. He would never rely solely on electronic equipment, especially at Camp Lemonnier.

The Peterson Group Office
1700 Hours

Rick, Carl and Ann watched as Roland panned the satellite imagery of the op-area. The presentation on the large screen was clear and impressive to say the least. Roland had already identified and placed markers on the ships in the area, including Roy's patrol boat, the *Seychelles Princess* and the pirates' mother ship. The marker indicated that the mother ship was on a southwesterly course and moving at eighteen knots.

"Roland, how far out was the mother ship the other day?" asked Rick as he looked at his notes and then back at the large screen.

"She was about two hundred miles offshore," answered Roland.

"And now it's within eighty miles and moving at quite a clip," observed Rick. "I wonder if that's normal procedure on their part?" he asked as he looked over at Carl.

Carl turned up the volume on the monitor that was positioned in the center of the conference table. As planned, it provided a live feed to Roy's CIC. Roy's attention was on his big screen. Carlos could be seen leaning over the wargaming table. He appeared to be moving one of the models. *Carlos must love this*, Ann thought to herself. It brought a smile to her face.

"Roy," summoned Carl.

Roy turned and faced the video conferencing monitor and switched the audio to speaker.

"Morning Carl," he answered as he looked directly into the camera. It was obvious that he hadn't shaved in a couple of days. There were small bags under his eyes that were probably more pronounced as a result of the lighting. He did look a bit tired.

"We noticed that the pirates' mother ship has moved considerably closer to shore and is on a southwesterly course. Appears to be maintaining eighteen knots. Is that normal?" asked Carl.

Roy was fully aware of the mother ship's position but glanced up at the large screen. He then leaned a bit forward and looked back into the camera.

"Sometimes they come in close when we are in the area escorting the Saudi tankers. I wouldn't read anything into it at this point. They've challenged us in the past...didn't make out very well as you know. They like to play games, probably just looking for a few crumbs," responded Roy.

"A few crumbs?" questioned Ann.

"They're trying to figure out which ships are vulnerable," answered Roy.

"I thought that most of the ships transiting the Seychelles had onboard security," said Carl.

"Most do, but not all. Depends on several factors. Some of the ships have more protection than others. Most of the oil tankers have hired guns. All of the supertankers have onboard security. You'll notice as the ships continue to enter the Seychelles, they queue up and form a loose convoy."

"Safety in numbers," said Ann.

"They seem to think so," replied Roy.

"False security," responded Rick. "No ship is going to allow their security force to leave their post and go assist another ship under attack. It's not like an aircraft in formation that can just peel off," added Rick.

"You're right about that Rick," Roy responded. "And quite frankly, the pirates have figured that out. Their challenge nowadays is to determine which ships do not have adequate protection," added Roy. "It's a bit of a game with them."

"With their paid sources, I'm surprised they don't have that information," said Rick.

"I believe they do know, but they want to give the impression that they're just looking for a target of opportunity," responded Roy. "Then they'll zero in on their prey," he added.

"Does the mother ship come in every time your assets are in the area?" asked Rick.

"No, just once in a while," responded Roy.

As they continued to talk, Roland zoomed in on the ridge where he assumed Guillermo and Rafael would be. He panned the ridge and switched to night vision. Guillermo and Rafael could be seen moving at a steady pace. They were more than halfway to their destination. Roland panned forward and zoomed in on the Liberty ship. He could easily make out two people near the brow. He could just see one person near the gun mount. Ann and Carl were watching the screen intently as Rick continued to talk with Roy.

"Can you pick up Courtney Evans and her friends?" asked Ann.

"In the Somali heat, the ship and Ms. Evans are just about the same temperature. If we had the Gulfstream over there, we might be able to pick up their movement," answered Roland. "Fortunately, we are able to pick up the people walking around on deck," he added.

Rick came over and sat next to Ann. He looked up at the clock and then over to the large screen. Roland had zoomed out and was panning the small fishing village. Everything seemed to be quiet.

"Roland, zoom in on those small boats that have been pulled up on shore," Rick directed as he looked at his notebook.

"I noted that there were three speedboats there yesterday when we dropped off Cody and Shaun. Where are they now?" he asked.

Roland zoomed out and panned the coastline. They were nowhere in sight.

"Could they have gone up the river into the city?" asked Carl.

Just as Roland was about to focus in on the river, Rick noticed something north of the main harbor.

"Hold it right there," said Rick as he leaned on the conference table. "Right there. Check out that small harbor to the north."

Roland zoomed in on the small harbor. The three speedboats were pulled halfway up on shore.

"Yeah, right there," said Rick. "Why would they be congregated there?" he said under his breath but loud enough for all to hear.

"I count eighteen," said Ann.

"Something is going on," said Rick.

"Where are Guillermo and Rafael?" asked Carl.

Roland zoomed out and easily picked up Guillermo and Rafael. They had stopped. Roland checked their position and announced that Guillermo and Rafael were at the predetermined location. He checked the distance to the Liberty ship. They were exactly eight hundred ten meters from the brow.

"Okay, they're well within range," said Rick.

Carl picked up the satellite phone and called Roy.

"Guillermo and Rafael are in position," he said when Roy answered the call.

"Good, the *Seychelles Princess* just entered the op-area," added Roy.

"Roy, we have three speedboats with eighteen people in a small harbor north of the main entrance to Eyl. What do you make of that?" asked Carl.

Roy didn't say anything for several seconds as he zoomed in on the small harbor. He zoomed in closer.

"They usually join up with the mother ship. They could be waiting till she's closer," responded Roy.

"Have you seen them do this before?" asked Carl.

"No, I haven't," responded Roy.

"Rick feels that something's up," said Carl.

"Could be. Let's bring everyone online," said Roy as he and Carlos donned their tactical headsets.

The Peterson Group office was already monitoring the secure network. Roland checked the circuit's integrity and gave a thumbs-up to Rick.

Rick thought back to his Navy days on the USS Nimitz. He never could understand why they would use the codes when they were employing a secure network. It made no sense when you had to write down the code, get out the codebook, decipher it…and fly an aircraft at the same time.

Roy was about to say, "check in" when he lost his satellite image. He called for everyone to check in. There was no response.

CHAPTER TWENTY-FOUR

Eyl, Somalia
Day 11
0230 Hours

Roy turned off the satellite system, waited thirty seconds, and then turned it back on. As the system was rebooting, he tried to contact Guillermo over the secure network. He tried several times but to no avail. All he could hear was static accompanied by an annoying clicking sound. As soon as the large display came online, the video presentation was immediately covered in wavy lines. Nothing on the screen was discernable. Roy looked over at the large screen monitor in the center of the conference table. He had also lost the video feed with The Peterson Group office. Everything that he tried, failed. The timing couldn't have been worse.

"You gotta be kidding me!" he yelled as he pounded his fist on the conference table, knocking his coffee cup to the floor.

"Carlos, would you go outside the building and see if you can make contact with Rick?" he asked as he leaned forward and turned off the video conferencing hard drive.

Carlos went outside and called Rick on his satellite phone. Rick answered almost immediately. He had his satellite phone in hand and was just about to give Carlos a call.

"What the hell is going on?" Rick asked, knowing that there was a problem at Roy's end.

"Seems we've lost all our communications, including the satellite feed," answered Carlos.

"Even the secure communications network?" asked Rick.

"We've lost everything," responded Carlos.

Rick didn't say anything for several seconds. He looked at his watch and was about to say something when Roland signaled him.

"Hold on a second Carlos, Roland is trying to get my attention."

Rick walked over and sat down next to Roland.

"Carlos, we're trying to access the CIC computer system from this end," said Rick.

Roland nodded in agreement as he continued to type code.

Inside the Combat Information Center, Roy was on his third reboot—still no connection with the satellite or the secure communications circuit with the guys in the field. The large screen was still covered in snow and a multitude of wavy lines. Roy shook his head in frustration. He had seen this before, but this was the first time he had a problem at Camp Lemonnier. He tried to contact the patrol boat. Still no success.

"They're being jammed," announced Roland.

"Are you sure?" asked Carl as he walked over and stood next to Roland.

"I'm quite sure," responded Roland confidently.

"Can you tell where it's coming from?" asked Rick as he leaned forward.

"Not precisely, but I'm confident that the signal is coming from Roy's building," answered Roland. "And by the strength of the signal, I would bet that it's coming from a space very close to the CIC," he added.

"How close?" questioned Rick.

"If I had to guess...I would say that it's coming from the space directly next to the CIC," responded Roland as he looked over at Rick and then up at Carl.

"How would someone know exactly when to start the jamming?" asked Ann.

That's a good question, Rick thought to himself.

"I'll bet Roy's space is bugged," declared Carl.

"Carlos," said Rick. "You guys are being jammed by someone in your building, quite possibly from a space next to the CIC."

"Can you override them from your end?" asked Carlos.

Rick asked Roland. The short answer was no.

"You're going to have to shut them down from your end," said Rick. "And Carlos...it's quite possible the CIC is bugged. Take the necessary precautions," warned Rick. "We'll take over the mission from this end."

"Thanks boss. We'll get back to you as soon as possible," said Carlos as he hustled back into the Combat Information Center.

Roy was still doing his best to get back online. He wasn't having any luck. His patience was wearing thin, and it showed.

"Did you talk with Rick?" he asked.

"No, I couldn't get through," responded Carlos, as he put his right forefinger in front of his lips. He leaned over the conference table and wrote on one of the pads: *We're being jammed and they believe there is a good chance the CIC is bugged.*

Roy silently acknowledged the note as he pursed his lips and made a tight fist with his right hand.

"Let's see what we can do here," responded Roy, his jaw relaxing as he ceremoniously looked around the room. He thought he knew the people at Camp Lemonnier. If his space was in fact bugged, he would find out who was responsible. They would pay dearly.

He picked up the pencil and wrote on the pad: *Any idea who is jamming us?*

Carlos wrote back: *Roland believes it's coming from a space very close to ours.*

Roy thought for several seconds and then wrote on the pad: *At this time of night, the only people onboard are the people working in support of the Combined Joint Task Force. They're in the space right next to ours.*

How many? scribbled Carlos.

Usually no more than three, wrote Roy.

Roy and Carlos didn't need to discuss what they were going to do next. They knew exactly what they were going to do. Roy stood up and walked over to his desk as Carlos checked his weapon. Roy retrieved a nine-millimeter Beretta from the center drawer, checked the magazine, and chambered a round. He slowly let the hammer down.

Neither man said anything as they went out into the hallway. Roy motioned to his right. There was a light on over a door about twenty paces east of the CIC. The light indicated that the space was occupied. It was the only space with an illuminated light over the door. There were two other spaces. Carlos checked the doors. They were both locked. He looked down at the floor. There was no light emanating from under either door.

Roy motioned to Carlos to try the door for the space next to the CIC. Carlos slowly turned the knob. It was unlocked. He looked back at Roy and nodded. Both men went inside and quickly scanned the room. They counted three men and one woman in the space. All four were at workstations. Two of the men and the woman looked up and maintained eye contact. They were surprised by the sudden unannounced entry by Roy and Carlos. They knew Roy Higgins but had no idea who Carlos was. Seeing both men with weapons drawn was unnerving.

The fourth person, a man who appeared to be in his mid-fifties, looked up and then immediately looked back at his computer screen. He didn't seem to be at all surprised. Carlos and Roy knew they had their man.

Rafael scanned the area with his spotter scope. Two pirates were standing by the brow smoking cigarettes. They appeared to be engaged in an animated conversation. They both had AK-47s over their shoulder. Rafael watched them for a couple of minutes and then turned his attention to the small fishing village.

He was about to look back at the brow when suddenly he noticed several men jumping into a pickup truck that was parked in front of a small A-frame house. The house was well lit. One of the men had an RPG. *This is not good,* he thought to himself as he nudged Guillermo and pointed in the direction of the small village.

"Something's up," he said as he handed the spotter scope to Guillermo.

Guillermo looked through the scope for several seconds and then back to the brow. One of the pirates appeared to be talking on a cell phone.

"You're right. This isn't good at all," he responded as he moved the mic closer to his mouth.

"Cody, you got several bogies inbound from the fishing village."

"How many?" questioned Cody.

"Looks like five, including the driver. One has an RPG," said Guillermo. "You have the guys by the brow?"

"I got them in my sights," responded Cody.

Carl, Rick and Ann were listening to the conversation. Rick looked over at Carl.

"We've been compromised," he said in a loud clear voice.

Just then, Roland interrupted. "I have three trucks inbound from the city. Quite a few guys on board. Looks like they're heavily armed."

"We need to shut it down, and shut it down now," said Rick, without a hint of discussion.

"I agree," concurred Carl.

"Stand down. Do not engage, repeat, DO NOT ENGAGE," said Rick over the secure network. "Acknowledge."

"Standing down," said Cody disappointedly.

"Roger, standing down," said Guillermo.

Cody knew that the order to stand down meant for them to immediately abandon the mission, get off the ship, and head for the extraction point. Guillermo and Rafael would hold their position and provide coverage until Cody and Shaun were well clear of immediate danger. Then they would follow close behind. Within twenty seconds, Cody and Shaun were heading into the shadows, past the old tug and toward the ridge.

At the same time, back at Camp Lemonnier, Roy and Carlos wasted no time as they headed for the one individual who didn't maintain eye contact. He was typing furiously on his keyboard and then yanked the plug from the wall. One of the men got up and said something to Roy.

"Sit your ass down and shut up," ordered Roy, aiming the Beretta at the man's head.

One of the other men picked up a phone and began to dial. Carlos ripped the phone out of the wall and threw it across the room. The woman didn't move. She was squirming in her seat. She had peed her pants. The "jammer" had already bolted for the back door. There was a large sign on the door that warned, *To be opened in an Emergency Only.*

"You have no jurisdiction!" yelled the woman, her voice cracking.

Roy and Carlos ignored her as they ran to the exit. The door was still ajar but closing rapidly. A horn was blasting, and the caged red light over the door was flashing. Carlos was the first one through the door. He had no trouble catching the man, grabbing him by the right shoulder, and spinning him around. The guy took a wild swing with his left arm. Carlos fended off the blow and hit the man with the butt of his weapon, breaking the man's nose. He dropped to his knees and put both hands up to his face. Blood was gushing through his hands. Carlos kicked him in the chest, knocking him to the ground. He pressed the muzzle of his gun to the guy's forehead.

"You move, and I'll blow your fucking brains out," said Carlos in a calm clear voice. Carlos was in his element.

Roy bent down and yanked the guy's ID from his shirt, nearly ripping the pocket completely off.

"André LaPointe," said Roy as he looked closely at the ID card and then at the bleeding man. "I know you, don't I," he said. It wasn't meant to be a question.

"Je ne parle pas anglais," he said in a heavy French accent.

"Don't pull that 'no speak the English' bullshit with me. I know you speak English. Now tell me what I want to know, or my friend here is going to start taking you apart…piece by piece."

"I don't know what you're talking about," responded LaPointe in English.

Roy looked at Carlos. Carlos pulled back the hammer on his weapon.

"Last chance," said Roy.

"Va te faire foutre connard," answered LaPointe as he followed the comment with a hand gesture that needed no translation.

Without hesitation, Roy shot LaPointe in the right knee. He then aimed his weapon at LaPointe's left knee.

"Wait, WAIT!" yelled LaPointe as he grabbed his knee, gasping in pain. He took a few deep breaths and moaned as he rocked back and forth.

"It was Booshay. Booshay gives the orders. I was just following orders. Please, don't shoot," he said as he rolled over on his left side.

Roy lowered his weapon and was about to say something when several well-armed soldiers came rushing through he door.

"Drop your weapons!" they demanded.

Roy and Carlos slowly laid their weapons on the ground and put up their hands. Two of the soldiers went over to attend to LaPointe. An Army major by the name of Carmondy walked over to Roy Higgins. He had known Higgins for well over a year.

"Mr. Higgins, what the hell is going on here?" he asked in a low voice.

"I've got a covert operation going on, and this guy started jamming my equipment," answered Roy directly.

"An operation...other than the tankers?" questioned Major Carmondy.

"I can't go into any detail at this time. I really need to get back inside," said Roy. "My people are in real danger," he emphasized.

The major looked back at André LaPointe. The soldiers had placed a tourniquet on his right thigh.

"Corporal Regano, get an ambulance over here—now," barked the major as he turned to Roy Higgins.

"Okay, but we need to talk. The colonel is going to blow a freaking gasket. He'll demand answers."

"I'll be available at the colonel's earliest convenience," Roy replied as he motioned toward their weapons.

"Yeah, no problem. Just don't shoot anyone else on my watch," smirked the major.

"I'll try not to," said Roy as he and Carlos went back into the building.

The equipment in the CIC appeared to be working normally. The first thing Roy did was contact Rick. Rick, Carl and Ann were already at the conference table.

"I'm back online. So where are we?" asked Roy.

"We stood down. We couldn't take any chances. The guys are on their way to the extraction point. Doesn't appear to be anyone in hot pursuit," said Rick. "Obviously you took care of business at that end," he added.

Roy didn't question the decision.

"Roland was correct. We were being jammed."

"Did you find out who was jamming you?" asked Carl.

"We did. His name is André LaPointe," answered Roy. "Says he got orders from a guy by the name of Booshay."

"Booshay?" asked Carl.

"Yeah, he said Booshay," repeated Roy.

"Roland, cross-check those names," said Carl as he rubbed his jaw.

Roland checked all his available databases for a connection between Booshay and LaPointe.

"No match," he said.

"Hold on a second," said Rick. "Booshay is the French pronunciation for Boucher."

Roland made several keystrokes and announced that he still didn't find a match.

"So our friend, Patrice Boucher, pronounced Booshay, is pulling the strings," said Carl.

"Looks that way," answered Rick.

"For some reason I keep thinking I know this guy," said Carl as he went over to his desk, sat down, and opened one of the file drawers. "Even more now that I've heard the correct pronunciation."

Carl thumbed through one of the folders and found what he was looking for. He then retrieved a flash drive from the center drawer and handed it to Roland.

"Bring this up on the screen."

The flash drive contained several folders. One was named Steinbrenner.

"Open Steinbrenner," directed Carl.

The folder contained twenty-three pictures. Roland put the pictures up on the screen one at a time.

"Hold that one," said Carl. "Can you blow that up," he said as he moved closer to the conference table.

"Holy shit! That's him…that's Patrice Boucher standing there almost in front of me," exclaimed Carl. "That son of bitch actually joined in on the conversation with me and Blackwell," said Carl as his memory of the conference became clear.

"So you actually had a conversation with him?" asked Rick.

"Yeah, I did. We talked a little about shipping and piracy. As we talked, I remember thinking to myself that there was really something familiar about him. I'm still not sure if I've met him before," said Carl as he continued to study the picture.

Rick sat down at the conference table. He appeared to be in deep thought. He then sat back in the chair and looked over Carl.

"If you remember, we thought this guy's biography was a bit prosaic," said Rick.

Rick was about to continue when Roland interrupted.

"There is one thing I've uncovered in my search through the Interpol database that's bothering me. It could be a coincidence, but it just seems a bit odd. While the info on Boucher appears to be authentic, I found that the computer code for all of Boucher's documentation was actually created at the same time."

"Maybe it was entered at the same time," offered Carl.

"That was my first thought, but upon further examination, I discovered that the computer code for each document has consecutive time stamps," responded Roland.

"Meaning?" asked Carl.

"Meaning that someone created them, in order, and at the same time," responded Roland.

"Couldn't they have just been scanned into the computer in that order and at the same time?" asked Rick.

"These weren't scanned documents," said Roland.

"So you believe they were fabricated?" asked Carl.

"I'm pretty certain they were," responded Roland. "And, there is one other thing…the creation of those documents coincides with the deactivation of another individual—an individual who is the same age with similar physical characteristics as Boucher," explained Roland.

"A coincidence?" asked Rick.

"Possibly, but I believe very unlikely," responded Roland.

"And who is that individual?" asked Rick.

"Does the name Jean Gendreau ring any bells?" asked Roland.

"You bet your ass it does!" exclaimed Carl, as he looked closer at the picture. "I thought that son of a bitch had been killed in Ottawa in a car accident several years ago," he exclaimed.

"I take it you two have a history," said Ann.

"That we do," responded Carl. "That we do," he repeated under his breath.

Carl continued to study the photograph. "That's why he seemed so damn familiar. I can't believe I didn't recognize him. Looks like he's had some cosmetic enhancements," rationalized Carl, still in disbelief that he couldn't see past the minor changes.

"Maybe Courtney Evans was just a pawn," said Rick. He was a quick study.

"A pawn? How so?" asked Carl.

"You, Blackwell and Boucher, a.k.a. Jean Gendreau, just happen to show up at the same conference. You and Gendreau have a history... one that I assume was not very pleasant. Blackwell's granddaughter is looking for a good deal on a sailboat and planning a trip around the world. Boucher just happens to own a company that brokers sailboats—one, by the way, that was captured by Somali pirates. And now we know that the same sailboat just so happened to be purchased by Ms. Courtney Evans. And JT Blackwell hires you to rescue his granddaughter. Could all that be just a mere coincidence?" asked Rick.

No one said anything—they just looked at Rick. Suddenly, he had everyone's undivided attention.

"Carl, I believe *you* are the real target...and always have been," concluded Rick.

CHAPTER TWENTY-FIVE
Old Town
Day 10
2200 Hours

Rick's hypothesis initially caught everyone by surprise. The sheer possibility of it being true left them momentarily speechless. Carl was uncharacteristically silent as he went over and sat behind his desk. He pulled out the bottom right hand drawer, sat back in his chair, and rested his right foot on top of some old brown folders that had been in there for several years.

Rick had already made a few notes and had started drawing little rectangles in his notepad. For Rick, everything had fallen into place, it had become quite clear…everything made perfect sense. Not only did he know what was really going on, but he also knew who had orchestrated the capture of Courtney Evans. At least in the short term, they had an answer for JT Blackwell. Rick was already three steps ahead and planning the team's next move.

Carl smiled to himself as he looked over at Rick. He was well aware of Rick's ability to think outside the box—to see things as they really were. Connecting the dots was one thing, but very few people had the ability to identify the dots. Rick was good at both, and he was great at figuring out what needed to be done next.

Roland was fully engaged in searching the Interpol database and extracting tidbits of information on Jean Gendreau and Patrice Boucher. Although there was considerable data available for both names, none of the biographical information on Jean Gendreau was even remotely similar to the information fabricated for Patrice Boucher.

The person, or entity, that had put together Jean Gendreau's new identity was good, really good…too good to be an amateur. Although Patrice Boucher's life history was a pure canard, every document that Roland retrieved appeared to be genuine and was traceable to other genuine documents. There were no flags or distinguishing characteristics that jumped off the page—nothing to cause anyone to dig deeper or question the information. Everything about Patrice Boucher seemed to be real, from his birth certificate, school transcripts, and previous addresses to his current location and banking information.

For the unaware, Jean Gendreau and Patrice Boucher were two completely different individuals who were living separate lives. Patrice Boucher's life was transparent in all respects. He could easily be the guy living next door. The only common thread between the two names was the fact that they were both in the Interpol database.

As Carl sat there, his thoughts wandered back to Camp Lemonnier and his last encounter with Lieutenant Jean Gendreau. It was certainly far from pleasant and one that he didn't relish or want to remember for that matter. Langley did not want Carl to say anything. In fact, he was told to let it go, to forget about it, and move on. However, in all good conscience, Carl couldn't let it go. Besides, he wasn't from New Jersey—he wouldn't *forget about it*. The relationship with Jean Gendreau would be history.

Carl picked up his pen and began to slowly twirl it like a baton between his thumb and first two fingers of his right hand. His expression changed as he mulled Rick's hypothesis over in his mind. *Could Rick be right*, he thought to himself. The more he thought about it, the more Rick's deduction made sense. Rick was right. Carl was about to say something when Ann finally broke the silence.

"So who the *hell* is this guy, Jean Gendreau, anyway?" she blurted out, looking directly at Carl. Ann had little patience. She was ready for some answers.

Rick stopped drawing and put down his pencil. He had been waiting for Ann to break the ice. He sat back and looked over at Carl. Carl had a slight smile on his face but didn't immediately respond. Rick knew that Carl would fill in the blanks when he was ready, and it appeared that he was just about ready.

Carl put the pen down next to his notepad and looked out the window. He then leaned forward and rested his arms on the desk as he looked over at Ann, then at Rick, and finally over at Roland who had also stopped to listen. They all wanted to know what the history was between Carl Peterson and this mysterious Jean Gendreau, a.k.a. Patrice Boucher.

"Do you want the long or short story?" he asked as he leaned back, resting both elbows on the arms of his chair.

Carl didn't seem to look at anyone in particular. He appeared to be relaxed. He made a little church steeple by folding his fingers together and extending his forefingers. He rested his chin on top of the steeple, lowered his chin slightly, and pursed his lips.

"We have time," responded Rick, looking at his watch.

Ann nodded in approval. She had the look of a little kid waiting to hear, "Once upon a time."

Rick smiled and thought about his only daughter, Brooke. Ann and Brooke were so much alike. Both wanted to hear the story—*right from the beginning.*

"And don't leave anything out," instructed Ann.

She is indeed just like Brooke, Rick mused to himself.

Carl got up and went over to pour a cup of coffee from one of the glass coffee pots that had been brewing for several hours. Although the coffee was hot, it had the unfortunate texture of molasses. His first swallow brought a profound scowl to his face. He looked into the cup but held on to it and walked back to his desk.

"I met Jean Gendreau quite a few years ago…nineteen eighty-nine to be exact. Actually, I liked the guy right from the start. He was from Montreal, Canada, and since both of us were avid hockey fans, we had something in common. His father was French and his mother was a half-breed…French Canadian and Huron if memory serves me," he added after a slight pause. "Actually, I believe that his mother was more Huron than French Canadian. However, and for reasons only known to Gendreau, he never wanted to be considered a Canadian citizen. He had no problem making it quite clear that he was French. In fact, he was born in Leone, France. Following his birth, his mother took him to Canada…and he would always emphasize the word *took* as if he were literally kidnapped."

"So the parents were divorced?" asked Ann.

"That I don't know. I would assume they were, or at the very least, separated," responded Carl, not expecting the question.

Carl started to take a drink of coffee, but didn't. He had remembered the first swallow. As he put the cup back down on the desk, Ann looked over at the coffee pot. She considered getting up and making a fresh pot but didn't want to be distracted. She didn't want to miss anything. Carl continued with his story.

"Somewhere during his childhood years, Gendreau became totally fascinated, even obsessed, with the adventures of the French Foreign Legion. I think he knew every French Foreign Legion movie ever made. When he was old enough, he left Canada for France and became a legionnaire. When I met him, he was already a lieutenant who had distinguished himself as an extremely competent strategist and battlefield tactician."

By now, Carl had everyone's undivided attention. He accidentally took another swallow of coffee and made a face that convinced Ann that it was time for a fresh pot. She went over to the coffee maker as Carl continued.

"When I met Gendreau, the U.S. had interests in the Sudan from oil, to human rights, to politics. In nineteen seventy-nine, Hassan al-Turabi became the Minister of Justice. At that time, a hardline Islamic fundamentalist, by the name of Gaafar Nimeiry, was the man in power. His efforts to unite Sudan were futile. Getting the various tribes to agree on any one course of action, or follow any one individual, was very difficult under the best of circumstances. Islam was certainly a common factor. Although Nimeiry had attempted to institute sharia law throughout the country, it was al-Turabi who was responsible for actually implementing it in the northern part of Sudan. As you know, atrocities like amputations and hangings are a common occurrence with sharia law. The Sudan was no different. As a result, the people were desperate for a more democratic and liberal government. Although he wasn't very popular with the people, al-Turabi was saying all the right things. He appeared to be embracing democracy, allowing women to become an active part of public life, and implementing sharia law on a more gradual and benign basis. As a result, in nineteen eighty-nine, a coup d'état ousted Nimeiry and brought al-Turabi and the National Islamic Front to power."

"However, as we all know, politicians say one thing and do another…our present Administration not excluded," interjected Rick.

"You got that right. And it was no different in the Sudan under al-Turabi," said Carl as he continued.

"Al-Turabi's regime was marked by harsh human rights violations, severe repression, purges, imprisonment, executions, banning of political parties…the list goes on. There wasn't a shred of any of the good things that he had promised. It was then that the CIA, along with a detachment led by Lieutenant Jean Gendreau, was dispatched to convince al-Turabi to reconsider his political promises."

As Carl was about to continue, Ann announced that the coffee was fresh. She brought a fresh cup to Carl and Rick. Roland was satisfied with a bottle of water. Carl took a healthy swallow, smiled, saluted Ann with his cup, and continued.

"My role was to meet with the leaders of the National Islamic Front and convince them that it would be in their best interest to allow a more relaxed democratic environment throughout the Sudan and encourage them to take advantage of their immense natural resources. I was to explain how the U.S. was willing to provide technological support to bring their vast oil supplies to market—and bring it in at a competitive price. Unfortunately, Gendreau had other ideas."

No one said anything as Carl got up and went over and stood by the window. He looked out as if seeing something again…something that he wanted to forget. He slowly lifted the cup but didn't take a drink. He turned and continued his recital of the events as he sat back behind the desk.

"Gendreau had put together a plan to visit one of the tribal leaders in a small town near Darfur. Supposedly, the tribal leader was an elder of influence. I was basically there to be a negotiator. I was the only one from the CIA along with Lieutenant Gendreau and twelve legionnaires. In retrospect, I should have realized from their look that this was not a refined bunch. They were a bunch of goons with other plans. We entered the small village late in the morning. Gendreau had brought food, some trinkets, and a small amount of medical supplies to gain their confidence. It was a small village with less than forty inhabitants. Basically, it was typical of the small villages scattered near the larger cities. Most of the inhabitants were probably from the same family. Everything seemed to be going well when suddenly, Gendreau's men opened fire. They killed everyone—little kids, old women, men, even their animals. The only one they didn't kill was the old tribal leader. They gave him a written message for al-Turabi. The message was simple. Change your ways, or the next time it will be you. Then they proceeded to hack the bodies into pieces. Gendreau seemed to enjoy the carnage. It was a side of him that I hadn't expected. Gendreau was an animal. He was brutal. I would have tried to stop him, but I was sure they would have killed me and used my death as an excuse."

No one said anything as Carl got up and poured a fresh cup of coffee. He looked out of the window and didn't say anything for several minutes. The silence in the room was deafening. Rick got up and poured himself a cup and motioned to Ann. She declined. As Carl continued to look out the window, he went on.

"When we returned to Camp Lemonnier, Gendreau and I had words. I told him that what he had done made no sense to me. He said that these people were animals. The only thing they understood was brute force, and that killing a few would save many. I asked him if he had received those orders from higher command. He said that he was given carte blanche to do what was necessary to gain al-Turabi's attention. I said that they were insane, that he was insane. He took a swing at me. I ducked, broke his nose, and knocked out several of his teeth. Against Langley's orders, I reported Gendreau to his superiors, to Geneva, and anyone else who would listen. I resigned before I was reprimanded. I knew then that my time at the CIA was over."

CHAPTER TWENTY-SIX
The Ritz Carlton
Day 11
0700 Hours

Carl met Rick at the Ritz Carlton in Pentagon City promptly at 0700 hours. Rick was looking over the *Washington Times* when Carl walked in. There were several other guests having breakfast. Briefcases were neatly tucked in next to the chairs. A couple of men in three-piece suits were so engrossed with their phones; they didn't notice their eggs Benedict getting cold. Rick looked up as Carl approached. Both men were tired from the previous night...and it showed.

"So what's new this morning?" asked Carl as he sat down across from Rick. He tried to get a glimpse of the headlines as Rick folded the newspaper.

"Same old thing. Scandals everywhere according to the Administration."

"Hell, the Administration *is* the scandal," declared Carl in a loud enough voice that it attracted some attention.

"Looks like Benghazi is finally boiling to the surface," announced Rick as he offered the paper to Carl.

"And who would you want to answer the phone at three in the morning?" questioned Carl sarcastically as he declined the paper with a wave of his right hand.

"Hillary is apt to be the one answering it in twenty sixteen," replied Rick as he put the paper on the chair next to him.

"Well she certainly didn't answer the phone when she was the Secretary of State, now did she? Do you really think she has a good chance at the Presidency?" asked Carl.

"Unfortunately, I think she has a very good chance. And if the Republicans don't learn how to address the issues, and learn to fight the battles they can win, they'll be history," said Rick quite seriously.

"Don't you think there are still more conservatives—people in this country who really know what's going on?" asked Carl.

"I used to think that conservatism would win out. But we have created a society that seems to value handouts over freedom," said Rick. "Look at the number of people on food stamps. Do you think for one minute the Democrats really give a crap about the poor? They just want them to be dependent. They have them in their back pocket. Couple that with a liberal press and a Republican party who can't articulate their platform...how can the Democrats lose?" he continued solemnly.

Neither man said anything for several seconds.

"I'm just afraid the U.S. is not a serious country anymore," said Rick, breaking the silence.

Carl knew that Rick was right, but he was betting on the resiliency of the American voting public—a resiliency that Rick no longer shared.

"If Benghazi had happened under Bush's watch, the press would have been calling for his head," said Rick as the server approached.

"Coffee," said Carl before the server had a chance to ask.

She was young, short and appeared to be from one of the Central American countries. She smiled and made a quick about-face as if given orders by her commanding officer. Carl watched her as she headed for the kitchen. He noted her ample hips but didn't comment.

"I need to give Blackwell a call and let him know what's going on," Carl said, getting right down to business. He seemed a bit antsy.

"Why don't you hold off on that call. I'm sure we'll hear from Blackwell soon enough," suggested Rick.

"I'll bet that Ibrahim has called him already," said Carl.

"Probably. And you can bet he's already demanded a higher ransom," offered Rick as he finished his first cup of coffee.

Carl was about to say something when the server approached. She placed a cup and saucer in front of Carl and filled his cup with piping hot coffee. She offered to refill Rick's cup. He accepted as he leaned back in his chair, staying out of her way.

"Have you gentlemen decided on breakfast?" she asked. Her accent was subtle.

"I'll have the eggs Benedict," said Rick without looking at the menu. Eggs Benedict was his favorite, and he always ordered it for breakfast at the Ritz. They were by far, the best in town.

"That sounds good. Make it two...Adriana," said Carl with a smile. Where he was looking, he couldn't help but notice her nametag.

She returned the smile and headed for the kitchen.

"So, where do you think our little server, Adriana, is from?" asked Carl.

"Little?" questioned Rick as he turned to check out Adriana. He watched her until she went into the kitchen.

"I was being nice," responded Carl. "Besides, size is relative."

"You just keep telling yourself that, my friend," said Rick. "I suspect that she's Nicaraguan," he added.

Carl nodded in agreement. That would have been his guess. Both he and Rick had been throughout Central America. There were certainly subtle differences among the inhabitants, but after a while everyone looks alike, especially at night...and especially after a few beers.

"So you don't think we should prepare Blackwell, let him know what happened?" asked Carl.

"Blackwell can take care of himself," Rick responded.

"You do know that Ibrahim has probably given him an earful," Carl added as he took a sip from the blue porcelain cup with the Ritz Carlton logo.

"It'll be better if Blackwell sounds totally surprised. He'll be more convincing if he really doesn't know anything at all about our mission," responded Rick.

"Ignorance is bliss," said Carl after several seconds. "So I take it we're going to deny everything," it was purely a rhetorical question.

"I'm sure that the team didn't leave any evidence. They're professionals, they know the routine, and they know how to cover their tracks."

"What about the communications?" asked Carl, playing devil's advocate.

"The plain communications were minimal. None of our secure transmissions could have been intercepted. Higgins' people were doing what they always do when escorting a Saudi ship. We'll deny that we were ever on shore," said Rick calmly.

"And what about this guy...LaPointe? He obviously knew what was going on when he jammed our equipment. He must have been in contact with someone in Eyl," continued Carl.

"He probably was, but don't forget that he's Boucher's man," responded Rick. "He reported what he *thought* was going on."

Carl didn't say anything as he cradled the coffee cup in both hands. It was still quite warm. He held the cup in front of his face and focused on the logo for several seconds. He took another swallow and then set the cup down. He was about to say something when Rick continued.

"If we're correct, and I believe that we are, Boucher would certainly have maintained real-time communications with LaPointe... and maybe Ibrahim," said Rick.

"And you believe Boucher was calling the shots?" asked Carl.

"If he's the tactician you believe him to be, he would assume that we would use the escort operation as cover for the extraction," responded Rick.

"And based upon LaPointe's input, Boucher decided to alert the pirates at Eyl," offered Carl.

"I believe so," said Rick.

Carl didn't say anything for several seconds as he thought about Rick's analysis of the previous night's events. It was certainly plausible. Besides, at this stage in the game, it was a moot point.

"I'll bet you thought about this all night," said Carl as Adriana approached with a tray over her right shoulder. She was carrying a stand in her left hand. Her right hip was providing needed ballast. With one motion, she opened the stand and placed the tray squarely on it. Rick and Carl didn't say anything as she moved around the table carefully placing the plates in the center of each placemat.

"Be careful, the plates are very hot," she warned. "May I get you anything else?"

"This will do just fine," responded Rick, gesturing to Carl with his left hand.

"We're fine," Carl concurred. "Please, just keep the coffee coming."

Adriana looked at the coffee cups, smiled, and left. They started to enjoy breakfast while it was hot. Out of habit, Carl touched the edge of the plate. Adriana was right. It was very hot.

"When you were at the Steinbrenner conference, how long did you, Boucher and Blackwell carry on a conversation?" asked Rick.

"Five to ten minutes at most. When they started to talk about sailboats, I excused myself. There were a couple of other people in the room that I wanted to meet," responded Carl.

"So Blackwell and Boucher spent some time together," observed Rick.

"They did, and that son of a bitch stood right next to me and I didn't even recognize him. I must be getting old," Carl said, shaking his head in self-disgust.

Rick thought for a few minutes as they continued with breakfast. Several other guests were being shown to their table. The room was nearly full. The noise level had risen slightly.

"He was testing you. Wanted to see how close he could get...see if you recognized him," said Rick.

"Well I didn't," Carl responded. He made a slight face. It still bothered him that he hadn't recognized Jean Gendreau.

"When Blackwell calls, ask him if he remembers Boucher from the conference. Find out if he can recall what they may have discussed," said Rick.

"And if he does?"

"If he does, tell him that we've obtained strong evidence that Patrice Boucher was the one who orchestrated the piracy and that we're fully prepared to go after him," responded Rick.

"And that's when Blackwell will tell me that he just heard from Ibrahim. And that Ibrahim told him that we were involved in a failed rescue operation," replied Carl.

"Then you deny that we were ever there," said Rick firmly before Carl could continue.

"And?" asked Carl.

"And that we fully expected that Mohamed Ibrahim would up the ante."

"You think Blackwell will buy it?" asked Carl.

Rick thought for several seconds before answering.

"No, but it really doesn't matter," responded Rick. "Just tell him that Ibrahim is playing the usual game."

"I hope that the conversation with Blackwell goes as easy as you make it sound," said Carl.

"Carl, I fully expect that Blackwell will be pissed."

"That's an understatement," exclaimed Carl.

"I believe the conversation will be awkward at first, but I have full confidence in your ability to put Blackwell at ease."

"Blackwell's no fool. He's been around a long time," offered Carl.

"That he has. And for that very reason, he'll know how the pirates operate...and how the negotiation process works."

Carl didn't say anything for a minute or two.

"And what about his granddaughter?" asked Carl.

"Well, the one thing we have going for us is that *you* are the real target, not his granddaughter," said Rick, saluting Carl with his coffee cup.

"Great. That's a comforting thought," said Carl.

"Well, since you're the target, you should have no problem convincing Blackwell that his granddaughter and her friends are in no immediate danger."

"No immediate danger?" questioned Carl.

"There's absolutely no reason for the pirates to harm them. The pirates just want the ransom money."

"And what if Ibrahim has, in fact, demanded more money?" asked Carl.

"Tell Blackwell not to worry. We'll take care of any additional ransom requirements," responded Rick without looking up from his meal.

"Yeah right," said Carl. "I hope you have something more in mind than paying the ransom with my money."

"I do. Trust me, I do," said Rick with a look that Carl had seen before.

"Assuming everything goes well with Blackwell, what do you see as our next step?" asked Carl, his thoughts still on the ransom.

"We need to gather some real-time intelligence on Boucher...find his Achilles' heel."

"Assuming that he has an Achilles' heel," offered Carl.

"Everyone has a weakness. We just need to find his and exploit it," said Rick. "I can't imagine that setting you up was purely an act of revenge," continued Rick after a slight pause.

"You don't know this guy," Carl responded. "I gave you the short story."

"And the long story?" asked Rick.

"Turns out that Jean Gendreau had a long history of brutality. He had gone over the top on several occasions."

"And why didn't the Legion deal with him accordingly?" asked Rick. Actually, Rick knew the short answer to his own question.

"The overall mission objectives were met. Thus, for political reasons, his actions were covered up," answered Carl.

"And the *fine* image of the French Foreign Legion remained intact," said Rick rather sarcastically.

"As fine as it could be," said Carl.

Rick hesitated before responding. He finished his second cup of coffee. Adriana was there to refill both cups. She left the silver carafe on the table along with a fresh supply of cream and sugar.

"You're right that I don't know this guy. But I believe that Boucher has an agenda, and it's not revenge," said Rick.

Carl thought about Jean Gendreau, a.k.a. Patrice Boucher. Since Rick didn't really know Boucher, Rick could be more objective in his analysis of Boucher's real game. Certainly, revenge was a motive; and in many cases, it was the only motive. But would a man who has established a new identity, and waited for such a long time, risk everything on revenge?

"I think our next move will hinge upon Blackwell's recollection of the conference and how well he recalls his conversation with Boucher," offered Rick.

"And if Blackwell doesn't remember him?" asked Carl.

"Well, having said that, I don't think it really matters," said Rick.

"Rick, you lost me," surrendered Carl.

"It would be nice if Blackwell could offer some supportive information. However, what we do know for a fact is that Boucher owns the company that sold *A Pirate's Dream* to Ms. Evans. No matter how that transaction came about, I don't believe for one minute that a chance encounter between you and Patrice Boucher was just a mere coincidence."

"I...I have to agree," said Carl hesitantly as he thought back to the conference and to the subjects discussed.

"I think Patrice Boucher is using Ms. Evans to coerce you into helping him achieve a much bigger objective."

"Any thoughts on what that objective could possibly be?" asked Carl.

"Not a clue," responded Rick.

"Assuming that you're correct, how do we find out what that objective is?" asked Carl.

"Parlez-vous français?" asked Rick.

CHAPTER TWENTY-SEVEN
Old Town
Day 11
0830 Hours

As soon as Carl and Rick entered the office, Elaine Drew informed Carl that JT Blackwell had already called three times.

"Sounded really anxious to talk with you," she added with raised eyebrows. She had the look of an old maid schoolteacher about to scold her problem student.

"Thanks Elaine. Give us a few minutes," said Carl as he looked around at Rick.

"Just tell him what we discussed," said Rick.

Rick turned, smiled, and said hello to Elaine as he followed Carl into his office. Carl wasted no time grabbing a bottle of water from the small fridge. Rick went over and poured a cup of coffee. Carl sat down behind his desk and drank nearly half the bottle of water. Some of it spilled on his shirt and the desktop.

Elaine had stacked the usual newspapers on the right side of Carl's desk. Several messages were placed neatly in a pile in the center of the desk. Little yellow stickies and paperclips identified areas that she knew would be of particular interest. Red stickies identified items that required Carl's immediate attention. There was only one letter next to the messages. She had drawn a large smiley face on the envelope. Some of the spilled water had fallen on the smiley face and had made the eyes run. It was an interesting contrast.

Carl wiped it dry and picked up the letter. It was a notice from the IRS. It simply stated that The Peterson Group's audit for calendar year 2012 had been completed satisfactorily and did not result in any changes to the 2012 tax return. Although that was particularly good news, there was no outward reaction from Carl. The audit cost him several thousand dollars and many wasted hours, just to verify that he and The Peterson Group had met all IRS requirements. He would deal with them later. Right now, his attention was squarely focused on his forthcoming conversation with JT Blackwell.

"Any last minute suggestions?" he asked as he finished the bottle of water.

"I can't think of any," answered Rick.

Carl managed a slight smile.

"When this is all over, you can let Blackwell know what really transpired in Eyl," said Rick as he slid into one of the soft Italian glove-leather chairs that faced Carl's desk. Carl's smile faded rapidly. The concerned look had returned, and it wasn't going away anytime soon.

"You know Rick, I have no problem stretching the truth, or even flat out lying to some people...but Blackwell is different. He's not one of those people. He's a good man. He certainly deserves the best from us...and he deserves the truth from me," said Carl.

Carl Peterson had always been a man of staunch character and unwavering integrity. Men of his ilk were few and far between in this day and age, especially in the D.C. area. Rick knew all along that it would be very difficult for Carl to avoid the truth, but it was a necessary evil in order to effectively deal with Patrice Boucher.

"Elaine," said Carl, pressing the intercom. "Would you please get Mr. Blackwell on the line?"

"Yes sir," responded Elaine. From the tone in Carl's voice, she realized that Mr. Blackwell was not the only one anxious about the call.

Carl went over and retrieved another bottle of Fiji water from the refrigerator. He opened it, took another long swallow, and swished it around in his mouth just as Elaine announced that Mr. Blackwell was on line one. Carl nodded to Rick and picked up the phone. His expression had changed. He had a look of confidence on his face.

"Good morning Mr. Blackwell," said Carl in a cheerful voice that he found surprisingly less difficult to muster when needed. Carl Peterson was back.

"Peterson, what the hell is going on up there?" demanded Blackwell in a clear strong voice that Rick could hear as Carl moved the phone away from his left ear.

Carl pictured the old man standing ramrod straight looking out over the harbor, *his* harbor, and the ships that *he* had built. The old man was tough as nails. Carl could only imagine the look on Blackwell's face when the President made the statement, "You didn't build that." *Yeah right, you go tell that to JT Blackwell Mr. President,* Carl mused to himself. Carl had expected Blackwell to get right to the point, but the fact that Blackwell did just that, still caught Carl a bit off-guard. It was certainly disarming. It was a technique that Carl had employed through the years. Hit them hard, and hit them first. Being on the other end of the stick was an interesting phenomenon that Carl had rarely experienced. He didn't enjoy the position.

"Well Peterson…will you explain to me what the hell happened in Eyl," asserted Blackwell again after a delayed response from Carl. The old man wanted answers, and he wanted them now.

"I'm afraid you have me at a disadvantage. With all due respect, I have no idea what you're referring too" said Carl after a slight pause.

"Listen. I'm too old for bullshit. Late last night I got a call from Mohamed Ibrahim. He wasn't very happy to say the least, and he was very direct. Told me that your people tried to rescue my granddaughter. Is that true?" asked Blackwell.

Rick motioned to Carl to put the phone on speaker.

"Mr. Blackwell, Rick Morgan is here in the room with me. Is it okay if I put you on speaker?"

"I don't care what you do, as long as I get some answers," responded Blackwell impatiently.

"Mr. Blackwell," said Rick.

"Morgan," was Blackwell's solemn acknowledgement.

"I happened to hear part of the conversation. I can assure you that our people did not attempt a rescue operation," said Rick in support of Carl's denial.

"Then why was this guy, Ibrahim, so emphatic. He claims his people stopped the attempt."

"I can only tell you that we would never risk the life of your granddaughter," reassured Rick.

"Then why would he call? Why was he so forceful?" demanded Blackwell.

Rick purposely hesitated in order to give the impression that he was contemplating Blackwell's question.

"He's playing the game. He's a negotiator," answered Rick.

"This is not a game," interrupted Blackwell. The tone of his voice suggested that he didn't like Rick's use of the word game.

"I understand perfectly well, but to the pirates, it is indeed a game. One they have played for many years. And they play it simply to get more money. He's fishing for a larger ransom," offered Rick.

"He wasn't fishing, he demanded a higher ransom," Blackwell responded, his voice again increasing in volume.

"How much?" asked Rick.

"Double. He doubled it. Ten million for their safe return."

Rick didn't say anything as he looked over at Carl. Carl had a wry expression on his face. He mouthed the words, "I hope you have a good plan."

"Mr. Blackwell, we'll deal with Ibrahim. Just don't worry. As long as there is the promise of money on the table, your granddaughter will be just fine," consoled Rick.

Blackwell didn't say anything for several seconds.

"I still don't understand why he thought your people were there. He was genuinely sincere in his statements to me," said Blackwell, sounding somewhat confused.

"I can't answer for him...or his emotion. I know that one of our contacts was involved with an escort operation in the Gulf of Aden, but I don't believe his operation involved putting anyone on shore. That would make no sense," said Rick calmly.

"I suggest you check with him," said Blackwell, still trying to maintain control of the conversation.

"I have all intentions of doing just that. But please understand that we have no control over what the pirates say or do for that matter."

Blackwell didn't say anything for nearly a minute or so. He was obviously mulling over Rick's explanation. Rick was about to say something when Elaine Drew came into the room and handed a note to Carl. It simply stated that Roy Higgins was on line two. Carl subconsciously looked over at the phone. Line two was blinking.

"Did he call for me or Rick?" whispered Carl.

"He asked for you," responded Elaine with her hand partially covering her mouth.

Carl handed the note to Rick and motioned for him to take the call.

"Mr. Blackwell, Carl needs to ask you a few questions. Unfortunately, I have another call that I must take. Understand that we are making very good progress," said Rick before Blackwell had a chance to respond.

Rick got up and went into the outer office. Elaine got up from her desk.

"You can use my phone. I need a potty break," she said as she went tiptoeing toward the ladies room.

"Thanks Elaine," said Rick as he sat down and picked up line two.

"Morning Roy...or good afternoon in your case," said Rick as he looked at his watch. It was already nearly 1700 hours at Camp Lemonnier.

"Hey Rick," answered Roy. There was a slight delay in the line. "How's it going at your end?" he asked.

"Not bad. Did the guys make it back okay?"

"They're on the patrol boat. The *Seychelles Princess* is in the queue at the Suez. We're going to meet at the club in a couple of hours."

"Was there a chance that anyone saw them in the harbor?" asked Rick.

"I suppose there's a chance...but I sincerely doubt it."

"So there was no hot pursuit?" asked Rick.

"There was no pursuit at all. Cody and Shaun weren't followed and neither were Guillermo and Rafael. I don't think the pirates even had a clue that they were there," said Roy. "Is there something I don't know?"

"Mohamed Ibrahim called Blackwell and got him all spun up," responded Rick.

"I assume Carl has talked to Blackwell."

"Carl is on the line with him as we speak," said Rick.

"And how's that going?" asked Roy.

"It started out a little rough. Ibrahim doubled the ransom."

"I'm sure that was no surprise," said Roy.

"It wasn't."

"I suspect that LaPointe was in touch with Ibrahim," said Roy. "Probably convinced him that a rescue attempt was imminent."

"Actually, we believe that LaPointe was in touch with Patrice Boucher," said Rick.

"Patrice Boucher...there's a connection between Boucher and LaPointe?" questioned Roy.

"Roland did some research, and it seems that LaPointe and Boucher, a.k.a. Jean Gendreau, go back quite a few years. Both were stationed together at Camp Lemonnier," responded Rick.

"Gendreau? Who the hell is Gendreau?" questioned Roy.

"It's a long story, but Patrice Boucher and Jean Gendreau are one in the same. And Gendreau and Carl have a history going back to the Sudan."

Higgins didn't say anything for several long seconds. He was putting two and two together. The total still wasn't four.

"I think I'm with you. I take it the history wasn't good," said Roy.

"It wasn't. Gendreau was thrown out of the French Foreign Legion as a result of an operation involving Carl."

"Thrown out...you're kidding," said Roy. "He must've been something special to get thrown out of the Legion. And I take it he blames Carl?"

"He does," said Rick.

"Is this a 'once upon a time story' or a 'no shitter'?" asked Roy.

"I'm afraid it's a little bit of both."

"So I take it you believe that Boucher is running the show. He's the one behind the piracy."

"It sure looks that way," said Rick.

"So what's next?" asked Roy.

"We need to find out just exactly what Boucher is after. I believe he's using Blackwell's granddaughter to get to Carl. We need to determine what he wants," said Rick.

"Could be a simple case of revenge."

"That was our initial thought, but we believe there's more to it."

"Knowing you, you'll figure it out. In the meantime, what about the guys?" asked Roy.

"Can you keep them busy for a couple days?" asked Rick.

"I can keep them busy for a couple weeks. We have a Saudi supertanker on the schedule."

"Good. What about LaPointe? Will you get another chance to interrogate him?" asked Rick.

"I don't know. The command is a little upset that I shot him in the knee. Guess I scared the hell out of a lot of people. They might not let me get to close to him."

Rick could visualize Roy's interrogation techniques. During a covert operation, time is of the essence. Lethal force is sometimes necessary and often used to get timely information. It's much easier to get results if you're interrogating two individuals at the same time. Shooting one in the forehead is a very effective way of getting the other one's undivided attention. The trick is to shoot the right guy and then convince the other one that you'll let him live.

"And by the way, my people informed me that the pirates have moved Ms. Evans and her friends into the city," added Roy.

Rick hadn't thought about Ozzie and Harriet. He never did trust anyone he really didn't know. And you never really *knew* anyone in his business.

"And you're sure that Ozzie and Harriet are clean and can be trusted?" asked Rick.

"I believe so, but as you know Rick, money buys a lot of trust."

Rick was about to say something when he noticed that the light went out on line one.

"Roy, Carl just finished his conversation with Blackwell. Hopefully he got some good information from him concerning his conversation with Boucher. I'll get back to you in a couple of days with a new plan."

"Keep me in the loop," said Roy.

Rick hung up the phone and re-entered Carl's office. Carl was pouring a cup of coffee. Rick walked over and picked up the coffee pot and began to refill his mug.

"Well?" asked Rick.

Carl smiled and gave Rick a thumbs-up.

CHAPTER TWENTY-EIGHT
Old Town
Day 11
1000 Hours

Carl had a genuine look of relief on his face as he sat down behind his desk. He picked up the letter from the IRS, looked at it again, and threw it unceremoniously into his out-basket for Elaine to file.

"Every time these assholes send me a letter, it costs me a thousand bucks just to have my accountants draft the initial response," said Carl.

"And you get it all back from the government…in spades," retorted Rick.

"Of course I do. And those morons have no idea that every audit costs the government three times what it costs me. They'll never learn. They're a bunch of morons," he repeated as he looked at the letter in the basket.

"Morons on our nickel. The fact is, they really don't care," said Rick. "So what did you find out from Blackwell?" asked Rick, trying to change the subject and avoid a thirty-minute diatribe from Carl on the virtues of the IRS.

"He was very informative. Seems you may be right about Boucher," said Carl.

"So I take it he does remember having a conversation with Boucher."

"That he did. He remembered it quite well. Actually liked the guy, if you can imagine that," said Carl shaking his head in disbelief.

"If I remember correctly, you liked Gendreau…*right from the beginning*. Your words," emphasized Rick.

"Touché," replied Carl pretending to pull a sword from his belly, checking it for blood.

"So what did you find out?"

"He said that he and Boucher exchanged the usual pleasantries—the you show me yours, and I'll show you mine phase. The conversation was cordial, and Boucher was quite talkative and open," said Carl, finishing his coffee.

Rick didn't say anything as he waited for Carl to continue.

"During the conversation, Boucher mentioned that among his various holdings, his primary business was brokering new and used sailboats."

"And that obviously got Blackwell's attention," commented Rick.

"It did. Blackwell mentioned that his granddaughter was in the market for a sailboat capable of circumnavigating the globe."

"Transition from a trivial conversation to one of real substance and opportunity," remarked Rick.

"That appears to be the case," responded Carl. "Boucher mentioned that he had recently come into possession of a Beneteau that would certainly meet her requirements."

"At that point, he had Blackwell's undivided attention," said Rick.

"That he did. Told Blackwell that he could make his granddaughter a very good deal if she was willing to pick up the boat in Saint Lucia."

"How convenient," said Rick. "Probably gave Blackwell his card," added Rick pointing to Carl.

"You know, he probably did," responded Carl as he leaned forward and pressed the intercom.

"Yes Carl," answered Elaine.

"Elaine, would you please call Blackwell and ask him if Patrice Boucher happened to give him a business card, and if he did, would he mind faxing a copy to us."

"Will do."

"Rick, is it possible Boucher hatched this whole scheme on the spur of the moment—based on a chance conversation with JT Blackwell?"

Rick didn't answer right away; although, he was convinced that Boucher's attendance at the conference was no mere coincidence. There was a good chance that Boucher had attended the meeting with the specific purpose of confronting Carl. The casual conversation with Blackwell may have unexpectedly provided him with another option.

"If I remember correctly, you said that Boucher was a very good tactician."

"I'll give him that. He was. He had a reputation for thinking on his feet," responded Carl.

"Then he probably did see an opportunity to use Ms. Evans to get to you," said Rick.

"To get to me...how?" asked Carl. "I'm still not so sure this whole thing isn't about revenge...plain and simple," he added as Rick was about to speak.

"Revenge is a two-edged sword," said Rick.

Carl finished the cup of coffee and leaned forward, resting his arms on the desk.

"Maybe I just don't see it...or want to see it."

"Carl, ask yourself this question—how would Boucher profit from your failure to rescue Ms. Evans?"

Carl sat back in his chair. His expression changed slightly as he thought about Rick's question. He didn't say anything as Rick went on.

"The fact is, he wouldn't," said Rick. "But if he could use Ms. Evans to coerce you into doing his bidding, then he could profit...and at your expense."

"Go on, I'm listening."

"There's more to this. He wants something from you...something more tangible. Something that he believes only you can deliver," said Rick.

"And you believe that whatever that tangible item is, in return, he'll release Courtney Evans once I deliver?" questioned Carl.

"Correct. Blackwell will get his granddaughter back safe and sound. Boucher will get what he wants, and the only guy who gets taken to the cleaners and left holding the bag will be our mutual friend, Carl Peterson."

"How comforting. Lucky me. Did you just come up with that scenario sitting here?" asked Carl.

"Actually, I've been thinking about it all night. It's the only thing that makes reasonable sense to me. And besides, when it comes to Ms. Evans, he holds all the cards."

"He does now. So how do we find out what he wants?" asked Carl.

"Finding out what he wants will be the easy part. You just need to ask him."

"Just ask him. Right, why didn't I think of that? And the hard part?" retorted Carl.

"The hard part will be to determine his weakness."

"And coming up with a plan to exploit that weakness," added Carl.

"Once we discover his weakness, the plan might be a little easier to develop than you think." said Rick confidently.

"I'm glad you think it might be," said Carl as he got up and went over and poured another cup of coffee. "I drink way too much coffee," he declared as he turned and asked Rick about his conversation with Roy Higgins.

"Roy mentioned that the pirates have moved Ms. Evans and her friends into the city of Eyl."

"Does he know where they're being held?" asked Carl as he took a drink of hot coffee.

"I believe so. His people are keeping him informed," said Rick.

"Ozzie and Harriet," mumbled Carl, taking a deep breath. "You know, we really don't know them. How do we know they didn't tip off Boucher's people?" said Carl motioning with his coffee cup, spilling a few drops on the carpet.

"Higgins trusts them," responded Rick.

Carl looked back at a picture on his credenza. Rick knew what Carl was thinking. They had trusted one of the locals in El Salvador with disastrous results. Trust was a commodity that could be purchased on the open market. Unfortunately, the opposition in El Salvador had paid a little bit more.

"What about Cody, Guillermo and the guys?" asked Carl.

"According to Higgins, they are on the patrol boat. Actually, they should be at Camp Lemonnier within the hour," said Rick as he looked at his watch.

"I assume they had no problem getting away *clean*," stated Carl. He placed added emphasis on the word clean.

"Higgins said they weren't pursued."

"Not at all?" questioned Carl. He seemed surprised that there was no pursuit.

"Not the least," answered Rick.

"So the pirates really didn't know that we were there...and on the Liberty ship," said Carl with a forced smile.

"Doesn't appear that they did," said Rick.

"So Ibrahim was really playing the game. He simply made a decision based upon the information provided by LaPointe," said Carl.

"Or he was following Boucher's directions all along," offered Rick. "For his plan to succeed, it doesn't matter how we got to this juncture," added Rick.

Carl sat back in his chair thinking about how close they were to rescuing Courtney Evans. He cradled the mug in both hands.

"I hated to stand down, but we just couldn't take a chance," said Carl.

"It was the correct decision given the circumstances," reassured Rick.

"It would take a small army to rescue them now," lamented Carl.

"The collateral damage would draw too much attention. It would end up being a small war."

"So what's next?" asked Carl.

"Are you up for a French holiday?" asked Rick.

"I'm always up for a holiday, especially to France. Fine cuisine, great wine and small-breasted women who have finally discovered the beneficial effects of deodorant."

Rick enjoyed Carl's cultural description of French amenities. Carl didn't ask who was paying for the trip. It had briefly crossed his mind, but he knew who would finally end up with the tab.

"Who was that contact we had in France? Marcel something or other," asked Carl as he continued to think about the French Riviera.

"André Marcelles," said Rick.

"Ah yes, André Marcelles. He's a good man. Isn't he about our age?"

"He's a little bit younger," said Rick.

"You think he's still active?"

"The last time I talked with him, he was still with the DGSE."

"Ah, the good ol' Directorate-General for External Security," said Carl. I would think the acronym would be DGES?" he mused.

"In French, it's actually the Direction Générale de la Sécurité Extérieure," said Rick.

"Your French accent is good," complimented Carl as he got up and retrieved a bottle of Fiji water from the small refrigerator. "You want one?" he asked, motioning to Rick.

Rick stood up and caught a bottle from Carl before he had a chance to say yes.

"I think the last time I saw André was in Brussels. Must've been thirty years ago," recollected Carl.

"Thirty-four years ago to be exact," said Rick as he took a long drink of water from the bottle.

"Good memory."

"Lynn and I were enjoying our tour at the Naval War College."

"Newport, Rhode Island," Carl said. "That was a great tour."

"For some," said Rick, raising his eyebrows.

Carl tried to suppress a smile.

"So I take it Ms. Lynn didn't believe your explanation that you had to do some on-site research at the NATO Headquarters in Belgium."

"Well she might have, if you hadn't picked me up at two in the morning in a black Ford with small hubcaps, several conspicuous antennas and Georgia plates."

"Those cars were a dead giveaway," laughed Carl. "Probably purchased by some pencil-neck geek who had never been in the field."

"She thought those days were behind me," said Rick.

"And you didn't tell her otherwise," admonished Carl.

Rick didn't say anything as Carl looked out the window. He could see the King Street Metro Station. The yellow line was leaving the station heading north. Several cabs were parked along the curb. The cabbies were huddled together in a group. One of the cabbies appeared to be reading an article to the others. Most of them wore turbans. Their English was limited to street names and buildings.

"That was a quick in and out. I don't think that the NATO guys had any inkling that we were there or that we were the ones who stopped the assassination attempt on Petrov."

"Thanks to some very good intel by André," added Rick.

"Wasn't Viktor Petrov related to Ann?" asked Carl.

"He was her uncle. That's why you and I were brought in. He had been in touch with her and she convinced him to trust us."

"Whatever happened to him?" asked Carl.

"He's here in the states. Teaches at one of the colleges in Colorado. I believe he and Ann communicate on the holidays."

Carl didn't say anything as he looked back at the King Street station. All the cabs had departed. *I wonder what they're up to*, he thought to himself as he turned to Rick.

"You think what we do has a positive affect on anything?"

Rick smiled. This wasn't the first time they had this discussion, and it probably wouldn't be the last.

"In the short term. I suppose it depends on one's definition of positive," commented Rick.

Rick should have been a politician, Carl thought to himself.

"I don't think Lynn will ever *really* like me," said Carl, changing the subject as he sat down behind his desk.

"Would you stop it. She likes you," said Rick. "But every time you showed up in the past, I disappeared for a few days. She had no idea where we went or if we were ever coming back."

"Good point. You think André is still at the DGSE?" asked Carl, jumping back to topic.

"Well, he certainly could be. I'm sure he's still connected one way or the other," responded Rick.

"Should we give him a call?" asked Carl.

"I would prefer to surprise him. Talk with him face-to-face. Check out his body language."

"So you don't believe he'll be forthcoming?"

"You know how these agencies are. Hell, look at us. I suspect that Sims knew much more about the Coughlins than he let on...and he certainly knew more about Patrice Boucher. I would prefer to be sitting across from André when we talk with him." responded Rick.

"I agree. So who do you have in mind for this French holiday?" asked Carl.

"You and me for sure, and we'll need at least one other operative who's not on Boucher's radar."

"You think our team has been compromised?" asked Carl.

"We don't know how long Higgins' space has been bugged. We have to assume that Boucher has all the names involved in the rescue attempt…except for Tony Ramos."

"Tony would be a good choice. He'll fit right in with the casino crowd," said Carl.

"He knows what to look for, and he can take care of himself if necessary."

"What about Lynn? Do you think she would like to go?" asked Carl.

"She's not particularly fond of the French, or for that matter, flying across the Atlantic. However, since she's been to Cannes, I sincerely doubt she is going to let me go alone…*especially* with you," teased Rick.

Carl was about to say something in his defense when Elaine buzzed him on the intercom.

"Yes Elaine."

"I have Boucher's business card," she said.

"Is there an address?"

"InterContinental Carlton Cannes, 58 Boulevard de la Croisette, 06414 Cannes, France."

CHAPTER TWENTY-NINE
Old Town
Day 11
1400 Hours

Ann Peters arrived at The Peterson Group office a little after 1400 hours. She had just finished a lengthy conversation with Carlos and was enjoying a cappuccino. She had brought one for Elaine. They were engaged in a discussion about one's diet and the pitfalls of gluten when Rick and Carl came in from lunch. They looked a bit surprised to see her sitting there.

They knew that Ann had a meeting that morning at the Pentagon. She had certainly dressed for the occasion. She set a striking pose in her tailored dark blue business suit and matching high heels. Her hair was pulled up into a French twist. *How ironic,* Rick thought to himself. Her earrings were dainty and unassuming. Ann was blessed with flawless skin. She hardly wore any make up and only a slight amount on her eyes. She looked well rested.

"I thought you had a meeting this morning at the Pentagon," said Carl.

"I did, but all this stuff going on in the Ukraine caused a change in the schedule. My client was called in for a special meeting with the Joint Chiefs of Staff. We're planning to meet first thing in the morning...unless there's a decision made."

"Well there's certainly no fear of anyone making a decision," said Carl sarcastically. "So who's the client?"

"I can't tell you," answered Ann expecting that Carl would ask.

"Yeah right," said Carl.

"Really, I can't. Confidentiality is part of the contract. I might be able to bring you in, but until then, his identity must remain a secret."

"Have you talked with Carlos?" asked Rick, as Carl was about to ask another question.

"Just got off the line with him. Higgins took them all to the club for a debrief. He sounded like he enjoyed the wrap up."

"Good place for a debrief," said Carl.

"A few beers can make any debrief bearable," added Rick.

"Anything new?" asked Ann as she patted Elaine on the hand and whispered that she would talk with her later.

She followed Carl and Rick into Carl's office. Carl was still wondering who Ann's client was.

"We thought that we'd take a vacation," said Carl winking at Rick.

"A vacation? What vacation? You're kidding...right?" said Ann as she looked over at Rick.

Rick and Carl didn't say anything for a couple of minutes. Rick tried to avoid eye contact with Ann. He had never been successful trying to con her. Her unbridled facial expressions would invariably cause him to laugh regardless if he was serious or not. Carl was much better at playing that game. Besides, Carl wasn't about to give up on finding out who Ann's new client was.

"You're not kidding. So where are we going?" asked Ann. Her anticipation was refreshing. Although Ann was a former KGB agent, there was a little kid running around inside, dying to get out and enjoy the playground.

"It's a secret," said Carl with a sinister look.

"I'll tell you when I'm allowed to tell you. It's a 'need to know' thing. You, of all people, should understand that," scolded Ann. She was starting to get annoyed. The KGB agent was back.

"Just kidding. I love it when you get all pissed off...and your nostrils flare. Rick, will you bring Ann up to speed? I need to talk with Roland," said Carl.

He purposely whispered in Rick's ear just to dig Ann one more time. She made a face that he had no problem interpreting, which she followed with a punch in the arm as he walked past her. He winched just enough to confirm that she had made solid contact. Ann grabbed Rick by the arm.

"My nostrils don't flare," she protested as she rubbed her nose.

Rick smiled and patted her on the back as they sat down at the conference table. It only took Rick about fifteen minutes to completely brief Ann on the morning events and his thoughts concerning what he believed to be Patrice Boucher's objective. Rick's analysis of the situation made perfect sense to Ann. Her only question was how she could contribute.

Roland was expecting Carl. He already had a Google Earth image of the InterContinental Carlton Cannes on his large screen. He was bringing up a street view as Carl entered the space. Roland stood up and greeted Carl. Carl immediately recognized the front view of the Carlton.

"Just as grand as I remember. Some things never change, especially in Europe," said Carl as he sat down at the small table that served as Roland's desk, conference table, workbench, and whatever else Roland needed it to be at the time. Today it was his desk.

"I've always heard that Cannes was a great place," said Roland as he started to manipulate the street view. "I believe this presentation is several months old. I can bring up the satellite if you wish," he added.

"No, this will do just fine. I wanted a visual to refresh my memory of the area. Can you zoom in on the harbor across the street?" asked Carl.

Roland panned counter clockwise toward the south. The harbor was full of high-end yachts, numerous sailboats and two tall ships. Roland was able to zoom in close enough to read many of the names on the stern.

"I could check the harbor log and determine the exact date that this image was taken," offered Roland in his quest for accuracy.

"No, this will do just fine," said Carl.

Roland maneuvered the street view toward the main entrance to the docks. He continued to move forward. A name on one of the yachts caught his eye. He zoomed in. The name *Bill Fisher* was neatly stenciled in large black script over a subtle image of a sailfish. Ironically, the yacht's homeport was Wilmington, North Carolina.

"Is that just a coincidence?" asked Roland.

"Probably is, but check it out anyway," said Carl.

Roland zoomed out. There were only a few empty berths that appeared to be available.

"Roland, I need you to look up André Marcelles. I believe his middle name is Paul. The last I knew, he was living in Paris. A good starting point would be the DGSE."

"DGSE?" questioned Roland, making a note of his name and organization.

"It's a French government agency. You can certainly find information about it on the net," Carl responded.

Roland made a few more notes as Carl went on.

"Marcelles may still be working for the French government. I need a current address. And Roland, I assume you can find that information without alerting him or the DGSE," said Carl leaning forward, as if someone may be listening.

"I'm pretty sure that can be accomplished," Roland responded, subconsciously looking around.

"Did you find out any more information on Patrice Boucher?" asked Carl.

"I did."

Roland leaned forward and retrieved a large notebook from the center of the table. He opened it to a page marked with a large blue paperclip. He threw the paper clip into a small bowl that was home for many paper clips of various colors.

"He has a suite at the Carlton. The billing information suggests that he's been living there for the past nineteen months. He makes an occasional trip to Ottawa, although he hasn't made the trip in nearly eleven months," answered Roland.

"A suite at the Carlton," mumbled Carl under his breath as he thought back to better times at Camp Lemonnier. Jean Gendreau always had a desire for the finer things in life. He fancied himself to be of the aristocracy. Unfortunately for Gendreau, the French Foreign Legion wasn't known for recruiting polished individuals. Even his position as an officer wouldn't offer the opportunity to mingle with the upper crust of French society. Gendreau was trapped from birth.

"Is he married?"

"Never been married. Seems he likes to...*rent* women," said Roland, searching for the right word.

"Rent them, huh. Roland you *do* need to get out more," said Carl. "Maybe we should take you to Cannes," he chuckled.

"The rent is probably much more reasonable here," answered Roland.

Carl looked over at Roland and smiled. *The kid's probably a virgin*, he thought to himself. Roland caught his gaze as if he could read Carl's mind.

"I've had a few girlfriends," he retorted defensively.

"And you spend money on them?" asked Carl.

Roland didn't say anything. He knew where Carl was headed. Fortunately, Carl changed the subject.

"Have you been keeping track of the Beneteau?" Carl asked.

Roland brought up the satellite coverage, made a few keystrokes, and quickly located the sailboat. It was heading west about fifty nautical miles northwest of Port Said. Roland zoomed in on the ship. One of the crew members could be seen leaning against the wheel. The other crew member must have been below. Roland zoomed in a little closer.

"They must have a steady wind. The wheel is lashed," said Carl.

"According to the forecast, they'll have a good wind until late tomorrow morning. Then, if the forecast is correct, they'll be lucky to make a couple of knots."

"What did they list as their final destination?" asked Carl as he continued to watch the ship. There was no doubt in his mind where they were headed.

"The manifest listed Cannes. They took on enough provisions to make it all the way."

A wry smile crossed Carl's face as he continued to watch the ship. *I wonder how many times this ship has been captured by Somali pirates*, he mused to himself. *How many times has the name on that stern been changed?*

"After we take care of Patrice Boucher, we're going to get that ship back for Ms. Evans," declared Carl in a low voice as he continued to watch the image.

"What was that Mr. Peterson?" asked Roland.

"Nothing Roland. I was just thinking out loud. Good work," he said as he left Roland's office.

Rick and Ann were having a good laugh when Carl came back into his office. He was still thinking about the sailboat and didn't question their laughter.

"The Beneteau is on its way to Cannes," he announced.

"That's good. We can retrieve it there," said Rick.

"Ann, how locked in are you with this new client of yours?" asked Carl.

"I just need to meet with him and finalize the statement of work. Then I'll turn him over to my project manager," responded Ann.

"So you could be available for a trip to Cannes?"

"I could, especially if he and I meet tomorrow as planned," she answered, trying to suppress a smile.

"Good. It appears that Boucher is living at the Carlton. Roland is checking on André Marcelles as we speak."

"Marcelles…he's still in Paris. I have his address and phone number," offered Ann.

"I should've known," said Carl shrugging his shoulders.

"I'll give Tony Ramos a call and fill him in," said Rick.

"Is Tony meeting us there?" asked Ann.

"He'll be there to cover us just in case," responded Rick.

"When do you think we'll be ready to go?" asked Carl.

"Well, actually I have all I need here. I'll need to give Lynn a little lead time."

"Tell her we'll pick her up at the Northwest Regional Airport," said Carl as he buzzed Elaine.

"Yes Carl."

"Will you get Captain Somerville on the line?"

"Yes sir," responded Elaine.

"We'll get Carlos to meet us in Cannes," said Carl, looking for Ann's reaction.

She smiled at Carl. Carl had given up on her client.

"I need to talk with Higgins," said Rick.

"You think we'll still need him?" asked Carl.

"Once we find out what Boucher is after, we may still want Higgins to coordinate the exchange and ensure safe passage."

"Good point. Have you thought more about what Boucher is after?" asked Carl.

"I have some ideas, but let's talk with Marcelles first. If I'm even close, we'll have some planning to accomplish, and we'll definitely need Higgins."

Carl was about to ask Ann a question when Elaine informed Carl that Captain Somerville was on line two.

"Captain," answered Carl.

"Yes sir, Mr. Peterson. How may I help you?"

"We're going to need you to schedule a flight to Cannes, France, with stops at Fort Walton and Paris."

"No problem Mr. Peterson. And when would you like to depart?"

Carl looked over at Rick and Ann. Rick looked at his watch.

"Thursday morning," said Rick.

Ann nodded.

"Thursday morning," answered Carl.

"And how many passengers?"

"There will be four of us. And Captain, I'm not sure how long we'll be over there, so plan on spending a few days."

"Will do," answered Captain Somerville.

"I'll call you tomorrow afternoon to confirm. Talk with you later," said Carl as he hung up the phone.

"I guess we need to pack our sea bags," said Carl.

"I need to call Lynn," said Rick.

"She'll be excited, I'm sure," offered Ann.

"Maybe, but the last time she and I were in Cannes, a lady of the night approached us while Lynn and I were walking hand in hand down the Boulevard de la Croisette. The lady was young and actually quite beautiful."

"No more so than Lynn, I'm sure," interrupted Ann.

"That's true. I can still see the look on Lynn's face when the girl placed both hands on my forearm and whispered in my ear. She was quite descriptive. I introduced her to Lynn and told her that Lynn was my wife. I explained that she and I were quite happy and that I had absolutely no interest. She looked over at Lynn, smiled, and said that she would be perfectly happy to make it a threesome."

"Oh, that must have gone over real well with Lynn," said Carl.

"Lynn still doesn't like the French," responded Rick.

CHAPTER THIRTY
Old Town
Day 11
1600 Hours

At first, Lynn had a million excuses. She wasn't about to entertain thoughts of going to Europe…and especially to France. Her initial reaction was not only predictable, but it was also exactly what Rick had expected. He remained silent as she went through a litany of reasons why she couldn't go…or didn't want to go.

Rick let her continue for several minutes, and then when she took a breath, he reminded her of the great time they had had on the French Riviera. Reluctantly, she paused long enough to hear Rick out. When he mentioned that Ann and Carlos were also going on the trip, she acquiesced. Lynn really liked Ann, and she was actually enjoying Carl's company more and more.

"So how long will we be gone?" she asked, sounding a bit defeated.

"Plan on at least a week. Ten days at the most," answered Rick. "We'll have a great time, you'll see."

"I'm sure that we will, but you know how I hate to fly…especially overseas."

"We're not flying commercial. We're going in one of Carl's planes," said Rick.

"Oh, now that I can deal with," she said after a slight pause. "Do you need me to pack some things for you?" Lynn asked, knowing that Rick had just planned on spending a couple of days in Washington. By now, he had to be running out of things to wear. He would buy something new before using one of the hotel's washing machines.

"Just a few things. Pick some outfits that will complement your selection. And honey, I will need you to pack my tuxedo and all the trimmings."

"Medals too?" she asked.

"No medals, strictly civilian attire."

"So I need to pack something…formal?" asked Lynn.

Lynn loved to dress up. She was quite elegant and would easily blend in with the French nightclub crowd. Rick had always thought that Lynn was born into the wrong time period. She would have done quite well at the turn of the twentieth century. She was definitely a *Downton Abbey* girl.

"A couple of nice evening dresses will do just fine," answered Rick. "I'm sure if need be, you and Ann will find something quite appropriate in Paris," he added.

Lynn didn't say anything as several outfits came to mind. She had bought one very nice black formal in D.C. recently and was saving it for just the right occasion. The French Riviera would certainly offer that opportunity.

"What's the current temperature in Paris?" she asked as she continued to make an imaginary journey through her walk-in closet.

Lynn was now in full planning mode.

"Just about the same as here. A little cooler at night, but the ten-day forecast looks very comfortable. You can bring it up on the computer."

"So when are we leaving?" she asked.

"Thursday morning. Will that give you enough time?" answered Rick, knowing that Lynn was probably looking at the calendar. He could only imagine her expression.

"It's tight. I'll have to make a few calls. What time do I need to be at the airport?"

"About ten. I'll call you with our ETA. We'll pick you up at the corporate terminal. And honey, we'll be landing at the Northwest Regional Airport."

"Northwest Regional not Destin?" asked Lynn.

"Correct. The runway at Destin isn't long enough," responded Rick.

"How long did you say we'd be in Paris?"

"A couple of days in Paris, and then we'll head down to Cannes," said Rick nonchalantly.

"Cannes. That sounds good. Hey, maybe your girlfriend is still there hanging out on Croisette Boulevard."

Women never forget anything, Rick thought to himself.

"If she is, we'll fix her up with Carl," Rick quipped.

"Good idea. I'm sure he'll like that. He may need to find someone else to make it a threesome," she said. Her sarcasm was real.

Rick decided to stop while he was ahead. By the sound of her voice, he knew that she was in travel mode and would make every effort to enjoy the trip…and especially the shopping in Paris. She just never liked the hassle at the airport. Flying on The Peterson Group's aircraft would be just fine. Plus, she knew that Carl's contract aircraft were well maintained, always immaculate, quite comfortable, and above all, very safe.

"Everything okay with Lynn?" asked Carl.

"She'll be ready. Said she has a lady in mind for you," said Rick with a devilish grin.

"Really," said Carl with a puzzled look. "I didn't know she knew anyone in France."

Rick gave Carl a look that seemed to jar his memory.

"Oh jeez! She actually mentioned your *friend* from the boulevard?" laughed Carl, who had finally caught on.

They all enjoyed a good laugh.

"Great. I'm so happy she's coming. I know some wonderful boutiques that she'll just love," said Ann. "All originals," she added.

Rick forced a smile.

"They have Bass Pro in France?" teased Carl.

Rick wasn't about to join in on that one. Ann just ignored him. Carl looked up at the two clocks on the wall. It was already midnight in Somalia.

"Ann, is it too late to give Carlos a call?" asked Carl.

She looked at her watch and then at the Somali clock.

"Heck no. He's a night owl. Besides, I told him I'd give him a call when I knew more about Rick's plan," said Ann looking over at Rick, knowing perfectly well they needed to confront Boucher before any plan would be on the table.

"I'd like Carlos to meet us in Paris. You might want to pack a few things for him," said Carl as Ann hit one of the keys on her satellite phone. "I assume Tony is heading straight for Cannes," he continued as he walked over and sat down next to Rick.

Rick was already making notes and drawing small rectangles.

"He is. I told him we'd determine a drop point when we got there. Said he only needed a stiletto. I'll pack one of the new SIGs just in case," answered Rick.

"He's an up close and personal kind of guy," remarked Carl, shaking his head ever so slightly.

As Rick and Carl were talking, Ann got Carlos on the line. He, Higgins and the guys were at the club. She told him their current plans and that Carl would like him to join them in Paris. Carlos tried to suppress a smile as he looked over at the guys. He certainly wouldn't miss Camp Lemonnier one bit, although he did enjoy the team's company. They were a great bunch with a myriad of stories. He especially liked Guillermo.

"Carl, do you need to speak with Carlos," Ann asked as she held the phone close to her chest.

Carl nodded that he did.

"I'll call you tomorrow. Love you babe," she said as she handed the phone to Carl.

"Hey Carlos. How's it going over there?" asked Carl, knowing that it was hot as blazes and that Carlos was probably working hard at not being miserable.

"Going well. Only thing to do here is to drink beer and watch the young guys bargain with the hookers."

"Glad you're being entertained," joked Carl. "So how's the food?"

"Typical for the region. I probably smell like couscous. I'm sure that I've put on a couple pounds already."

"Well...cheer up my friend. We're heading to Paris tomorrow morning, and as Ann mentioned, I'd like you to meet us there."

"That'll be *no* problem," responded Carlos, stretching out the word no. "Do I need to make reservations?"

"I'll get Elaine to make the reservations. I was thinking about the Castille on Rue Cambon. I've stayed there before but it was quite some time ago."

"I've heard Higgins mention the Renaissance Paris Arc de Triomphe Hotel. Supposed to be quite modern and very nice. Also, it's just steps away from the famous Champs-Élysées, which I'm certain the girls would enjoy."

"That does it then. I'll have Elaine check the availability," said Carl.

"I'll plan on flying out tomorrow. There are several military flights in and out of here every day," said Carlos.

"Well, you decide. You're certainly welcome to fly commercial if you desire. I'd assume there are several flights out of Djibouti to Paris. Either way, I'll have Elaine book a room for you tomorrow. She'll contact you with the details."

"Great. And Carl...I'll need some hardware," said Carlos.

"We've got you covered, and Ann will pack some things for you," said Carl.

"Look forward to seeing you."

"Is Higgins available?" asked Carl.

Carlos handed the phone to Higgins and ordered another round for the team. They suspected that something was up and that Carlos would be leaving soon. His whole mood had changed. He was having a difficult time suppressing a smile.

"Hey Carl," answered Roy. "Anything new?"

"Nothing yet. We're focusing our efforts on Boucher. We've decided to go to Cannes, and flat out ask him what he wants with me...face-to-face."

"That'll be interesting. I've always liked the direct approach. Do you need some backup?" asked Higgins.

"If Rick's hypothesis is correct, and I believe that it is, we won't need any backup. Besides, Tony Ramos is on the way, and as you know, he's perfectly capable of providing any backup if necessary."

"Well...be careful. France isn't what it used to be. I can break Guillermo and Rafael loose just in case," offered Roy.

"I'll let you know as soon as we have something concrete. We're planning a stop in Paris. Need to drop in on an old friend."

"An old friend?" questioned Roy.

"Do you happen to know André Marcelles?" asked Carl.

"I've heard the name, but I don't know him personally," answered Roy after a slight pause.

"Rick and I have had some dealings with him in the past. We believe he's still with French external security. If so, he might be willing to share some pertinent information on Boucher."

"That reminds me," said Higgins. "Did you hear about the jewel heist that took place at the Carlton?"

"I did see an article, but I haven't looked into it," answered Carl.

"You don't think Boucher had anything to do with that, do you?" asked Higgins.

"I have no idea. I wouldn't put it past him," responded Carl making a note.

"It was big...somewhere north of a hundred and thirty million. Maybe he wants you to help fence the jewels," offered Higgins.

"Boucher has a suite at the Carlton. I can't imagine that he'd pull off a heist of that magnitude in his own backyard," said Carl.

"A hundred and thirty million is a lot of incentive," said Higgins.

Carl thought about the prospect but dismissed any serious consideration that Boucher would have been involved.

"We'll look into it. But I'd really be surprised if he had anything to do with that. By the way, you mentioned you could keep the guys busy. Is that offer still on the table?"

"It is. I've got several escort operations in the queue. If they're available, I can keep them real busy," said Higgins.

"Good. I'll let you know as soon as we have a plan," said Carl as he hung up the phone and handed it back to Ann.

Tony Ramos cancelled his plans to meet his lady friend in Panama City. He had already scheduled a flight to Atlanta with a connecting flight on Air France to Paris. The flights from Paris to Nice were presently booked. However, the agent informed him that cancellations were not uncommon, and his chances of flying standby were very good. If time were of the essence, another option would be to charter a small aircraft. But flying in a single engine aircraft, serviced by a French mechanic who probably doubled as the pilot, was not a comforting thought. Tony decided that he would make that decision when he got to Paris. Besides, he could always rent a car. For Tony Ramos, driving had always been a time to reflect...and plan.

Tony hadn't been on the French Riviera in several years. The last time he was there, he lost nearly thirty thousand dollars playing the French version of baccarat known as chemin de fer. He was determined that he wouldn't be so foolish this time around. He would no longer play a game that was strictly a game of chance—a game where players are called "bankers" and eight decks of cards are used. The banker controls the shoe. If the banker loses, he passes the shoe to the next player in order. That player becomes the new banker and may set any bank they see fit. Counting cards would have been hard... even for Rain Man.

Tony probably would have lost a lot more if it weren't for a young Danish girl by the name of Tofi Nieesen. She soon recognized that the James Bond atmosphere, opulent surroundings and numerous martinis were having a negative impact on Tony's judgment. For whatever reason, she decided to come to his rescue. Actually, he was looking for the right excuse to give up his seat at the circular table. Tofi Nieesen offered that opportunity. She bent down and whispered something in his ear. The other players smiled as Tony excused himself from the table.

His time with her proved to be quite enjoyable. They spent several days together touring the French Riviera, ending up in Monaco. He smiled as he thought about her. He opened the bottom drawer to his desk and shuffled through several small stacks of paper until he found a faded lilac colored envelope with the single inscription, *My Anthony*. He passed the envelope back and forth under his nose. There was still a faint aroma of a wonderful time. It brought a smile to his face along with a fond memory that would last forever. She was a remarkable woman who had absolutely no inhibitions whatsoever.

On the second day, she asked him if he were married. He told her that he wasn't. The twinkle in her eye indicated that she didn't believe him. She had no problem telling him that she was happily married and this was her vacation...no questions asked. Tony was fully aware that separate vacations were the norm among European married couples...especially those from the Scandinavian countries. Actually, Tony didn't care if she was married or not. He knew that he would never see her again. So he had decided to fully enjoy the moment.

He read the note several times, smiled, and put it to rest in the drawer. He then searched and found the folder marked, *Baccarat*. He put it in his briefcase, sat back in his chair, poured a scotch on the rocks, and smiled.

What the hell, he thought to himself.

CHAPTER THIRTY-ONE
High over the Atlantic Ocean
Day 13
1700 hours

The flight from Northwest Regional to Paris Charles de Gaulle Airport would take a little over eight hours. The weather was forecast to be clear with unlimited visibility. So far, the weather guessers were correct. The flight was extremely smooth. Lynn and Ann settled in quite nicely. They enjoyed the plush surroundings and friendly attention offered by the crew. They sat back, took off their shoes, got comfortable, and talked for the first couple of hours before having a light lunch. Following lunch, it was obvious that Lynn was going to take a short nap. Ann would join Rick and Carl.

Rick and Carl were consumed with the material that Roland had put together on Patrice Boucher. Most everything in the record was benign to the point of sheer boredom. In reality, it was too benign for someone with Patrice Boucher's temperament and penchant for money and power. It was quite obvious to Rick that someone with experience, abundant resources, and well-compensated connections had fabricated Patrice Boucher's record.

Everything about Patrice Boucher was too clean. There were no violations...not even a single parking ticket. By all accounts, Patrice Boucher was the model citizen. He was the guy next door who was always friendly and accommodating and who would set up your garbage cans when they fell over. Everything in the record was verifiable. There was absolutely no connection between Patrice Boucher and Jean Gendreau. Rick sat back and lowered the material to his lap. He took a long drink from his water bottle, screwed the top back on, and looked over at Carl. Carl was turning a page. He had a pensive look on his face that seemed to be frozen in place.

"You know Carl, this guy's record is way too clean."

"You got that right my friend," responded Carl as he sat back in the seat.

"There are only a few agencies outside of the U.S. that I'm familiar with that are capable of fabricating a record this good—this complete."

"The Brits are pretty good at it...and so is Mossad," said Carl.

"The KGB was no slouch for that matter. They were very good at creating new identities," offered Ann.

"Yeah, but they usually started when the kids were in grade school. Hell, they created people that didn't exist. But they're no longer active," said Carl. From the tone of his voice, his last statement sounded more like a question.

"The KGB may not be active, but the reserve unit is. And you can bet your ass that most of the old agents are still around...and doing the same job," replied Ann.

"I would actually bet that some of them are drawing a paycheck from the Russian mafia," added Rick after thinking about Ann's statement.

Carl's expression changed as he looked over at Rick.

"Are you suggesting that the Russian mob is behind Boucher?" asked Carl.

Rick didn't answer right away. He looked down at the information resting on his lap, and then over at Carl. Carl's mind started racing.

"It crossed my mind," Rick responded after a minute or so.

Carl didn't say anything as he thought about the Russians. The last thing he wanted to do was have a run in with the Russian mafia. With them, it was always about shooting first and asking questions later. Ann certainly wasn't thrilled with the thought of a run-in with them either.

"Maybe I should've taken Higgins up on his offer," said Carl as he slid back into his seat.

"And what offer was that?" asked Rick.

"He offered to send Guillermo and Rafael to provide backup."

"That might've been a bit premature. We still have no idea what Boucher is really after...or if he is even working with anybody for that matter," answered Rick.

Carl nodded but didn't say anything. He knew that they needed more information before they could make an informed decision on how to proceed. Rick checked the flight monitor and looked at his watch.

"Looks like we'll be landing a little after midnight Paris time."

"We'll check in at the Renaissance, have a few drinks, and play it by ear," said Carl. "I have a feeling that Lynn is going to be wide awake," he added as he motioned toward Lynn.

She was sound asleep. Lynn had a blanket pulled up under her chin. She was in another world.

"Is Carlos meeting us at the airport?" asked Rick, looking at Ann.

Before Ann could respond, Carl announced, "I told Elaine to tell him to wait in the hotel bar for us. There was no sense for him to drive in Paris traffic at night. Besides, it's nearly an hour drive to the airport."

"You said the Renaissance. I thought we were staying at the Castille Paris," questioned Rick.

"It was actually Carlos's recommendation. It's the Renaissance Paris Arc de Triomphe Hotel. He said it was just steps away from the Champs-Élysées. I figured it was probably a better location," he said as he looked over at Ann, gave a little nod, and smiled sheepishly.

Ann sensed he was subtly waiving the white flag from his dig the day before.

"Lynn can walk everywhere. Elaine was able to book three suites," continued Carl.

"Lynn will like that," said Rick just as Carl's satellite phone vibrated. It began a little dance across the small table adjoining Carl's large leather seat. Carl picked it up and checked the caller ID. It was Roland.

"Afternoon Roland," answered Carl.

"Afternoon Mr. Peterson. How's the flight?"

"Going very well."

"Sir, I've put together some information on André Marcelles."

"Is he still with the DGSE?" asked Carl.

"He is. Looks like he might be on limited duty. I just sent you an email with all the information that I was able to gather," said Roland.

Carl looked over at the imbedded computer just as a tone indicated that he had an email.

"Hold on a second. It just came in," said Carl as he got up and clicked on the email icon. There was only one email in the inbox.

"Got it," said Carl as he opened the attachment.

"Looks like he meets someone every Tuesday and Thursday at a small café on the Champs-Élysées," said Roland.

"Really."

How convenient, Carl thought to himself.

"How did you discover that little fact?" asked Carl, not sure that he actually wanted to know the answer.

"Well, let's just say that French security leaves a bit to be desired. They protect what they consider to be most important. For whatever reason, they don't think that logs warrant the same protection."

"And our friend, André Marcelles, logged in and out each day," said Carl. It was really a question.

"That he did. And he always included a destination when he logged out."

Carl thought about the log. Sometimes logs were used in order to provide false information. Most experienced operatives would give little credibility to the information provided in a log, especially logs that were placed in the open for anyone to view.

"And you're certain that he does frequent the same establishment?" asked Carl.

"Receipts indicate that he frequents two places…one more than the other. And from the amount on the bill, I suspect that he's not alone," responded Roland.

"I would think one would have to speak French in order to hack into a French computer system," Carl declared, wondering how Roland was able to obtain receipt information from a French café.

"I speak French," answered Roland, sounding a bit surprised that Carl didn't know. "My grandfather was from Lyon. He lived with us. He passed away when I was seventeen. He could only swear in English. Consequently, I learned French at a very early age."

Carl felt a little embarrassed that he didn't know, or worse yet, had forgotten that Roland could speak French.

"We should have brought you along on this trip," said Carl, trying to recover. "Thanks for the information. Next time you're coming with us," apologized Carl.

"Is there anything else?" asked Roland after a slight pause.

"I think this will do it for now. Thanks again," said Carl as he put down the phone.

"Did you know that Roland spoke French?"

"I had no idea," said Rick.

Ann shrugged in harmony with Rick.

Carl printed a couple copies of the material. There was a current headshot of André Marcelles on the last page that included a full-length image of him boarding a large sailboat. His hair was almost all gray. It was long and appeared to be pulled back into a small ponytail. His eyebrows were still dark and quite bushy. He had no other facial hair. The lines on his face were characteristic of someone who used facial expressions to emphasize a point. The crow's feet were permanent. Although André Marcelles was a bit younger than Rick and Carl, he looked ten years older. Carl studied the picture and then handed it to Rick. Lynn had awakened and was stretching.

"He's not aging very well," noted Carl.

"Or he's living *too* well," offered Ann as she put the picture on the counter next to the computer.

"Roland indicated that André has lunch every Tuesday and Thursday at one of two cafés on the Champs-Élysées," said Carl.

"He doesn't vary his routine?" asked Rick somewhat surprised.

"According to the receipts, he hasn't," responded Carl as he thumbed through the information.

"He must not be active in the field anymore," said Rick.

"Limited duty," said Carl.

"This might explain it. Looks like he's been battling colon cancer for several years," said Rick as he perused one of the pages.

Rick didn't say anything as he read over the report. Both he and Carl had lost a lot of friends to cancer, especially in the last couple of years. It was an insidious disease that didn't discriminate. Cancer didn't care if you were young or old, rich or poor. You could be a victim of poor choices or unfortunately, in many cases, a victim of your DNA. As Rick, Carl and Ann continued to go over the material, the flight attendant entered the cabin area and asked if they were ready for dinner.

"We'll be landing in about an hour," she said with a broad smile that was genuine.

"Dinner sounds good. What's on the menu?" asked Carl as Rick looked over at Lynn and Ann. They were ready for dinner.

"Beef Wellington, or Copper River salmon," responded the flight attendant.

Rick knew what Lynn's choice would be. Everyone gave their preference as the flight attendant went back into the small galley that served the aircraft. She returned with plaid linen napkins and silverware that appeared to be new.

"Would anyone like a glass of wine?" she asked as she set each of the tables.

Lynn was the only one who wanted the salmon. Accordingly, she preferred to have a white wine. The flight attendant handed Lynn a short wine list. It was actually quite impressive. She chose the Pinot Grigio. Since Ann, Carl and Rick had chosen the beef Wellington, they opted for a Chilean Malbec that the flight attendant highly recommended.

As the flight attendant was preparing the meal, Carl's satellite phone vibrated again. He picked it up expecting that Roland had some more information for him.

"Yes Roland," he answered, without looking at the caller ID.

"Carl, this is Tony Ramos."

Carl had a surprised look on his face as he checked the caller ID.

"Sorry Tony, I just got off the line with Roland. Where are you? Are you in France?"

"I'm at the Carlton. Got a flight to Nice and drove over a couple of hours ago," said Tony.

"You made good time. I assume the accommodations are adequate?"

"The accommodations are superb," answered Tony.

"Have you had an opportunity to locate our friend?" asked Carl.

"I have. He's in one of the back rooms playing chemin de fer as we speak."

"Be careful. You can lose your shirt in that game," warned Carl.

"How well I know," lamented Tony.

"Was he with anyone?" asked Carl.

"No arm candy if that's what you're asking. He did have a couple of goons close by."

"Bodyguards?" questioned Carl.

"I'm not sure. At first glance they appeared to be bodyguards, but they seemed to hang back. They didn't show him any respect," answered Tony.

"Could they be Russian?" asked Carl as he looked over at Rick.

"Could be...they're ugly enough."

Tony's comment brought a smile to Carl's face as he looked over at Ann.

"By the way, this place is crawling with gendarmes, plainclothes police, news people and quite a few paparazzi," remarked Tony.

"It's because of the jewel heist," said Carl, remembering his conversation with Roy. "It may be a blessing in disguise. Could make our job a little safer," he added.

"Maybe, but I don't think the goons care. The gendarmes seem to give them a lot of space, if you know what I mean," said Tony.

"Probably on the payroll," said Carl.

"I suspect so. When will you and Rick be here?" asked Tony.

"A couple of days. We're going to meet with an old friend and see if he can provide some information on Boucher," answered Carl.

"I'll keep a low profile and see what I can dig up from this end," said Tony.

"Well, you know what to do. If the cops are indeed on the payroll, Boucher will know if someone is snooping around."

"Don't worry, I'll be discrete. I'll keep in touch. If you find out anything from your friend, let me know," added Tony.

Carl hung up and told Rick what Tony had said.

"The Russians might be involved after all," said Carl.

"If Boucher is involved with the Russian mob, he's probably in way over his head," said Rick as Ann and Lynn joined in on the conversation.

"Maybe he's actually involved with the jewel heist," stated Ann.

"If he's involved with the heist and the Russians, he must be desperate," said Rick.

"Desperate enough to use Blackwell's granddaughter to get me to do his dirty work," said Carl.

"Ann, do you still have any friends who could answer a few questions?" asked Rick.

"Quite frankly, I hope not. Most of the ones that wanted to make me disappear are dead. The others are teaching school in the states."

"Keep your friends close and your enemies closer," said Carl.

CHAPTER THIRTY-TWO

Paris, France
Day 14
0100 Hours

The ride down the Champs-Élysées toward the Renaissance Paris Arc de Triomphe Hotel reminded Rick of his last trip to Paris. Although he had been to Paris on several occasions, the last excursion was a quick in and out at midnight. Ironically, he wasn't on the Champs-Élysées...he was under it. A slight smile briefly crossed Rick's face, as Carl continued to chauffer them down the Champs-Élysées.

Lynn noticed the smile on Rick's face.

"What are you thinking?" she asked.

"Just of times past," he responded, still seeming to be lost in thought.

Lynn had no idea what was going through Rick's mind. *He couldn't possibly be thinking about the Boulevard de la Croisette*, she thought to herself. She almost asked him; however, she decided to let it go and allow him the pleasure of whatever fantasy had surfaced. Besides, there was so much to see on the Champs-Élysées. Even at one thirty in the morning, the sidewalks were crowded with people window-shopping, couples walking hand-in-hand, and some enjoying French wine and little pastries at one of the many sidewalk cafés.

Lynn tried to take in everything as they headed west toward the hotel. Even though the Champs-Élysées was just a little over a mile long, she would love to have had a map in hand. She was making mental notes of the fine shops along the way—Cartier, Louis Vuitton, Gaultier, Nina Ricci and Prada just to name a few. The number of fine shops was overwhelming. Rick would have no problem encouraging her to go shopping as he, Carl and Ann went off to ambush their friend, André Marcelles.

Carl turned right on Avenue de Wagram. The Renaissance was ahead on the left. The five-star hotel presented a modern design, which seemed a bit out of place among the older architecture gracing the

Paris skyline. Lynn was aware that in many European countries, "five-star" sometimes meant that the water was still on after nine at night... and if you were lucky, there was an outside chance that it would still be warm. Hopefully, it was five-star by American standards.

Carlos was waiting patiently in the lobby when the group, led by Ann, entered the hotel. He had a dry martini in his left hand and looked quite relaxed until he saw Ann. A couple of martinis had heightened his anticipation. He spilled nearly half of the glass as he wiggled forward trying to escape the confines of an oversized soft leather chair.

The last time he and Ann were in France together was during a rest and relaxation following a mission to East Germany. Unfortunately, due to a complete misunderstanding on Ann's part, her feelings for Carlos at that time were strictly limited to one of a professional nature. She was there because she had to be there. Twenty years went by before Ann learned the truth from, of all people, Carl Peterson. This time, Paris would be much different.

Ann had spotted Carlos as soon as she entered the hotel. A broad smile crossed her face as she walked briskly toward him. He put what was left of his martini on a small coffee table. Two little plastic swords were resting on a folded black napkin. Ann and Carlos embraced for more than a minute or so. The patrons took little notice of the lovebirds.

"I'll check us in and meet you guys in the lounge area," said Carl as he put his briefcase on the floor and opened it momentarily.

"Do you need any help?" asked Rick.

"With this...certainly not. Go ahead. I'll meet you in the lounge," insisted Carl. "They just need my credit card," he added with a smile as he pulled it from one of the many slots and waved it like a small flag in the air.

"Napoleon brandy?" asked Rick as he turned to follow Lynn.

"But of course," responded Carl, giving Rick a thumbs-up. Carl's persona had changed. Carl always liked to role-play—to be in character. If they were in Arizona, Carl would have worn boots and a cowboy hat, and he would have referred to Rick as "partner."

Ann and Carlos had already secured a small circular table in the corner. It had just been cleaned and reset with a new gold-colored tablecloth and appropriate silverware. Carlos borrowed a chair from a small empty table for two that was near the passageway to the kitchen. A middle-aged server pulled out chairs for Lynn and Ann. He greeted everyone in English as he went around the table handing each one of them a black leather-bound menu with a raised gold emblem of the Arc de Triomphe set in the center. The emblem was angled just enough to give it a three-dimensional look. A second server seemed to appear out of nowhere. He placed water glasses on the table along with several bottles of chilled Perrier. Carl was approaching before Rick had a chance to order.

"Not bad," he said as he looked around the room as if expecting to see someone he knew.

The lounge was still about three quarters full even at two in the morning. Several bottles of champagne were resting in large silver coolers. Everyone seemed to be engaged in conversation, although it was fairly quiet—not like the din which was characteristic of most establishments in the States where you had to shout to be heard.

"Did you order yet?" asked Carl as he took a seat between Ann and Lynn.

"Not yet," answered Rick.

"Is anyone hungry?" asked Carl. It was a rhetorical question since a little over an hour ago they had dined on salmon and beef Wellington.

"I'm not," said Lynn as she continued to look through the menu. She particularly enjoyed the descriptions. Besides, she was curious by nature.

"Me either," added Ann.

"Let's have a couple of drinks and maybe something to eat later," said Rick.

"Would you ladies like a bottle of champagne?" asked Carl as he noticed a server pouring two glasses at a table nearby.

"A mojito would do me just fine," said Ann.

"Make it two," added Lynn as she placed the menu on the table.

"Carlos?" asked Carl.

"I suppose a Modello Especial in a frosted glass with a slice of lime would be out of the question," mused Carlos as he looked around the room. He didn't see one bottle of beer, or even a tall glass for that matter.

"Maybe not," said Carl. "How about you Rick. What's your preference?"

"I'll have what you're having," responded Rick, remembering Carl's request.

"Ah yes...Napoleon brandy," said Carl as he signaled the server.

Carl ordered the drinks, and much to Carlos's surprise, the hotel had an ample supply of Modello Especial. Carlos wasn't sure if that was a good sign. Certainly in the posh surroundings of the Renaissance, he wouldn't be drinking straight from the bottle. Unfortunately, the lounge did not offer a frosted mug. He would have to drink from a tall glass.

"So Rick, what do you think? Should we head up to the swimming pool?" asked Carl as both servers returned with the order. Carl knew that the swimming pool comment would get Lynn's attention.

Rick didn't say anything until the servers were finished. The older server asked if there would be anything else. Carl told them that they were fine for now and would let them know.

"The swimming pool?" asked Lynn, wondering why Rick and Carl would be going for a swim, especially this late at night.

"The 'swimming pool' is a metaphor for the building that houses the Directorate-General for External Security, which we refer to as the DGSE," responded Rick. "Our friend André Marcelles has an office there."

Lynn looked over at Carl and smiled. He just loved digging a hole.

Rick looked at his watch. It was already 0215 Paris time.

"If André sticks to his routine, we might just find him on the Champs-Élysées at one of the cafés that Roland mentioned," said Rick.

"So we have about ten hours?" said Carl as the server approached with their order.

Carlos was surprised to find his Modello in a tall frosted glass. There were little crystals of ice on top of the beer. More crystals were forming before his eyes as the server placed the glass in front of him. He was wearing a heavy glove.

"Be careful. It is really cold," said the server.

"I don't believe I've ever seen one quite so cold," said Carlos as he looked over the tall glass. He didn't touch it.

"The chef has one of those nitrogen bottles. He broke two glasses trying to get it just right," added the server.

They all had a good laugh, which caused several patrons to look in their direction.

"I think I'm going up to the room to get ready for bed," said a tired Lynn as she took a sip of her drink. "May I take this with me?" she asked the server.

"Of course," he responded.

"Give us a few minutes and I'll be up," said Rick.

When Lynn was out of sight, Carl moved next to Rick. He signaled the waiter and ordered another round.

"So tell me Carlos, were you able to get any information out of LaPointe?" asked Rick.

"Not as much as we would have liked. As you can imagine, the command was very reluctant to let us interrogate him alone."

"They probably know Higgins," said Carl.

"How long had the space been bugged?" asked Rick.

"From what we gathered, it appears it had been bugged for nearly a month."

"So LaPointe heard the planning session?" asked Carl.

"No. Higgins didn't trust anyone. We briefed at the club over a few beers."

"What about the team members? Do you think LaPointe knew who they were?" asked Rick.

"He did. Roy had him write down all the names he had passed to Boucher. I copied the list," said Carlos as he reached into his pocket and retrieved a small green notebook. He thumbed through it, stopping on one of the pages. He handed the notebook to Rick.

Rick went over the list as the server delivered the second round of drinks. The server asked if there would be anything else. Carl said that there wouldn't be and asked for the bill.

"This is interesting," said Rick in a low voice as he went down the list of names. "And you're sure this is the complete list?" asked Rick.

"I copied the names from Roy's list. Roy asked him again when we were just about finished, just to be sure. The list was the same."

"What is it Rick?" asked Carl.

"There are a couple of names that are conspicuous by their absence," answered Rick as he handed the notebook to Carl.

Carl looked over the list for a couple of minutes and then smiled.

"Ozzie and Harriet," said Carl.

"If LaPointe had been listening for a month or so, wouldn't he have heard their names?" asked Rick. "At least once?"

"I never trusted them," said Carlos.

"Higgins didn't notice?" asked Carl.

"I really don't know. Our time was limited. Higgins asked the questions, and I took notes. Following the interrogation, I had to catch my flight. We didn't have a chance to do a thorough debrief."

"Did you guys record the interrogation?" asked Carl.

"They wouldn't let us use a recorder. However, there were mics in the room. I'm sure that the interrogation group has a recording," Carlos responded.

"You think they're dirty?" asked Carl.

"I really don't know, but in either case, we can use them to our advantage if and when the time comes," responded Rick.

CHAPTER THIRTY-THREE

Paris, France
Day 14
1130 Hours

Carl held her tightly in his arms. He pulled her close and kissed her gently. Ronnie Lake was everything he had expected her to be…and much more. His excitement was peaking as their breathing intensified. He could feel her hands moving down his body. She arched her back slightly as he kissed her neck. She moaned. Carl could feel her warm breath as she nibbled on his ear. They were just about to make love when his satellite phone began a little dance across the small marble-topped table that was snuggled up to the left side of the bed. Carl rolled over onto his left side trying to ignore the buzz and hold on to Ronnie, but she started to slip away. She held out her hand and was saying something, but he just couldn't understand. His heart was pounding as he tried to reach her, but no matter how hard he tried, he couldn't move fast enough. His arms and legs felt so heavy. They didn't want to move.

"Don't go…don't go," he called out. "Please, don't go."

He moved as fast as he could and was about to grab her hand, when she just faded away…and was gone.

Carl lay there for a minute or so, refusing to open his eyes. He squeezed them tightly, trying desperately to bring her back. He reached over and felt the bed. It was warm. The sheets were ruffled. He was still breathing hard when he realized that the buzzing sound was not in his head—it was coming from his phone. Reluctantly, he opened his eyes and tried to focus. Little slivers of light came uninvited into the room from around the edge of the room darkener. He looked over at the curtain. He didn't remember closing it. Suddenly, he wasn't quite sure where he was. There was just enough light entering the room to add a modicum of confusion.

What happened to Ronnie, he thought to himself as he continued to look around the room, expecting to see her standing there in the dim light.

Carl fumbled for the phone as he tried to figure out where he was. How much did he drink the night before? He looked at the clock. It was 1130. The phone continued to vibrate. Carl finally sat up on the edge of the bed and rescued it just before it would have fallen to the tile floor. He looked at the caller ID. It was Roland. *Shit, I'm in France*, he realized as he answered the call.

"Roland, what's going on?" he asked as he vigorously rubbed the back of his head. He was back; he was wide-awake…and Ronnie Lake had never been there.

But she seemed so real, he thought to himself as he looked over at the other side of the bed.

"Good morning Mr. Peterson. Thought you'd like to know that your friend André Marcelles has logged out for lunch."

Carl looked at the clock again. It was now 1133. He was suddenly aware of the time difference and that it was only 0533 in Old Town.

"Jeez Roland, what the hell time did you get to work?"

"A bit early. I figured the only way I could provide the team with effective support was to be on French time."

Carl smiled as he envisioned Roland sitting at his computer wearing a short sleeve shirt, khaki pants and loafers with no socks.

"You're amazing Roland. So, what was it that you just said about André?"

"He just logged out of the DGSE. Listed his destination as Café George."

"Café George?" repeated Carl.

"Yes sir, that's correct. The café is located on the corner of Champs-Élysées and Boulevard Saint-Germain," added Roland. "It's real close to where you're staying," he added.

Carl didn't say anything as he looked back at the bed. *It seemed so real,* he thought to himself again.

"You wouldn't happen to know if he has a car?" asked Carl, knowing that many people in Paris use the public transportation system.

"He does, but I don't think he drives it to work. I believe he uses the Paris Métro. In fact, line one travels right under the Champs-Élysées. There are four stops. One station is named in honor of George the Fifth."

Carl didn't say anything for several seconds as he looked at the clock again. He was surprised that it was nearly noon. He knew that he could be ready in about twenty minutes.

"Good job Roland. I really appreciate your resourcefulness. I'll give you a call later," Carl said as he put down the satellite phone.

He got up, stretched, and went over to the window. He moved the curtain aside slightly. It was a beautiful Paris morning. He could see the Eiffel Tower off in the distance. Carl went back and sat on the edge of the bed. He yawned as his thoughts went to Ronnie Lake. *Maybe I should have invited her,* he thought to himself.

"Probably a bit presumptuous," he said out loud, for no one to hear. He looked back at the bed and sighed ever so slightly. He picked up the satellite phone and called Rick. Rick answered right away. He had been expecting the call.

"You up?" asked Carl.

"Carlos and I just finished a continental breakfast. We figured that after your fourth brandy, you might need a little extra time this morning."

"Rick I hate to admit it, but I don't remember that last one. Where are the girls?" he asked, wanting to change the subject.

"They're getting dressed. Looking forward to their venture down the Champs-Élysées."

"Well, you can afford it," laughed Carl. "By the way, I just got a call from Roland. He believes that André is on the way to his luncheon engagement."

"Any idea where?" asked Rick.

"Looks like he's heading for Café George. Are you down in the restaurant?"

"We are," said Rick.

"Good, I'll be down in about twenty," said Carl as he put down the phone and headed for the small bathroom.

Carl got ready in less than fifteen minutes. He took out his Paris map and checked the location of the café. Roland was right. It was just a few blocks away. They could easily walk there in less than ten minutes.

Rick and Carlos were enjoying their second French roast coffee when Carl entered the restaurant. He was stepping quite lively and looked refreshed.

"Bonjour," he said smiling at the hostess. He pointed in the direction of Rick and Carlos. She accompanied him to the table and handed him a lunch menu.

"Bon appétit!" she said. Her smile was genuine.

"Merci," Carl replied as he took the menu and opened it. While he was practically fluent in the language, he kept things brief.

"Morning guys," he said as a young female server approached with another French press. She was tall and slender. Her hair was a bright purple color and cut extremely short on one side, giving her a butch-like appearance.

"Coffee?" she offered, knowing that the trio was American.

"By all means," Carl responded as he sat back in the chair. He looked her over. She noticed but didn't smile.

"Looks like Café George is no more than a ten minute walk," Carl said as he selected one of the large breakfast rolls.

"I assume it'll take André about forty-five minutes to get here, so we have some time," said Rick as he rotated the outer dial on his watch.

"Do you want me to go with you guys?" asked Carlos.

"What do you think Rick?" Carl asked as he started to butter the roll.

"Three of us might be a bit over powering. I don't want to send André the wrong signal," responded Rick.

"I agree," said Carl.

"Carlos, why don't you follow us from a distance and watch to see if we've been followed," said Rick.

"You think we're being followed?" asked Carl as he subconsciously looked around the room.

"I sincerely doubt it, but you never know. Boucher seems to be one step ahead of us," responded Rick.

"Good point," said Carl as he selected another roll and tore it in half. He covered it in butter and one of several preservatives that were stacked neatly on a three-tiered tray.

"And if we don't locate him?" asked Carl.

"Then I hope you brought your bathing suit," said Rick with a cunning smile.

Carl chuckled as he took a healthy chomp out of the hard roll. Crumbs went everywhere.

Fifteen minutes later, Rick and Carl were heading east on the Champs-Élysées. Carlos followed from a distance. There were people everywhere. The majority were obviously tourists. Several women in burqas passed by heading toward the Arc de Triomphe. They were covered from head to toe. Not even their eyes were visible behind the screen-like mesh that served as their only window to the western world.

There could be anyone under that garb, Rick thought to himself. Carl was having similar thoughts.

Several groups of men wearing turbans were looking into the shops. None carried shopping bags. *The Champs-Élysées is a Petri dish that will eventually produce nothing good,* Rick mused.

As they walked east on the Champs-Élysées, Café George could be seen ahead on the left. All of the tables along the sidewalk appeared to be fully occupied. Rick and Carl were engaged in conversation as they walked past the café. However, they were indeed checking out each of the tables. Rick was first to notice a man resembling André Marcelles sitting at a table one row removed from the tables that lined the sidewalk. Rick tapped Carl on the forearm.

"Second row in," he said without pointing.

"Got him," responded Carl.

André was reading a newspaper that was folded accordion-style—typical of people who ride the metro. A demitasse was sitting on the table near his right hand. André fumbled with the cup as he read the paper. He had placed a napkin on the back of one of the four chairs to signify that he was expecting a guest. André's hair was long and pulled back into a ponytail—a hairstyle that many European men seemed to prefer.

Rick and Carl continued down the Champs-Élysées for another block and then turned around. They were about halfway back when they saw Carlos being seated at a small table for two near the main entrance to the café.

"Let's go surprise our friend," said Rick.

They entered the café and informed the maitre d' that they were meeting a friend and pointed in André's direction. The maitre d' nodded as Rick and Carl proceeded to André's table. They pulled out two chairs and sat down.

"Excusez-moi, ce siège est pris," announced André as he lowered his newspaper slightly. He peered over the top of Ben Franklin-style wire rim spectacles.

Rick and Carl didn't say anything. André started to raise his newspaper and then dropped it on the table.

"Oh mon Dieu!" he exclaimed.

Rick and Carl leaned forward.

"How are you my friend?" asked Rick as he held out his hand.

André looked a bit bewildered. He searched his mind as he looked at both men in front of him. Then he smiled broadly and grasped Rick's hand with both of his hands.

"My God...Rick Morgan and Carl Peterson. How long has it been?" he exclaimed.

"Certainly too long," responded Carl as he shook hands with André.

"I can't believe this. You both look well, a bit older, but time has been kind," said André.

"And you?" asked Rick, knowing that André has had some physical problems.

"I'm doing quite well. Had some problems that appear to be behind me, if you know what I mean. As you say…no pun intended.

"André, are you still with External Security?" asked Carl getting right to the point.

"You found me here…you must know that I am," answered André, raising his eyebrows.

"Touché," said Carl.

"Actually, I'm on limited assignment. I'm in the process of turning over my case files to one of the younger agents."

"You will always be on call," said Carl.

"I suppose that is true. We are never really retired…are we?" said André. It was purely a rhetorical response. "So tell me, is this a social call or just plain business?"

"Actually André, it's a little bit of both," responded Carl.

"Ah, that is good," he said as he checked the front of his shirt. "There is no laser dot on my forehead, is there?" he laughed. "I was beginning to wonder if I had fallen out of good graces with the… *company*."

"I apologize for not alerting you. But as you know, in our line of work, events are not always as orderly as we'd like them to be," said Rick.

"And what is it that I can do for you my friends?" asked André.

"We need some information. Would you happen to know the name Patrice Boucher?" asked Carl.

"Ah, quand on parle du loup," responded André.

Rick looked over at Carl.

"Speak of the devil," Carl translated.

"In fact, his name just came up the other day when we were looking into the jewel heist in Cannes," continued André.

"Do you think he had anything to do with that?" asked Carl.

"Actually, we don't think he was involved. But he is certainly no angel. How do you know him?" asked André.

"I worked with him when he was with the French Foreign Legion. We worked together on an assignment in the Sudan. But his name then was, Jean Gendreau," said Carl, again getting right to the point.

André looked surprised and was about to say something, when a middle-aged woman approached. She was elegant to say the least. She had dark hair with streaks of gray that appeared to be natural. She wore a loose fitting purple dress that seemed to have a life of its own. It moved just enough in the slight breeze to draw everyone's attention. André stood up, embraced her, and kissed her on both cheeks.

"Let me introduce the love of my life. This is Cerise Renaud," he said with the sincerity of a man who was truly in love.

Cerise smiled as she sat down in the seat that André had pulled out from the table.

"Please forgive the intrusion," said Carl, as he and Rick remained standing. "André, is it at all possible that we can get together a little later?" asked Carl.

"Where are you staying?" asked André.

"The Renaissance," responded Carl.

"I will meet you there later. I can provide the information you requested. I would like to hear more about Monsieur Gendreau," said André as he handed a business card to Carl.

"Call me."

CHAPTER THIRTY-FOUR

Renaissance Paris Arc de Triomphe Hotel
Day 14
1600 Hours

Carl planned on giving André plenty of time to make it back to the DGSE Headquarters before he would make the call. Both he and Rick were convinced that André could provide some valuable intelligence on Patrice Boucher. Moreover, they were equally interested by André's reaction when Carl mentioned that he had known Patrice Boucher by another name—Jean Gendreau. André appeared to have zero knowledge that Boucher had a prior identity. Consequently, Carl had something of significance to trade.

The telephone number that André had given to Carl went directly to his private phone. However, Carl was certain that all calls going into the DGSE Headquarters were monitored. They certainly were at Langley. André was looking forward to the call, and the tone of his voice confirmed his anticipation. He was also looking forward to another meeting with his old friends. He answered on the second ring. There was only one other person that ever called André's private number.

"Bonjour mon ami," answered André.

"André, it was great seeing you. I must apologize for our serendipitous assault on your privacy. Quite frankly, Rick and I wanted to surprise you."

"I understand perfectly well," said André, knowing that Carl wanted to avoid any questions or interference from the DGSE.

"I would like very much to continue our conversation…say over diner?" asked Carl.

"Oui, dinner would be just fine," responded André. His enthusiasm was genuine.

"And please, bring Cerise," said Carl.

"I would love too, but unfortunately, Cerise doesn't get out of work until nine. Maybe she could meet us for some after-dinner drinks," offered André.

"By all means," said Carl. "Do you have a particular dining preference?"

"The Makassar is wonderful, and it's right there in your hotel," offered André.

"You don't mind coming here?" asked Carl.

"Of course not, and Cerise is within walking distance. It will actually be quite convenient for both of us."

"Then it's settled. How about 1900 hours?" said Carl.

"That will work. I will see you there mon ami," confirmed André.

Carl made a reservation for six at the Makassar Lounge Restaurant and let the others know of the plans. Since the weather was exceptionally nice, the maitre d' convinced Carl that dining on the terrace would be a most pleasurable experience. Carl agreed, as he picked up the menu that was strategically positioned on the desk that was located in his room. The Makassar Lounge was known for its combined French and Indonesian cuisine. There were numerous positive reviews included with the menu.

The ladies will certainly enjoy this, he thought to himself. Actually, he really didn't care where they dined, he just wanted to have an opportunity to question André.

Carl put the menu down and sat on the edge of the bed. He fondly placed his left hand on Ronnie's side of the bed and smiled. He thought about the night before and a dream that was so real—so vivid that it still gave him a rise. He couldn't get Ronnie Lake out of his mind. For Carl, the physical as well as the emotional connection with Ronnie Lake was genuine. He lay back, shut his eyes, and hoped for another encounter.

Rick was sitting in his room flipping through the channels when Lynn came bouncing in. The first thing she did was to reach down and pull off her shoes. She dropped her bag on the floor and fell backward onto the bed with her hands over her head. She had surrendered. She took a deep breath and looked over at Rick.

"Next time, I'm wearing tennis shoes. I'm pooped," she said as she turned her gaze toward the ceiling.

"No packages?" questioned Rick as he looked back at the door.

"Ann said that today was a recon day…whatever that means. We traveled up and down both sides of the street checking out all the shops."

"So have you narrowed down your targets?"

Lynn propped herself up on both elbows.

"You know honey, the shops are really nice, but it's not me. There's no way that I would spend that kind of money on just one outfit. I could buy twenty outfits at Anthropologie for the cost of one on the Champs-Élysées."

"If you find something really nice, you should buy it. Make a memory of Paris."

"There is a Gap," she said after a slight pause.

Rick smiled. Lynn was indeed a trip. Besides, she looked good in anything.

"So you had a good time?" he asked.

"I did, and Ann is a delight. I love her. Carlos better hold on to that girl," she added shaking her finger. "Or he will answer to me." She was serious—all one hundred and ten pounds of her.

"I'm sure that he will. Will you be up for dinner at seven?" asked Rick.

Lynn looked over at the clock. It was already four thirty.

"I just need a short nap. Where are we going?"

"Carl made reservations for all of us right here at the Makassar Lounge. We're eating on the terrace." Rick knew that Lynn would eat anywhere if it were on a terrace.

"I saw the menu. It really looks quite nice. Not sure that I know what some of the items are," confessed Lynn.

"I'm sure the servers will explain the fare," said Rick. "By the way, André Marcelles will be joining us. You'll really like him. His lady friend will be joining us after dinner."

"I'm sure that I will," responded Lynn, as her eyes were already getting heavy.

Rick knew that Lynn was about to dose off. She didn't even ask one question about André's lady friend. Within seconds, she was sound asleep. She didn't move when Rick's satellite phone vibrated. He picked it up and looked at the caller ID. It was Tony Ramos. Rick went out onto the balcony to take the call.

"Tony, how are you doing?" answered Rick as he went and stood by the railing. The Eiffel Tower was clearly visible off in the distance.

"I'm doing quite well. When will you guys be heading this way?"

"I suspect late tomorrow afternoon. Lynn and Ann will probably want a few more hours on the Champs-Élysées."

"The Champs-Élysées. From what I remember of that street, that could be an expensive proposition," warned Tony.

"Lynn is quite frugal when it comes to shopping. She'll hardly ever buy anything unless it's on sale."

"Everything is always on sale," added Tony.

He's right, Rick thought to himself.

"So how is our friend?" asked Rick.

"That's a good question. Basically, he hasn't left the hotel since I've been here. He did walk across the street to the marina. Checked out one of the empty boat slips, and then went straight back to the hotel," answered Tony.

"Was he alone?" asked Rick.

"Not really. The muscle was trailing behind. They never let him out of their sight."

"He probably has everything that he needs right there at the hotel," said Rick.

"I'm not so sure that is the real reason. I get the impression that he's not being allowed to leave," Tony responded.

Rick didn't say anything as he drew a mental image of Boucher being led around in chains. Rick really didn't know Boucher, but from Carl's verbal account, he wasn't one to be controlled.

"The goons are definitely Russian," added Tony before Rick had a chance to respond. "I picked up a few words. Maybe Ann can do a little eavesdropping…find out what they're saying."

"I'm sure she can."

"Rick, I get the feeling this guy is on a real short leash. He smiles a lot, plays the part of a high roller, but I get the impression it's all for show."

"You may be right. Just keep an eye on him and stay loose. By the way, I brought some hardware for you," said Rick.

"Better leave the hardware on the plane. Security here at the hotel is tight as a drum due to the jewel heist. They've even set up metal detectors," said Tony.

"A little late for that, isn't it?" questioned Rick.

"Well, you would think so, but you know the French, always showing up late for the dance."

Rick smiled as he looked back into the room. Lynn hadn't moved.

"I'll call when we're on the way," said Rick. "Take care," he added.

"See you tomorrow," responded Tony as he ended the call.

Rick walked back into the room. Lynn was breathing heavily. Every once in a while her feet twitched slightly as if she were walking on hot pavement. She was off into the world of fine shops. Rick watched her for a few more minutes. He decided that he wouldn't disturb her until he was ready to head down to the lounge and meet with the guys. He would give her plenty of time to rest.

Makassar Lounge
1845 Hours

Carl, Rick and Carlos were in the lounge enjoying martinis when André Marcelles entered. He was carrying an attaché case and what appeared to be a gift.

"Bonjour mon amis," he announced in a loud booming voice when he saw them, and while he was still several feet away. His greeting attracted the attention of several patrons who appeared to be annoyed. André paid them no mind.

Carl and Rick greeted him and introduced Carlos.

"And how do you know these two scoundrels?" asked André, as he shook hands with Carlos. "A strong grip," he said as he twisted

Carlos's wrist. "I saw you when you were seated in the café," he added with a grin.

"Was I that obvious?" asked Carlos. Surveillance was not one of Carlos's strong points...and he knew it.

"No, but I have a few years on you. I never liked sitting around pretending to read a newspaper either," André confessed.

"And was the young lady in Versace jeans and dark blue sweatshirt with you?" asked Carlos, still holding André firmly by the hand. Carlos twisted André's wrist ever so slightly.

"Good...he's good," said André as he looked over at Rick and Carl.

"Actually, she follows me everywhere. I'm not sure if she's supposed to be watching me...or watching out for me," he laughed as he patted Carlos on the shoulder. "I'm not even sure if she's aware that I know that she's following me."

Carl picked up the gift and looked at the design on the carton.

"Belgium chocolates," he said with a smile. He resisted the temptation to shake the box.

"Our last mission together. Mon Dieu...it was a long time ago," lamented André, his French accent seemingly stronger.

"It was indeed," said Rick.

"By the way, whatever happened to the lovely Ms. Petrov?" asked André.

"She's here with us. She and Lynn will be joining us for dinner," said Carl.

"Wonderful. And if I remember correctly, Lynn is your wife, n'est-ce pas?" said André, looking over to Rick.

"You have a good memory," answered Rick.

"Some things you don't forget. And what about you, Carl? Non Madame Peterson?"

"Not yet. I'm still looking for the right one," answered Carl.

"Well, you had better hurry. You're not getting any younger my friend. My advice to you is to find one that can cook...they can all make love mon ami," said André with a smile.

They all had a good laugh.

"A toast to good cooks everywhere," said Rick as they touched glasses.

"I don't seem to remember Cerise," said Carl, knowing perfectly well that she was not André's wife.

"Ah, that is because she is about to become my second wife. It was Claudette that you probably remember."

"It was indeed Claudette," responded Carl.

"Claudette is with the Lord," said André solemnly, as he lifted his glass high over his head in a gesture of salute.

"I'm sorry to hear that. When did she pass away?" asked Carl.

"Oh, don't be sorry. She didn't *die!*" he exclaimed. "She ran off with Lord Kensington," he added, pronouncing each syllable distinctly.

André smiled broadly. They all laughed enthusiastically at André's revelation. They finished their drinks and ordered another round.

"Frankly, it was difficult at first. But now, I find it quite amusing to tell everyone that she is with the Lord. I love their reaction when I finish the story. Truly tears of joy."

"And Cerise has wiped away the tears," said Carl.

"Completely," confirmed André.

The lounge was nearly full when Lynn and Ann made their way toward the end of the bar where *the boys* were telling stories. Carlos was first to notice them as several men turned to check them out. Lynn and Ann paid the voyeurs no attention.

"The ladies are here," announced Carlos as he stood up to greet Ann.

"Oh mon Dieu, they are beautiful," exclaimed André, as he kissed the ends of the fingers on his right hand.

Carlos hugged Ann as Rick introduced Lynn to André.

"Rick, she is beautiful," said André as he hugged Lynn and kissed her on both cheeks. "You're a lucky man, Rick Morgan," he added with a smile.

"And Anya. What can I say? You are as beautiful as ever."

André hugged her and kissed her on both cheeks. He was about to say something when he looked over at Carlos.

"Oh, mon Dieu. How foolish of me. I must be getting old. You are *that* Carlos, n'est-ce pas?"

"It was a long time ago," said Carlos as he put his arm around Ann and kissed her on the cheek.

"I believe our table is ready," said Carl as he noticed the maitre d' approaching.

As they proceeded onto the terrace, André leaned toward Carl.

"We can talk after dinner," he whispered.

CHAPTER THIRTY-FIVE

Makassar Lounge
Day 14
2115 Hours

Cerise Renaud purposely didn't make eye contact or return any of the smiles as she entered the lounge area. She presented a striking pose as she hesitated momentarily while looking for the entrance to the terrace. A server went past her with tray overhead. She followed close behind. She moved gracefully through the lounge. Her low-cut black evening dress seemed alive as it tried to cling to her in all the right places, only to fall off and start all over again with each step. She wore a small cross, adorned in diamonds, suspended from a silver necklace. Her earrings were modest and sparkled in the light that was purposefully dimmed in order to foster a romantic atmosphere. She carried a silver clutch in her left hand. Her hair was swept up into a twist that was complemented by a black bow that had been fashioned from the same material as her dress. For having worked all day, she looked quite refreshed.

Everyone at the table stood as André introduced his angel to Lynn, Ann and Carlos. She had already met Carl and Rick and was still wondering who they really were...and what their connection was to André. Why were they here after all these years? Her guarded expression confirmed that her suspicions had not been satisfied. Unfortunately, André still referred to Ann as Anya Petrov, thus adding to the mystery. It might have been better if he had introduced her by her adopted name, Ann. Cerise smiled as she shook each of their hands.

"I remember you two," she said in near perfect English as she looked at the girls. There was only a hint of a French accent. Cerise was most certainly from a family of stature and means. In fact, she had attended finishing school in England.

Her comment surprised Ann and Lynn as well as André.

"You peeked into my shop," she said before they had a chance to respond. "I was with a customer."

"Which shop?" asked Ann.

"Sephora," responded Cerise.

Sephora was one of Lynn's favorites.

"We were on a mission," said Lynn in defense, as she looked over at Rick.

Rick smiled. No one said anything for several long seconds.

"I do the same," admitted Cerise. "So how do you like Paris?" she asked, temporarily breaking the ice.

"We have only been on the Champs-Élysées," answered Lynn.

"Oh...there is so much more to see in Paris," consoled Cerise. "How long will you be staying?"

"Unfortunately, we have business in Cannes," said Carl. "Maybe when it's over, we can come back and spend a few days," he added.

"And what is it that you do?" asked Cerise pointedly. She was direct and was still looking for answers.

"What do you say we order some dessert," interrupted André, trying to change the subject in an attempt to rescue Carl. It only intensified Cerise's desire for answers.

Carl smiled and leaned forward. He knew that he needed to provide a response to comfort Cerise's legitimate concerns. Otherwise the night would be long and cold.

"Right now, I am...or I should say, *we*," said Carl with a sweep of his hand to include Rick, Ann and Carlos, "are working for a client whose granddaughter has been captured by Somali pirates. We're working to secure her safe release," answered Carl.

He maintained eye contact. Her reaction was somewhat predictable.

"And they are holding her where?" asked Cerise.

"In Somalia, but the key to her release is being held by a person of interest in Cannes," answered Carl.

"In Cannes?" she repeated, not intending it to be another question. She looked over at André.

"It's complicated my angel. When it's all over, I'm sure that Carl will be more than happy to let us know the outcome."

Cerise smiled and leaned back in her chair. She crossed her arms in front of her body. It was a classic defensive posture.

"And my André has information concerning the pirates?" she asked as she glanced over at André.

"We believe that André has some information about our person of interest. Information that we believe will help us with the negotiation process," offered Rick.

The explanation seemed to satisfy Cerise's curiosity. She was well aware who André's employer was, but she had absolutely no idea what his past job description entailed. For that matter, she was not fully aware of his present role. But she was very much aware of the fact that André was about to retire, and she didn't want anything to jeopardize his decision, or their future together. She looked over at André, put her hand on his, and smiled. It appeared that she was satisfied with Rick's answer...at least for the time being.

Rick looked over at Lynn and then at Cerise. When women become more mature, security becomes a priority. And when they are secure in their relationship, everything else falls neatly into place. He certainly understood Cerise's concerns and her desire for candid answers. Even after all these years, Lynn still wanted a full explanation of what Rick was doing, where he was going, and most importantly, when he would return.

"Cerise, would you like something from the menu?" asked Carl.

"I'm fine. Maybe a little dessert when you are ready to order," she answered.

"Angel, will you be so kind to excuse us while we go over a few things? It shouldn't take too long," asked André as he kissed her on the hand. "You understand. Je t'aime ma chérie," he added with a child-like expression that was hard for her to resist.

"Does anyone need to go to the restroom?" asked Lynn as she stood up.

"I'll join you," said Ann. "Cerise?"

"That sounds good," agreed a reserved Cerise.

She's still not sure, Rick thought to himself as the girls stood up.

"We'll find a spot in the lounge. You ladies enjoy the comfort of the terrace. Enjoy dessert. André is right, we won't be long. I promise," insisted Carl.

The men went into the lounge. Well-dressed middle-aged women occupied most of the seats at the bar. Several men stood by hoping to engage them in meaningless conversation. It wasn't clear if any of the men were actually with any of the women, although a couple of the men seemed to have hit pay dirt. The scene reminded Carl of the night he met Ronnie Lake. He realized how intriguing she was…and how much he had enjoyed his dream the night before.

André looked around the lounge. There were only three empty tables. He pointed to one that was furthest from the bar. As soon as they were seated, a female server came by and placed little white circular napkins in front of each of them. André and Rick ordered a Crown Royal on the rocks. Carlos ordered his usual, a Modello Especial, and Carl ordered his favorite, a Napoleon brandy. He asked for a heated snifter.

"That is the only way we serve it at the Renaissance," snipped the server as she turned and headed for the bar. She had obviously had a long unrewarding night. Unfortunately, Carl was the recipient of her frustrations.

"So tell me about Jean Gendreau?" asked André as he opened his attaché case and removed a brown manila folder with no markings. It was at least an inch thick.

"I was on a mission to the Sudan back in the eighties. Gendreau was an officer in the French Foreign Legion. Without going into a lot of boring detail, suffice it to say, I didn't approve of his tactical methods. Consequently, I wrote a scathing report, which resulted in him losing his commission and being mustered out of the Legion," said Carl.

"Mustered out?" repeated André. "He must have been an extraordinarily bad character to be thrown out of the French Foreign Legion," he added as he looked at Rick and Carlos for confirmation.

"Well, he was that indeed. I believe he went back to Canada. Several years later, I heard that he was killed in an automobile accident. However, that information proved to be wrong," said Carl.

"Or contrived," added Rick.

André listened intently but didn't say anything as Carl continued.

"One of my people discovered that Gendreau had assumed a new identity altogether. Jean Gendreau and Patrice Boucher are one in the same."

"And when did this happen?" asked André.

"Nineteen ninety-two," answered Carl.

André looked a bit perplexed.

"And where did they find that information?" asked André as he leaned forward placing both elbows on the table. He rested his chin on folded hands. He was sure that he knew the answer to his question. He wasn't sure if he wanted to hear the answer.

"The Interpol database," answered Carl.

André shook his head. His unspoken assumption was correct.

"Of course. It amazes me that the data can be so...flawed," said André, searching for the right word.

"The data is what it is," said Rick. "It all depends on how good your data entry people are, and whether or not they are entering the data under the guidance and feedback of the field agents."

"Obviously they're not as good as they used to be," said André.

"And they probably never were," remarked Carlos.

"If you had gone forward with the name, Jean Gendreau, you would have discovered that he was killed in a car wreck in Ottawa. The people who created his new identity were professionals. Unless you really knew what you were looking for, there was no way that you would have stumbled onto the fact that Gendreau was Patrice Boucher," said Rick without going into too much detail.

"So simple to just die and start over again," confessed André.

André was about to continue when the server arrived with the drinks. She served Carl last. Her expression confirmed that, for whatever reason, she really didn't like Carl. The others noticed her obvious dislike for him. When she left, André was first to speak.

"You can make it up to her with a nice tip."

"Fat chance," quipped Carl. His expression confirmed that she wouldn't be getting anything from Carl Peterson. The only tip she would get from him would be verbal.

"So what can you tell us about Patrice Boucher?" asked Carl.

"Boucher is somewhat of a rogue. When he first came to France, he bought into a partnership with a fellow by the name of Laurent Duval. Duval and his wife, Melanie, were the owners of a large marina on the Riviera. It was strategically located between Nice and Cannes. Duval was quite the businessman. He was one of the few licensed Beneteau sailboat dealers in all of France. In fact, he became a leading broker for Beneteau. And, as you may know, Beneteau is considered to be one of the best sailboats for sailing around the world. Duval had a real niche."

"It is indeed. In fact, my client's granddaughter purchased a Beneteau from a broker in Saint Lucia," remarked Carl.

"Interesting," responded André. "Duval had several brokers throughout the world," he added. "Anyway, within a couple of years, Boucher and Duval had a falling out of sorts. Duval and his wife decided to take a short sabbatical and sailed out into the Mediterranean on their way to Barcelona. Several weeks later, their sailboat was found adrift south of Palma de Mallorca. Duval and his wife were not aboard...and they were never found."

André swirled the Crown Royal around in the glass and then took a healthy swallow. He studied the glass for several seconds.

"And the authorities suspected foul play?" asked Rick.

"No...not at first, but Duval and his wife were considered to be well-experienced sailors. To somehow be swept overboard seemed out of the question," responded André.

"That would seem to me to be the very reason to investigate," said Rick.

"You are obviously correct. The authorities began the usual inquiries. Part of their investigation led them to Palma de Mallorca. Duval and his wife had stopped there for a few days, made some acquaintances, and left for Barcelona with another sailboat following close behind. The investigators discovered that the two men on the sailboat were of questionable character; although, they couldn't prove anything. It was discovered later that the men knew Patrice Boucher."

"Did they question the men?" asked Rick.

"They did, but they claimed that their only connection to Boucher was through the purchase of a sailboat."

"How convenient," commented Carl. "So was Boucher ever considered a real suspect?"

"Well, he ended up with everything. A partnership is a lot like a marriage…with different benefits. So he was indeed a prime suspect," said André as he finished his drink.

Rick signaled the server and ordered another Crown Royal and one Modello Especial for Carlos.

"So I take it there was no hard evidence?" asked Rick.

"No evidence, and the boat was fairly clean," said André.

"Could the weather have been a factor?" asked Carlos.

"The weather was a bit rough but nothing that an experienced sailor couldn't handle," answered André. "The sailboat they were on could have been easily handled by one sailor."

"Where was Boucher when they went missing?" asked Carl.

"He was in Cannes," answered André.

"Maybe it was a coincidence," commented Carlos.

"A coincidence that benefited Patrice Boucher quite handsomely," responded André.

"Did he have other acquaintances?" asked Rick.

"Just about everything that I have on Boucher is here in this folder," said André as he pushed it over toward Carl.

Carl lifted it as if he were checking its weight. He handed it to Rick.

"And why did the DGSE take an interest in him?" asked Carl.

"He came under our radar a few years ago due to his dealings with the Russians," added André.

"Are we talking the Russian mob?" asked Rick.

"No, not initially. Actually, he had dealings with a Russian oil company that was looking to do some drilling off the north coast of

Cuba. Zarubezhneft, I believe is the correct pronunciation. It's all there in the material," said André pointing to the folder.

"Cuba? What was his connection to Cuba?" asked Rick.

"It appears that Boucher had some connections in Cuba, and in particular with a close friend of Raul Castro's by the name of Eduardo Peña. Boucher had met Peña in Montreal. As it turns out, Peña controlled Cuba's oil leases in the Gulf of Mexico. Voilà...the connection," explained André. "Not only that, Peña happens to be related to Rafael Ramirez who served as the Venezuelan Minister of Energy. When it comes to oil, everyone seems to be related."

As André continued his short brief, Rick opened the folder and began to thumb through the material. A page of known associates caught his eye. There were several names on the list. One name in particular caught his attention. He pushed the folder toward Carl and put his finger under the name.

Carl looked at the name for several seconds and then interrupted André.

"Son of a bitch. Osman Mohamed Ali," exclaimed Carl.

"Higgins' man, Ozzie," confirmed Rick.

CHAPTER THIRTY-SIX
Renaissance Paris Arc de Triomphe Hotel
Day 15
0900 Hours

The meeting with André Marcelles had lasted a lot longer than Rick and Carl had anticipated. The information provided by André confirmed Carl's suspicion that Boucher hadn't changed at all. He was still a villain. Both Rick and Carl were convinced that whatever Boucher wanted from Carl, it probably had something to do with oil.

Following the discussion, the ladies joined then in the lounge area where they continued to enjoy a few more drinks and light conversation. They finally said their goodnights well after one in the morning with a sincere promise to meet when the mission was over. Lynn could hardly keep her eyes open. On the way up to the room, she told Rick that in the morning, she would tell him about her conversation with Cerise. She said that she had a lot to tell him. Lynn could always sleep like a baby and was sound asleep by the time Rick finished brushing his teeth.

At 0900 hours, the team met in the restaurant as planned. Ann and Carlos were already on their second cup of coffee and enjoying the continental breakfast when Rick and Lynn arrived. Carl was right behind them. He was stepping lively as he tried to catch them before they got to the table. He almost made it. As soon as they sat down, a server was there with three menus and a carafe of hot coffee.

"So, how did it go with Ms. Renaud last evening?" asked Carl as he added cream to his cup.

"She's very..." Lynn hesitated as she was searching for the right word to describe Cerise.

"French," declared Rick, completing her thought and finishing her sentence.

"French. That she is, but we like her in spite of her heritage," said Lynn, looking over at Ann.

"Actually, she warmed up quite a bit. And she really knows the shops on the Champs-Élysées," said Ann.

"Especially the ones that offer the best deals," said Lynn.

"It appears that her feelings for André are genuine," offered Rick. Lynn had debriefed him earlier.

"She is deeply in love with André, and she is quite protective of him," said Ann as she squeezed Carlos's left arm. Both Ann and Lynn knew what it was like to care deeply and to have a man who returned the affection.

"Good for her," said Carl.

"And guess where she's from?" asked Lynn.

"I have no idea," answered Carl.

"And neither do I," said Rick, quite surprised that Lynn left out a piece of information during her debrief.

"She's from Dijon. Do you know what Dijon is known for?" asked Lynn.

"Mustard," blurted out Carlos without looking up from his sweet roll. Carlos was a man of few words.

"That's right, but did you know that Dijon is located in Burgundy, which is one of France's main wine producing areas. Her family is in the wine business. They have one of the largest vineyards in all of France," announced Lynn.

"Nice. So she knows her wines...or should I say grapes," said Carl.

"Not only that, she knows the wine business," said Lynn.

"So what did you learn?" asked Rick.

"We learned that the best French white wines are made exclusively from Chardonnay grapes," said Lynn with a nod of her head. "Oh, and guess what?" she asked before anyone could ask another question. "She is an only child," said Lynn answering her own question.

"So she could, or will, inherit all of it," said Carl.

"That she will," confirmed Lynn.

"I guess we know where André will be living when he retires," added Carl.

"A vineyard has always been one of Rick's secret dreams," confided Lynn.

"Is that true Rick?" asked Carl.

"I've always been fascinated with the whole wine making process," responded Rick.

"You realize Virginia has some very good vineyards. Maybe we should look into buying one," said Carl. His expression indicated that he was quite serious.

"So how long do you ladies need on the Champs-Élysées?" asked Carl.

"Not long at all," said Ann. "Cerise helped us narrow our targets to just a couple of shops. Let us know when you want to head out," said Ann.

"Let's be ready to leave the hotel by 1600 hours. Will that give you enough time?" asked Carl.

Ann looked over at Lynn.

"That'll be fine," responded Lynn as she got up and kissed Rick on the cheek.

Carl leaned over toward Lynn trying to solicit a kiss on his cheek as well.

"Yeah right," she said with a smile as she patted him on the shoulder. Ann kissed Carlos and then kissed Carl on the forehead as the girls smiled and headed out.

"See, she really doesn't like me," said Carl, looking over at Rick. He feigned a hurt expression.

"She just knows how to pull your chain," responded Rick as he signaled the server for more coffee. Carlos was already in the process of selecting another sweet roll from what was left of the once impressive assortment.

"Higgins has no idea that his man, Ozzie, is on Boucher's payroll," said Carl.

"What about Harriet?" asked Carlos.

"Mohammed Yusef was not on the list. But he could be working both sides of the harbor," answered Rick.

"We need to treat both of them as hostiles," said Carlos.

"I really need to give Higgins a call," said Carl as he pulled his satellite phone from his belt and looked around the room. "I should probably give Blackwell a call for that matter," he added as he looked at his watch. "Way too early for Blackwell," he said under his breath.

Roy Higgins was sitting in his Combat Information Center at Camp Lemonnier. He had all the equipment up and running. The pirates' mother ship was clearly visible in the center of the large screen that was the focal point of the room. The resolution was good enough to count the number of AK-47 magazines each pirate carried. Another monitor was set to a much larger scale. A Saudi tanker was about four hours southwest of the Seychelles.

Shaun Spencer had fallen asleep. The Saudi tanker schedule was on his lap and about to fall on the floor. Higgins had several documents spread out on the conference table and was holding an area map that was folded in half when his phone rang. From his expression, it was obvious that he wasn't in the mood for a phone call. He considered ignoring it until he noticed that the call was from Carl Peterson.

"Morning Carl," he answered. He sounded tired, and he was.

"Roy, we were just thinking about you guys. How are things going?"

"Going well. Getting ready for another escort mission. I'll be sending the guys out in a couple of hours. How about you? How did your meeting go with your friend?"

"It went very well. André had quite a bit of information on Boucher. By the way, he provided a folder with information that included a list of Boucher's known associates."

"I assume that LaPointe was on the list," said Higgins as he continued to look over the area map.

"He was indeed…as was Osman Mohamed Ali," said Carl after a short pause.

That revelation got Higgins' full attention. He put the map down, sat back in the chair, and didn't say anything for a minute or so. Carl didn't interrupt the silence. He certainly knew what must have been going through Roy's mind.

"You're absolutely sure it's *my* Ali?" asked Roy, hoping that it could have been a mistake. "So many of the Somali names are similar. A minor lapse in attention, or a simple transposition, could easily result in a wrong name being entered. You know the saying, 'garbage in, garbage out,'" he rationalized.

"There's no mistake," confirmed Carl.

"What about Yusef?"

"His name was not on the list," responded Carl.

Higgins remained silent for several long seconds. Carl could hear him fidgeting with his pencil. He was expecting to hear it snap.

"I would never have suspected that Ali was dirty. Yusef possibly... but not Ali," said Higgins. The tone of his voice indicated that he was very disappointed with the prospect that Ali was a double agent. Ali's loyalty had never once crossed his mind.

"Maybe the command will let you question LaPointe again," offered Carl.

"I can try, but I doubt they'll let me within a mile of him," answered Roy. "Are you in Cannes?" he asked, taking a deep breath that Carl could hear. Carl sensed that Higgins needed some time to consider the whole Ali situation.

"Not yet. We'll be leaving this afternoon. I'll keep in touch."

"Talk with you later," said Higgins.

Carl put down his phone. He felt a slight twinge for Roy Higgins. Finding out that one of your people isn't who you think they are, is always discomforting. Unfortunately, when dealing with locals, ideology and money are in a constant battle. Money usually wins the war.

"How'd he take the news?" asked Rick.

"As you can imagine, he's disappointed. Said that it wouldn't have surprised him if Yusef was dirty but not Ali."

"Hell, Ali is related to the President of Puntland. I can understand Higgins' surprise," said Rick.

The server returned with fresh coffee and a few more rolls—rolls that weren't needed. Carlos already had three and was eyeing the replacements.

"I went over most of the material that André provided. Looks like the deal that Boucher tried to set up with the Cubans turned out to be a scam," said Rick.

"Boucher tried to scam the Russians? I know that he's crazy, but I didn't think he was stupid," said Carl.

"There's a fine line between stupid and crazy," offered Carlos.

"Actually, from the information, it would be easy to conclude that Boucher was the one who got scammed," said Rick.

"Did Boucher take money from the Russians?" asked Carl.

"Ten million to grease the skids in Cuba," responded Rick.

"Ten million…and the deal didn't happen?" asked Carl.

"It didn't."

Carl didn't say anything for a few minutes as he selected a sweet role from the fresh assortment.

"Is it possible that the Russians suspect that Boucher was part of the scam?" asked Carl.

"It's certainly possible. And they might even suspect that he orchestrated it," said Rick.

"If he did, he's got some cojones," said Carlos.

"It appears the Russians have been leaning on him ever since. One way or the other, they're going to get their money back," said Rick.

"So Tony was right. The goons are definitely Russian. We're just not sure if they are Russian oil, government or mafia," said Carl.

"Whoever they represent, you can bet they are there to make sure that Boucher doesn't disappear," said Rick.

"Maybe the Russian government has made a deal with the mob to get their money back," said Carl.

"And the mob gets something in return for their…help," said Rick.

"Ann will be able to determine who these guys are and who they're representing," said Carlos.

"And more importantly, who we're up against," said Rick.

"It wouldn't be the first time that a government partnered with the mob," said Carl. "Kennedy teamed up with Trafficante in the early sixties trying to get to Castro."

"And at the same time, Bobby Kennedy was going after the mob," added Rick.

"And look how that turned out," said Carlos.

Cannes, France
1800 Hours

Since the runway at Mandelieu Airport in Cannes was not long enough to accommodate Carl's Gulfstream IV, Captain Somerville landed the aircraft at Côte d'Azur Airport in Nice. The flight took a little over an hour. During the short drive to Cannes, Carl called JT Blackwell and gave him an update. Carl purposely didn't tell Blackwell where they were or that he was on his way to confront Patrice Boucher. He felt that the less Blackwell knew about the team's real plans, the better. Blackwell was still concerned that the negotiation process seemed to have stalled. Carl assured him that everything was going according to his plan. Blackwell accepted Carl's update, but from the tone of his voice, it was clear that Blackwell was concerned with the perceived lack of progress.

The security at the Carlton was exactly as Tony Ramos had indicated. It was clear that the jewel heist hadn't been solved. Why the French felt that it was necessary to maintain security after the fact, was not clear...unless there was something else in the hotel that was extremely valuable.

Lynn and Ann went through the metal detectors first, followed by Carlos, Rick and Carl. The bags were scanned and taken by the bellhops. Carl, Rick and Carlos proceeded to the check-in counter. Lynn and Ann took a seat in the lobby. Tony Ramos was sitting and reading the *London Times*. He saw them when they entered the hotel, but he purposely didn't make eye contact.

"Let's plan on dinner in about an hour," said Carl.

"If your friend, Boucher, is on a short leash, you might run in to him," reminded Rick.

"Did you notice Tony sitting in the lobby?" asked Carl.

"I did."

"When I get up to the room, I'll give him a call and have him give us a heads-up when he spots Boucher. I really want to surprise that asshole," said Carl.

"Why don't I just get a table for four," said Rick. "You may want to hang out in the lounge. Might just surprise him there," added Rick.

"That's a good idea," responded Carl.

Carl was sitting at the bar when Tony called.

"Boucher is on the way—goons in tow. Looks like he's heading for the lounge."

"Thanks Tony," said Carl as he used the mirror behind the bar to watch the entrance.

Patrice Boucher entered the lounge area and selected a table for four next to the wall. He went over, sat down, and ordered a dry martini. The two goons took a seat at the bar and ordered vodka tonics. Carl ordered another drink. He sat there momentarily, waiting for the bartender. He watched Boucher in the mirror. The goons seemed to ignore Boucher. When the bartender delivered the drink, Carl slid off the stool, and without hesitation, walked directly to Boucher's table. He pulled out a chair and sat down directly across from Boucher. Boucher seemed a bit startled at first and then regained his composure.

"Carl Peterson," he said with a moderate French accent.

Carl didn't say anything as he looked intently at Patrice Boucher. Boucher looked around the room and then back at Carl.

"I must have died and gone to hell."

CHAPTER THIRTY-SEVEN
InterContinental Carlton Cannes Hotel
Day 15
1900 Hours

Carl Peterson and Patrice Boucher just stared at each other for several long uncomfortable minutes. The mutual dislike for one another was obvious, even to the casual observer. The Russians at the bar immediately took notice of the stranger who pulled out a chair and sat down across from Boucher. One of them stood up and was about to go over to the table, when the other one grabbed him by the arm. He said something in Russian, which caused the big guy to sit back down. They had a few words and then were silent. They just watched from their stools at the bar. Tony Ramos had already come into the lounge and had taken a seat several feet from where Carl had been sitting. Carl's tab was still resting in the clip holder next to an empty glass. The bartender knew where Carl was.

Carlos came in and sat at the far end of the bar where he had a good view of all the players. He ordered a scotch on the rocks and pretended to take a swallow. He then stirred the drink more than need be as he watched the Russians. Carlos and Tony didn't make eye contact or acknowledge each other's presence. They were there just in case all hell broke loose. Knowing Carl's temperament and his professed dislike for Jean Gendreau, an altercation was not out of the question.

"So, what is it that you want from me?" asked Carl directly as he leaned in toward Boucher. His voice was calm and controlled.

Patrice Boucher leaned back in his chair. He wasn't ready for Carl to invade is personal space. A wry smile crossed his face.

"After all these years, not even a 'how do you do?'" said Boucher.

"How the fuck are you, asshole," obliged Carl.

"I guess that is better than nothing."

"I had heard that you were dead," said Carl.

"Tsk, tsk. And now you know differently. You look disappointed."

"I am disappointed…very much so," responded Carl. "I had heard you were killed in a car wreck in Ottawa. I liked you much better dead," he added.

"I had some unfinished business in Ottawa…thanks to you," said Boucher.

"Thanks to me?" questioned Carl.

Carl searched his memory for a minute or so. In the back of his mind he remembered an event that, at the time, made him think of Jean Gendreau. The memory surfaced.

"The attack on al-Turabi? That was your doing?" asked Carl.

Boucher smiled and leaned in toward Carl.

"He was not a good man. He held back the Sudan. Look where they are today. If you hadn't interfered, things for the Sudanese might have been much different."

"*Might* being the operative word. So your solution was to hire someone to nearly beat him to death?"

"He was supposed to beat him to death. I guess a coma is just about as good," said Boucher.

"And what did it accomplish? Where are the changes?"

"You Americans never learn. You can't make one statement and expect immediate changes. It takes several sentences to form a paragraph and many paragraphs to make a chapter. The book on the Sudan is still in work," said Boucher, defending his position.

"There are better ways to make a point, and certainly better ways to influence a culture that is centuries old," offered Carl.

"And you think your methods have worked in Iraq, Afghanistan, Egypt…Syria? The Brits tried it. Look where they are today."

"It can work with the right diplomacy," answered Carl.

Boucher laughed and sat back in his chair.

"Diplomacy is a joke. These people only understand strength and brutality."

"You would have killed them all," responded Carl.

"And what did God tell the Israelis when they went into battle? Be nice, be compassionate…no, he said kill them all, including all their animals. Leave nothing alive. Take no prisoners. They didn't obey, and look what they have gone through. You think the Holocaust was an accident?"

"You're not God," responded Carl.

"And you're still a fucking boy scout. You probably still help old ladies cross the street," said Boucher smugly.

"In the long term, our ideology will prevail," said Carl.

"You won't live that long. You didn't even recognize me at the Steinbrenner conference...and I stood right next to you," said Boucher, changing the subject slightly. "I could have stuck a blade into your bleeding heart. How soon we forget our friends."

"You are not my friend. Besides, since I thought you were dead, I wouldn't have expected to see you there. What is it that you want?" said Carl, raising his voice slightly.

Carl was tired of playing cat and mouse with Boucher. He would never agree with Boucher's philosophy or methods. There was no way that Boucher would convince Carl otherwise.

"You know...when I saw the name Carl Peterson on the conference list, I couldn't resist the temptation of traveling to New York. It was an added benefit that the conference addressed all the latest methods to combat piracy.

"Piracy—something you certainly know quite a bit about," said Carl.

"How ironic, wouldn't you say. I must thank you again for giving me the opportunity to make that lucrative career change," said Boucher. "And now you have to deal with me," he added with a forced smile.

"What is it that you want?" asked Carl for the third time. He knew the game Boucher was playing. Boucher was trying to control the conversation by frustrating Carl to the point of anger. Carl wouldn't fall for that old trick.

"My initial plan was to just show up and confront you...but I had the fortunate opportunity of meeting Mr. Blackwell. As fate would have it, his granddaughter was in the market for a sailboat—one that was capable of sailing around the world."

"And there you were, a pirate in the sailboat business," said Carl. "And you just happened to have the perfect boat moored in Saint Lucia. Had you planned on selling her a new one, or the same one you sold to the Coughlins?" asked Carl, trying to turn the conversation in his direction.

"Ah yes, the Coughlins. I see you have done your homework," responded Boucher.

"You are so predictable," said Carl as he took a sip of his dry martini.

"Then you should know that I mean business."

Carl leaned back in the chair, swirled the glass carefully in his right hand, and took another swallow.

"Did your friend at MI6 fill you in?" asked Boucher, letting Carl know that he was aware of his relationship with Sims.

"What is it that you want from me?" asked Carl for the fourth time. "I'm not going to ask you again," he promised.

"Maybe you should be asking me what *I can do for you*," said Boucher smugly.

Carl didn't want to lose any advantage he had just gained by issuing his ultimatum. Carl knew down deep inside that as far as Courtney Evans was concerned, Boucher did have the upper hand at this point. He hated playing games with Boucher, but the only road to Courtney Evans passed through Boucher's backyard.

"And what can you do for me?" asked Carl reluctantly.

"I can guarantee safe passage for Ms. Evans and her three friends," answered Boucher. "And it won't cost you or Blackwell a dime," he added with a sinister smile.

I can't believe this prick has gotten the upper hand again, Carl thought to himself. However, he needed to play along. Getting Courtney and her friends safely out of Somalia was his priority, and Boucher knew it.

"What if I don't want to play your little game?" asked Carl.

"Then Blackwell will never see his granddaughter again," responded Boucher unemotionally. "You think you and your team can just waltz into Somalia, shoot a few skinnies, and walk out with Ms.

Evans and her friends? I suspect your people are good, but they're not that good. Short of a full blown military operation, you don't have a chance in hell of even finding them, let alone extracting them safely."

"So this whole thing is really about you and me," said Carl.

"It always has been. I just needed the right vehicle. Quite frankly in the beginning, I just wanted a piece of you. I would have been quite satisfied with beating the shit out of you, but I find myself in a situation where we can both gain something for our mutual cooperation."

"Does your situation have anything to do with the two Russian goons sitting up there at the bar watching us in the mirror?" asked Carl.

Boucher smiled and signaled the server. He ordered a refill and another martini for Carl.

"They do stand out, don't they?" said Boucher. "Let's just say that I had a deal with the Russians that didn't go quite as well as I had planned."

"The Cuban deal," said Carl. It wasn't meant to be a question.

"My, my…you *have* done your homework. So how much do you know?" asked Boucher.

"Enough to know that the Russians are never going to let you off the hook."

"That may be. And now they're wondering who this fellow is talking with Patrice Boucher. Do you think for one minute that you and your friend, Carlos over there, can handle them? They were both Spetsnaz combat training instructors, then they were KGB."

"Were KGB?" interrupted Carl. "So who do they work for now? Are they connected with the Russian mob?"

"To whom they are connected is irrelevant," said Boucher.

"So what do you owe them?" asked Carl.

"That doesn't matter."

"If you want…or I should say need, my help, I want to know right here and right now what my people are up against…or I'm walking away."

"The boy scout is walking away," mocked Boucher. "And what about your commitment to Blackwell…you're just going to give up on Ms. Evans? Say what you will, but we both know that is just not your style, now is it?" said Boucher as he finished his first drink.

Carl knew that Boucher was right. Carl would never walk away from a commitment. He was about to say something when Boucher continued.

"Actually, my dealings with the Russians began as a legitimate venture. The Russians wanted a stake in the drilling operations off the north coast of Cuba. I had a contact that supposedly controlled the leasing operation. He said that he could guarantee several of the high probability sites."

"And of course for that guarantee, there would be a fee," said Carl.

"I gave him ten million dollars to guarantee the leases."

"You mean the Russians gave you the ten million."

"True," said Boucher.

"And your contact disappeared and left you holding the bag with the Russians," said Carl.

Carl couldn't help but think that what goes around comes around.

"That's it. Simple as that," said Boucher.

Carl sat back and nursed his drink. Surprisingly, Boucher still seemed to be in control of his own situation. The only reason Boucher was still alive was because he owed the Russians ten million dollars. For that amount, they would tolerate his excuses and give him an opportunity to return their investment. How long they would give him that opportunity was questionable.

"So you think I can help you out of your situation?" asked Carl. "I don't see that happening."

"I convinced the Russians that I could pay them back...with interest."

Carl didn't like where the conversation was heading. The last thing he and Rick wanted to do was get involved with the Russian mob. They were a very unforgiving bunch. But they weren't as bad as the Serbs.

"You obviously have a plan in mind," said Carl.

"Your friend Higgins has a nice deal with the Saudis," said Boucher. It almost sounded like a question.

Carl had no problem considering a deal with Boucher in order to secure the release of Courtney Evans. However, in good conscience, he would not entertain any thoughts of involving Roy Higgins.

"Whatever you are planning, Higgins is off-limits," said Carl sternly. "Off-limits," he repeated.

"It's the only way you'll ever get Ms. Evans back...in one piece!" exclaimed Boucher.

"You could get your ten million out of Blackwell," said Carl.

"It's not that simple. The Russians aren't going to let me off the hook that easily, and I couldn't let you off the hook even if I wanted to. You're in this if you like it or not."

Carl thought about just walking away. However, Boucher had him by the short hairs, and he knew it. The son of a bitch had gotten them all in the Russian mob's crosshairs.

"So what do you think my team can provide to salvage your miserable life?" asked Carl.

"It's simple...I want you to hijack a supertanker."

CHAPTER THIRTY-EIGHT
InterContinental Carlton Cannes Hotel
Day 15
2000 Hours

Carl joined Rick, Lynn and Ann in the dining room. He ordered another drink and informed the server that he had started a tab at the bar. The server said that he would take care of it. Rick was anxious to hear about Carl's confrontation with Boucher. Another server appeared with a chair in hand and quickly set a new place at the table. Carl forced a smile and sat down. He had a look of frustration on his face that wasn't going away soon. His expression spoke volumes.

It was rare for Carl to be frustrated, let alone show it. Carl had always been a cool customer. Rick didn't push him for any information. Carl would be forthcoming when he was ready. Besides, Rick didn't want to discuss details in front of Lynn. She would only worry and have a million questions.

Carlos was close behind. On his way past the two Russians, he purposely went well out of his way to bump into the larger of the two, just for the hell of it. It wasn't a casual brushing—it was obviously a deliberate encounter. Carlos could feel the Russian's shoulder holster. They immediately made eye contact. The larger Russian had one eyebrow that needed trimming.

"You'll need it," said Carlos as he slapped the Russian's weapon with the back of his hand.

The Russian didn't respond. The muscles on the sides of his face twitched involuntarily, broadcasting his extreme displeasure. He wasn't used to being on the receiving end of a threat, especially from a guy smaller than he. Both Russians stared intently at Carlos. Carlos smiled and said something in Spanish that the Russians didn't understand. The tone of his comment suggested that he had no respect for either of them, or their supposed prowess. Just because they were big and ugly, didn't mean they were tough. Carlos had just thrown down the gauntlet. The Russians snickered in return. All knew that they would meet another day.

One of the Russians wrote something on a napkin and showed it to his comrade.

"Maricone?" he questioned.

Neither of them knew what it meant. They wouldn't be happy when they found out. Carlos had a big smile on his face as he walked away and headed for the restaurant.

Tony Ramos had been watching from the far end of the bar. He had reached over and retrieved a small paring knife that was resting next to a bowl filled with sliced lemons. He felt the tip. It was sharp. The blade was dull, but it would do. Tony was prepared to back up Carlos in the event the Russians decided to take him up on his unspoken challenge. Tony held the drink in front of his face with both hands and watched intently. He smiled to himself knowing that Carlos was itching to take the Russians down. He knew that Carlos could easily handle the Russians one at a time, but they were not known for fairness. This wasn't the movies. There was no script. No one would wait his turn.

Tony had watched as Carlos strategically placed himself in a position where the second Russian would have to move off the stool in order to get clear of his partner and be within range to deliver a blow. He would never get that chance. Carlos was good. He had been in this situation on many occasions. Certainly the Russians were sizing him up. If they were as good as they thought they were, they probably sensed that Carlos was no slouch. He knew what he was doing. Tony relaxed as Carlos went on his way without looking back. He took another drink of scotch and causally put the paring knife into his pocket.

"Are you up for some dinner?" asked Rick as he handed the menu to Carl. "We have already made our selection," added Rick, knowing that Lynn would most likely have a few questions for the server. Rick couldn't remember a time that Lynn didn't have questions in a restaurant.

Carl looked at the menu. It didn't take him long to select his favorite choice, chateaubriand…an end cut if possible. He closed the menu just as the server arrived with his third martini. Three drinks was his normal limit. Tonight would be an exception. Everyone ordered. Surprisingly, Lynn had only one question. Since Ann also spoke French, she had answered almost all of Lynn's questions concerning the fare.

Following dinner, Lynn excused herself. She knew that Rick was chomping at the bit to know what Carl and Patrice Boucher had discussed. Besides, it had been a rather long day, and she was ready for her nightly ritual. Rick watched as Lynn made her way through the restaurant. She looked back one time and smiled. Rick blew her a kiss.

"He's a real son of a bitch," said Carl as soon as Lynn was out of earshot.

"That bad, huh?" said Rick.

"Rick, you were right. This whole thing has been about me right from the very beginning," said Carl as he finished his martini. He held the glass in the air as if he were in an officers' club. It was a rude gesture, but at the moment, he felt like the proverbial ugly American.

The server sauntered over to the table and retrieved the empty glass. He didn't say anything. His expression said it all. Carl ordered a Modello Especial for Carlos and Napoleon brandies for him and Rick.

"Forgive my rudeness," he said as the server forced a smile and headed for the bar.

"I take it that you found out what he's after," said Rick.

"Oh yeah. I found out all right," responded Carl as he looked around the room.

Rick knew that Carl was saving the best for last.

"And the Russians? Are they part of it?" asked Rick.

"Seems he owes the Russians a hefty amount," said Carl.

"How hefty?" asked Carlos.

"Ten million," responded Carl matter-of-factly as the server approached with their drinks.

After the server left, Carl continued.

"Seems he tried to work a deal with the Cubans to secure some offshore oil leases. Long story short, the deal went south."

"Along with their ten million," said Ann.

"So Boucher got taken," smiled Carlos. "Karma," he added.

"That he did," responded Carl as he swirled the brandy in the snifter. He put the glass up to his nose and savored the fine aroma. "This is good stuff," he said as he took a drink.

"They're not going to let this guy off the hook," said Carlos.

"He's lucky they didn't take him out on a fishing trip," said Ann.

"Ten million is just enough to keep him alive. He's probably convinced them that he can pay them back," said Rick.

"He has a plan?" asked Ann.

"He does, and unfortunately, he's using Ms. Evans as leverage to get us to implement and execute his plan," said Carl.

"So what does he want us to do to solve his problem?" asked Rick.

"He wants us to hijack a supertanker," said Carl calmly as he took another drink from the snifter. He looked around the table.

Carlos nearly spit his beer out on the table. Some of it actually came out through his nose. He needed a napkin to wipe his shirt.

"Are you shitting me?" exclaimed Carlos as he checked his lap.

"That's precisely what he wants," said Carl.

Carl actually felt some relief after telling them what Patrice Boucher wanted. Carl went on and told them about his entire conversation. Rick didn't say anything as he listened intently. Carlos continued to dry his shirt. The server came by and handed him a dry napkin and another Modello.

"So what do you think?" asked Carl as he casually looked around the table.

"He's a real nut case if he thinks for one minute that we would even consider hijacking a supertanker," said Carlos.

Rick still didn't say anything. He appeared to be in deep thought.

"Rick, you haven't said a word," said Carl. "Rick," he said again.

Rick leaned back in his chair and picked up the snifter. He swirled it around, but didn't take a drink. He watched the little fingers of brandy as they ran down the sides of the glass.

"What are our options?" he asked calmly.

Carl and Carlos didn't say anything. Ann was about to say something when Rick continued.

"Carl, are you willing to give up on rescuing Ms. Evans?" asked Rick.

"Certainly not," responded Carl.

"And, according to your conversation with Boucher, there is only one way that he will even consider releasing her and her friends, correct?"

"Correct," responded Carl reluctantly.

"Shit," said Carlos as he drank nearly half of the new bottle of Modello. He knew where this was heading.

"He's got us by the balls," said Carl. "Most of us," he added as he looked over at Ann.

"He thinks he does," said Rick.

"Why a supertanker? He only owes the Russians ten million. Shit, I can't believe I just said, *only* ten million," said Carlos shaking his head.

"Ten million seemed like a lot of money a few minutes ago," said Carl.

"So how much crude are we talking about?" asked Carlos.

"Over two million barrels," said Rick.

"And the current value of a barrel of crude is just over a hundred dollars," offered Ann.

"So we're talking…holy shit, that's two hundred million in crude," said Carl as he did the calculation in his notebook.

"And that doesn't even take into consideration the value of the tanker," said Rick.

"We're screwed," said Carlos. "Do we have any other options? What about a smaller tanker?"

"Do you think he'd negotiate for a smaller tanker?" asked Ann, looking at Carl.

"I have no idea. Knowing him, he has probably already made a deal with another buyer," said Carl. "Leaving us holding the bag with the Russians."

"We really need to find out who is pulling his stings," said Rick as he looked over at Ann.

"I might be able to find out that information," she responded.

"Do you still have some contacts in this part of the world?" asked Carl.

"No, but my Russian contacts in the states would be able to find out," said Ann.

"Rick, are you really considering hijacking a supertanker?" asked Carlos.

Rick didn't answer right away. He took a drink of brandy and put the snifter back into its holder.

"Big ship, little ship, there's no difference in the sentence," he responded.

"Oh, that's comforting. So how many in the crew on a supertanker?" asked Carlos, accepting his fate.

"Not as many as you'd think...probably no more than twenty," answered Carl.

"Obviously, we'd want to take over the ship without firing a shot," said Rick.

"Man...I don't believe this," said Carlos as he finished the bottle.

"What about Higgins?" asked Carl.

"He'll know the schedules and which ships are being escorted," responded Rick.

"Do you think he'd go along with us...help us?" questioned Carl.

"He's a good friend. I need to talk with him, preferably in person," said Rick.

"That's no problem. Somerville can fly you there in the morning," said Carl.

"Ann, we really need to know who hired the goons," emphasized Rick.

"It's either the Russian government or the Russian mafia," said Carl.

Rick didn't respond right away. He signaled the server and ordered another round.

"What are you thinking Rick?" asked Carl, realizing that Rick's mind was in overdrive. He was in full scenario development mode.

"I'm thinking there's a remote possibility that Boucher has hired them himself," offered Rick.

"I'd be surprised if they're working for him," said Carlos.

"Maybe that's his plan," responded Rick.

No one said anything as the server arrived with another round of drinks. When he left, Rick continued.

"Do you think for one minute that the Russian government really cares about ten million dollars?" asked Rick.

"It's chump change to them," said Carlos.

"The Russian mafia probably does," responded Ann.

"They probably do, but they're more interested in their reputation. I don't think they'd spend a lot of time messing around with this guy. They'd most likely make an example of him," said Rick.

"So if he's conning us, what is he planning on doing with a supertanker?" asked Carl.

"That is what we need to find out," said Rick.

"And what if he's working his own deal?" asked Carl.

"It doesn't matter...we'll give him what he wants," said Rick as he took a healthy swallow of brandy.

CHAPTER THIRTY-NINE
Camp Lemonnier
Day 16
0900 Hours

On the early morning flight to Djibouti, Rick sat back, rested his head against the headrest, shut his eyes, and focused all his energy and thoughts on Patrice Boucher. According to Carl, Boucher was the worst kind of villain—not only was he cold-blooded and ruthless, but also he was a very skilled tactician. Boucher was fully capable of thinking on his feet and could rapidly adapt to changing situations. In Rick's mind, the evidence was mounting in support of his contention that Boucher was in fact the one pulling the strings…all of the strings.

Whatever Boucher's initial intention was when he made the trip to New York City, it had all changed when he ran into JT Blackwell. When he learned that Blackwell's granddaughter was in the market for a sailboat capable of circumnavigating the globe, Boucher saw an opportunity to entrap his old nemesis, Carl Peterson.

Rick was fully convinced it was during this chance meeting with Blackwell that Patrice Boucher decided to remain incognito and develop a plan to ensnare Carl. The fact that time did not appear to be of the essence was further confirmation in Rick's mind that Boucher could not have been under the thumb of the Russians. There was no way that the Russians would have played games with Boucher. It's not how they operate. For Rick, the fog of confusion was lifting…and lifting rapidly.

Roy Higgins was waiting at base operations when Rick disembarked from the aircraft. He walked out onto the ramp, shook hands with Rick, and placed his hand on Rick's shoulder as they continued toward the terminal. It was already over a hundred degrees. Higgins didn't seem to mind the heat. Rick could feel sweat running down his sides.

"Good flight?" asked Higgins as he looked back at the aircraft. "Nice plane. That's different than the one that picked me up in

Homestead. Carl must be doing very well," he added, noticing The Peterson Group logo on the tail of the aircraft.

"Well, you know Carl. He always liked the best toys. I believe he just got that one a couple of months ago. It has all the bells and whistles," responded Rick.

Higgins motioned to a gate that was a few feet to the right side of the terminal. It was protected by a cipher lock. He entered a code. The gate opened into a small parking area where Higgins' Range Rover was parked in a space marked, *Colonel and above*. The Range Rover was covered in sand, dust and an abundance of bird droppings—some freshly baked.

Rick had a computer and a small duffle bag with him that he placed on the back seat. The seat was hot to the touch. He jumped in the front and fastened his seatbelt. Higgins started the vehicle and put the air conditioner on full. The cool air was refreshing. It would cool the vehicle down by the time they got to Higgins' command center.

"So what is so important that you needed to fly here and talk with me face-to-face?" asked Higgins as he headed toward the main drag. He suspected that something was up, and it included him.

"As you know, Carl confronted Boucher."

"I would like to have been a fly on the wall," said Higgins as he made a right turn and headed toward the command center.

"Boucher made his demands known," said Rick, getting right to the point.

"So how much does he want?" asked Higgins.

"He doesn't want any money," said Rick, looking over at Higgins. Higgins looked back. The lines in his forehead deepened. In Higgins' mind, money was always the primary reason—the great equalizer.

Rick didn't say anything for several seconds. Higgins suddenly looked over at Rick.

"He wants you to hijack a ship…one of *my* ships," he declared after a short, but meaningful, pause. He subconsciously took his foot off the gas.

"That's just about it," answered Rick tentatively.

"Just about?" questioned Higgins. "What the hell could be worse?"

"He wants us to hijack a supertanker," said Rick.

"A supertanker!" laughed Higgins as he looked back at Rick.

Rick didn't say anything. He just looked over at Higgins.

"Shit! You're not kidding, are you? You're serious," declared Higgins as he realized the car was hardly moving.

Higgins didn't say anything as he pushed on the accelerator. He looked over at Rick a couple of times. Rick pretended to be taking in the sites around Camp Lemonnier. Rick knew very well what Higgins' initial response would be. Higgins certainly wouldn't want to jeopardize his contract or relationship with the Saudis. He had an extremely lucrative deal with them that included a lot of nice weaponry.

Higgins turned into the parking lot at the command center and pulled into his assigned parking space. They both got out of the SUV. Rick grabbed his bag and computer from the back seat. Both men headed toward the building. Just before they got to the door, Higgins put out his arm and stopped Rick.

"Damn it Rick, this is not what I wanted to hear."

"I know," said Rick as they entered the building and went into Higgins' command center.

Higgins didn't say anything for several minutes. He took a few deep breaths and poured them both a cup of coffee.

"A supertanker," repeated Higgins, shaking his head as he took a drink from his mug. He looked fondly up at the large screen. A small tanker was being escorted by one of his patrol boats. *This has been a good gig*, he thought to himself.

"Roy, I'm just here to go over a few ideas. You know that there's no way that Carl or I would pressure you into a situation that would jeopardize our friendship...or your contract with the Saudis for that matter."

"What about the granddaughter? Can't we just negotiate her release?" asked Higgins. "I know some of these people. I'm sure we can work a deal," he added.

"If we could, that's exactly what we would do, but Boucher has made it quite clear that he'll never release her or her friends unless Carl does what he wants."

Higgins didn't say anything for several minutes. He just watched the screen.

"We could put together a formidable team, and just go in and take her and her friends out of there," said Higgins as he sat down at the conference table. He was quite serious.

"Even if we knew where she was being held, that would be a major undertaking at best. Besides, Boucher said that he has split them up. They're all at different locations throughout Eyl," responded Rick.

Higgins stared at his cup for several seconds.

"He probably has. The pirates are notorious for moving the captives around, keeping the local citizenry involved and on the take," said Higgins.

"If we did attempt another extraction, we would need reliable intelligence to locate them," said Rick.

"Like Ozzie and Harriet," said Higgins sarcastically.

"Maybe we can use them to our advantage," said Rick.

"*Maybe* is the cousin to *hope*. Neither is a good strategy," mimicked Higgins, using one of Rick's sayings. "You must realize that all the supertankers have onboard security. Even if we wanted to take one, we would have to deal with several experienced contract personnel," added Higgins. "They wouldn't give up the ship without a battle. Are you absolutely sure there's no other way?"

"I've had some time to think about our position," said Rick.

"Our position? Shit, we're occupying the low ground my friend," offered Higgins.

"True," said Rick as he finished the coffee and went over and poured another cup.

"So what do you have in mind?" asked Higgins, acquiescing to friendship.

"I have a couple of scenarios in mind, but first I need to confirm Boucher's relationship with the Russians."

"Do you think they're backing him?" asked Higgins.

"I did at first, but the more I think about it, the more I believe he's working on his own," said Rick.

"And if he is indeed on his own, he must have a customer for a supertanker," said Higgins.

"My thoughts exactly," said Rick.

"And you believe he could have a paying customer without the Russians knowing what he's up to?" asked Higgins.

"He might be giving them a small cut, but I still don't believe they have an active role."

Rick looked at his watch and sat back in his chair.

"I'm expecting a call from Ann. She's contacting an old friend who may be able to provide some insight concerning Boucher."

"Rick, there's not too many countries that can handle a supertanker. Even offloading to a smaller tanker presents challenges for many," offered Higgins.

Rick was familiar with lightering operations and was about to say something when his satellite phone rang.

"It's Ann. Hopefully she has some answers," said Rick as he answered the phone. Realizing that he just said "hopefully," he smiled as he looked over at Higgins.

"Morning Ann," answered Rick.

"Hi Rick. I hope you had a good trip."

"I did. I'm here with Roy Higgins. I'm putting you on speaker."

"Hi Roy," said Ann in a cheerful voice. "Carlos really misses you guys," she joked.

"Yeah right," laughed Higgins. "I'm sure that he does."

"So, what do you have for us?" asked Rick.

"Boucher did have a deal with the Russian government. They provided the funds for the deal in Cuba."

"And they let him off the hook?" asked Rick.

"You remember how Carl said that Boucher's contact in Cuba disappeared?"

"Yes, a guy named Peña. Boucher said that he took off with the ten million," answered Rick.

"Well, that appears to be partially true. He's definitely among the missing, but not before the Russians got all their money back," said Ann.

"So Boucher doesn't owe them anything?" asked Rick.

"Nothing. As far as the Russian government is concerned, he's clean."

"What about the Russian mob?" asked Rick.

"Just some minor gambling debts. Nothing of any real significance," answered Ann.

"And the goons?" asked Rick.

"Looks like you were right about them. They are working for Boucher."

Rick didn't say anything as he made a few notes.

"Roy believes he must have a client for the supertanker," continued Rick.

"This is where it gets a bit interesting," continued Ann. "There's a rumor that Boucher could be involved with the recent jewel heist at the Carlton. Interpol strongly suspects that the Pink Panthers pulled off the heist. They also believe that Boucher may have played a pivotal role."

"How so?" asked Rick.

"The authorities suspect that Boucher gave them access to the hotel."

"It wouldn't be the first time the Pink Panthers pulled off a heist in Cannes," said Higgins.

"So, he's actually being held there by the gendarmes," said Rick.

"Basically, he's under house arrest, although he hasn't been officially charged with a crime," responded Ann. "They just want to keep him under wraps."

"A person of interest," said Higgins as he got up and poured another cup of coffee.

"So what is the connection between the Pink Panthers and a supertanker?" asked Rick. "Seems to be out of their expertise," he added.

"My contact has heard that Boucher is trying to work a deal to deliver two million barrels of crude oil to the Rijeka oil refinery in Urinj."

"Hence a supertanker," said Rick.

"That's a deepwater port," interrupted Higgins. "In Croatia, I might add. If I remember correctly, aren't the Pink Panthers from Serbia?" asked Higgins.

"They are," said Rick as he made a few more notes.

"I can't imagine the Serbs and Croatians working together on anything," said Higgins.

"The Croatian Democratic Union, or HDZ, is the ruling class. They're just a bunch of gangsters," offered Rick.

"And money is the common thread that ties them all together," said Higgins.

"Did your contact provide any names?" asked Rick.

"Just a first name...Milenko. He appears to be a member of the Pink Panthers," said Ann.

"Is Milenko a real name?" asked Rick.

"It's a code name," answered Ann. "Many of the Serbs use the same name," she added.

"So it looks like the Pink Panthers may be getting into the oil business," said Rick.

"That's the rumor," said Ann.

"Anything else?" asked Rick.

"Just that my friend said to be very careful dealing with the Croatians. They're a ruthless bunch...and just as bad as the Serbs. Boucher is taking a real chance dealing with any of them."

Rick didn't say anything for a minute or so, prompting Ann to ask if he were still on the line.

"I'm here. I need a little time to go over everything."

"I'll enter all my notes into the computer and send it to you within the hour," offered Ann.

"Thanks for the information. Tell Lynn I'll call her a little later."

"We'll be here," said Ann as she ended the call.

Rick put the phone down and looked over at Higgins. Higgins was already typing on his keyboard. He changed the input to the large screen. A listing of all tankers, locations, times of departure, destinations, and their ETA appeared on the screen. Higgins began scrolling down the list. He stopped and highlighted a supertanker that was scheduled to depart Saudi Arabia in three days. Rick moved over next to Higgins and took a seat. They both sat back and looked at the screen. Higgins highlighted the destination and looked over at Rick. Rick got a little smile on his face. Several scenarios were going through his mind. He knew the one that he wanted to develop.

"Do you think the Saudis will work with us?" asked Rick.

"I can talk to them," said Higgins as he pulled out his little green book.

CHAPTER FORTY
Camp Lemonnier
Day 16
1100 Hours

Rick continued to make notes as Roy Higgins sat in front of the computer and re-established satellite coverage with his current escort operation. Since he hadn't heard from his people, Higgins assumed that everything was going according to schedule. The ship was already in the Red Sea and moving toward the Suez Canal at eight knots. The escort would continue until the ship was in the queue and scheduled for the early morning transit to the Mediterranean.

Higgins made a few keystrokes and looked up at the large screen. He used a small joystick to zoom out and pan the area to the southeast. He located the pirates' mother ship and zoomed in on the bridge. The mother ship was heading on a southerly course at six knots. Several pirates could be seen sitting along the port rail. They were sharing what appeared to be a homemade cigar.

They're probably high as a kite, Roy thought to himself.

Roy watched the ship for several minutes then sat back and thumbed through his small notebook. He stopped on one of the pages and wrote down the private number of Prince Saud al-Faisal. Higgins was circling the prince's name when Rick came over and sat down next to him. Rick looked down at the pad.

"I believe I have a plan in mind that will solve all of our problems. The key will be to get the Saudis to go along," said Rick as he handed a one-page outline to Higgins. "How about a refill?" he asked as he got up. He hesitated, waiting for a response from Higgins.

Without looking up or saying anything, Higgins handed his cup to Rick. He was already engaged as he went down the list of items. A slight smile crossed his face when he came to one of the items that Rick had circled several times. A note to the side simply stated, *this is the key*.

"Shit, this just might work," he said as he put the page down on the conference table.

"The real key is…can you sell it?" asked Rick.

"If the Saudis believe they'll get their ship back, and we can eliminate the head of a major piracy organization…they just might go along with it," responded Higgins.

"I assume you have a good contact?" said Rick, looking over at the paper in front of Higgins.

"That I do," he said as he pushed the paper in front of Rick.

"You don't beat around the bush…right to the top. You know the prince well?" asked Rick, recognizing the name.

"Actually, I know him very well," responded Higgins. "You might say that he owes me one."

"Does he owe you one big enough to risk nearly three hundred and fifty million in assets?" asked Rick.

"We'll see," said Higgins as he underlined the name of the supertanker on Rick's outline and shook his head. A sly smile briefly crossed his face.

"How ironic," said Higgins not expecting Rick to hear him.

"What's ironic?" asked Rick.

"The *Sirius Star* is owned by Vela, which is a subsidiary of Saudi Aramco. She was launched in two thousand eight and was hijacked by Somali pirates in November of the same year. They asked for twenty-five million in ransom."

"Did they get it?" asked Rick.

"No, they didn't. They settled for three million in U.S. currency. The exchange took place far out at sea during some really bad weather. Several of the pirates drowned when they left the ship in small boats. A couple of them actually washed up on shore with their share of the money in plastic bags."

"A fitting end. So how long did they keep the ship?" asked Rick.

"About three months," answered Higgins.

"You have a good memory," said Rick.

"Well, I should. It was that event that triggered the Saudis to hire my company to provide escort operations," said Higgins.

"Maybe it was meant to be," said Rick.

"I hope it's not flagging the end of my contract," said Higgins as he looked over at Rick.

"If Prince Faisal agrees, and this works out as I expect it will, you'll be in with the Saudis forever," said Rick confidently.

"Or out forever," lamented Higgins. "I wish I shared your optimism, but what you've outlined here is going to require a hell of a lot of coordination. And, if we want to use this particular ship, we don't have a whole lot of time," said Higgins as he picked up the sheet of paper and waved it in the air.

"Then we need to get busy," said Rick as he dialed Carl Peterson.

Carl and Carlos were having lunch at the Carlton when Rick called. The girls had already finished breakfast and were out visiting a few of the shops near the hotel. Carl was expecting the call.

"Hey Rick," he answered. He sounded enthusiastic.

"I trust you're enjoying the nice weather," said Rick, sounding as if he missed the milder climate.

"I take it that it's really warm there," said Carl.

"It's not warm…it's hot," responded Rick.

"Any progress?" asked Carl.

"We have a plan. Just need to get the Saudis to go along with us," said Rick.

"The Saudis?" questioned Carl.

"We'll be hijacking one of their ships," responded Rick.

"Oh great. How does Higgins feel about that?"

"He has legitimate concerns."

"I'm sure that he does. I really hate putting him on the spot," said Carl.

"He was a bit tentative at first, but he's fully on board with us," said Rick as he looked over at Higgins.

"Well I would certainly understand if he didn't want to go along," said Carl after a slight pause. "He's got a great deal to lose," he added.

"So do we…but true bonds matter," said Rick.

"So I assume Higgins is working that end with the Saudis," said Carl. It was more of a statement than a question.

"He is."

"So what's the plan?" asked Carl, sounding like a little kid that was just given permission to enter a toy store.

Carl had already dismissed any thoughts of remorse for Higgins' position. Rick envisioned Carl sitting there, rubbing his hands together, waiting for the good news.

"Let's see how Roy makes out with the Saudis before I go into any details."

"You gotta give me something," pleaded Carl.

"Look up the *Sirius Star*," offered Rick.

Carl didn't say anything for several long seconds as he wrote down the name.

"I seem to recall that name," he said. It sounded like a question.

"Look it up, and say a little prayer that the Saudis go along with us. If they do, I have a plan that I strongly believe will work."

"When will you know something...solid?" asked Carl, searching for the right word.

Rick looked over at Higgins. Roy was pacing back and forth and engaged in conversation. He didn't notice Rick looking over in his direction.

"I believe Roy is talking with Prince Faisal as we speak," answered Rick.

"Faisal, huh...Higgins doesn't mess around, does he?" responded Carl.

"I suspect we'll know an answer momentarily," said Rick as he heard Higgins laugh. Laughter was usually a good sign, especially when dealing with a sensitive situation.

Higgins turned toward Rick, held out his right hand, and without making eye contact, gave him a thumbs-up.

"Seems we're in business," said Rick.

"So what's the plan?" asked Carl again.

"It's simple. We give Boucher what he wants...a supertanker loaded with crude."

"I know you Rick Morgan. What do you have up your sleeve? Higgins must have given Prince Faisal some concrete assurances.

The Saudis aren't about to give up one of their ships, especially one loaded with crude. You've got to give me something. What have I guaranteed?"

"Let me work this out with Higgins. I'll let you know soon enough. You need to focus all your attention on Boucher," said Rick.

"And what do you want me to tell that son of a bitch?" asked Carl.

"Tell him we'll deliver the ship in a few days. But in order to make the deal happen, we need twenty-five million upfront, and we want Courtney Evans and her friends released."

"He'll never agree to that," said Carl.

"Of course he won't, but it'll be a starting point," said Rick.

"So what do you really want from this prick?" asked Carl.

"I want twenty-five million upfront."

"What about Courtney Evans?" asked Carl.

"She can be his ace in the hole. He can have his people hold on to her and her friends until we have delivered the ship. But you need to make it clear that we expect her release immediately upon acceptance of the ship."

"Twenty-five million is a hefty sum," said Carl.

"It is, but remind him that he's getting a package deal worth over three hundred and fifty million dollars. Twenty-five million is a drop in the bucket. It's not even ten percent, and that doesn't even take into consideration the profit on a liter of gasoline."

"What if he doesn't go for it?" asked Carl.

"Then get up from the table and tell him that's the deal. Take it or leave it."

"You actually think he'll take it?" asked Carl.

"He won't at first, but he'll do the math. He'll probably make five million himself when he collects the down payment. Besides, I'll bet you that he's made promises that would have severe consequences if he fails to deliver," said Rick.

"You're probably right about that," said Carl. "Okay, so how long do we have?"

"Three days...four at the most."

"Shit, that's cutting it close."

"It's a lot closer at this end. Tell him we have a potential target in mind. And Carl, whatever you do, don't mention the name of the ship."

"What if he asks? What if he insists?"

"Hold on a second," said Rick.

"Roy, I need the name of another supertanker that'll be heading into the Med about the same timeframe."

Higgins brought up the tanker schedule and went down the list.

"The *Aries Star* will work."

"Carl, try to avoid giving him a name. Use any excuse you want. However, if he insists, tell him our potential target is the *Aries Star*. Don't give him any other information than that."

"You got something cooking...what is it?" asked Carl.

"Trust me. It's a surprise."

Carl didn't say anything for a minute or so. He looked over at Carlos. Carlos couldn't hear Rick's side of the conversation. But from what he did hear of Carl's side, he knew that Rick was in the zone. He was on a Morgan roll.

"All right. You're killing me, but I trust your judgment. You know that I'm not good with surprises. I'll work on Boucher. Let me know when the action starts."

"It'll start when you have verified the twenty-five million is in your account. Talk with you later."

Rick put the phone down on the table and looked up at the screen. Higgins had zoomed in on a large ship that was heading to the northwest at ten knots.

"That's our ship," said Higgins as he zoomed in on the bridge.

"I'm surprised the Saudis didn't ask you to escort the ship," said Rick.

"There's a crew of twenty-four, including six well-trained contractors with RPGs on board. The pirates would have their hands full...and they know it," responded Higgins.

"I assume your friend, the prince, will let the captain know of our plans?"

"I just need to give him a call," responded Higgins. "Do you think Boucher will bite?"

"I believe he will. Carl is a very good salesman. Once Boucher realizes that Carl means business, he'll come through."

"And you trust that Boucher will hold up his end of the bargain?" asked Higgins. His expression confirmed his total lack of trust in Boucher.

"No, I don't trust him at all, but I do trust Carl's ability to set up a failsafe exchange."

Higgins didn't say anything as he panned the *Sirius Star*. The ship was impressive. It still looked new. One of the contractors was standing close to the bow. He wore desert cammies. He had an AR-15 over his shoulder and a handgun strapped to his left leg. He was scanning the horizon with binoculars. Higgins moved the view back to the bridge. Two more contractors were standing by the railing. They appeared to be engaged in conversation.

"Prince Faisal wants his captain and two essential crew members to remain aboard the ship," said Higgins.

"He understands the risk?" asked Rick.

"He does, but that was the only way he would agree to the plan. Said they were essential to the safe operation of the ship."

Rick didn't say anything for a few minutes as he thought about his plan. He went over and poured another cup of coffee. The coffee was black as coal. *Crude*, he thought to himself as he swirled the coffee around in the cup, *black gold*.

"That's fine. We can deal with that. It is the captain's ship. Besides, his presence will add legitimacy and certainly help to accomplish the plan I have in mind," said Rick. "What's the minimum crew required to operate a ship of that size?" he asked.

"I believe nine well-qualified crew members could handle the ship in an emergency situation," answered Higgins.

"Then I would assume the other two individuals that the prince wants to remain with the ship are most likely crew members well-trained in the onboard computer systems," said Rick.

"That would be my guess," answered Higgins.

"I would like Guillermo and Rafael to be part of the team that picks up Courtney Evans and her three friends. We'll need to discuss their role in the exchange. Will you be able to provide six more people for the ship?" asked Rick.

"Assuming that I'll have Cody and Shaun, I see no problem," responded Higgins.

Rick made a few more notes and sat back in the chair. He appeared to be deep in thought. He made one more entry and looked over at Higgins.

"We'll need another ship's captain," he said as he put his pencil down on the table.

CHAPTER FORTY-ONE
InterContinental Carlton Cannes Hotel
Day 16
1700 Hours

Carl spent the better part of the afternoon in his hotel room thinking about Patrice Boucher. He knew the approach he would take and what he was going to say. He just needed to play hard ball—no room to negotiate. Carl was aware that Rick was working hard on the scenario and was close to finalizing a workable plan. Rick was extremely good at developing a myriad of scenarios that would yield the desired results while minimizing risk. However, no matter how good the plan and how good the people, you could never totally eliminate risk. Risk was an inherent part of every mission. Carl would like to have known more of the details, but it was probably best that he didn't.

Carl looked at his watch. He wasn't expecting the girls for at least an hour or so. Carlos had gone to meet them. Carl knew that Carlos would be bored silly, but Carlos was head over heels in love with Ann—he would do anything to please her. Carl went over to the desk and picked up his satellite phone. He dialed Tony Ramos. Tony answered as soon as he felt the phone vibrate.

"Good afternoon," he said in a low voice, not wanting to attract any attention.

"Hey Tony. Let me know as soon as Boucher shows up, will you?"

"He's already sitting at the bar," responded Tony, faking a smile just in case anyone had taken notice.

"Is he alone?" asked Carl.

Tony was sitting at the far end of the bar. He used the mirror behind the bar to keep an eye on Boucher and the Russians.

"He's alone for now. But it looks like he's expecting someone. He has placed a napkin over the back of the stool next to him."

"Either that, or he doesn't want anyone to sit there. What about the goons? Are they close by?"

"They're sitting at the far end of the bar...one on each side of the corner. They are stacking the empties in front of them."

"Okay. I'll be down in a few minutes. I need to talk with Boucher again. Might get a little heated. Whatever you do, don't compromise your position unless it's absolutely necessary," cautioned Carl.

"After the second punch?" asked Tony with a hint of a laugh.

"Depends on who is delivering the blows," responded Carl.

"I'll have your back," said Tony as he signaled the bartender for a refill.

Carl put the satellite phone down on the bed and took off his shirt. He went into the bathroom and washed his face and brushed his teeth. He looked up at the mirror.

"Here we go again," he mused as if he were talking to an alter ego that occupied the world on the other side of the mirror.

Carl stared at his reflection for several seconds. Time had been kind. He was still in good shape, and he certainly didn't look his age. He flexed his muscles, dried his face, and threw the towel on the counter. He then went back into the bedroom and put on a fresh shirt. He rustled his hair with both hands, checked the room, and headed out the door.

Boucher immediately saw Carl as he entered the bar. Although Carl knew exactly where Boucher was sitting, he pretended to search the lounge for him, and then walked over to where he was sitting. Boucher was nursing a scotch on the rocks and didn't acknowledge Carl.

"Are you expecting someone?"

"I have a guest who'll be joining me in a little while," he answered without making eye contact.

"We need to talk," said Carl as he looked around the lounge for a suitable table.

Carl spotted and empty table in the back of the lounge area. He motioned toward the back of the lounge. Boucher looked over at the table and glanced toward the goons. They were very much aware of Carl's presence. They had already looked around for Carlos, but he wasn't there.

"Save these two stools," said Boucher to the bartender as he got up with glass in hand. He followed Carl to the table.

As they sat down, a server approached with two menus.

"Just a dry martini for me," said Carl, motioning to Boucher's half-full glass.

Boucher waved the server off, saying that he was fine for now.

"So you have considered my offer?" asked Boucher.

"Your offer...that's putting it generously. You know what I would really like to consider?" said Carl, leaning in toward Boucher. It was a rhetorical question.

"I know...but you won't. So when will you deliver?" asked Boucher.

"We'll deliver when you release Ms. Evans and her friends...and wire twenty-five million to one of my offshore accounts," said Carl quite clearly.

Boucher didn't say anything for several seconds as he swirled the drink in the glass. There was a lot more ice than scotch. He nearly finished the drink before setting the glass on the table with a discernible thud. Carl's demand didn't seem to faze him one bit.

"You seem to forget who is holding all the cards," he responded calmly.

The fact that Boucher didn't balk at Carl's demands, convinced Carl that Boucher had expected certain concessions.

The server arrived with Carl's drink. Boucher picked up his glass and took one last long swallow. He then ordered another as he held out the glass for the server. From the server's expression, it was obvious that he didn't care for Boucher.

Boucher waited until the server was well out of earshot.

"There is no way that I will release Ms. Evans until I have full control of the ship...and you know it. And twenty-five million," laughed Boucher, "what are you smoking?"

"The twenty-five million is non-negotiable," responded Carl.

"And what about Ms. Evans?" asked Boucher. "She's suddenly expendable?"

"You're the one who set the conditions," said Carl.

Boucher didn't say anything as the server approached with his drink. Boucher took a drink from the glass, set it on the table, sat back, put his fingertips together, and studied Carl.

"Twenty-five million is out of the question," he said after a long pause.

"A supertanker has a crew of twenty-four and a security force consisting of six well-armed contractors. As you well know, it'll take a considerable amount of resources, many that I'll need to hire and pay for upfront in order to successfully take control of a ship that size."

"As I said, twenty-five million isn't going to happen," reiterated Boucher.

"Then we don't have a deal," said Carl as he stood up and started to walk away.

Boucher let him get a few steps away before he summoned him.

"Peterson, hold on a second."

Carl stopped, turned, and slowly returned to the table. He sat down and took another drink. He didn't say anything.

"Twenty-five million is way too much," said Boucher.

"I'm not going to waste my time and put my whole team in jeopardy without a tangible commitment from you. The ship alone is worth one hundred and fifty million. The cargo is worth in excess of two hundred million. Twenty-five million is a drop in the bucket. I'm putting a whole bunch of people at risk. It's not going to happen without your vested interest."

"Fifteen million…maybe," said Boucher after a long pause.

Carl immediately knew that Boucher was merely the broker. He would have to get both permission and the money from his cohorts.

"Twenty-five million is the bottom line or no deal," said Carl as he slid the chair back and stood up.

"I'm going to need to know the name of the ship," said Boucher before Carl had a chance to walk away.

"You don't need to know," said Carl as he turned around and started to walk away again.

"If you want twenty-five million, and I'm not saying you'll get it, I'm going to need to know the name of the ship. It's that simple."

Carl walked back over to the table. He didn't sit down. He stood there for nearly a minute just looking down at Boucher. Boucher had a smirk on his face that Carl would have loved to wipe away. He took a pen from his pocket and wrote the name, *Aries Star*, on the coaster.

"Twenty-five million upfront. And when we turn over the ship, your people will release Courtney Evans and her three friends," said Carl.

"For a guy who's not in the driver's seat, you got some set of balls. At one time, I actually liked that about you," said Boucher as he picked up the coaster, looked at the name, and put it into his pocket.

"You may own all the cards, but you played your hand, and now I'm calling you," said Carl as he walked away without looking back.

"I'll be in touch," yelled Boucher as he signaled the Russians.

Carl left the lounge area. He purposely didn't make eye contact with Tony Ramos. The Russians went over and stood next to the small table waiting for instructions. Boucher watched Carl as he left the area.

"When this is over, I want you to take care of that guy... permanently!"

Earlier that afternoon at Camp Lemonnier...

Rick finished what little water was left in the bottle as he got up and moved over next to Roy Higgins. Roy was working the joystick. He zoomed in on the area where he expected to find his patrol boat. It didn't take him long to find it. The boat was heading south at fifteen knots. The escort operations had been completed successfully. Higgins zoomed out and checked the distance to Camp Lemonnier.

"They'll be home in a few hours," he announced as he leaned back in his seat, interlocked his fingers, and placed his hands behind his head.

"Do you have someone who can do this?" Rick asked as he pushed a piece of paper in front of Higgins. He pointed to the name on the ship. He had made a few modifications with an accompanying diagram and comments.

Higgins smiled.

"I have just the person if I can find her," said Higgins as he continued to look over the drawing.

"Find her?" questioned Rick.

"She goes off the grid every once in a while. The last time I talked with her, she was living in Rome."

"If you can locate her, and she's available, I can send the aircraft," said Rick.

"Let me make a few calls," said Higgins as he pulled out his small green government-issued notebook. It was very old and held together with small strips of duct tape that had long since dried out. Little white threads were everywhere.

"And you believe she can do this?" asked Rick again.

"Rick, this girl is the best I've ever seen. The Italian government actually pays her an annual stipend to stay in *retirement*."

"She's that good," remarked Rick. It wasn't a question.

"She is indeed that good my friend," responded Higgins.

Rick got up and retrieved another bottle of water from the refrigerator.

"You want one," he yelled to Higgins.

Higgins indicated that he did. He was about to say something when a woman answered his call. He immediately recognized her voice. He put the phone on speaker.

"Mona, this is Roy Higgins."

"Roy Higgins, you old fart. How long has it been this time? You married yet?" she asked. Her voice was a bit gravelly.

"It's been way too long, and no, not married," responded Roy.

"You'll be too old for making bambinos," she said.

"I'm already too old, but I still enjoy trying. Are you available?" he asked.

"For marriage...or a job?" she asked with a chuckle.

"Tempting," he said after a slight pause. "A job. I need your special talents. The gig will pay extremely well," said Roy, looking over at Rick for confirmation.

Rick nodded in the affirmative. He loved spending Carl's money.

"How well?' she asked.

"That will be your call. There's someone I'd like you to meet. We need to talk in person."

"When?" she asked.

"We can be there in about five hours."

"Five hours? Where the hell are you?"

"I'm at Camp Lemonnier in Djibouti."

"Lucky you," she said. She didn't mean it.

"I'm available. I assume you'll be landing at Fiumicino?"

"I'll call you with an ETA. And Mona, plan on flying back with us if you accept," said Roy.

"I'll be there, and you know I'll accept. How many days?" she asked.

"Four to five days should do it. Oh, and by the way, four of those days will probably be at sea."

"At sea? My price just went up," she said as she ended the call.

Higgins put the phone down and smiled to himself. He had worked with Mona on several occasions. Each time proved to be quite interesting...and most rewarding. Whatever she wanted, it would be worth the cost.

"I need to call Captain Somerville," said Rick. "How soon can you be ready?"

"Fifteen minutes, assuming we can clean up on the plane," responded Higgins. "I have everything I need right here in the locker."

Rick looked at his watch. He realized that with the time difference, they could make Rome at a reasonable hour.

"The plane will give us some time to finalize the plan," said Rick as he dialed Captain Somerville.

"When will the *Sirius Star* enter the Adriatic?" asked Rick.

Higgins brought up the schedule on the screen and made a few calculations. She'll be off the coast of southern Italy late tomorrow night.

"That should give us enough time. I suppose we could do a quick turnaround. Somerville would have to make that decision," said Rick.

"Or we could spend the night in Rome at my hotel suit," smiled Higgins.

"You have a suite in Rome?" asked Rick.

"It was part of the contract. The Saudis pick up the tab."

"Sweet deal," said Rick.

"It is indeed. I hope I can keep it. I let my team use it between operations. If they had to hang around here all the time, I'd be looking for new people every other week."

Rick looked at his watch and made a few mental notes.

"I thought you wanted to take over the ship in the Med?" asked Higgins.

"I did at first, but I have changed the plan slightly."

"And what about the onboard security personnel?" asked Higgins.

"We'll employ them. Besides, the Croatians have no idea who they are. For all they know, they're our people," answered Rick.

"Good point. And I should be the one to go aboard the ship," said Higgins.

"Are you sure you want to do that?" asked Rick.

"Rick, it makes perfect sense. I know how the tankers operate. I know all the Saudi tanker captains, and I probably even know some of the contractors on board."

"And you know Mona," added Rick.

"Yes I do. I have worked with her on several occasions."

"Okay then. I need to make sure Carl tells Boucher that we'll deliver the ship right to the refinery. No at sea transfer bullshit. Once she's pumping crude, our part of the deal is complete."

"And what if he doesn't authorize the release of Ms. Evans?" asked Higgins.

"Then I'll kill the prick myself, and we'll go to plan B."

CHAPTER FORTY-TWO

Rome, Italy
Day 16
1830 Hours

Captain Somerville reduced the power slightly as he crossed the threshold on runway 34R at Leonardo da Vinci International Airport in Fiumicino. The wheels touched down on the numbers precisely at 1830 hours on day sixteen of the mission. As he cleared the active runway, the tower directed him to terminal three, gate six. Within thirty minutes, Rick Morgan and Roy Higgins were on the way to the Hilton Rome Airport Hotel. The hotel was conveniently located less than a mile from the airport.

During the flight, Roy Higgins had called the woman he referred to as Mona—Mona Lisa to be exact. He told her the ETA and that they would meet her in the hotel lounge. She said that she was familiar with the hotel and would be there. She also said that she was looking forward to seeing her old friend and meeting Rick Morgan. She seemed to linger on the word, old. Higgins subconsciously looked down at his waistline and sucked in what little belly he did have. He was getting older, but he was still in very good shape.

Captain Somerville and the rest of the flight crew remained at the airport until the plane was fully serviced. As he waited, he filed a flight plan to Sigonella for a 0730 departure. Higgins had reserved a couple of rooms for the crew. Captain Somerville said that it would be a welcomed change from the officers' quarters at Camp Lemonnier and not to worry since he was the designated driver. Higgins wasn't sure if the good captain was kidding or not. By the captain's unwavering expression, Higgins still wasn't sure. Higgins was aware of the twelve-hour "bottle to throttle" rule. He looked at his watch—they were already inside that timeframe. Somerville smiled as if he knew what Higgins was thinking.

The flight had given Rick plenty of time to continue refining the plan. Basically he was at the "what if" stage. The plan consisted of two separate scenarios connected by a single objective...the safe passage of Courtney Evans and her friends.

About one hour into the flight, Rick had finalized the first part of the plan, which involved the takeover of the *Sirius Star*. Rick went over the plan several times with Higgins. They both agreed that the scenario could be accomplished with minimal risk. When they had finished planning, Rick asked when Higgins would call Prince Faisal.

"I'll give him a call right now," said Higgins as he took his satellite phone from his briefcase.

"Do you know the captain of the *Sirius Star*?" asked Rick.

"I do indeed. He's a crusty old British captain by the name of Lewis Early. As with many British captains, he's extremely direct. However, he's also quite competent."

"Do you think he'll have a problem going along with our plan?"

"I'm sure that he will, but he'll follow orders. He'll do whatever Prince Faisal tells him to do," responded Higgins as he dialed the private number of the prince. The prince had been expecting the call.

"Yes Mr. Higgins," he answered with an English accent.

"Good afternoon Your Majesty," said Higgins.

"Ah...so formal from my American friend. I thought by now we had dispensed with the formalities. I assume you are ready to proceed with your, or maybe I should say, with *our* mission?" responded the prince.

"I am indeed...Sir," responded Higgins. At this point, he wasn't quite sure how to address the prince. They had met on several occasions in the past. Only one time could their encounter have been considered somewhat informal. They would never speak of that time.

"When do you plan on boarding the *Sirius Star*?"

"Tomorrow night off the coast of southern Italy. There will be three of us," answered Higgins.

"Just three?" asked the prince, sounding a bit surprised.

"Yes, just three. I'm planning on using the onboard security team... with your approval."

The prince considered the request for nearly a minute or so. Higgins could hear him talking with someone in the background. The prince had obviously placed the phone against his robe.

"I see no problem. I'll let the captain know of our plans. I assume you'll be briefing the captain and security personnel when you go aboard."

"That is correct."

"Then I'll call you right after I talk with him."

"Thank you Sir," said Higgins.

"And Higgins…what is that—that American warning? Oh yes, you break it, you buy it," said the prince as he ended the call.

Higgins smiled to himself as he set the phone down next to his seat. He looked at it for several seconds thinking about the conversation and his relationship with the prince.

"You heard?" asked Higgins.

"I heard enough," responded Rick.

There was no doubt in Higgins' mind that Prince Faisal would make his desires known to the captain. No matter how the captain felt about the operation, he would comply unconditionally.

"I particularly liked the part where the prince said that if we break it, we buy it," said Rick.

"You do understand that he's not kidding," responded Higgins.

"Maybe one day you'll tell me what he owes you," said Rick.

"One day," responded Higgins.

Rick respected the fact that Higgins was loyal to whatever promise he had made to the prince.

Both Rick and Higgins were very much aware that neither the Serbs nor Croatians could be trusted. Both ethnic groups were extremely brutal in their dealings, not only with the outside world, but also with each other. Their demonstrated hatred for one another was a matter of record. The only common thread that could postpone their intense animosity toward one another was, as always, the lust for money. However, each would do whatever was in their best interest, or at least what they considered to be in their best interest.

Ironically, the saving grace for the mission was that Boucher, along with his Serbian partner, known only as Milenko, was brokering the deal with the Croatians. And when the ship entered the port, as far as the Croatians knew, the ship was under the control of the hijackers— hijackers who were employed by none other than Patrice Boucher.

Rick was fully convinced that the plan would work, especially with Roy Higgins at the helm. Although Rick didn't know Mona, he did know that Higgins had full confidence in her ability to make the modifications that he had clearly indicated on the drawing of the *Sirius Star*. The unique modification was indeed the most critical element for completing the mission successfully.

Once the ship was moored at the refinery and pumping crude, Carl Peterson's part of the deal with Boucher would be satisfied. Then it would be up to Carl to ensure that Boucher followed through with his part of the bargain. It was extremely important that Boucher made the call to the Somali negotiator, Mohamed Ibrahim, before the ship was fully unloaded. Higgins picked up the plan and looked over at Rick.

"This could really work," he said.

"*Could* is not an option my friend," said Rick. "It *will* work. It *has* to work."

"The Croatians are really going to be pissed," said Higgins, shaking his head.

"They certainly will, but no matter how pissed off they are, they won't do anything."

"You're sure about that?" asked Higgins.

"You can never be absolutely sure, but they'll be caught between the proverbial rock and a hard place," replied Rick.

Higgins smiled as he continued to look over the plan and follow Rick's block diagram.

"Do you trust that the Somalis will hand over Ms. Evans?" asked Higgins.

"Well, that is certainly the great unknown," responded Rick. "And it's imperative that we have her in our custody before the crude is completely offloaded," he added. "By the way, how long will it take to pump two million barrels of oil?"

"The port is capable of pumping one hundred thousand barrels per hour," responded Higgins.

"So basically, we have twenty-four hours once the ship is hooked up," said Rick as he did the calculation in his head.

"And then if Boucher double-crosses us..." started Higgins.

"He's dead, and we go to plan B," interjected Rick before Higgins finished.

"Plan B," laughed Higgins. "There's always a plan B. And what is plan B, my friend?"

"Plan B is simple. We'll complete the first phase of the operation. Once Boucher learns what has happened, he'll be scrambling just to save his ass. I suspect that, one way or the other, he'll disappear. When the Somalis don't hear from him for a few days, they'll be more than willing to deal directly with us. All they want is the money," explained Rick.

"And we'll have twenty-five million to play with," added Higgins.

"I'm sure the Somalis would settle for five million. I would only make that offer if we're forced into plan B. I prefer that everything goes according to schedule and Boucher makes the call."

"Are you planning on going to Eyl with the team?" asked Higgins.

"I need to be there. The Somalis will expect to meet with someone they've talked with. Since Carl has talked with Mohamed Ibrahim, he can pave the way for me."

"Maybe I should give Ali a call just to keep him in the loop so he doesn't become suspicious," said Higgins.

"Ah yes, Ozzie. The only thing we need from him is confirmation that the Somalis are gathering Courtney Evans and her friends. Let him believe that we're expecting to conduct a routine turnover."

"And what about all the weaponry?" asked Higgins.

"They'll be expecting us to be carrying insurance," responded Rick.

Hilton Hotel
1915 Hours

There were quite a few people milling about in the lobby of the Hilton. Although Higgins had told Mona that they would meet her in the lounge, he fully expected that she would be lurking about in the lobby in order to catch the first glimpse of her *old* friend, Roy Higgins. He looked around the lobby and wasn't disappointed. Mona was leaning against a large Roman-style column. Higgins hadn't seen her in quite some time. She smiled as he caught her eye. She pushed herself away from the column and headed toward Higgins. Higgins elbowed Rick.

"There's Mona," he said.

Mona wasn't exactly how Rick had pictured her in his mind. Many of the operatives he had worked with were nondescript. They could easily blend into a crowd, never to be seen again. Mona was certainly an exception. She appeared to be about five foot six. She had long auburn-colored hair, green eyes and a body that was much more than Higgins could handle.

"Rick, this is my friend Mona," introduced Higgins as he tried not to be too obvious. He was having a hard time not staring at her abundant cleavage…and she knew it.

Mona extended her right hand and smiled. She was truly a beautiful woman. She was probably in her late forties and quite fit.

"Nice to meet you. Actually, Roy might be the only one who still refers to me as Mona. My real name is Maria Lucci. Maybe you knew my father Salvatore?" she said with a subtle smile, revealing perfect teeth—a rarity in Europe.

Rick didn't know Salvatore Lucci personally.

"Only by reputation," said Rick, knowing that Salvatore Lucci was a well-known forger who could copy anything…and did for many years. The old man died under house arrest in Milan.

"What do you say we head to the lounge," offered Higgins.

All of the bar stools were taken. There were at least three times as many men as women. Most of the women, if not all, were working girls. Rick pointed to a table that had just been cleared. The three of them went over and sat down. A server pointed to the wine list. However, the three of them ordered martinis. Maria asked for hers to be extra dry with two olives, "on those little swords," she added with a thrusting motion.

"So what is the gig?" she asked as she put both hands on top of Roy's right hand. Her hands were very warm and smooth. She rubbed his hand.

Rick reached into his pocket and pulled out a folded piece of paper. He opened it and placed it in front of Maria. A slight smile crossed her face as she looked at it and read the notes in the margin. One of the notes had an asterisk by it that was circled several times. The word *key* was written in large capital letters next to the asterisk.

"I assume this is possible?" asked Rick.

"No problem," answered Maria as she handed the paper back to Rick.

"And you have the material?" asked Higgins.

"I have everything I will need in my storage area," responded Maria.

"We are planning an early morning departure. Will that present a problem?" asked Rick.

"Not at all. After dinner, I'll pick up my things and stop by the storage area. Then I'll be back. You do have room for me, don't you Roy?" she said with an inviting smile as she again placed her hands on top of Roy's.

Roy moved around in his seat. There were some strategic readjustments that needed to be made. Maria squeezed his hands ever so slightly. She knew that she had gotten a *rise* out of Roy. It was refreshing for both of them.

"I do," said Roy looking over at Rick, hoping that there was still "room at the inn."

CHAPTER FORTY-THREE
High over the Mediterranean
Day 17
1000 Hours

The Peterson Group aircraft was well on its way to Djibouti by the time Roy Higgins and Maria Lucci arrived at the home of Captain William C. Maheu. Maheu had a sprawling villa next to a vineyard in Catania, Italy. The villa had been built sometime in the eighteenth century. It had a musty aroma that, by now, Maheu didn't notice. Higgins had called Captain Maheu the night before while he was waiting impatiently for Maria to return. He had re-shaved and brushed his teeth several times in anticipation of a long awaited renewal of their "friendship."

Higgins had known Maheu for nearly ten years. It wasn't a very long time, but it was enough time for Higgins to determine that he liked and respected the captain. After a little catching up, Higgins provided a brief overview of the mission and what he needed him to do. Ironically, Captain Maheu had worked for Vela, Saudi Aramco's subsidiary headquartered in Dubai, and had lived in the United Emirates for several years. He was very familiar with both the *Sirius Star* and *Aries Star*. In fact, his last assignment before retiring to Catania, was to take the *Aries Star* to the Louisiana Offshore Oil Port in the Gulf of Mexico.

Soon after Maheu retired, he met a hot little number by the name of Angelina D'Angelo. Angie, as she liked to be called, had all the physical attributes any man would desire, which regrettably included an insatiable sexual appetite. Unfortunately for Captain William C. Maheu, *Little Willie* couldn't quite keep up—literally—with Angie. However, Maheu's young gardener and teenage pool boy could, and they had no trouble filling in for *Little Willie*.

Captain Maheu became suspicious of her activities when he paid the monthly bills. For the amount he was paying for yard work and pool maintenance, the condition of both should have been much better.

As a result, Maheu decided to do some investigating on his own. One day, he hid in the closet to confirm his suspicions. He soon discovered that Angie was getting more service from the crew than both the lawn and pool combined. In fact, she was doing both of them at the same time. She was only momentarily surprised when he popped out of the closet and confronted them during their weekly ménage à trois. Angie rapidly regrouped, and in her nakedness, made the mistake of telling him that he could watch. Fortunately for her, Maheu didn't keep the shotgun in the closet. It was under the bed.

The gardener and pool boy were smart enough to vacate the scene. Although Maheu was mad as hell, the sight of their skinny butts as they ran from the bedroom brought a slight smile to his face. He had been there himself many years ago. However, Angie couldn't keep her big mouth shut. She went on and on. Finally, Maheu had had enough. When he pulled back both hammers on the double-barreled shotgun, she finally got the message loud and clear, including some of the birdshot that made its way through the old door. Fortunately, her butt was large enough to absorb several of the pellets that hit the mark. Suffice it to say, Captain Maheu was ready for a change and jumped at the opportunity to work on an assignment that he knew he would enjoy and could complete.

By early afternoon, Roy, Maria and Captain Maheu were sitting on the back of a small charter fishing boat enjoying a couple of beers. The boat was flying across the top of the water at nearly thirty knots. Maria was fast asleep. She had the ability to sleep anywhere, at any time, and under any condition. She claimed she had no trouble falling asleep, because she had a clear conscience.

"She's a fox," said Captain Maheu as he took a drink from a longneck. Some of the beer spilled out on his shirt. He looked down and wiped it off with his free hand.

"That she is," answered Higgins. The memory of his night with Maria was still lingering in his mind. It made him feel young again. His heart rate increased as he thought about it. He could still smell the aroma of love on his hand as he put the bottle to his mouth.

"Have you known her long?" asked the captain.

"Not long enough," responded Higgins as he looked over at her again and smiled fondly.

"If you find the right one, don't let her go," said Captain Maheu as he opened the ice chest and rescued another longneck from its temporary ice grave. "Would you like another one?"

"I'm fine for now," said Higgins.

"I've had a few dealings with the Croats. Don't like them one bit... none of them," said Captain Maheu, getting down to business. "Is Captain Early still at the helm of the *Sirius Star*?" he asked without taking a breath, as he changed the subject.

"He is. You know him?" asked Higgins.

"We were in the Royal Navy together. He's a good man. May not like it that I'm going to take over *his* ship...even if it is for a short period of time," said Captain Maheu as he took several swallows from the cold bottle.

"Do you guys have a history?" asked Higgins, wondering if there was any animosity between them.

"No more than any other former shipmates. Turning your ship over is like giving your wife to a friend with a big dick and then telling him to take it easy on her. She comes back a little sore but is never quite the same."

Higgins was trying to understand the analogy when his satellite phone rang. It was Rick.

"Hey Rick. You back?" he asked.

"Landed about twenty minutes ago. Where are you guys?"

"We're heading to rendezvous with the ship. Should be alongside in a couple of hours," responded Higgins.

"Have you heard from the prince?"

"I did. Everything is a go."

"Everything is kosher with Captain Early?" asked Rick.

"According to Prince Faisal, he and the security personnel will cooperate fully. How about at your end? Have you contacted any of our people?"

"I just got off the line with Guillermo. He's going to get everyone together. We're meeting at the club a little later."

"Sounds good. I'll let you know when we're aboard the *Sirius Star*."

"I assume everything went well with your captain friend?"

"It did indeed. By the way, his last cruise was aboard the *Aries Star*."

"How ironic, same layout...he'll be right at home. Look forward to hearing from you later," said Rick as he ended the call.

The phone call didn't wake Maria. She hadn't moved for at least an hour. As Higgins looked at her, he thought about Maheu's comment, "When you find the right one, don't let her go." Sounded like the lyrics from *South Pacific*. He really liked Maria, but he wasn't sure that she considered him anything more than a close friend—a close friend with benefits.

Higgins looked at his watch. He would make contact with the *Sirius Star* in about an hour.

InterContinental Carlton Cannes
1900 Hours

Carl and Lynn met Carlos and Ann in the restaurant. Carl had made reservations for four. Since most of the French dine at a much later hour, there were only a few tourists scattered about the dining room. Carlos had seen Tony Ramos head into the lounge area. Tony wasn't alone. The lady with him was a little taller than he, quite attractive, and most likely on the clock.

"Did you see Tony?" whispered Carlos.

"I did indeed," responded Carl, looking in the direction of the lounge.

"I wonder how much she is costing him?" asked Carlos.

"You mean how much she's costing me," said Carl as he pulled out a chair for Lynn.

They had just sat down and were looking at the menus when one of the Russians approached the table. Carlos put his hand on his weapon. The Russian didn't say anything. He just handed Carl a folded note. He purposely bumped Carlos's shoulder and made eye contact as he left. Carlos smiled and then looked over at Ann, but he didn't say anything. Lynn caught the exchange. Carl opened the note.

"Looks like we're in business," he said as he got up. "I'll be right back," he added as he went into the lounge.

Tony Ramos and his newfound friend were sitting at the bar, seemingly enjoying each other's company. The two Russians were sitting at the far end of the bar. They both watched as Carl looked around for Boucher. Patrice Boucher was sitting at the same table that he and Carl had occupied the day before. He was alone. Carl went directly to the table, pulled out a chair, and sat across from him. Carl reached into his shirt pocket and pulled out a card with the name of a bank in the Caymans. He placed the card in front of Boucher. Boucher picked up the card.

"The Royal Bank of Canada. I have an account in the same bank," he said with a forced smile as he placed the card against a water glass.

"My people are already in position to board the ship," said Carl. "And when I verify that the funds are in that account, we will proceed with the operation."

"It will be there within the hour," said Boucher.

"All twenty-five million?"

"All," said Boucher reluctantly.

"Then we have a deal," said Carl as he slid the chair back and stood up.

"Don't fuck with me Peterson," said Boucher.

"Don't worry, you'll get the ship. And as soon as we're pumping crude, I expect to take custody of Ms. Evans and her three friends."

"I've already talked with Mohamed Ibrahim. He'll move them to Eyl sometime tomorrow."

"And he knows that we're just there to pick them up. No ransom?" confirmed Carl.

"He knows," responded Boucher.

Neither man said anything for a minute or so. They just continued to make eye contact, waiting for the other to blink. It wasn't a game.

"When this is over Boucher, I don't ever want to see you again," said Carl, placing both hands on the table and leaning in toward Boucher.

"When this is over, I'm certain that you won't," responded Boucher, still maintaining eye contact. He didn't blink. Neither did Carl.

Carl knew exactly what Boucher meant. He was sure that the Russian goons had their orders. Carl just needed to determine when the goons would make their move. His ace in the hole was Tony Ramos. Carl was convinced that neither Boucher nor the Russians had made Ramos...yet. He needed to provide Tony with a weapon.

Camp Lemonnier
1900 Hours

Rick met Guillermo and the rest of the team at the officers' club. The entire team was there. The current escort operation had gone without a hitch. Rick ordered a round as more people filtered into the bar. Several of the local hookers had already latched on to the younger guys. The younger troops had money, and it didn't take much time to fulfill their desires. The girls would probably take on several customers each before 2200 hours. It was a nightly ritual that had gone on for years. The only thing that ever changed was the price.

Guillermo was first to ask about the mission. "So where are we?"

"Well, Roy is about to board the *Sirius Star*," answered Rick as he looked at his watch.

"That simple?" asked Rafael.

"Roy greased the skids with the Saudis," said Rick as he went on and brought them up to speed on the first phase of the plan.

No one said anything for several minutes as they enjoyed watching the action in the club.

"I love it," said Guillermo as he finished his first beer and signaled for another round. He was referring to the first phase of the plan.

"The only thing that I don't like is that we're dealing with the Serbs and Croats," said Cody.

"I share your concern, but I think when Higgins' friend, Mona, does her thing, the harbormaster will have no recourse but to release the ship," responded Rick. He decided to continue to refer to Maria Lucci by her alias when talking with the team.

"How do you think of these things?" asked Guillermo. It was purely a rhetorical question. "I love it," he added again. He saluted Rick with the bottle.

Rick reached into his pocket and brought out a folded piece of paper. He opened it on the table and was about to go over the rescue operation, when his satellite phone vibrated. It was Carl.

"Hey Carl," he answered.

"We're in business. Boucher transferred the funds. I just completed the verification, and I transferred the money to another account," said Carl.

"The full amount?" questioned Rick.

"Full amount," confirmed Carl, knowing that he would have settled for less. "Where are you?"

"I'm at the club with Guillermo and the rest of the guys. Just about to go over the rescue portion of the plan," said Rick.

"Boucher said that he made contact with Mohamed Ibrahim. The Somalis are supposed to move Courtney Evans and her friends to Eyl sometime tomorrow. I suspect they could end up back on the old Liberty ship. My gut tells me not to trust them."

"I trust your gut," responded Rick. "We'll need to employ Roland's talents to follow the pirates and confirm that they do move Courtney and her friends," he added.

"Could we possibly use Ozzie and Harriet to our advantage?" asked Carl.

"I can make contact with them, but if Ali is truly playing both sides, he might sell us out," responded Rick.

"Then let's leave them out altogether," said Carl. "Have you decided how you'll handle the transfer?"

"Heavily armed," responded Rick.

CHAPTER FORTY-FOUR
Aboard the *Sirius Star*
Day 17
2150 Hours

The initial meeting between Captain Early and Roy Higgins was cordial at best. Captain Early had been a ship's captain for over twenty years. His demeanor was that of a man who had full confidence in his position with demonstrated ability to command the ship. He was tall, thin and well tanned from too many years in the sun. He was well past the point of sun block. He had extremely large hands that rivaled his size sixteen shoes. He was neat in all respects except for eyebrows that seemed to have a life of their own.

Captain Early was very apprehensive and immediately made it known that he wasn't the least bit comfortable with turning his ship over to William Maheu, or anybody for that matter…even if it was for a short period of time. He would comply, but only because he was directed to do so by Prince Faisal. However, for the record, he had made his concerns known to the prince. He also made it quite clear that he wouldn't be held responsible for any shenanigans that resulted in a less than favorable outcome. Higgins couldn't remember the last time he heard anyone use the word, shenanigan. However, it was not his intention to do anything that was deceitful. Boucher might have thought differently.

Following the brief encounter with the captain, Higgins asked to speak with the leader of the security team. The security team was under the control of a former Army Ranger by the name of Travis Lattimer. Lattimer had come up through the ranks and retired at the rank of major. He had distinguished himself in Iraq and Afghanistan. His decorations included the Silver Star, Bronze Star with Cluster and two Purple Hearts. He was nearly six foot four and weighed close to two hundred and thirty pounds. Lattimer was built like a tight end, and in fact, had received numerous college offers as a high school All-American—all of which he turned down in order to follow in his father's footsteps to pursue a career in the Army. It was a decision that he did not regret.

Although he did not know Roy Higgins personally, Lattimer was aware of Higgins' stellar reputation and was obviously quite eager to work with him. Even before he knew what the mission entailed, Lattimer made a point of telling Higgins that he and his men would have no problem following his orders. Higgins told Lattimer that he appreciated his enthusiasm and that he would like to brief the entire security team at 2200 hours.

As Captain Early and Higgins resumed their conversation, Maria was left to move freely about the bridge. It didn't bother her one bit that she was basically left to tour the bridge on her own. Maria was inquisitive by nature, to say the least. As far as she was concerned, nothing was out of bounds or out of her reach. The computers and impressive array of electronics that controlled the ship soon captured her attention. She stood back, crossed her arms, and watched as the computer operators monitored the equipment and made slight adjustments when necessary. Nothing went unchecked. The computer system and the two men sitting at the station controlled every aspect of the ship.

"So Ms. Lucci, what do you think of our system?" asked the captain as he came up on her left side.

"Impressive," she responded as she turned toward the captain. "Is there a place where I can spread out my things and get to work?" she asked, not wanting to get into a lengthy discussion with the captain.

"Do you need privacy?"

"Preferably," responded Maria.

"There is a large desk in my quarters that should meet your requirements," responded the captain as Maria continued her unaccompanied tour.

Captain Early couldn't quite figure out who this woman was, or what unique skill she possessed. Whatever it was, he was about to find out. He continued to watch her as she moved about the bridge. She didn't just glance at things; she took the time to examine every detail.

"Do you have the ship's specs and maybe some pictures that I can borrow?" she asked as she looked back at the captain.

"Any pictures in particular?"

"I'm most interested in pictures that show the bow and stern," Maria responded.

"I'm sure that we do. I'll have the first mate check and bring those items to you. Is there anything else?" asked Captain Early, sounding a bit sarcastic. His patience with Ms. Lucci was beginning to wane. He was having a difficult time dealing with her indifference.

"No, that should do it for now," she responded, ignoring his obvious tone and apparent dislike for a woman being on *his* bridge. She sensed his displeasure. She picked up his binoculars and scanned the horizon.

Higgins smiled, knowing that she was purposely trying to get the captain's goat. The captain was getting more annoyed by the minute, but since he was under specific orders from Prince Faisal, he would refrain from taking her bait. Higgins decided it was time to rescue the captain from Maria before she totally violated the captain's personal space. He wasn't sure why she was testing him. He suspected that he knew the answer; however, he would ask her later.

The first mate led Maria to the captain's quarters and said that he would return shortly with the items she had requested. The captain's quarters were quite impressive. Everything was spotless and neatly stowed. The desk was large enough to provide a sufficient work area. The usual items were laid out on the desk. Everything was placed at right angles to the edge of the desk. Being a confessed obsessive-compulsive, Maria liked the order. She smiled as she sat down and retrieved her computer from her briefcase. She plugged it in and brought up a graphic program that she had created from various sources. She connected to the Internet via satellite and did a Google search on the *Sirius Star*. She downloaded several good shots of the bow and stern. She did likewise for the *Aries Star*.

One of the sites listed all the supertankers, including an impressive array of diagrams. Many of the diagrams included dimensions. Maria changed the scale on the computer program to accommodate a silhouette of the *Sirius Star.* Once the diagram was inserted, she brought up several pictures of the ship with the name *Aries Star* clearly visible. She highlighted the name on the bow and cut and pasted it onto the port side of the silhouette. She made a few adjustments, and within several minutes, she had created the image necessary to complete her initial part of the mission. By the time the first mate made it back to the captain's quarters, Maria was fully prepared to create the banner that would be used to cover the first part of the name of the ship. She would use the specs and additional photos of the ship to confirm the dimensions needed to make a perfect overlay.

While the first mate was still there, she retrieved a four-foot long cylinder from her sea bag. She opened one end and pulled out a roll of what appeared to be an ultra thin sheet of plastic. In fact, it wasn't plastic at all. It was actually a sugar-based parchment that was accidentally discovered by a baker who was a life-long friend of her father, Salvatore Lucci. When it was discovered that the sheet was fairly strong, but could be completely dissolved, Salvatore Lucci immediately saw the parchment's potential. Consequently, Salvatore used the baker's services on numerous occasions to provide the unique material. Maria had certainly learned from the best.

She spread a length of the parchment out on the desk and used a small measuring tape to measure and then cut the material to exactly the size required to completely cover and replace the name, *Sirius.* The only thing she needed to do was to get a digital image of both sides of the bow and stern to compare the color requirements and ensure that the dimensions she had calculated were correct. She would do that first thing in the morning.

"Will there be anything else?" asked the first mate, wondering what she was doing.

"Is there a paint locker aboard the ship?" she asked without looking up.

"We have a modest supply," responded the first mate.

"I assume you have paint that matches the hull?"

"We do," responded the first mate.

"I may need a small amount of that paint. I will let you know. Thank you," she said in a rhythmic tone that was clearly meant to dismiss the first mate.

She didn't turn or make eye contact as he left the captain's quarters. He smiled to himself as he left.

Captain Early stood ramrod straight as he talked with Captain William Maheu. Reluctantly, he began to show Maheu around the bridge. Captain Lewis Early had been with Vela several years longer than William C. Maheu. Since both were on very different schedules, their paths only crossed on one occasion during their time in the Royal Navy. Although Captain Early didn't say it, he was confident that Maheu could easily run the ship and would have no problem masquerading as the ship's captain.

Since the *Sirius Star* and *Aries Star* were nearly identical in all respects, the familiarization process wouldn't take very long. Captain Early had briefed the crew that Captain William C. Maheu would be taking command temporarily. He didn't go into detail but indicated that there would be a crew briefing in the morning. The crew suspected that something was up, rumors were abundant, but they had no idea what was about to take place.

Since Maheu once had command of the *Aries Star*, his old uniforms would be perfect...if they still fit. He had put on a few pounds in recent years but certainly not enough that would fill out a jump suit with an elastic band at the waistline. Both jump suits were still in the plastic bag from a dry cleaner in Catania. Fortunately, they didn't smell like mothballs...or garlic. He would try them on later.

Higgins met with Lattimer and his team in the galley precisely at 2200 hours. The other five members of Lattimer's team were already sitting in the galley, drinking sodas and eating crackers smothered with copious amounts of peanut butter. They were young and fit. The youngest looked to be in his late twenties. The oldest was probably no more than forty, give or take a year or two. The galley was quite small but large enough to accommodate half the ship's crew at any one time.

The security team seemed to be eager to assist. Following the customary introductions and handshakes, Higgins went over the basic plan in full detail. However, he purposely didn't mention Maria's part of the mission. He had his reasons. There were several questions, all of which Higgins addressed to everyone's complete satisfaction.

"Do you think we'll engage the Croatians?" asked a team member with a sewed on nametag that identified him as Mule. There were no quotation marks around the name. It had to be a nickname.

Higgins sat back in the chair and took notice of Mule's impressive forearms. He was by far, the largest of the group.

"Where are you from Mule?" asked Higgins.

"Kansas, Sir," responded Mule, clinching his fists as if he needed to defend the state. The kid fought back the urge to stand at attention.

Of course you are, Higgins thought to himself.

"Well Mule, if everything goes as planned...the short answer is no. We shouldn't have to engage anyone. But, as all of you well know, things usually do not go entirely as planned. There is always that possibility. The key is to be prepared," responded Higgins as he made eye contact with each security team member.

"We've been practicing for such an occasion," said Lattimer.

"I assume your team is well armed," said Higgins. It was meant to be a question and not a statement.

"We are very well armed. All the usual weapons, including a couple of RPGs," answered Lattimer.

"Then we should be fine," responded Higgins. "We just don't need to go looking for trouble...especially if we are not in immediate danger."

"And if trouble finds us?" asked the youngest of the group. His nametag identified him as Morty.

"Then Morty, we'll respond with full force," answered Higgins.

A slight smile crossed Morty's face as it did with a couple of the others. Higgins took notice.

"And the lady?" asked Lattimer. "May I ask what she's doing here?"

"She is a painter...actually, she is an artist," responded Higgins after a long pause.

"An artist?" questioned Lattimer.

"Let's just say that she has a unique talent," smiled Higgins as he looked at his watch.

Cannes, France
2030 Hours

Carl, Lynn, Ann and Carlos had just finished the third course of a five-course meal when Carl's satellite phone vibrated. The vibration momentarily startled him. The girls smiled as he jumped. Carl retrieved the phone and looked at the LED display. He announced that Higgins was on the line.

"Good evening," he answered.

"Evening Carl. Just wanted to let you know that we are aboard the *Sirius Star*. We're right on schedule," said Higgins.

"Good. What is your ETA?"

"We'll be docking the ship at twenty hundred hours tomorrow night."

"I'll let Boucher know that you're in control of the ship and heading for the refinery at Rijeka."

"I assume that Boucher will be making contact with the Croatians," said Higgins. It was meant to be a question.

"I'm sure that he will as soon as I let him know."

"Carl, I really don't want a boat load of Croatians, armed to the teeth, coming out to meet us. The security team aboard the ship is a young group, and they are itching for a fight," added Higgins.

"I understand," responded Carl. "I'll see what I can do."

"Captain Early indicated that the people at the deepwater port are very efficient. We should be offloading oil within an hour of being moored."

"Okay. Keep me posted."

"Will do. See you soon," said Higgins as he ended the call.

Carl returned the phone to his belt and let everyone at the table know the status.

"Are you going to let Boucher know?" asked Carlos.

"Not yet. I don't want to seem too eager. How about another bottle of wine?" he asked as he signaled the waiter.

CHAPTER FORTY-FIVE

Camp Lemonnier
Day 17
2200 Hours

Rick Morgan and the Higgins team met at the club for the scheduled mission debrief. In recent months, the debrief merely served as an official excuse for the team to gather at the club and have a few beers and enjoy the local scenery. On only one occasion in the last six months was there an actual debrief, and that event was about to be revisited.

The escort missions had become more benign with every passage. There was hardly a hint of a threat from marauding pirates. They knew what they were up against, and accordingly, maintained a respectable distance from any Saudi ship being escorted by Roy Higgins' people. Besides, there were many other targets of opportunity ripe for the picking. Every once in a while, the younger pirates would feint an attack, only to turn at the last moment just before warning shots were fired. It had truly become a game to see how close they could get. Sometimes they got too close…and paid a fatal price.

Rick had ordered the first round. In Roy's absence, Guillermo Bonafonte was in charge of the team. Rafael Gonzaléz, Raul Sanchez, and the newest members, Shaun Spencer and Cody Taylor, were seated at the larger of the two round tables in the club. The table could handle eight comfortably. Roy Higgins had purchased the tables and given them to the club. Everyone knew that the larger table was off-limits and reserved exclusively for Roy Higgins, or his people. There could be standing room only at the club, but that one table would always be available for the Higgins team. No one would dare sit there without Roy Higgins' written permission.

The club was busy as usual. Music from the seventies was being piped over the antiquated speaker system. It was too loud and scratchy for Rick's taste. He asked one of the servers if he would be so kind to lower the volume just a tad. The server complied. No one else in the club seemed to notice, or care for that matter. Several of the usual prostitutes had made their way into the bar area and were parading their wares for all to see.

"So who wants in?" asked Shaun as he tore a piece of paper into seven pieces.

Rick smiled as they all took a piece of paper and watched as the different pairs around the room were deep in the negotiation process. Each member of the team threw in a five-dollar bill as they continued to drink beer and wait. Within a couple of minutes, one of the girls led a young soldier by the hand out toward the communal van. He smiled at his friends as if he had just won a prize. She was certainly no prize. She had been unwrapped and re-gifted more times than a fruitcake at a Shriner's Convention. She had a faraway look on her face. The only thing that would make her smile was the money count at the end of the night.

"Ah, *Speedy Gonzalez*," announced Shaun. "Sorry guys, no offense," he laughed as he looked around the table at Guillermo, Rafael and Raul.

They didn't say anything. Shaun was the gambler. He was the kid in high school who ran the sports pool starting with the playoffs. In Shaun's eyes, Camp Lemonnier was just another playground. The only thing different was the name of the game. The rules were simple. Time was the measure, and the one closest to predicting the time was the winner. Since Shaun won so many of the pools, the other team members suspected that he was keeping a detailed account of the *Johns* and how long they took in the van.

"We'll go by the clock on the wall," he said, eager to start the game.

They all looked at the clock as they wrote their name and put down the time they expected the twosome to return. The second hand was in play.

"You better hurry. I know this guy," snickered Shaun.

They folded the piece of paper and threw it in among the five-dollar bills and continued to observe the bargaining process among the other patrons. It was interesting to watch since the price hardly ever changed. Part of the foreplay was talking about what you wanted to do…and then getting the price right. The price would come down a bit as the night wore on and the girls lost interest in bargaining. Last minute deals were commonplace. Two bucks could get you just about anything after midnight, including an STD if you had too much to drink and weren't careful. By that time, most of the prostitutes were tired and had to get home to their kids. After midnight, they could be real quick.

Nothing changes. It's the same everywhere, Rick thought to himself.

Guillermo ordered the second round as the young soldier and prostitute returned.

"Six minutes and thirty-five seconds," announced Shaun as he looked up at the clock and retrieved the pieces of paper from the pot. "And the lucky winner is…oh, would you look at that…it's me," he announced with a big smile as he raked in the five-dollar bills.

"Let me see those. I think this is fixed," protested Rafael. "You're buying the next round," he added as he looked at each piece of paper and threw them on the floor.

Rick let them have their fun for a while. Shaun won the next two pools. Rafael won the fourth as things began to slow down. It was similar to the seventh-inning stretch. The girls hit the bathroom, cleaned up a bit, and then things picked up again for an hour or so. By midnight, the discounts would start and just about anything would be up for grabs.

"We need to talk some business," said Rick as he leaned in and placed both elbows on the table, his chin resting on folded hands.

Surprisingly, everyone paid attention. They had been briefed on the overall mission plan prior to Higgins' departure.

"The first part of the mission is going according to plan. Roy has taken over the *Sirius Star* and is heading for the refinery at Rijeka as we speak. Once they start pumping crude, Boucher is supposed to call Mohamed Ibrahim and authorize the release of Courtney Evans and her three friends."

"And you trust Boucher to keep his end of the deal?" asked Guillermo as he finished his second bottle of beer.

"No, I don't. But I trust Carl will see to it that Boucher keeps his end of the bargain," answered Rick, expecting the question. "That is why we need to be fully prepared, and ready to move."

"An at sea transfer would be nice," offered Guillermo.

"That would be my first choice. Carl is going to tell Boucher that I'll be dealing with Mohamed Ibrahim to confirm the details of the transfer."

"I'd be surprised if they agree to an at sea transfer," added Rafael.

"They won't, but it's a starting point from which we can bargain. I suspect we'll go back and forth and then I'll accept a compromise. They'll view a transfer in Eyl as a moral victory," said Rick.

"If we have to go into the city, we'll need a lot more fire power," said Guillermo.

"That is why I'll insist that the exchange take place at the harbor in Eyl."

"And you think Ibrahim will go for it?" asked Guillermo.

"Since no money is involved, there's no reason why he wouldn't."

"So, we are not paying a ransom?" asked Guillermo.

"No. That was part of the deal with Boucher," answered Rick.

"We better hope the pirates are on the same page," said Guillermo.

"I intend to make that point very clear when I talk with Ibrahim," said Rick.

"Well, we certainly don't need any surprises," said Cody.

"Assuming Ibrahim agrees, how can we be sure that he moves Ms. Evans and her friends to the harbor?" asked Rafael.

"That's a very good question. Roland Carpenter has been keeping track of their current location. He'll continue to monitor them via satellite. When...and if...the pirates move Ms. Evans and her friends, Roland will be able to make that confirmation," answered Rick.

"If? And if they don't move them?" asked Guillermo.

"Then we'll wait," said Rick as the server approached to check on the table.

No one said anything for several minutes as they watched the action in the bar. While they were talking, several transactions had taken place. Shaun had made a few notes. Rafael took notice. A wry smile crossed his face. The server returned with another round, compliments of Rafael.

"Having dealt with pirates, I don't trust them one bit," said Raul.

"I don't either," said Rick.

"They're not a refined bunch. Money is the only thing they understand," added Raul.

"The young ones may be expecting to see plastic bags of money," offered Guillermo.

"They might indeed. That's why we're not going to take any chances. Guillermo, I would like you to determine another location to cover the harbor," said Rick.

"Are we going to take up a position on the Liberty ship?" asked Cody.

"Not this time. They might expect us to try that again," answered Rick.

"Again? They didn't know we were there the first time," said Shaun.

"Probably not, but they suspected we were," responded Rick.

"So where do you want us?" asked Shaun.

"I want you guys with me. They'll be expecting us to show up fully armed. I don't want to disappoint them."

"We had selected two sites for the first mission," Guillermo chimed in. "Rafael and I will use the secondary site this time. It's just north of the harbor and well within weapon range."

"Good, then we'll plan on dropping you guys off late tomorrow night," said Rick. "We'll use the same communications package."

"So this could happen real soon?" asked Raul.

"Higgins will be at the deepwater port around twenty hundred hours tomorrow night. The deal was that Ms. Evans would be released as soon as they were hooked up. That will give us a twenty-four-hour window to make the extraction," responded Rick.

"Why twenty-four hours?" asked Cody.

"Because if all goes as planned at the refinery, after twenty-four hours...the shit will hit the fan," said Rick.

No one said anything for a few minutes as they wondered what was going to take place at the refinery.

"And what happens after twenty-four hours?" asked Guillermo, breaking the silence.

"That's a surprise," answered Rick. He had everyone's undivided attention.

Cannes, France
2130 Hours

Following dessert, Carl decided it was time to let Boucher know that Higgins had taken control of the *Aries Star*. Carl was actually looking forward to the confrontation. He fully expected that Boucher would try to take control, since he still had Courtney Evans in his back pocket. However, somewhere in the back of Boucher's mind, he had to know that the simple solution for Carl Peterson would be to just eliminate Boucher and deal with the pirates directly. Carl Peterson already had twenty-five million of Boucher's money tucked away in an offshore account. What incentive did Peterson have to continue playing the game? However, Boucher would rely upon on what he believed to be Peterson's fatal weakness...that of character and integrity...not to mention the fact that Carl had witnessed Boucher's ruthlessness firsthand.

Boucher had moved from the bar with one of his lady friends. They were sitting close together at one of the small tables near the back wall. They were laughing and enjoying a couple of after-dinner drinks. The two Russians had taken up residency at the far end of the bar. They had used the empty shot glasses to construct a small pyramid as testimony to their drinking prowess. Although the construction wasn't complete, they had to be feeling no pain, unless they were dumping the contents on the floor—as was Tony Ramos. Tony was sitting at the other end of the bar. His female escort had long since departed. She got paid well for doing nothing except massaging Tony's left thigh.

As Carl approached the table, Boucher whispered something into his lady friend's ear. She got up, took her small purse, excused herself, and smiled cordially as she walked past Carl on her way to the bar. Carl took a seat across from Boucher. The lady's perfume lingered just long enough. It was pleasant and quite expensive.

"Higgins has control of the ship," said Carl as he signaled the server.

"Napoleon brandy," he said.

"Monsieur Boucher?" asked the server.

Boucher waved him off without comment.

"So how do I know that Higgins has control of the ship? I'm supposed to just believe you?" asked Boucher.

"I'm here, there's no reason to lie since we have an agreement," said Carl as the server approached with a snifter of brandy. When the server left, Boucher spoke up.

"I will honor that agreement when the ship is moored and pumping oil."

"That wasn't our agreement," said Carl, leaning in toward Boucher. He pretended to be annoyed.

"Things change. You've got twenty-five million of my money. All I have is your fucking word. When the offload starts, I will make the call," said Boucher.

Carl had fully expected that Boucher would want to verify that the ship was at the deepwater port and pumping crude before he would make the call to Mohamed Ibrahim. Carl took a sip of brandy and held the warm snifter between both hands. He took his time enjoying the brandy before responding.

"No problem. The ship should be at the refinery by twenty hundred hours tomorrow night."

"We'll talk then," said Boucher, believing he had gained the upper hand.

Carl decided not to push. He got what he expected. If he seemed too eager, Boucher might become suspicious. Waiting for the right moment was crucial. How one responds, separates the professionals from the amateurs. Many a deal had fallen through because one of the parties got antsy and didn't have the patience to wait for the right moment. Carl knew how to play the game. He wouldn't make that mistake, especially with Patrice Boucher. Boucher was a lot of things, but stupid wasn't one of them.

"Tomorrow night we'll complete the deal. And Boucher...as soon as the *Aries Star* is hooked up, I *will* expect you to contact Mohamed Ibrahim. No changes."

Carl finished the brandy and stood up. Boucher didn't say anything he just nodded. He didn't like being on the fat end of the stick.

"And when you make that call, I'll call Higgins and tell him to start transferring crude. Your Croatian friends can provide verification."

Boucher watched as Carl walked away. Boucher had a lot on the line. Five of the twenty-five million was his. The rest of the money had been provided by Milenko and the Serbs. At this point in the game, failure to deliver was not an option—and he knew it.

CHAPTER FORTY-SIX

Adriatic Sea
Day 18
0815 Hours

Maria had spent several hours the night before working diligently on the banners that would be used to cover up the name *Sirius*. With the specs and pictures provided by the first mate, she had no problem determining the exact dimensions and was certain that the banners would fit perfectly. Each one had taken her just a little over an hour to fabricate. As she stood back and looked at them, there was a knock on the door.

"Yes," she answered as she continued to look over the banners that she had placed carefully side by side on the floor.

"Maria, it's Roy," came a voice from the passageway.

Maria opened the door. Her smile was genuine and inviting. Even in the morning, and with little or no makeup, she was certainly a beautiful woman. Her olive skin was smooth, and her eyes sparkled. Roy couldn't take his eyes off her.

"Come see," she said, pulling Roy into the captain's quarters.

She led him to the far side of the room. She stood over the banners like a little kid looking for approval.

"I see you have been a busy lady. These really look good," he said as he squatted down and looked more closely at the banners.

"Are they dry? Can I touch them?" he asked.

"They're dry. Just don't push on them. They're a bit fragile."

"How fragile?" asked Higgins.

"Fragile enough that they need to be handled with kid gloves. But once in place, they'll do quite nicely."

"These must have taken some time," he said as he gently touched the banner with the fingertips of his right hand. The texture was fairly smooth and mirrored the texture of the paint on the ship's hull.

Roy stood up and continued to examine the banners from different angles.

"Actually, it didn't take quite as long as you would think. Once I had the template made, the rest was a piece of cake. I could make another one in twenty minutes if need be," said Maria as she admired her work.

Roy continued to look them over. He was impressed with the results.

"Where did you get the paint?" he asked.

"There is a modest supply on the ship. Should match perfectly,"

"How long did it take them to dry?" he asked.

Maria reached over and picked up an aerosol can and turned toward Roy.

"Thirty minutes tops with this additive. It makes things hard," she added as she looked down at Roy's fly. She had a mischievous look on her face.

"This is going to be good," he said, trying to stay focused.

"I'll need someone to help me put the banners in place," she said as she moved very close to Roy and fondled the top two buttons on his shirt.

She was close enough that he could feel the warmth of her body emanating through her silk robe. Her hair was still damp from the shower and fell across her shoulders.

"If you get much closer, we'll never get this job done," he said as he looked into her big green eyes.

"You're right. Let's get the first mate. I'll tell him what I will need."

I know what you need—what we both need, Roy thought to himself.

"Is it difficult to attach the banner?" asked Roy.

"Not if the sea cooperates," said Maria.

"Then we should be fine. It's almost like glass out there," said Roy.

"I need to make up the paste. Once I make it, we'll have about thirty minutes before it's dry," she said as she retrieved three containers from her sea bag and placed them in a row on the desk.

"And the paste will dissolve?" asked Roy.

"Like a bad relationship," she answered.

"I'll go get the first mate and tell him what we need. He should have no problem setting up the necessary rigging."

"And tell him I'll need one person to help with the banners," reminded Maria.

"I can help with that."

"Then as soon as he's set up, I'll mix the paste," Maria said as she shed her robe and reached for a pair of jeans.

Seeing Maria in nothing but a G-string was almost too much for Roy to bear. Maria looked back at Roy and smiled. She knew what he was thinking. His reaction was exactly what she knew it would be.

"You're killing me," he said as he moved away from the door and took her into his arms.

She was warm and felt like a part of him as he hugged her gently. Everything seemed to be touching, to fall into place.

"We've got plenty of time," she said as she looked into his eyes and undid his belt. "Oh my, we don't even need the spray," she added, looking down at his manliness.

Camp Lemonnier
1015 Hours

Rick and Guillermo had gone over the plan several times. They were close to finalizing the details and bringing in the rest of the team for the briefing. Since the helicopter was a high-value target, and quite vulnerable to an RPG, Rick had decided that they would take Courtney Evans and her friends out in one of the Zodiacs. The patrol boat would remain two thousand meters offshore and well out of RPG range. That would allow the helicopter to maneuver at will and provide cover.

Guillermo and Rafael would set up on the hill just north of the harbor. They would blend in with the environment, maintain their position, and continue to provide sniper coverage until the Zodiac was at least five hundred meters offshore. Once Courtney and her friends were well clear of the harbor, Guillermo and Rafael would head for the beach, where they would be picked up by the second Zodiac.

Rick poured a cup of coffee as Guillermo made a few notes.

"This looks good to me," said Guillermo as he sat back in the chair.

"Do you see any obvious holes—any fatal flaws?" asked Rick.

"Not really," said Guillermo.

"Not really?" questioned Rick.

"Well, I suppose we could run into another bunch of pirates looking for some scraps," said Guillermo.

"We'll have satellite coverage. Roland will keep us informed of the tactical environment," said Rick.

"And if we do run into another group?" asked Guillermo.

"No warning shots. We'll blow their ass out of the water with the drone."

Guillermo nursed the coffee. He still seemed a bit uneasy.

"Something's bothering you. What is it?" asked Rick.

"It's nothing," he answered. His response was far from convincing.

"Spit it out," said Rick.

"Actually, I would feel more at ease if we were handing over a ransom. Money is the name of this game. I just think it would mitigate any thoughts of a confrontation."

Rick didn't say anything for several minutes. He fully understood Guillermo's concerns. They were certainly relying very heavily on Boucher keeping his part of the bargain, especially the payment to the pirates. The real question was, how much did the pirates trust Patrice Boucher.

"If they show up with an RPG or two, they might have something else in mind," said Rick.

"They usually show up with at least one, just for intimidation purposes," said Guillermo.

"We don't trust them…and they don't trust us," said Rick. "We'll have to play it by ear," he added.

"If things go south, Rafael and I will take out the RPGs first."

"And Cody and Shaun can take out Ibrahim and whoever else is with him. Things could happen real fast," said Rick.

"It's just that I've never been involved in a hostage situation that didn't involve money in one form or another," said Guillermo.

"How many pirates can we expect?" asked Rick.

"Well, if you discount the whole fishing village, there will be Ibrahim and probably two to three guards, one to two additional guys with RPGs, and probably two guys guarding Ms. Evans and her friends."

"And the weaponry?" asked Rick.

"Most likely they'll be carrying AKs. Some carry handguns, but that is not their weapon of choice. However, Ibrahim will most likely be carrying a handgun. Fortunately, the AK is not an accurate weapon," said Guillermo.

"With a thirty-round magazine...it doesn't have to be," offered Rick.

"Touché," said Guillermo.

"I assume the heavy hitters will be accompanying Ibrahim?" said Rick. It was a rhetorical question.

"Most likely the more experienced ones will be up front. The young ones will be guarding Ms. Evans and her friends," said Guillermo.

"We'll need to evaluate the firing order," said Rick.

"That's no problem. The only unknown is the real young ones. There's no in-between with them. They either drop their weapons and run like scared rabbits, or they start shooting in all directions."

Rick didn't say anything as he made a few notes in preparation for the brief with the rest of the team. Guillermo got up and poured a cup of coffee. He offered to refill Rick's cup.

Adriatic Sea
1000 Hours

The first mate and two crew members had fashioned a small scaffold and secured it with block and tackle. Maria and Roy wore harnesses that were attached to the railing with safety lanyards. The two crew members lowered them over the port side of the bow. Maria had placed everything she needed into a basket that was firmly attached to the scaffold. She and Roy held one of the banners between them. They held on to the scaffold with the other hand. The two crew members lowered them slowly until Maria yelled for them to stop. She used a medium-sized paintbrush to apply a thin layer of paste over the name *Sirius*. She was very deliberate. She and Roy then centered the banner and carefully smoothed out the wrinkles and pesky air bubbles. She then went around the edge and finished securing the banner. From their vantage point, the match was nearly perfect. From several feet away, it was perfect. They continued the process, and within the hour, the *Sirius Star* had been miraculously transformed into the *Aries Star.*

"That was much easier than I thought it would be," exclaimed Roy.

"It is when you know what you're doing," said Maria.

"You're still the best," said Roy.

"Roy, I get the feeling that the crew has no idea what we're doing here."

"They don't," said Roy simply.

Maria had a puzzled look on her face. She didn't say anything as they walked back toward the captain's quarters.

"Are you going to brief them?" she asked.

"Actually, what they don't know won't hurt them."

"Don't you think they'll suspect the worst when we get to the refinery and the Croats come aboard?" she questioned.

"I don't think they'll have the slightest clue," said Roy.

"And if they do?" asked Maria.

"Then Captain Early, along with Captain Maheu, will brief them."

"And what if they panic?"

"It will just add to the realism."

"Sounds too simple," said Maria.

"If it goes as planned, it will be simple," said Roy.

"You hope," said Maria.

"Rick Morgan always says that *hope* is not a strategy."

"You should listen to your friend. He's right," said Maria as she opened the door to the captain's quarters.

Camp Lemonnier
1200 Hours

Rick had lunch brought in for the team. The entire team was present with the exception of the patrol boat operator. The helicopter pilot was a former Marine major who simply went by the initials, "TD." He was in his late thirties and had a large scar that went from the right corner of his mouth to his right ear lobe. He had received the wound in a crash just north of Kandahar. Following his third tour, and second crash, he decided it was time to pursue a new career. As they say, he basically jumped out of the frying pan into the fire. He fit right in with the Higgins team. Rick went over the scenario in detail. There was only one question that got everyone's attention.

"Will I be dropping the ransom?" asked TD as he rolled an unlit cigar from the right side of his mouth to the left side.

"It's my understanding that Patrice Boucher has taken care of the ransom," answered Rick. "When this brief is over, I'll give Mohamed Ibrahim a call and confirm that the ransom is not an issue."

"That would be my only concern," added TD.

"Well you're not alone. Guillermo has the same concern," said Rick. "Are there any other questions?" he asked.

"Is the ship on schedule?" asked Rafael.

"Unless I hear otherwise, she's scheduled to dock at twenty hundred hours," answered Rick.

"Then the clock starts," said Cody.

"Then it starts," confirmed Rick as he handed each member of the team a copy of the scenario with times based upon the actual start time. "Let's plan on heading out at sixteen hundred."

As the team was finishing lunch, Rick's satellite phone rang. It was Roy Higgins.

"Good morning Roy," answered Rick as he looked up at the clock on the wall.

"Morning Rick. Just wanted to let you know that the *Aries Star* has risen and is on schedule."

"Good. I just briefed everyone. We're going to be heading out in about four hours," said Rick.

"I'll give you and Carl a call when we're hooked up and pumping," said Higgins.

"It's important that we get Courtney Evans and her friends out of Somalia before you finish the offload," said Rick.

"I understand. I'm sure we could delay a bit if we have to."

"You probably need to stay on schedule. No sense in raising any unnecessary flags," said Rick.

"I think a very large flag will go up when Maria pops the name," said Higgins.

"I'd like to see the look on the harbormaster's face when he sees the name on the ship," said Rick.

"I'll take a picture," laughed Higgins.

Rijeka Refinery
1950 Hours

Dag Kadic and two of his bodyguards along with the harbormaster stood on the dock. The harbormaster was looking through a large set of binoculars.

"It's the *Aries Star*," he announced as he looked over at Kadic.

The harbormaster handed the binoculars to Kadic. Kadic watched as the tugs maneuvered the *Aries Star* into position. Thirty minutes later, Kadic and his people met with Captain Maheu and Roy Higgins on the bridge. Mule and two of his security people stood guard.

"Once the offload is complete, I will send in a couple of my people to accompany you to the Limassol Port," said Kadic.

"The offload will take a little over twenty-four hours," said Captain Maheu.

"Good, let's get started," said Kadic.

"I assume you'll let Boucher know that you have the ship," said Higgins.

"I've been dealing with Milenko. I don't know this Boucher. Milenko can deal with him," Kadic said as he and his men left the ship.

As soon as they were gone, Higgins called Carl Peterson and told him of the brief conversation with Dag Kadic. He told Carl that Kadic would let Milenko know that the ship was in. Carl said that he would let Boucher know, and that he would call Rick.

"What is this guy, Kadic, like?" asked Carl.

"Rough looking guy. He's all business. Curt and to the point," answered Higgins.

"Didn't ask for a bill of lading?" asked Carl.

"He didn't ask for anything. Seems he bought it hook, line and sinker," answered Higgins.

"Okay, let me know when you have finished the offload," said Carl as he hung up.

As a fisherman, Carl knew how easy it was to lose a fish...even when you thought it was well hooked.

CHAPTER FORTY-SEVEN
Eyl, Somalia
Day 20
0400 Hours

Guillermo Bonafonte and Rafael Gonzaléz were nestled in among several large rocks. Their modified desert ghillie suits blended in perfectly with the environment. At night, they were completely invisible. In the daylight, even an experienced sniper would have a difficult time spotting them. For the Somalis, it was already too late.

Rafael panned the small fishing village with his night scope. There was the usual early morning activity—activity that was expected. Well over a dozen Somalis were getting ready to move out with the rest of the fishing armada. There were still several nets draped across boats that didn't look to be seaworthy. Drying didn't take very long in the one hundred degree temperature.

Guillermo focused in on the old Liberty ship and checked the range.

"Twelve hundred twenty-seven meters," he said to himself, making a mental note. He could hit the center of a penny at that range.

There were two young Somalis sitting on overturned buckets next to the makeshift brow. Both were smoking cigarettes and drinking coffee. They had AK-47s slung over their shoulders. Both weapons had thirty-round magazines attached. An old rusted pickup truck was parked alongside the base of the brow. The front bumper of the truck was up against the lower part of the railing. It had actually hit the post and bent it. The generator was on and vibrating as it tried to dance across the deck. It was still held in place by strips of cloth that appeared to have been torn from an old sheet.

The two Somalis just sat there leaning forward with their elbows resting on boney knees. They weren't talking—they just sat there staring aimlessly at the deck. Guillermo looked at his watch. *They're expecting someone*, he thought to himself as he focused on the old truck. The truck would be easy to take out with a bullet to the tank and another bullet to light the fire. He had lost count of the number of vehicles he had caused to go up in flames—several with occupants who were unaware that they had just taken their last breath.

Rafael peered through his scope and checked the range and wind. He made a few minor adjustments. He opened another bottle of water and drank half of the contents.

"I haven't seen Ms. Evans or her friends yet," said Guillermo as he continued to watch the two Somalis. They hardly moved. They seemed to be frozen in place.

"Do you think they're aboard the ship?" asked Rafael.

"They could be. Might have been moved there yesterday. Rick will know," answered Guillermo as he continued to sweep the area.

"If they aren't, I suspect they'll bring them at the last minute," offered Rafael.

Guillermo looked at his watch. Although they weren't expecting to do the exchange for several hours, they knew it could happen at any time. Rafael lowered his head onto his forearms.

"Think I'll take a short nap," he said in a low voice. He was asleep in less than 30 seconds.

Both men were well acclimated to desert environments. Guillermo had always maintained that "comfort" was merely a state of mind. The key was to stay well-hydrated. They had brought plenty of water and ammunition with them. However, they weren't planning on being there for very long.

Three miles offshore
0430 hours

Rick looked out across the bow of the patrol boat. Several seagulls were perched on the railing, facing into the wind. They stood on one leg and moved instinctively as they adjusted to the boat's movement. Rick scanned the horizon. He counted four large ships that were heading toward the Gulf of Aden. They would be too late for the morning transit. Rick looked over at Raul Sanchez. Raul had fallen asleep. A day-old copy of *USA Today* was draped across his legs. The business section had fallen to the deck. A *Financial Times* was folded and set atop a small stack of old magazines that had been read many times. Rick went over and retrieved the *Times* from the pile. He was about to sit down when his satellite phone vibrated. He looked at the LED display. It was Roland Carpenter.

"Evening Roland," answered Rick, knowing that Old Town was eight hours behind Somalia time. It was 2230 hours in the SCIF at The Peterson Group office.

"Good morning," he responded. "Just wanted to let you know that the pirates are on the way with Ms. Evans and her friends."

"And you're positive that it's Ms. Evans?" asked Rick.

"I'm positive. They're about twenty minutes out."

"How many pirates?" asked Rick.

"Three in the truck with Ms. Evans and her friends, and four in the other truck. One of them is carrying an RPG," answered Roland. "They're moving right along."

Rick looked at his watch again. According to his last conversation with Mohamed Ibrahim, he expected that the transfer would take place early in the morning. However, Ibrahim made it very clear that he wouldn't release Ms. Evans until he had received confirmation from Boucher that all of the oil had been transferred from the *Aries Star*. There would be no negotiation on that issue. Rick would have liked to be well on his way with Ms. Evans before there was even the slightest chance that the Croatians would notice that the *Aries Star* had somehow vanished, and the *Sirius Star* had miraculously taken her place. The timing was becoming more critical with every sweep of the second hand.

"Is Mohamed Ibrahim with them?" asked Rick.

"No, he's not," responded Roland.

That meant that he would be showing up later and would probably be accompanied by a bodyguard or two.

"How about the pirates' mother ship?" asked Rick.

"She's one hundred fifty-six nautical miles to the southeast. Won't be a factor," said Roland, expecting the question.

"Have you heard from Carl?" asked Rick.

"Heard from him a few hours ago. Said he was going to get some sleep and then get up early so he could monitor your mission."

"Okay Roland, hang in there...I believe the action is about to start," said Rick.

"Got you covered Mr. Morgan," said Roland.

Patience was always the hardest part of a mission that was dependent upon separate, but related events. It wasn't like a SEAL operation where the team was dropped off, stormed the site, shot everyone, grabbed the target, and then on their way out the door in twenty minutes. An exchange involved a face-to-face confrontation that could fall apart at any second. A simple sneeze could start bullets flying in all directions.

Rick let Guillermo know that the pirates were inbound with Courtney Evans.

"What's the count?" asked Guillermo.

"Seven pirates. Doesn't appear that Ibrahim is with them. One of the pirates is carrying an RPG."

"There are two here already. Probably end up with a dozen when Ibrahim shows up," said Guillermo.

Rick visualized the scene in his mind. The team could easily take out six guys before they knew what hit them. They just needed to keep Ms. Evans and her friends out of the line of fire.

"Have you heard from Roy?" asked Guillermo.

"Not yet. I expect to hear from him anytime now," answered Rick.

"Is Roland up on the circuit?" asked Guillermo.

"I'm listening," responded Roland.

"Hey Roland. Good to hear your voice," said Guillermo. "Watch our back."

"Will do," responded Roland.

"If Ibrahim doesn't show up soon, I'll give him a call," said Rick.

"Hold on a second. Believe I have the two trucks inbound," said Guillermo. "I'll call you back."

Rick looked at his watch. It was already 0500. The sky was beginning to show faint signs of the rising sun. There were only a few thin clouds. It was going to be a clear morning in Eyl...a nice day was yet to be determined. Rick poured a cup of coffee, sat down, and opened the *Financial Times*. Thirty minutes later his satellite phone rang. It was Roy Higgins.

"Hey buddy, how's it going?" asked Rick.

"We just finished taking care of the banners."

"How did it work?"

"Like a charm. I sprayed the banner on the stern myself. Within seconds, the banner was unrecognizable, and then it slipped off unceremoniously into the sea."

"And no one is the wiser?" asked Rick.

"There hasn't been anyone in the vicinity since we stowed the equipment. The harbormaster is probably sound asleep.

"And Captain Early has taken command?" asked Rick.

"That he has. Should be real exciting when he gives the command to single up all lines and prepare the ship for departure."

"Hold off as long as you can. I'd sure like to be well out of here when the Croatians find out they've been had."

"We should be good for a couple more hours. Have you heard from Ibrahim?" asked Higgins.

"Talked with him late yesterday. He was noncommittal. Said he was waiting for confirmation that the oil has been transferred."

"Rick, he should know that by now. I was there when the harbormaster called Dag Kadic and told him the offload was complete. I let Carl know right away."

"How long ago was that?" asked Rick.

"About two hours ago."

"Two hours," repeated Rick. "Then Ibrahim knows."

Roy didn't say anything. Rick could hear Maria in the background. She had completed her part of the mission and was ready for some undivided attention.

"Okay, hang in there. Let me know as soon as you are underway," said Rick.

Harbor at Eyl
0545 Hours

Guillermo watched as the two pickup trucks raced into the harbor and headed over to the old Liberty ship. Dust flew into the air as they abruptly stopped the vehicles. One of the pirates dropped the tailgate and motioned for Courtney Evans and her friends to get out of the truck. Guillermo and Rafael watched through their scopes and verified that it was indeed Courtney Evans, Scotty Blackwell and the Bradleys. They were handcuffed with plastic ties. They looked okay considering their ordeal. Since they weren't blindfolded, Guillermo assumed that the pirates were expecting to release them soon.

Two of the pirates pushed them in the direction of the brow. They were then led up and into the crew deck. The other pirates remained out on the main deck. Guillermo watched as seven of the pirates lit cigarettes and drank coffee. They talked amongst themselves and seemed to be relaxed. As planned, Guillermo called Rick.

"They're here," said Guillermo.

"And you've made a positive identification?"

"That's affirmative."

"And Ibrahim?" asked Rick.

"He wasn't with them," responded Guillermo.

"Okay, I'm sure that he's heard from Boucher by now. If I don't hear from him in an hour, I'll call him," said Rick.

"How far out are you?" asked Guillermo as he looked out to the east.

"About two miles out. We're slowly making our way toward the harbor."

Roland interrupted, "I have an SUV inbound. Looks like two individuals. Haven't been able to make a positive identification, but I suspect it's your man."

"Guillermo, did you hear that?" asked Rick.

"I did. I don't have him in sight yet," said Guillermo as he looked in the direction of the city. "Are you coming in?"

"Not until he calls. He might get overly suspicious if we just happen to show up the same time he does," said Rick.

"Hold on, I've got a vehicle inbound," said Guillermo.

"I'm picking up some conversation," announced Roland.

Rick and Guillermo remained silent.

"Okay, it's definitely Mohamed Ibrahim. He just told his people that he was inbound."

"The SUV just turned toward the Liberty ship," said Guillermo.

Rick didn't say anything as he waited for Guillermo to identify the occupants.

"It's Ibrahim and one heavily armed bodyguard," said Guillermo.

"Hold on guys, my phone is ringing," said Rick as he answered the call.

"Morgan," he answered.

Rick left the circuit up so that Guillermo and Roland could hear the conversation.

"Morgan, this is Mohamed Ibrahim."

"Ibrahim" responded Rick simply.

"Where are you Morgan?"

"A few miles offshore," answered Rick.

"I have your people here at the harbor as we agreed. I think you know where the old Liberty ship is located," said Ibrahim, still believing that The Peterson Group had attempted to rescue Ms. Evans.

"We can be there in thirty minutes," said Rick, purposely ignoring the inference.

"We?" questioned Ibrahim.

"There are four of us."

"All right, we'll be waiting."

Mohamed Ibrahim put the phone in his pocket and slowly walked up the brow. Guillermo continued to watch through the scope. He had a clear view of everyone. He counted eleven targets.

The patrol boat operator reduced the throttle to idle. The bow fell sharply. Raul Sanchez jumped into the Zodiac. He pulled the line tight and held the Zodiac steady. Rick, Cody and Shaun jumped aboard and checked their equipment. Raul gave a thumbs-up to the patrol boat captain as they rapidly moved out in the direction of the harbor. The patrol boat followed close behind.

CHAPTER FORTY-EIGHT
Rijeka Refinery
Day 20
0400 Hours

The Port Security Vehicle was making its scheduled rounds and had just passed the *Sirius Star.* Suddenly, the truck came to an abrupt halt and backed up rapidly. The passenger rolled down the window, leaned a little forward, and looked up at the name on the bow. He checked his clipboard and told the driver to back up. He then checked the name on the stern. He leafed through the clipboard again, shaking his head.

"I thought the *Aries Star* was here," he said looking over at the driver. He had a puzzled look on his face.

"You're the one with the clipboard," answered the driver sarcastically.

"This doesn't make any sense. I need to call the harbormaster," he said as he dialed the number.

"It's your ass," said the driver as he looked at his watch.

"What is it," demanded a gruff voice on the other end of the line.

"Sir, this is Marco Stanek."

"What is it Stanek?" barked the harbormaster. "This better be a life-threatening situation."

"I'm looking at a ship…" said Stanek.

"Are you fucking kidding me?" interrupted the harbormaster. "We're in a port. What would you expect to be looking at, you moron?"

"Sir, I'm looking at the *Sirius Star,*" said Stanek respectfully.

The harbormaster didn't say anything for several long seconds.

"What are you talking about? You're not making any sense," said the harbormaster as he sat up on the edge of the bed, yawned, and scratched the right side of a belly that served as a potato graveyard.

"I said, I'm looking at the *Sirius Star.*"

"And your point."

"What happened to the *Aries Star*?" asked Stanek.

The harbormaster sat on the edge of the bed still scratching. Suddenly, it dawned on him what Stanek was saying. He jumped up, grabbed the binoculars, and looked out the window.

"Shit!" he exclaimed in a loud voice. "Shit! Stay right there, I'm coming down," he said. "You get the captain of that ship," he demanded in a booming voice.

Within five minutes, the harbormaster was going up the brow of the *Sirius Star*. Captain Early was there to greet him. They had known each other for several years.

"Good morning Captain Markovic," said Captain Early as he shook hands with the harbormaster. "Is there…is there a problem?"

At first, the harbormaster didn't know what to say. He stood there with his mouth partially open. He had a confused look on his face that wasn't going away. He looked up and down the ship and then back at Captain Early who had a look of confidence on his face. Captain Early was in full control, and it was quite obvious.

"No…no problem," answered the harbormaster.

"Good. I'm getting ready to single up the lines. I would like to be underway within the hour," said Captain Early. "As you well know, time is money," he added with a slight smile that spoke volumes.

"I'll call the harbor pilot. Good to see you Captain," said the harbormaster as he turned and left the ship.

He jumped into his SUV and called Dag Kadic. He dreaded making the call. But not making it would have disastrous results. The phone rang six times and then went to voicemail. The harbormaster hung up and dialed the number again with the same results. He started to drive away when his phone rang.

"You better have a good reason for calling me at this hour," said Kadic.

Kadic had been up late, playing his weekly game of poker.

"We've got a problem," said the harbormaster.

"What's the problem?"

"The *Aries Star* is gone."

"What do you mean, it's gone?" asked Kadic after a slight pause.

"I mean, it is *not* here. I'm beginning to think that it was *never* here."

"You're not making any sense. I saw it myself. We offloaded over two million barrels of oil. What the fuck are you talking about? Are you back on the vodka?"

"I'm sitting in front of the brow. I just talked with Captain Early. He said he was getting ready for departure."

"Who the hell is Captain Early?" asked Kadic.

"He's the captain of the *Sirius Star*."

"The *Sirius Star*," repeated Kadic.

"Yes, the *Sirius Star*."

"Wait a minute. Are you telling me that somehow we just hijacked our own oil? Is that what you are telling me?" asked Kadic.

"I'm afraid that is exactly what I'm telling you," said the harbormaster.

Kadic wasn't silent for long. He was now wide-awake.

"That Serbian son of a bitch, Milenko, fucked us good. I knew I shouldn't have trusted that prick. Hold on to that ship. Don't let it leave."

"I can't. We have contracted with the *Sirius Star*. There's a paper trail—there are records. Too much would be at stake—they could shut us down. We have no choice but to let her go," said the harbormaster.

Kadic mumbled a few words. He knew that the harbormaster was right. He began to pace back and forth. The harbormaster could hear Kadic throwing things. Something made of glass shattered.

"I'm going to grind that bastard Milenko into hamburger and serve him to his family," said Kadic as he slammed the phone down.

Kadic went over to his desk and retrieved a small notebook from the center drawer. He dialed the private number that Milenko had given him. Surprisingly, Milenko answered on the second ring.

"What is it Kadic," answered Milenko, sounding like he hadn't been to sleep yet. There was no telling where he was.

"You prick, you sold me my own oil."

Milenko didn't respond right away.

"What are you talking about?"

"I'm talking about the *Sirius Star*. I don't know how you did it, but you owe me fifty million. And if I don't have it today…I will find you and cut you up into little pieces, you piece of dog shit," said Kadic as he slammed the phone down and yanked it from the wall. He stood there with it in his hand for several seconds, looked at it, and then threw it across the room.

Milenko immediately called Patrice Boucher.

Eyl, Somalia
0610 hours

Guillermo and Rafael confirmed the firing order just in case all hell broke loose. Rafael would take out the pirate with the RPG first. Guillermo would take out Mohamed Ibrahim. Rick's job was to take care of the bodyguard. Guillermo would then work from right to left, and Rafael would work from left to right. Cody and Shaun would take out the pirates guarding Courtney Evans and her three friends. That had always been the contingency plan just in case things went south.

As the sound of the Zodiac filled the air, Courtney's heart began to pound. She had no idea what to expect, or what her grandfather had negotiated. She just knew that she couldn't wait to get back to the civilized world and tell him how much she loved and missed him.

Lynn Bradley was silent. Tears rolled down her cheeks, believing that they were about to be rescued. Scotty and Dan didn't say anything. They just watched the two pirates that were guarding them. Dan knew to stay calm. Scotty was fighting an urge to attack the pirates.

There was enough light for Courtney and her friends to see the Zodiac and the three men who jumped ashore. They wore desert cammies, were well armed, and walked with authority toward the brow. Rick Morgan led the way. Raul Sanchez stayed at the controls of the Zodiac. He had an HK416 by his side. The safety was off. He was fully prepared to use it if necessary.

Mohamed Ibrahim walked part of the way to meet Rick and his team. The bodyguard was to his immediate left and carried an AK-47 with a thirty-round magazine. He also had a shoulder holster with what appeared to be a Beretta. His right thumb was covering the safety. Rick assumed the weapon was ready to fire. It was. The men stood there for several seconds as they sized each other up and down. Mohamed Ibrahim was first to speak.

"You must be Morgan. I expected to hear a helicopter," said Ibrahim, looking toward the sky.

"I didn't think we would need one," said Rick. "I understand your demands have been met," he added.

"So far, they have," said Ibrahim as he signaled his men to bring Ms. Evans and her friends.

Courtney Evans and her friends moved slowly down the brow with the two young pirates behind them. Raul Sanchez stayed at the controls of the Zodiac. Just as Courtney Evans stepped off the brow, Mohamed Ibrahim's cell phone rang. He made a half turn to his left as he answered the call.

"Mohamed, they double-crossed us! Don't let them out of there!" exclaimed Boucher. "Did you hear me?" he repeated.

"Yes, we'll take care of it," Ibrahim said as he put the phone in his breast pocket and slowly reached for his Beretta.

Rick immediately knew that something was up. He reached behind his back and grabbed his SIG. Courtney Evans was about to yell as Ibrahim swung around with weapon in hand. He was about to shoot when a bullet hit him in the right side of his head, just above his right eye. Before he hit the ground, Rafael took out the pirate holding the RPG. Without hesitation, Rick shot the bodyguard in the forehead. The next several shots were not heard as the pirates went down in unison. One of the young pirates who was guarding Courtney and her friends, threw down his weapon and raised his hands high in the air. He had wet his pants. The other pirate made the mistake of turning his weapon toward Courtney Evans. Cody shot him through the left eye. He fell backward, still holding the AK-47 in front of his body.

There was an eerie silence as Rick, Cody and Shaun slowly checked the bodies. Scotty Blackwell picked up an AK-47 and aimed at the young pirate who had surrendered.

"Scotty no!" yelled Rick Morgan as he ran over and placed his hand on the weapon and pushed the barrel down toward the ground.

"Enough is enough," said Rick.

Scotty's heart was racing as he looked at Rick and then back at the young pirate. He wanted to shoot him full of holes. No one moved as Scotty finally relaxed and let go of the weapon. As Rick took the weapon, Scotty punched the young pirate, knocking him cold.

"Feel better now?" asked Rick as he looked back at Scotty.

Scotty didn't say anything. He just nodded as he hugged Courtney.

"Don't look at any bodies. Just get on the boat," said Rick as he motioned toward the Zodiac.

"What about this one?" asked Cody, looking down at the young pirate.

"Tie him to the old truck," said Rick as he bent down and retrieved the Beretta that was still in Mohamed Ibrahim's hand. He also took Ibrahim's cell phone.

"Get all the weapons," said Rick.

Guillermo and Rafael continued to watch from their position. Guillermo panned to the west and checked the road from the city. Rafael kept an eye on the old fishing village and the entrance to the harbor. There was no activity. The people in the shacks knew what had happened, and they remained inside.

Raul Sanchez gave Courtney and her friends life jackets, water and some snacks. Cody and Shaun jumped aboard with a handful of weapons, including the RPG. Rick was last to board. He took one last look at the old Liberty ship as Raul slowly added power and headed for the entrance to the harbor. Within two minutes, the Zodiac was in open water and moving at full throttle.

"Guillermo, we're clear," announced Rick.

"Looks good from this end. We're heading for the pickup point," answered Guillermo. Rafael was already standing up.

Rick sat back and looked over at Courtney Evans. She had a satisfied smile on her face.

This one is a tough cookie, Rick thought to himself as he dialed Carl Peterson. Carl answered right away.

"Looks like you had some action," said Carl.

"You saw?"

"Roland sent me the feed."

"Ibrahim must have gotten a call from Boucher," said Rick.

"I'm sure that he did. I just heard from Roy. The *Sirius Star* is underway."

"You better watch your backside," said Rick.

"I'm not too worried about Boucher. I suspect that he's packing as we speak."

"What about the Russians?" asked Rick.

"Ann, Carlos and Tony are keeping an eye on them," said Carl. "How are Ms. Evans and her friends doing?"

"They're fine. Thought I would give Blackwell a call," said Rick.

"That's a great idea. Call me when you're back at the base."

Rick brought up Blackwell's number, dialed it, and handed the phone to Courtney Evans. As soon as JT Blackwell answered the phone, she burst into tears.

EPILOGUE
Northeast of Eyl
Day 20
0830 Hours

Rick Morgan, Courtney Evans and her three friends heard the helicopter approaching as Raul maneuvered the Zodiac up onto the beach. The landing area was approximately fifty miles northeast of Eyl on a stretch of beach that was desolate and ideal for a landing. As soon as everyone was strapped in, the helicopter lifted off and headed out over the Indian Ocean. The flight to Camp Lemonnier would take about seven hours. They would make a fuel stop at Berbera. As soon as they were airborne, Courtney Evans adjusted the mouthpiece that was attached to the left side of the headset and pressed it against her lips. She held it there with her left hand.

"Mr. Morgan," she summoned.

"Yes, Ms. Evans," responded Rick.

"Where is my sailboat?"

Two weeks later...

Marina Café in Destin, Florida
1900 Hours

Carl Peterson had invited the team for dinner at Marina Café. The maitre d', Wally, had set a table for eight in the main dining room. The table provided a wonderful view of the harbor. The sun had gone down. There was a slight breeze from the southwest. It was another pleasant night on the Emerald Coast. Several boats were in the queue heading toward the Destin Bridge. Carl had ordered three bottles of Nickel & Nickel Cabernet Sauvignon. Wally was talking with Lynn as he pulled the cork from the first bottle. It made a popping noise that caused Carlos to reach for a weapon that wasn't there.

"It's okay Garcia," Ann said with a comforting smile.

Wally handed the cork to Carl for examination. He then poured a small amount of wine into Carl's glass. Carl was in the process of swirling the wine when he noticed Roy Higgins and Maria being directed to the table. Carl took a sip of wine. He held it in his mouth for several seconds before swallowing it. He let Wally know that the wine was wonderful.

As Roy and Maria approached, Rick, Carl and Carlos stood up. Roy seemed to have a permanent smile on his face since renewing his relationship with the lady he had always referred to as "Mona Lisa." Roy re-introduced her as Maria Lucci to everyone at the table. Her smile was refreshing. Her interest in Roy was obvious.

"So you're still with this old scoundrel," teased Carl.

"Well, he's not so bad…and not *that* old," responded Maria as she smiled fondly at Roy. She gently placed her right hand on his forearm. Roy squeezed her left hand ever so slightly.

Wally had already pulled out the chair next to Carlos. Maria smiled at Carlos and Ann as she sat down. She really liked Lynn and Ann.

"If you need anything, please don't hesitate to call on me," said Wally as he patted Lynn on the shoulder and left. He said something to one of the servers and motioned toward the table.

"Before we start, I just want to say that I really appreciate everyone's dedication and commitment to the successful accomplishment of another well-planned and well-executed Rick Morgan mission," offered Carl.

"Hear, hear," everyone said in unison as they lifted their glasses and toasted Rick.

"So, what have you heard from the front?" asked Rick as the women began to discuss the menu items.

"Got a call from André Marcelles a couple of days ago. As we suspected, Boucher had left the Carlton right after he got a call from Milenko. He didn't even take time to pack."

"He was running for his life," offered Higgins.

"He did take the time to call Mohamed Ibrahim," said Rick.

"Do you think the Croatians caught up with him?" asked Carlos.

"I wouldn't be a bit surprised. There is a large Croatian population in France. Quite a few on the Rivera," responded Carl.

"He's in the wind," offered Higgins.

"Or the Mediterranean," responded Carlos, raising his wine glass in what he believed to be a post-mortem salute.

"And the Russians?" asked Rick.

"Well, that's another story," said Carl as he looked over at Ann and Carlos. "Seems they were found behind the Carlton in between a couple of large dumpsters. Both had been shot twice in the chest and once in the head."

"A familiar signature," said Rick as he took a sip of wine and looked over at Lynn. She appeared to be engrossed in the menu.

"Any clues?" asked Higgins.

"Nothing of significance. The gendarmes did find a small paring knife at the scene. It had been wiped clean. They weren't sure if it was at all connected to the crime, especially since the Russians had been shot," answered Carl.

"The French are the French, but they can be relentless in their pursuit," said Higgins.

"According to André, there is little to no interest at all in finding out who may be responsible," said Carl.

"Is Boucher still a person of interest in the jewel heist?" asked Rick.

"More so since he disappeared so suddenly. In fact, they are now going under the assumption that he played a major role in the heist," responded Carl.

"Anything on the jewels?" asked Higgins.

"So far, none of the jewels have surfaced," responded Carl.

"Not even in the usual places?" asked Higgins.

"Nothing," responded Carl.

"Carl, do you really think Boucher was involved?" asked Rick.

"Well...I wouldn't put it past him. André said that the French were aware of his relationship with Milenko, and they strongly believe that Milenko was a member of the Pink Panthers."

"We may never know," said Rick.

"Hopefully, we've seen the last of Patrice Boucher," said Carl.

"Have you talked with JT Blackwell?" asked Rick, changing the subject slightly.

"He called me right after he talked with Courtney. Wants to get together to settle the bill. I told him that someone else had paid the ransom. He was a bit confused, especially when I told him that they had also covered our fee. He wondered who would have been so kind. I told him that they had no idea that they were participating in the negotiation process."

"So he was even more confused," said Ann, joining the conversation.

"He was. I told him that one day in the near future we'd get together, and I would fill him in on the details. By the way," said Carl reaching into his pocket, "a little bonus," he said as he pulled out two envelopes and handed one to Rick and the other to Roy Higgins. "I wasn't sure where to include Shaun and Cody, so I'll leave it up to the two of you to figure it out and take care of everyone," said Carl.

Rick and Higgins were about to thank Carl when the server approached to take their orders. When the server left, Carl asked about Tony Ramos.

"You think Tony likes Ms. Evans?" asked Carl.

"Since the Bradley's had had enough of sailing, I believe he just wanted to help her and Scotty Blackwell sail the boat back to Wilmington," answered Rick.

"She's not ready for a relationship right now. Tony knows that… but he likes her," said Maria, delighted to talk about the possibility of a new love.

"Women know these things," said Higgins with a telling smile.

"They do indeed," added Ronnie Lake as she reached down and placed her hand on Carl's inner thigh.

Carl nearly spilled his wine as he tried to ignore Ronnie's roving hand.

"So," he said, his voice cracking.

"Ronnie Lake," said Maria as if she just remembered something. "I know that name. You wouldn't happen to know a fellow by the name of…"

"Charlie Lake?" interrupted Ronnie, anticipating Maria's question.

Later that night, Rick and Lynn were getting ready for bed. Rick had placed the envelope on the dresser. He hadn't opened it.

"So what happened in Eyl?" asked Lynn, remembering that Rick had said Boucher called some guy by the name of Mohamed Ibrahim.

Women hear everything, Rick thought to himself.

"Just made things a bit more complicated," answered Rick, not wanting to tell Lynn what really happened.

Lynn didn't say anything as Rick opened the envelope from Carl. The contents caused him to make a comment under his breath.

"A nice bonus?" asked Lynn.

"Not bad," said Rick as he handed Lynn a one-page document from the Royal Bank of Canada. "Seems we have an offshore account in the Caymans," he added.

Lynn looked at the document and then over at Rick. Her expression was priceless.

"This can't be right. Is this right? Five million dollars isn't a bonus...it's a retirement," she said after a long pause. She sat on the edge of the bed and looked at the document again, wondering if Carl had made a mistake.

"Do you think Carl made a mistake?" she asked.

"Carl never makes a mistake when money is involved," said Rick.

"Did Carl give the same amount to Roy?"

"I don't know...but I'm sure that he did. We both have employees to take care of," responded Rick.

"You *will* save us some?" asked Lynn, knowing that Rick could be overly generous.

"I'll save a couple of bucks just for you," he smiled. "I promise."

Lynn kissed Rick and laid back in the bed thinking about the night. There were so many questions she wanted to ask. She still couldn't believe the bonus check.

"What was the name of Courtney's sailboat?"

"The original name was *A Pirate's Dream.*"

"If I remember correctly, that wasn't the name on the sailboat in the harbor at Cannes."

"The Somalis had changed the name to *Westward Ho*," answered Rick.

"And the plan was that Patrice Boucher would sell it again?" asked Lynn.

"There's no telling how many times that boat had been sold to unsuspecting sailors, only to be hijacked by the same pirates," said Rick.

"Didn't Courtney ask Maria to change the name?"

"She did," answered Rick.

"Did she change it back to the original name?"

"Nope. Courtney came up with a new name."

"And what name did she choose?"

"*Corsaire*," said Rick as he turned out the lights.

CPSIA information can be obtained at www.ICGtesting.com
Printed in the USA
BVOW05s0535220514

354229BV00002B/140/P